Bloodfeather Symphony

Blood Song Trilogy 3

Amber L. Werner

Contents

NORTHERN DEPTHS
NORWICH
DOLN
MIDSPORT
GRANSEA
KINGDOM OF
DRACWOOD
MAGEHAVEN
EPRORA
OCEAN
ORDDON
OCEAN
GREENVALE
BOGSMOUTH
FLAMESMOAT
THE BOGLANDS
STONESHORE
RAIMIRE
SLINAS
MUDO ISLANDS
SALT CLIFF
SULAND
WASTE
JORIA
SOUTHERN SEA

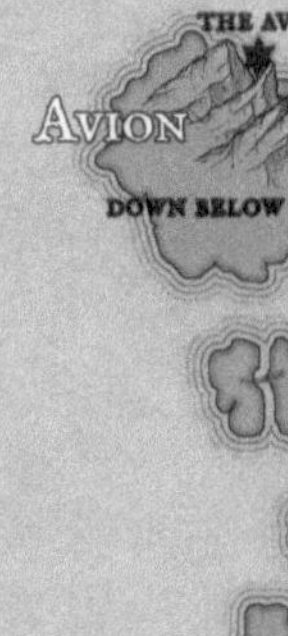

THE AVIARY
AVION
DOWN BELOW

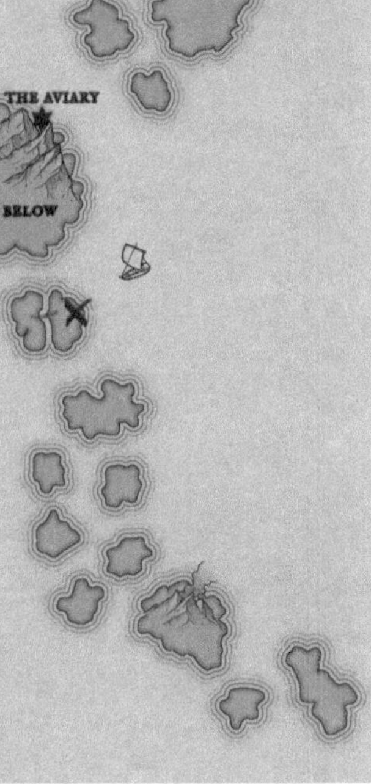

THE STILL SEA
SALT CLIFF
JOLIT ISLE

Prologue

Jurdan rapped his nails on the arm of his throne. "Well?" He shot a glare at the slob of a champion he'd been stuck with for the last half-century. "Anything worth noting with this group?"

He wasn't sure why he bothered asking. It was bound to be more of the same. Year after year, more men stepped forward to don the masks and receive the gifts he offered. It was just as well they covered themselves from head to toe afterward. Their faces had long ago begun to blur in his mind, one man indistinguishable from the next.

Crow leaned forward, a black bird perched on each shoulder. "There is one peculiar addition."

"Really?" His hand stilled. He turned to Crow. "Do tell."

"Remember that dark-skinned man who washed up on Jolit Isle a few years back?"

Of course he did. The shipwreck that ended with a single survivor stranded on the island his men used to slake their immoral desires had been no mistake. But Crow didn't need to know about that.

Jurdan cocked a dark brow. "What about him? The last I recall, he was struck dumb and incapable of taking care of himself." He smiled cruelly. "Has he finally died?"

Wouldn't that be nice? It would be a sweet little morsel to whisper into that wretched *queen's* ear when his plans finally came to fruition. It was the only reason he hadn't ended the foreigner years ago. Not when he might trot out the shell of a man who remained when the time was right. Or spin the tale of his many years of suffering before his tragic demise.

"No." Crow nodded to the empty ring that stretched out beneath them. The same ring that would soon hold the next class of men who'd wear the mask. Who'd chosen to serve him for the rest of their lives. "He's here."

This was even better than the wretch dying.

A muscle in his cheek twitched, but he buried the slow smile that fought to spread across his face. "I see." Jurdan stared stoically ahead. "And how did this come to pass when I was assured he was knocking on death's door?"

"An old washer woman on Jolit took him in and helped him recover. Seems he heard enough men talking about your greatness, Supreme, and he begged for a chance to train as a masked. Someone on leave took pity on him and brought him back. He's been living with the trainees for the last year." Crow scoffed, shaking his head. "Can you believe it? A grown man, training with the youths. Shadowing a masked like a lap dog." He laughed cruelly, his lips twisting into a sneer that made the ugly scars marring his face beneath his beard look even more hideous.

Jurdan sucked in a deep breath through his nose, fighting to remain calm. One of *them* had been living in his city for a year without him knowing? He wanted to rage. To find the kind sod responsible for giving that scum a chance and rip his head off his shoulders.

No. We cannot show weakness. Besides, this is most propitious. It does not matter how it came to be. We must use it to our advantage.

Yes. The possibilities flickered to life in his mind. There were so many things he might learn with such a man under his thumb. So many things he could accomplish.

"Well. That is unusual." Jurdan tossed his straight black hair over his shoulder. "But of course, all are welcome in the masked."

As long as they chose correctly...

He finally allowed the smile to spread. Perhaps that death would still be there to whisper about. And how much sweeter would it be if he were around to watch it happen? If he described in excruciating detail how the light faded from her *dear friend's* eyes as he drew his last breath... What a delicious parting gift for the witch who'd evaded him.

Either that, or her man would be his. Irrevocably twined with him in so many ways. All the ways that mattered most.

Jurdan's blood sang. To think, he'd been sitting there, certain he would be forced to trudge through another monotonous ceremony. But no. He was about to pluck a prize out of that silly girl's grasping fingers.

Might as well get on with it...

"Send them in." Jurdan strolled to the rear of his box, pausing at the door. "I'll meet them in the ring." His boots thudded on each step as he descended the stairs.

It had been seven years since the battle that changed the face of the world. Seven long years since he'd learned that another like—No. That wasn't entirely true, was it? The idiot who had tried—and failed—to destroy the land he was currently stuck in wasn't the same. He'd failed to do the one thing that set them apart. The thing that ensured Jurdan would one day prevail.

And now we are one step closer.

Sure, a single man wouldn't make the difference between winning and losing. But he could be a tool. In an expert craftsman's hands, even the most shapeless lump of clay could be molded into a masterpiece. And after all these years, what was he if not an expert at bending men to his will?

Jurdan emerged into the ring. Dirt kicked into the air with each step he took toward the semicircle of kneeling men. They were clothed in long white robes, their gazes downcast.

A dozen black-clothed masked flanked them, there to bear witness to the trainees' success. Or their failure.

A masked stepped forward from the pack. He cocked his head as Jurdan strolled closer, making the black-and-white eagle carved into his mask twitch in a birdlike fashion.

"Supreme." Eagle bowed his head. "The men here have trained long and hard to prove they deserve to serve you. They would be grateful if you found them worthy of your gifts."

Jurdan trailed leisurely in front of them, appraising each one in turn. The first four were what he'd come to expect from Thalass recruits. Dark hair and dark eyes that stayed humbly fixed on the ground. Each of them barely old enough to be called a man, yet strong and fit despite their youth.

The fifth was a good decade or two older than the rest. His skin was far darker than Jurdan's had ever been, even after Jurdan spent endless days basking in the sun when he'd first arrived in this world. The same shade as that fool prisoner who'd sat in one of his cells for decades.

There was no doubt in his mind that this trainee had been sired in the sundrenched waste across the sea. But then why would he choose to be masked?

"I must hear it from their own lips." Jurdan projected his voice loudly, making the four youngsters flinch.

But not *him*. The foreigner sat stolid, even as the Supreme's voice echoed off the walls.

Jurdan snapped his fingers, and one of the masked rushed forward. He carried a golden tray with three items upon it. First, a golden goblet encrusted with gemstones—gaudy as it was, he'd always maintained that moments like these called for a bit of theatricality. Next to it, a pitcher of water wobbled in the man's unsteady hands. And last, a blade, polished to a mirror shine, the hilt even more ridiculously adorned than the goblet.

He plucked the goblet off the tray and filled it with water. He took it and the knife, then stopped in front of the first lad. "Eyes on me."

The boy trembled, lifting fearful eyes to meet his.

"Do you swear to serve me, your Supreme, as masked for all the years of your life?" he asked.

"Y-yes. I swear it." For all his apparent nerves, the boy didn't hesitate to give his answer.

Jurdan nodded once, sliced his palm with the blade, and lifted his fist over the goblet. A slow stream of blood dribbled into the water, tinging it pink. He thrust out his hand. "Drink."

The boy gobbled the water greedily. So eager. There was never a shortage of men willing to sign over their lives to his service. Not when they knew what they'd receive in return.

The next three lads spoke the words and drank deeply. Surely it was the most momentous moment in their lives. Yet for Jurdan, the ceremony took on the dreamlike quality of a task done a thousand times. Even the sting of the blade tearing through his flesh scarcely registered in his mind.

But when he got to the last man, Jurdan shook himself into full awareness. This foreigner was different. Why was he here?

We'll know the whole of it soon. If sinister plans lurk in his heart, we can end him here and now.

It was true enough. "Eyes on me."

The foreigner met his gaze for the first time. This was no quivering lad. Even more curious, his dark-brown eyes held no malice. No hint of the barely contained rage of a man bent on revenge. Just the same reverence that he'd grown so used to seeing in the gazes of his people.

How curious. He'd been half-convinced the fool would leap at him at the last instant, a blade in hand and his beloved queen's name on his lips.

But no. This was the moment of truth.

"Do you swear to serve me, your Supreme, as masked for all the years of your life?" he asked.

"Yes." The foreigner's voice rang out, strong and sincere. "I swear it."

Jurdan lifted the bloodstained goblet. He sliced his palm again. After four cuts, he hardly needed to—warm blood leaked freely down his wrist and smacked into the dirt already—but ceremony was ceremony. This time, when he lifted his fist over the cup, the water wasn't merely tinged pink. So much blood spilled into the goblet that it overflowed.

He thrust it out. "Drink."

The foreigner clasped the bloody cup and lifted it to his lips. Though he'd expected some hesitation, there was none. The man only scrunched his nose before sucking down the liquid in a few quick gulps.

Jurdan backed away from the kneeling men. All the youngsters wore wide smiles. The one on the end began shifting, readying to stand.

Little did they know... "Seize them."

The masked rushed forward, two for each trainee. They clamped a hand on the men's shoulders, forcing their knees firmly into the dirt. The recruits' smiles faded, replaced with blinking owlish eyes and shuddering lips.

"This is only a small part of what I will ask. You're waiting for your gifts, yes?" Jurdan paced ahead of them and spotted a few men nodding in his periphery.

"My gifts come at a cost. You've pledged your lives to me. I will have your obedience as well." Jurdan stopped and spun to face them. He stretched out his uninjured arm, and with a thought, he called forth a crow.

"When I ask you to kill, you will do it without question." The crow landed on his palm. Jurdan lifted his bloodied hand and strangled the creature. Sure, he could've snapped the bird's neck. Put it out of its misery quickly. But ceremony was ceremony.

The men watched with various levels of dismay. The one in the middle sat stoically, a cruel glint in his eye. Two of the others looked like they might be ill. The foreigner sat stone-faced, but Jurdan didn't miss how he clenched his fists at his sides.

After an eternity of convulsing, the beast fell limp. Jurdan released it, not bothering to watch it slam into the dirt. He stretched out his bloodied hand. "Those who obey will be rewarded."

The sick looks disappeared. Eyes widened and jaws dropped.

Jurdan smiled. He never tired of watching the awe wash over his men's faces. Who wouldn't be impressed, seeing flesh heal before their eyes?

He flipped his hand down, brushing the last traces of blood on his fine purple robe. He flashed his palm again. "This is no trick."

Now for the final step. The step that would prove whether these men would become his in truth. Or if they were about to land in the dirt, as lifeless as the crow at his feet.

Jurdan strolled forward and plucked the ceremonial knife off the golden platter. He snapped his fingers three times.

A door on the far wall opened. Masked streamed in, leading five people in their midst. They were from all walks of life. An elderly couple, white-haired and slow-moving. A young woman cursed with a deformity that covered half her face. Two prisoners wearing rags and covered in bruises and scars.

Each of them carried a crow in their arms. A pair of masked directed each person forward and made them kneel facing one of the trainees.

Jurdan strode into the slim aisle his masked had left between them. "Now is the moment that will define you. Are you ready to wear the mask of my elite?"

He stopped in front of the trembling lad at the end. With a single swift motion, he thrust the ceremonial blade into his stomach. Gasps exploded, nearly loud enough to drown out the trainee's scream.

"W-why?" the lad asked after his screaming subsided.

Jurdan didn't answer. He merely pulled the ceremonial blade out of the recruit's gut and straightened. Then he dug into a pocket on his robe and dropped a small, unadorned blade in front of him.

He moved on to the next lad. And the next. They tried to struggle, now that the surprise had passed. It did them no good. Not with the masked holding them down. By the time he approached the fourth youth, the boy trembled uncontrollably but put up no fight. And when the blade sank into his gut, he hardly even screamed.

The foreigner, on the other hand, didn't even blink. His gaze stayed locked on the old man who sat in front of him.

Jurdan spared the elderly volunteer a glance. From the glazed eyes and dribble of spittle on his cheek, he would guess this one to be feeble-minded, but he couldn't say for sure. He typically didn't pay much mind to the fools who signed up for this unenviable task. Gullible and weak, the lot of them.

He turned back to the foreigner and lifted his blade. When the hilt kissed his flesh, the foreigner met Jurdan's gaze.

What was that he spied in its depths? Not pain, though surely he must be feeling that in spades. No. He'd bet his life the raw emotion he sensed was regret.

Too late for that.

Jurdan pulled the knife free from the foreigner's gut and tossed a blade in front of his knees.

Swiveling on his feet, Jurdan scanned the mess he'd left in his wake. The trainees' white robes weren't so white anymore. Blood spattered the dirt and coated the hands of the lads who frantically sought to stem its flow.

They needn't have bothered. It had taken a bit of trial and error, but after countless years, his aim was true. Their wounds would take hours to kill, yet kill they would. A slow, painful demise for any who couldn't stomach what came next.

"Obedience." Jurdan's voice boomed over the pained moans of the wounded men. "This is your first and only test before you take up your mask."

Jurdan walked to the platter and dropped the blade with a resounding *clack*. The move was a signal his masked knew well. They unclamped their hands from the trainees' shoulders, allowing them freedom once again.

"Kill them." With his words, the crows flew out of the volunteers' arms.

"But..." the lad on the end shouted, lifting the blade from the dirt in front of his knees, "we can't fly."

"You don't have to." A cruel smile spread across Jurdan's lips. "Gifts belong to the obedient." He stared at the men and women still held in place on their knees, one for each trainee. "Now, kill them. I won't ask again."

The Library

"Are you sure we should be in here?" Ryon asked.

Violet pushed open the door to the library in the northeast wing of Kings Keep. Shelves packed with books lined the walls, the spines stacked in neat, colorful rows. The musty stench of old paper tickled her nose. Fire crackled in the hearth, warming the drafty space.

"Better here than back in the Great Hall. All those guests are bound to be crabby with the non-stop questioning." Violet sank into a fluffy armchair with a sigh, gathering her long silvery-white hair over one shoulder. "Besides, Kayda said to make ourselves at home."

They'd left her aunt in the sitting room shortly after reintroducing her to her old friend Jayan. It had been a whirlwind of a day. They'd flown halfway around the world only to thwart an assassination attempt and heal a blind queen. And they still had daylight left somehow...

Ryon placed Orry in Violet's lap and wandered over to the huge bay window, throwing the curtains open. "At least it's quiet here." He smoothed a hand down his dusty black trousers before he sat in the window nook and leaned his dreadlocked head against the wall. "Do you think the Castle Guard will find who poisoned Kayda's wine?"

"Who knows?" Violet shrugged. "I'm just glad we were here in time to stop it." Truly, they had Mena to thank for that. If not for the albino fire dragon bonding with Kayda at the moment she'd been in danger, they'd have likely never known that the goblet was rigged to kill the Queen of Dracwood.

Orry shifted in her lap. Violet glanced down, watching her golden-feathered bondmate's head flick around as she studied the entire room before landing on the window.

"*You all right?*" Violet asked.

"*No.*" Orry narrowed her golden-rimmed black eyes at Violet for a heartbeat before returning her focus to the window. "*Something feels off.*"

"*Off?*" Violet's heart stuttered. If Orry thought something was wrong, Violet wasn't about to take her feelings lightly. "*How?*"

"*Not sure...*" Orry cocked her head. "*Notes are out of tune. Discordant.*"

Violet frowned, her stomach sinking.

"Anything wrong?" Ryon asked.

The library door banged open before Violet answered. A barrel-chested bald man with a neatly cropped red beard strode in, his tailored plum suit superbly styled yet stained with perspiration.

"Taul." Violet sat up straight, trying not to fidget in her chair due to how underdressed she was. She and Ryon wore simple traveler's attire that was wrinkled from hours of flying on dragonback. Of course, they'd had no clue they were about to barge in on her royal aunt's pre-wedding feast.

She wasn't surprised to see the Doln warrior had been cleared to leave the Great Hall. She'd met him countless times at Harvest Festivals and royal events in the past. He was a good man. She'd never suspected he'd poisoned Kayda's wine—even if the vintage was from his home county and he had the most to gain from her suddenly dying.

"Vi." He stopped at her chair, his gaze trailing around the room. "Where's your aunt?"

"I left her in the sitting room with Jayan."

Clearly Taul was familiar with the name. He jolted slightly, then plopped in the chair beside her. "I thought I recognized him." He massaged his temples, chuckling humorously. "This is an utter mess, isn't it? I can't keep her safe on the eve of our wedding, and now Jayan shows up out of the blue."

"I'm sorry." Violet wasn't sure what to say. And after what she'd witnessed in the sitting room earlier, she wasn't sure her aunt would be so keen to marry tomorrow. She had a feeling Taul sensed it too.

Violet glanced at her lap. Was that what had Orry feeling so off?

But Orry hadn't moved. Her gaze was still zeroed in on the window.

Violet's gaze darted across the room, and she spotted Ryon examining Taul with a sympathetic expression on his face.

Perhaps they could take Taul's mind off the wedding for a time. Violet cleared her throat. "Where are my manners? I should introduce you to my companions."

Taul shifted in his chair and dropped his hand from his face. "Of course," he replied automatically, though from his flat tone she gathered he was only being polite.

Violet pointed to Orry. "This is my bondmate, Orry, an orecoln from the island of Avion."

"Orecoln?" Taul cocked a brow. "I've never heard of them."

"They're a new species we discovered out east, gifted with rare magic." Violet lifted a single shoulder in a lopsided shrug. "Honestly, I still don't understand it entirely myself."

"I see." Taul leaned forward, scanning Orry with undisguised curiosity.

Then she waved toward the window. "Ryon of Avion. Meet Clan Chief Taul of Gransea."

Taul perked up as she finished the introductions, and his voice held a hint of interest when he replied, "Avion, eh? I'd love to hear more about your homeland."

Ryon took his cue, strolling over with a hand outstretched. "It's nice to meet you. I'd be happy to share some stories, if you'll do the same. I've heard so much about Doln from Violet." They shook, both so tall she was forced to crane her neck up to see their smiles.

Violet scooped Orry into her arms and vacated her seat. Ryon sat in it, and he and Taul launched into a conversation about their respective homelands that Violet quickly tuned out. She walked to the window seat and sank down in it. Orry hopped off her lap and settled on the sill.

"*Is the wedding what has you feeling so off?*" she asked Orry, though she had an inkling before her bondmate answered that it wasn't.

"*No. It's not that.*" Orry closed her eyes. "*I keep replaying their songs in my mind.*"

"*Kayda and Jayan?*" Violet flashed back to earlier in the sitting room. She'd used Orry's boon to listen to their heartsongs, too. The sweet melodies entwining together had stolen her breath. She smiled, recalling the soul-searing harmony of the reunited pair's heartsongs playing alongside each other. "*They were beautiful, weren't they?*"

"*Beautiful, yes. But the more I think about it, the more I wonder...*"

Violet joined Orry, staring out the glass at the castle grounds. She'd only been bonded to Orry for a few days. That didn't give her much time to practice using her boon. It was entirely possible she was missing something.

If Orry couldn't figure out what it was, then what chance did she have? Even though the obvious answer was not much at all, Violet's mind began replaying what she remembered of their songs. A soft smile lit her face as the glorious melody carried her away.

A flash of black flew past the window, breaking her concentration. The crow locked eyes with her as it darted past, and Violet flinched. Silly bird. She'd started attracting them lately. The crow today. Then there was that silly hat bird she'd thought was spying on her in that alley.

Violet gasped, and icy fingers clutched her heart.

"*What is it?*" Orry asked.

"*The hat bird. What if it wasn't a hat bird at all?*"

Orry chuckled. "*You still never explained what a hat bird—*"

"*Shh...*" Violet stood abruptly and turned to Ryon. "Mariun said crows were Jurdan's messengers, didn't she?"

"Yes." Ryon cut off whatever he'd been saying to Taul midsentence. "Why do you ask?"

Boots tapping on the polished floor, Violet paced, wringing her hands. "I saw a bird back on Avion. I thought it was a different black bird, but what if it wasn't?"

"You think it was a crow?" Ryon glanced at the window. "Did you see one just now?"

Violet nodded so forcefully her neck twinged.

What if Jurdan was watching them right now?

Taul leaned forward, waving a hand. "There are crows all over Dracwood. Doln, too."

But his words didn't calm Violet. Not in the least. Especially not when she considered Orry's feelings.

Her mind raced, making connections at lightning speed. The song was off. The crows were watching. If that was a crow in Avion, it had shown up at the same time as Jayan. What if the crows weren't there to watch her? What if they were there for Jayan?

He was the one with the discordant note!

Violet bolted for the door.

"Where are you going?" Taul called.

"Kayda's in danger!" Violet threw open the door and tore into the hall, certainty ringing through her even when she shouldn't truly be certain at all. But as soon as the words passed her lips, the truth of them struck a chord that played in her blood, chilling her to the bone.

Violet raced down the hall and through the door out of the northeast wing. The thump of footsteps echoed behind her, but she didn't turn to see if the others were following. Her heart slammed against her chest as hard as her boots smacked the tile floor in the corridor leading to the sitting room.

"Open the door!" she choked out.

Guard Captain Gawain stood with his back to the closed door. "Violet? You know she's asked to not be—"

"Open the door now," Taul demanded, stopping next to her. His pale skin was flush from the short run, but he wasn't nearly as out of breath as Violet. "The queen may be in danger."

That got Gawain moving. He grabbed the knob, twisting it firmly. He frowned. "It's locked." Gawain backed away, scrambling to tug off the key ring on his belt.

An ear-splitting scream rent the air. Violet's eyes bulged and her stomach twisted. It was coming from inside. They were too late!

"Move!" Taul shoved Gawain out of the way, lifted his huge muscled leg, and kicked the door. Wood splintered and the door groaned but didn't break.

"Where is the blazing thing?" The keys jangled in Gawain's fingers as he searched for the right one.

Ryon lined up next to Taul, and together they kicked it again. The door surrendered to the brute force, smacking against the wall with a deafening *thwack*.

The men were thrown off balance, which meant Violet was the first to duck inside. And the scene she was met with almost made her heave. Charred flesh and burnt hair perfumed the air. A figure was sprawled on the ground face down, writhing and screeching incessantly. "Kayda?" For half a heartbeat, Violet feared the worst.

But her aunt spoke from where she stood beside the open window. "I'm all right."

Kayda was breathing heavily, an arm wrapped around Mena's white-scaled head where it poked through the sitting room window. Taul raced to her side. "What happened?" He brushed his hand up and down her free arm, scanning her closely. "Are you hurt?"

"N-no." Kayda stiffened. "Stop. Please, Taul, stop touching me." The last word escaped as a shriek. Taul backed away, his jaw clenched.

"Gawain, get him out of here." Kayda waved at the figure on the ground who'd yet to stop moaning and yelping. "Take him to the healer but keep him in irons."

When Gawain kneeled and lifted the figure, Violet finally recognized him. She covered her eyes, unable to look any longer.

"I don't understand how this happened." How had she been so wrong? She'd been so certain that Jayan had changed. She'd listened to the song in his heart. He'd been worthy enough for the wishes he'd made. Was that all a lie?

Now she realized she'd missed something major. She'd been so sure that when she and Ryon left, Jayan and Kayda would spend the rest of the day getting reacquainted.

What happened after they'd left?

Orry flew in through the open door and landed on the arm of a yellow settee. "*I see. This is very disconcerting. After listening to the two of them earlier, I would've never expected this outcome.*"

As soon as Gawain lugged Jayan's screaming charred body out of the room, Kayda visibly eased. "Lock the door."

Ryon paced over to the doorway and did his best to shove the mangled door in place. "Sorry. It won't lock."

"It's fine." Kayda sighed. "That'll do."

Violet inched away from the blackened spot on the otherwise spotless carpet. "Maybe we should go to another room."

Kayda shook her head, leaning on Mena for support. "I just need a moment."

She looked at her aunt again—really looked at her. Kayda's hands quivered, and her breath sped in and out of her chest. Her fine plum dress and auburn curls were dappled with black soot.

Taul clenched his fists at his sides. His gaze darted from the spot on the floor to Kayda and back again. With each repetition, his anger increased, threatening to burst out of his skin.

Kayda left Mena at the window and walked to Taul. He startled when her hand landed on his forearm. "I shouldn't have yelled at you like that. It's just... the screaming." Kayda shuddered. "I forgot how awful the screaming could be."

"Don't apologize." Taul turned to her aunt, his gaze softening. "I shouldn't have assumed—" Kayda wrapped her arms around him, and Violet was left feeling like an intruder on her aunt's private life for the second time that day.

Taul breathed out a sigh and hugged her back. Then he eased her away from him and softly brushed her long red curls off her neck, revealing a dark-purple bruise. "What happened, Kayda?" he asked softly.

Violet scrubbed a hand over her face, dullness spreading through her chest and her throat burning with bile.

She hadn't saved her aunt. She'd brought the danger to her.

Miscalculation of a Lifetime

"Take it easy," Nox growled, a sharp pain shooting up his spine.

The masked wolf paid him no mind, only shoved his back more roughly.

Nox shuffled down the darkened hall, the howls of animals ringing off the walls. The same sound lived in his nightmares. One he'd hoped to never hear again.

He must have rot between his ears to have returned here.

He'd been so optimistic. So foolish. He'd thought that a stolen mask and the ability to speak their language would allow him to sneak in. Nox smiled grimly. It had been the miscalculation of a lifetime.

"Don't worry." The voice of his dead bondmate, Flint, filtered into his mind. *"You escaped once. You'll do it again."*

"Any luck getting through to her?" Nox asked.

"None. But we'd been expecting as much."

Nox sighed. He'd lost contact with Gwen the moment he'd breached the walls of the massive undersea city. Luckily, he still had Flint to keep him company. Otherwise, the plaintive cries of the animals locked away in the gloomy cells might drive him insane.

What was it about this place that stopped him from communicating with his bondmate on the outside? He'd never experienced the same thing anywhere else. No matter the distance or whatever obstacles separated them, he'd always been able to reach his bondmates.

Even though he'd only met Gwen recently, the cheeky green earth dragon had quickly begun to feel like family. Now, her absence ate at him. He felt her loss like an open wound that refused to close. He sensed the same loss overcoming Flint.

Gwen must be feeling it even more intensely. She was alone, in truth. Separated from her siblings for the first time, and now from him. And for what? So he could be imprisoned again?

Regret washed over him, seeping into his marrow. He should've never asked Gwen to sacrifice so much. But it might still be worth it. If only he could escape these cells and find Mariun.

Nox's chest burned. He'd come for her, desperate to save her from the evil clutches of her would-be father, Jurdan the Supreme. She'd been taken right out from under his nose. Stolen and carted back to the man who'd made her life miserable.

As soon as he'd woken, healed from the injuries he'd earned trying to stop the masked from taking Mariun, he'd left to save her. He'd barely even paused to form a plan, one that involved him sneaking in wearing a stolen mask and clothing. The thought of Mariun—the woman who'd come to mean so much to him—alone with that vile *thing* made his blood boil. He *had* to save her.

He'd have a hard time doing it down here.

They'd been waiting for him. Dozens of masked holding poles were posted in the massive room they'd used last time to enter—and escape. He should've suspected as much. But he'd been blinded by his need to find Mariun as soon as possible.

Nox hadn't even put up a fight. It would've been foolish to try against those odds. He'd attempted to brazen it out instead, pretending to be Spider and acting like he had every right to be there. It didn't take half a heartbeat for the men to surround him and pull the stolen mask off his face, revealing bronze skin that few men in this sunken city possessed. Even if his looks hadn't stuck out like a downpour in the desert, the guards remembered him from his fight with Crow, so he had no way to sweet talk his way out of imprisonment.

Wolf jabbed him in the back again. Nox glared at the man's black-and-white mask. "What do you want from me? Do I need to jog?"

"Shut your trap." Wolf snickered, lifting the gleaming metal pole in his fist. "Or I'll shut it for you."

Nox shuddered, recalling the pain of those poles all too well. He ground his teeth, choking down an angry retort. If he wanted to find a way out of this prison, he needed to be smart. Picking fights with the guards wasn't exactly a brilliant start.

Wolf shoved through a doorway, leading him into another long corridor filled with cells. The rank stench of unwashed flesh and stale gruel made his eyes water. Still, the cries of animals faded away to nothing.

This block must be populated only with men. Far better that. There was nothing Nox hated more than an animal in distress. If he had to listen to them wailing for hours on end, he wasn't sure if he could stand it.

Men, on the other hand, he could handle. True, their cries were disturbing. They might even be heartbreaking, like those of the young lad he'd met on his last round of imprisonment. Yet, they didn't make him want to claw out his ears.

Wolf halted in front of a cell and unlocked the door. Nox darted inside, dodging the man's beefy fist before it thumped his back once more. The barred door slammed closed behind him, and Nox's stomach sank.

It was as bad as last time. A filthy cell, barren except for the dozen or so bruised and bloodied men sprawled on the floor. On second thought, maybe it wasn't quite so bad. At least this time he wasn't unconscious.

"Well, well. The champion returns." The sound of his own tongue on a prisoner's lips made Nox certain he knew who'd spoken even before the dark-skinned man stepped out of the shadows in the rear corner.

"Iggy." Nox forced a grin, and from the nervous way Iggy retreated, he sensed the look had its intended effect. "I've got a bone to pick with you."

"With me?" Iggy chuckled, his fingers twining in his beard. "Come now. I've been a great help to you, haven't I? Might even say I'm the closest thing to a friend you have in here." He waved one skinny arm at the other men, all of whom stared at them with suspicion and glazed eyes. "Who else have you got to talk to?"

Nox advanced on him, not stopping until they stood toe-to-toe. He stared the older man down, pleased to see him quaking from the threatening glare he leveled on him. "I don't know." Nox switched to Thalassian. "How about whoever I damn well please?"

The other men in the cell who hadn't been paying attention turned to watch.

"H-how?" Iggy continued speaking in the native tongue they shared. He cocked his head, making the twin plaits he'd fashioned his long black beard into bob across his chest. "You sound more natural at that than me. Have you been doing nothing but studying Thalassian since you escaped?"

"Wouldn't you like to know?" Nox sneered, continuing in Thalassian. He wasn't about to let Iggy get away with keeping their conversation private. Not when the men in this cell deserved to know what kind of snake they were stuck with. "You're gonna tell your buddy Jurdan all about it, right?"

Excited murmuring broke out. Nox didn't stop glaring at Iggy, but he spotted disgusted looks painting the faces of the few men in his peripheral vision.

"Oh. Now I get it." Iggy backed up until his shoulders rammed into the cell wall. He wrung his hands, replying in Thalassian. "You can't fault me for that. I'm just trying to survive. Same as every man here."

"I can't fault you? Why shouldn't I?" Nox jabbed a finger into Iggy's bony chest. "Flint might still be alive if you hadn't blabbed everything I shared with you!"

"Y-you can't know that. I had nothing to do—"

"Save it." Nox balled his fists at his sides. "I don't want your excuses or your apologies."

"What are you doing back here, Nox?" Iggy frowned. "We all thought you'd done the impossible. I swore when you picked that map instead of your freedom you were a fool, but you proved us wrong."

Nox smiled. "Get used to it. I make a habit of doing the impossible."

A man seated on the filthy floor snorted. "Fool probably just got himself captured again." Laughter rained down.

Iggy's eyes narrowed. "No. I'm not buying it. You're here for a reason. Why have you returned?"

Nox considered keeping his plans to himself. Was he being even more of a fool to share anything with Iggy? But in the end, the need to know what he was up against won out. The prisoners might not be privy to all the information in this city, but they knew more than he did.

"Mariun. I'm here to save her."

Snickers and cruel chuckles exploded from the men in the cell. Nox scanned their faces and choked down the urge to scream.

Iggy shook his head and smiled slyly. "I should've guessed. You won't be the first man she's bewitched."

Nox gritted his teeth. "She's *not* bewitched me."

He didn't need to lay it out for Iggy and these prisoners. He knew what he and Mariun had was real. She'd shared things with him she'd never told another soul, and he'd done the same. They'd connected on a level he hadn't experienced with anyone else. And he still remembered the way she felt in his arms. None of the idiots "bewitched" by her looks could claim the same.

"Sure." Iggy chuckled, rolling his eyes. Nox barely resisted the urge to slap the stupid grin off his face. "I think you're going to have trouble with that."

"Don't be so sure about that." Nox echoed Flint's words, fighting to hang on to his bondmate's optimism no matter how dire his current situation seemed. "I escaped this cell once. I can do it again."

"Oh, I'm sure you could. But you might have trouble saving what isn't here."

"What?" Nox barked. The cell exploded in more guffaws.

"I hate to tell you this, my friend... The Supreme offered a reward to any masked that brought his daughter back. There hasn't been a whisper from the guards about anyone collecting it." Iggy dared to pat him gently on the shoulder, compassion filling his dark-brown eyes. "Mariun hasn't returned. Sorry, but you got yourself captured for nothing."

More Secrets

Ryon stepped away from the ruined half-closed door and crossed the room to Violet's side. He slipped his hand into hers, and she clutched it like a lifeline, her pale fingers threading between his.

Guano. What a mess.

His gaze locked on the ruined carpet where they'd found Jayan writhing, his skin and clothes charred so much he'd been unrecognizable.

How had it come to this?

He could only imagine that the man had attacked Queen Kayda, and Mena stepped in to scorch him. The question was, why? Had Violet been wrong to assume Jayan had changed? Had he been secretly working for Jurdan all along, just waiting for a chance to assassinate the queen?

Something about that idea rubbed Ryon the wrong way. He'd seen the way they'd acted when they first reunited. If he had to guess, he'd have sworn they were once lovers—at the least, very close friends. He still couldn't picture what would change so much in the short time they'd left them together to cause Jayan to attack Kayda.

How had Violet known? She'd torn off, screaming that Kayda was in danger. He ought to be used to Violet doing incredible things by now, but it had still stunned him.

Kayda cleared her throat, interrupting his musings. Ryon gave her his full attention, beyond interested in what had happened after they'd left this room. She backed away, dipping her head to hide the bruise on her neck again. "It was foolish of me to remain here with Jayan alone. I know that already, so save your breath."

Taul frowned, lifting his arms in surrender. "I didn't say anything."

Kayda glared at him. "You didn't have to."

"It's all right, Auntie," Violet cut in, holding her own neck and gazing at her aunt with sympathy. "No one's blaming you. If Jayan tried to hurt you, then he's the one at fault."

"Violet's right. Tell us what happened. Please," Taul added.

Kayda paced to the window, returning to Mena's side. "I just want-ed some time alone with my old friend. After he used that wish to return my eyesight, I hoped the letter was wrong."

"What letter?" Ryon asked.

"Wait." Taul's jaw dropped. "He wished to return your eyesight?"

Violet grinned. "Guess you haven't heard the news yet? Kayda can see through Mena's eyes now."

A radiant smile crossed Kayda's face, and she patted Mena's head.

"Is that true?" Taul asked.

"Yes." Kayda sighed. "Today's been overwhelming. Gaining a bondmate. Finding out the friend I thought I'd sent to his death still lived. Regaining my sight. I thought—" The queen doubled over, gagging.

Ryon frowned, until he spotted Mena's gaze cut across the room to the charred spot on the floor.

"I think Violet was right," Ryon said. "Isn't there somewhere else we can go to talk about this?"

Kayda nodded. "Let's move to the music room."

Taul glanced at Mena. "There are no windows. Are you sure—"

"Yes." Kayda stepped away from the window. "Mena needs to go to her brothers. Come."

Violet's grip on his hand tightened as they turned to leave. Ryon let her lead the way out of the sunny room with chairs too fancy to sit on and into the hall. Orry hopped along beside them.

They didn't travel far. They stepped inside a door a few steps down the hall, leaving behind the stomach-turning stench of charred flesh. Polished instruments hung on the walls and sat on the floor propped up in stands.

Ryon tried not to gape, but it was a hard feat to manage. The wealth displayed in Kings Keep boggled his mind. Violet walked around like it wasn't anything out of the ordinary—and perhaps for her, it wasn't—but they had nothing like this back on Avion. His heart twinged as he took it all in. Was this what Violet expected out of her life? To live in opulence with so many instruments on her walls that no one could hope to master in their lifetime?

"Close the doors," Kayda said.

Ryon dropped Violet's hand and strode across the room to the large double doors in the back. The door they'd entered through banged closed as Taul shut that too.

"I received a letter today from Ereni," Kayda announced.

"From my mother?" Violet brightened. "I was wondering why my parents weren't here." Her face fell. "Wait. Why *aren't* they here?"

"Your parents are fine." Kayda's tone was firm but gentle, like she could hear the panic in her niece's voice. "They left weeks ago for Magehaven, hoping to meet you upon your return."

"Oh." Violet pursed her lips. "I guess they were expecting me to come back on a boat."

Kayda grinned. "I imagine so." Her smile vanished. "It's a good thing they were there, or I would've had no warning."

"A warning for what?" Ryon asked.

"Ereni watched the three of you fly overhead while she was in Magehaven. She wrote to tell me about it. Sent me a letter by dove."

Ryon tried to hide his surprise. His little island was small enough that messages were carried by foot. But for a county as big as this one, using birds was genius.

"In her letter, she described what she saw with her seer sight," Kayda continued.

"Seer?" Ryon frowned. "What's that?"

Violet turned to him. "My mother possesses a rare talent. She can see when someone has access to magic. She describes it like a glow or aura wreathed around them, with different colors representing different types of magic." Violet's nose wrinkled. "What did she see?"

"Ereni noticed two auras that startled her," Kayda continued. "The first was silver, which is a color she'd never encountered before."

"I bet that was you, Ryon." Violet beamed at him.

"Me?" Ryon lifted a brow. "Are you sure?"

"From the feathers you're carrying," Violet added.

"She could see that?" Ryon's heart skipped a beat. No one else had known about the bloodfeathers hidden in his hair, but it sounded like Violet's mother would be impossible to fool.

Violet nodded. "Yes. Remember the vision I told you about? The Winter Witch uses the same fish that Orry spoke about. She's used that magic so often it changed her aura even though she's getting it from an outside source. I bet it's the same with you."

"Well, that explains the silver," Kayda cut in. "But that wasn't the aura that made your mother rush to pen me a letter."

Violet gasped. "Was it me? Is there something wrong—"

"No, Vi. It was Jayan. I didn't want to believe it, but after that..." Kayda thrust out a hand toward the sitting room and shuddered.

"What color was Jayan's aura?" Taul asked.

"Black." The single word reverberated through the room, leaving silence in its wake. Dread pooled in the pit of Ryon's stomach.

Violet blinked repeatedly, then shook her head. "Black? Mother has never said anything about seeing black..."

"Ereni had only seen it once before. During the battle in the Abandoned Lands, the men who'd been connected to the Unseen were all wreathed in black." Kayda sighed. "Of course, I hadn't been sure when you arrived. Without another seer, there was no way to know which of your companions had the black aura."

Ryon frowned as he considered the implications of the queen's claims. The Unseen was the monster responsible for almost destroying Dracwood two decades ago. Violet and her aunt Lark had both agreed they'd felt something vile standing in Jurdan's presence. The same feeling Lark admitted she'd sensed while with the Unseen. Did they both possess the same magic?

"It was a test." Taul stiffened. "That's why you were alone with him."

"I had to know." Kayda shrugged. "It was the fastest way to be sure."

"Surely we could've sent for another seer." Taul tugged on his beard.

"And waited how long?" Kayda crossed her arms. "I couldn't take that chance. It was better to learn now than allow him to wander around with all our guests."

"I suppose you're right," Taul admitted grudgingly.

"What happened after we left?" Violet stacked her fists on her hips. "Funny that you even let us leave, considering what you were debating."

"Gawain sent some of his men to watch over you discreetly. But by then, I already suspected Jayan." Kayda's head dipped. "It was too perfect to be believed. A friend returning from the brink of death and healing what could never be healed? Almost like the whole thing was staged to get my guard down. So, I let him believe that he had."

Taul crossed the room and grabbed Kayda's hand.

"We sat and talked for a long while, but it wasn't until Mena left to check on her brothers that Jayan made a move." Kayda paled and traced her collarbone idly. "Within moments of Mena leaving, his hands were wrapped around my neck."

"I'll kill him," Taul growled.

Kayda clasped his arm when Taul stepped away. "No, you won't. When the healer saves him, he needs to be questioned."

Taul glared at her but made no other move to leave.

"It's lucky Mena made it back to you in time to scorch him," Ryon said.

Kayda chuckled humorlessly. "She didn't."

Violet frowned. "I don't understand. If Mena didn't..." Her eyes widened.

"You aren't the only one who's never touched that willow," Kayda said quietly.

"I'm lost," Ryon blurted. It was clear he'd missed something important. Taul and Violet were both gaping at Kayda like she'd told them the grass was red and the sky was purple.

"H-how?" Taul dropped Kayda's hand and backed away slowly. "That's why there's always a candle burning. Everywhere you go..."

Ryon gulped, scanning the walls. He'd hardly given it a moment's thought when they'd strolled into the brightly lit music room. But Taul was right. The ornate oil lamps had been lit when they'd entered. Candles in three armed holders lined the halls. The hearth in the sitting room had a fire blazing when they'd arrived. The library, too.

"You've had magic all this time?" Violet asked.

"Just a little." Kayda smiled wryly. "When Lark called for a circle after the battle and sank the mages' magic into the ground, I wasn't with them."

"Wait. Weren't you dead?" Taul chimed in.

That's right. Ryon remembered the story now. Kayda had to be brought back with a wish from a golden bloodfeather.

"Yes. When I was revived, I discovered that I still had a small bit of magic left, like all the children born with magic before the Unseen's death."

"Like me." Violet scanned her aunt's face. "And you kept it hidden all this time?"

"I suspected one day I'd need it." Kayda smiled in Violet's direction. "Your mother swore the other seers to secrecy."

"More secrets." Violet groaned. "Why am I not surprised?"

"Secrets can keep you safe. They did for me today, at least." Kayda sighed, ruining the impact of her grave statement.

Did that mean... "You burned Jayan?" Ryon's stomach churned. She'd only just gotten her friend back and then had been forced to set him ablaze. Guano. He couldn't even imagine how hard that must've been.

Kayda merely nodded. Taul inched closer. "I'm sorry."

"It's—" Kayda's lip wobbled, and she sucked in a deep breath. "I'm fine."

"I'm sorry, too." Violet stared at the floor. The hardwood was polished to such a magnificent shine the frown she wore reflected up at him. "I shouldn't have trusted him. I knew he spent all that time with Jurdan, but I thought he'd changed."

"So did I, Vi. So did I." Kayda sighed again.

"What now?" Taul drifted past a tall harp and trailed his fingers lightly across the strings. "We try to pull information about this Jurdan out of him?"

"Yes." Kayda tilted her head. "And there's the problem with the dragons, too."

Ryon cocked a brow. "Problem? Is it the guard?" That overweight Guard Captain had given them his word they'd be safe, but he wouldn't be surprised if the younger guards were bothering them.

"No." Kayda shook her head sharply. "The three here are fine. Mena is worried about her sister."

"Gwen?" Violet gasped. "Did something happen? Is Nox all right?" She shot the questions out, barely pausing to breathe.

"She's not sure. Gwen hasn't talked to him in days." Kayda frowned. "Not since she dropped him off above the underwater city."

"The same thing happened to Lark, remember? While she was in Thalassia, Muse couldn't reach her either," Violet explained.

Kayda straightened the sleeves of her dress. "I remember. Still, it sounds like Gwen isn't happy about it. Or about leaving Nox alone for so long."

Nox had departed before them, determined to rescue Mariun on his own. He wouldn't have had nearly as long of a flight either.

"How long has he been down there?" Ryon asked.

"Three days." Kayda bit her lip. "I hate to say it, but what if he's been captured?"

"We have to help him. We already promised to meet Nox after we came to warn you, but now we need to leave right away." Violet walked to Kayda's side and hugged her. "I'm sorry to leave before the wedding, Auntie."

"Don't worry. You won't miss anything," Kayda said.

"I won't?" Violet asked.

"What do you mean, Kayda?" Taul choked out, his voice pained.

Kayda set her shoulders straight. "Jurdan stole my sister. He's infected my friend with his foul magic. He almost succeeded in killing me—twice. I refuse to stay here and let everyone else fight him alone. I'm coming with you."

Taul blanched. "You're kidding."

"I'm not." Kayda turned to him. "My bondmate needs me."

"Your bondmate? What about your country? And our wedding?"

Kayda didn't bow under the weight of Taul's questions. If anything, she relaxed a hair once he'd asked the last. "There will still be a wedding. And I'll leave the kingdom in good hands." Kayda smiled coyly. "Just think of it as practice, Husband."

"Son of a—" Taul cut himself off before he finished the oath. "I can't be your husband without a damn wedding."

"And you'll have it once this threat is neutralized and I return." Kayda crossed the room with her hands outstretched. Taul's face was red, but he wasn't angry enough to step out of the path of his soon-to-be wife's grasp. She halted when her palm landed on his chest, her touch trailing up to his shoulder. "I know this isn't how either of us pictured our wedding. This is supposed to be a celebration of our countries uniting in peace. Can you honestly say you'd be happy marrying with so much uncertainty hanging over our heads? When we're almost positive that peace is further away than we ever imagined?"

Taul frowned. "I suppose you're right. Again."

"I usually am," Kayda quipped.

Taul and Kayda drifted closer to each other, and the air shifted. Ryon tugged on Violet's hand and nodded to the door.

Violet cleared her throat. "Ryon and I will be in the library. Looks like you two need to *discuss* things."

They didn't make it further than the hall before Violet sank into a crouch, clutching her stomach.

"Violet? What's wrong?" Ryon cringed. What a stupid question. Her uncle was in danger and her aunt's wedding was postponed—and that wasn't the only bad news that'd been heaped upon her in the last few moments.

Orry crouched beside Violet and must've said something more useful than he had. Violet popped up a heartbeat later. "Sorry. I-I just pictured Jayan." She shuddered, and Ryon nodded gravely. Out here in the hall, the sickening stench wafted around them again. It was no wonder she was flashing back to that dreadful scene.

Ryon looped his arm through Violet's and led her away slowly. "You're right. That was awful. But it's over now."

"It's all my fault. I should've never—"

"Don't say that. There's no way you could've known. Unless you're a seer, too?"

Violet shook her head. "No."

"Well then, I stand by my statement. No way you could've known. But you're still ready to return and help Nox. The way I see it, you're part of the solution."

"I guess you're right." Violet sighed.

Ryon grinned, sensing an opportunity to lighten the mood. He cleared his throat and pitched his voice ludicrously high in a poor imitation of Queen Kayda. "I usually am," he said, echoing her parting words. Then he puckered his lips theatrically and leaned close to Violet.

"Puh-lease." He wasn't surprised when she rolled her unique violet-hued eyes and shoved him away. But then she started giggling.

Yep. That was the reaction he'd been hoping for. A bright smile spread across his face as they opened the door to the northeast wing.

"You're an idiot, you know that, right?" Violet said once she'd stopped laughing.

"Yeah. I know. But you're stuck with me anyway." He winked. Maybe this journey wouldn't be so bad after all. As long as he could keep her laughing like that, then maybe it wasn't too much to hope for.

Limbo

Nox squinted as the overhead lights shone down on the cell. He'd spent a long night tossing and turning only to wake less than rested with a thousand tiny pains plaguing him.

He reached out with his thoughts. *"You awake?"*

"Yes. Morning already, hm?" Flint replied. *"How'd you sleep?"*

"Rotting awful." A crowded cell full of snoring, stinking prisoners wasn't exactly an ideal resting place.

Flint chuckled. *"More of the same, then."*

It had been three long days and nights of this boring limbo. Long days with nothing to do but sit around and try to squeeze more information out of the prisoners—unsuccessfully so far. And long, sleepless nights wondering where his plan went wrong.

Mariun. If she wasn't here, then where was she?

Nox groaned as he sat up, rubbing the sleep out of his eyes. *"Doesn't get any easier just because I'm used to it."*

"I recall." Flint had been here last time. He knew all too well the monotony Nox was facing. *"At least they're feeding you."*

"*True.*" Nox shuddered at the same moment his stomach rumbled. The mere thought of food was enough to trigger a deep longing. The disgusting fish-and-porridge combination they served—in a single bucket for the men to fight over—was hardly worthy of being labeled food. Still, Nox had forced himself to gobble a few mouthfuls each day.

"*You've been eating, haven't you?*" Flint asked.

"*Yes, Mother,*" he replied sarcastically.

"*You need to keep up your strength.*"

"*I know. I know.*"

Nox sighed. He'd overheard chatter about a new game. It was only a matter of time before he'd be forced back into that ring. He was the *champion*, after all.

A sneer crossed his lips. The title had earned him a measure of respect with the prisoners. No one sought to fight him. On the first day, he'd shoved a man away from the bucket, knocking him to the ground. Now, the prisoners stood aside and offered him the first turn with the slop, only pouncing on it after he'd choked down a few nasty bites and washed it down with tepid water.

He'd endured it all. The food that he struggled not to spit up. The pitying looks and whispers. All to prepare himself to fight. Nox shivered. If they forced him to battle another starved, broken animal, he wasn't sure what he'd do. The thought of it sickened him far more than the food.

It was criminal what Jurdan was doing here. Forcing men to fight to the death to survive. Starving animals until they were ravenous enough to kill. If Nox had his way, he'd end it all. He'd sink this sorry excuse for a city, and all the revolting, cheering spectators with it.

"*I sense your thoughts have taken a dark turn,*" Flint said.

Nox flinched. It was unusual for bondmates to share thoughts they didn't purposely project. Flint was a bit of an enigma in that. Perhaps it was what happened when two creatures spent so many years bonded together in the flesh. Either way, he had a knack for sensing Nox's emotions, even when he wasn't keen to share his exact thoughts.

"*It's this place.*" Nox wandered to the cell wall, a familiar tingle passing through his hands. "*It makes me so furious, what they're doing to these innocent animals.*"

"*I get it. Once you're out of there, you'll find a way to stop it. I know you will.*"

"*It's not only that.*" Nox frowned. "*I felt it last time too. Something is off. Something I can't put my finger on.*"

"*Hm. I remember that feeling all too well. Still can't figure it out?*"

Nox placed his hand on the wall as a wash of emotions flooded him. The feelings simmering in his bones spread through his blood. The rage, the pain, the fear—all of it rose to the forefront of his mind, so strong and so swift it was overwhelming. He pulled his hand away.

What *was* that? His own emotions reflected at him? Or something else?

"*No. I don't have a clue,*" he admitted.

"Morning." Iggy yawned and scratched his belly.

Nox rolled his eyes inwardly but forced his face to remain stony. Iggy didn't know when to quit. Nox had learned his lesson. The oceans would freeze over before he shared any details of his life with the Jorian prisoner. But his tight-lipped treatment hadn't slowed Iggy's attempts to chat in the least.

"I think today's the day." Iggy sauntered over to the barred door. "You excited for your return to the ring?"

Nox scowled. "No."

"Oh, come on now. At least you'll get a break from these four walls. A little exercise." Iggy pressed his face between the bars, briefly looking in both directions before giving up, spinning around, and leaning against the door. "It's not like you'll need to worry about losing."

"What do you mean? Of course I could lose."

Iggy shrugged. "The champion never loses." He cut a glance at Nox and quirked a half-smile. "Well, almost never." Iggy leaned closer and lowered his voice. "The last fellow, Crow, he wasn't always so unnatural. It wasn't until he was crowned champion. There's a rumor Jurdan gifts each champion with powers."

Gifts. Shivers spread down Nox's spine. That was what Jurdan had offered him. What was it he'd said? *The next time we meet, you'll beg me for my gifts.*

Nox bit back a smirk. No chance that was happening. Jurdan could choke on his *gifts* for all he cared.

"So did he?" Iggy asked.

"Did he what?" Nox barked.

Iggy blanched, but that didn't dissuade him from asking, "Give you powers?"

Nox let the smirk spread this time. "Wouldn't you like to know?"

A door slammed. The men perked up. A few licked their lips, clearly anticipating breakfast.

As footsteps echoed down the hall, a memory assailed Nox. It wasn't so long ago that Mariun wandered those corridors. She'd sashay past in a floor-sweeping dress, all long legs and silky black hair. Her big gray doe eyes would peer in, and she'd meet his gaze.

He could recall it so clearly. She'd always been stunning, but back then she'd been the lone light in his dreary days. A single glimpse of beauty among all the ugliness drowning him.

But Mariun wasn't out there today. He knew it even before he spotted the masked man in the hall. The footsteps were too loud. Her musical voice wasn't bouncing off the walls. There was no swoosh of fabric sweeping the filthy floor.

Nox's chest ached. Where was she? Would he ever find her?

The footsteps halted outside their door, and a masked man peered in.

Who was this? Nox studied the bear mask. He'd been expecting the wolf. It was always the wolf who brought them their morning gruel.

Bear didn't have a bucket. Nox's pulse kicked up, drumming through his veins like a battle dirge. And as luck would have it, the guard stopped directly in front of him.

"Well, well. Look what we have here." Bear shook his head, making his mask look like it was ready to leap off his face and strike. "You know, I bet Wolf that the news of your return was a rumor." Bear chuckled dryly. "Three rotations on scum duty. That's what you cost me."

"Happy to be of service." Nox's stomach churned. Who was this guy? Some fool with a vendetta? It wasn't his fault the idiot lost a bet.

Bear cocked his head. "A joker, huh? Don't worry. We're gonna have a lot of fun together, you and I." Though he couldn't see his face—couldn't even see a stitch of skin beyond the all-black outfit complete with gloves and hood—Nox heard the smile in Bear's voice.

He gulped. That didn't sound good. Still, he'd be damned if he showed a smidgen of fear in front of the men in his cell. Or in front of this chucklehead of a guard.

"Great. I could use some fun in my life," Nox replied coolly.

Bear dug in his pocket and pulled out a key.

"Good luck," Iggy whispered at his elbow.

Nox grabbed Iggy's sleeve when he tried to dart away. "Who is this guy?" he hissed in the man's ear.

Iggy shuddered, making his braids shake. "Cleaning crew. Just keep your mouth shut and it will be over before you know it." The fabric ripped in Nox's fist, and Iggy made his escape, shooting to the cell's far corner.

"Someone's here from the cleaning crew," he explained to Flint. *"Looks like they're planning to put me to work this time."*

"Strange. What do they need cleaned?"

"The other cells, maybe?" His stomach clenched. Someone had to clear out the filth in the animals' cells. Clearly not very often, if the smell was anything to judge by. Was that where they were taking him?

He didn't have long to ponder the question. Within moments, Bear tugged the cell door open, a shining pole clutched in his fist. "Out with you, then."

"Stay sharp. Maybe this is the chance you need to escape."

Nox obeyed, knowing it was useless to struggle. If he refused, they'd only pierce him with one of their darts and lug his unconscious body wherever they wanted him. Then he'd be forced to endure hours of brain fog while he recovered.

He couldn't take that chance now. Flint was right. He had to stay sharp if he wanted to figure out an escape plan. Even after questioning every man in that cell, he'd come up with nothing. He had to hope that something on this little cleaning expedition would give him the edge he needed to escape.

The cell door clanged behind him. None of the other men had been pulled out with him. Nox frowned, his nerves sparking to life. What did they want with him all alone? Surely cleaning animal cages would take more than just him. Unless forcing him to complete the task alone was meant to be his penance for costing the bear his bet.

He followed Bear through the doors to another block of cells. And the next. The pungent scent of feces bombarded him. Nox held his breath, praying his guess wasn't correct. He might pass out if forced to clean those cages.

To his surprise, Bear kept walking. Corridor after corridor slid past until they arrived at a stairwell. Was he to clean the ring, then? He'd wondered what happened to the blood after the matches. Unless he was mistaken, this were the same stairs that led there.

Or it might be another match... After all, how much could he trust Iggy, anyway? What if all that talk of cleaning was his way of throwing him off his game? Who knew what angle Iggy would try? Surely that snake would do anything to put him in Jurdan's good graces.

Would Jurdan want him to fail? Nox honestly didn't know. It wouldn't say much about his old champion if the man who beat him fell in his first match as the reigning victor. Although, Nox had laughed at Jurdan when he'd offered his gifts. Then he'd helped Mariun escape. Could Jurdan's desire to punish him outweigh his pride?

If rumor proved true, then Jurdan wasn't in Thalassia, either. Would they even hold a game without the dark king there to watch?

It appeared his questions wouldn't be answered yet. Bear didn't ascend to the top. He stopped on the second landing and shoved open a door.

"Go on." Bear waved him through.

Nox slipped past Bear and jumped when the door slammed shut behind them. Bear nudged him forward into a dimly lit chamber that reeked of chlorine. Moisture dappled the walls, and a long black coil snaked across the floor. Bear stopped beside it and lifted the end.

"Strip," Bear barked.

Nox's stomach clenched. *Think I had it wrong. They're not making me clean. They're cleaning me.*

"*Careful,*" Flint ordered. "*You can't let them see it.*"

Flint was right. His lone advantage was tucked into his tunic, hidden on the string necklace Violet had given him. But how was he going to keep it hidden with Bear staring at him?

"You mind?" Nox sneered at the bear mask, forcing a mocking lilt to his words. "Oh. I get it. You want a private show."

Bear bristled. But his taunt accomplished what he'd been hoping for. Bear looked away, staring at the ground and shaking his head.

Nox pounced on the opportunity, slipping his tunic off his head and making sure to pull the necklace off with it. By the time Bear's head snapped up, he'd folded the precious feather inside his black tunic, out of sight.

"You ain't got nothing I haven't seen before." Bear smacked his pole against the tile wall, making a clang reverberate in the air. "Hurry or I'll show you what true pain feels like."

Nox stripped, tearing off his pants and undergarments. They'd stolen his boots before sending him to the prison level, so it didn't take long. He balled the fabric up, clutching it against his chest.

"Drop those in there," Bear instructed, nodding to a bin in the far corner.

Nox creeped sideways, keeping his gaze trained on Bear while his heart slammed against his throat. *"He's making me put it in with the laundry. What am I going to do?"*

"Relax. You'll get it back once this is over. One problem at a time."

Flint's words calmed him until he peeked into the bin. *"Rot and decay. It's not a bin. It's a chute."* Kings Keep had the same contraptions built into the walls. If he tossed his clothes inside, they'd be gone for good. Lost in some massive laundry pile who knew where.

"Think, Nox. There must be a solution." Panic bled into Flint's calm demeanor. *"Can you hide it?"*

"Where? There's nowhere, and he won't stop staring—"

The door eased open and a man in a striped cat mask sauntered in, pushing a cart loaded with an assortment of bottles, towels, and brushes.

"There you are. Thought I might have to hunt you down." Bear turned to the newcomer.

Perfect. Nox quickly disentangled his tunic from his balled-up pants. He dropped the shirt on the floor behind the chute and dumped the rest into the hole. He swallowed, watching the black fabric flutter as it disappeared into darkness.

"*I stashed it behind the chute.*"

"*Good,*" Flint said.

"Move it," Bear demanded.

Nox sauntered away from the chute into the center of the room. The two masked watched him, the uneasy way they shifted their stances and followed his every move betraying their curiosity.

Maybe these men who spent their entire lives covered from head to toe would be embarrassed if subjected to the same treatment, but Nox couldn't care less about his nudity. Where he grew up, no one batted an eye when exposed to unclothed flesh. It was practically an everyday occurrence.

The blast of frigid water that drenched him he could live without. Nox did his best to stand stoically while the icy stream pounded his limbs. Then he remained still while the cat rushed forward and dumped liquid soap on his head and roughly scrubbed him with a long, bristled brush.

Was it demeaning being washed like a pet? Of course. But he refused to let his feelings show. He'd suffer through anything if he could just save that feather after...

He stared straight ahead, even while his eyes itched to flick over to the bin. Was his tunic still hidden? Maybe if he complied, they'd allow him a bit of privacy to redress?

"I don't get it. Why the cleaning now? They were happy to let me sit in my own filth last time we were prisoners."

"Don't remind me." Flint's sardonic reply had Nox recalling the way his tail always twitched when he was annoyed. *"I almost licked you clean to save myself from smelling you."*

Nox fought the urge to chuckle. The masked finished scrubbing his hair and moved on to rubbing sudsy cleanser on his back. The soap was scentless, but he was thankful for it all the same.

Cat finished and backed away. Bear lifted the hose again, and Nox braced himself. Another icy blast washed off the dirt and soap. He endured it long enough that his teeth chattered when the bear killed the spray. A towel flew toward his chest. Nox caught it and started drying off. Cat bent beside his cart. When he stood again, he held folded black fabric in his hands.

New clothes. But what about the old ones? His gaze darted to the chute. The smallest bit of black peeked out from behind it.

"What do we have here?"

Nox cursed inwardly when he looked back and found Bear staring at the chute.

No! He was so stupid. If he'd only kept his attention off it a little longer...

Bear stepped toward it, and Nox lunged. A blast of pain in his temple was his reward. He stumbled, clutching his head and groaning.

"No one told you to move." Cat slid the metal pole he'd whacked Nox with back on his belt. He cocked his head toward Bear. "What is it?"

"Nothing." Bear lifted the balled-up tunic and dropped it in the chute. Nox's stomach sank with it. "He's just clumsy is all."

Nox breathed through the pain, blinking back dizziness. What was he going to do now? It was gone. His feather—and his one chance at making a wish—had disappeared.

Wait... A flash of gold caught the corner of his eye. He blinked again, his eyesight clearing in time to see the bear shove his hand into his pocket.

Maybe it wasn't lost after all. "*The bear has it.*"

"*The guard? He took your bloodfeather?*"

Nox gritted his teeth. "*Yes. The rotting greedy bastard.*"

"*It's all right. You'll get it back. Chances are good he doesn't even realize what it is.*"

Flint was right. For once, he was thankful for these people's sheltered upbringing. He still had a chance. He just had to figure out how to reclaim his feather...

Nox struggled to his feet.

"Hey. What did I say about moving?" The cat pulled his pole off his belt.

Bear strode forward. "Put that away. Or do you want to clean him again?" Bear nodded to the pole in the cat's hands. "You heard the Supreme. He doesn't want to be subjected to that scum's stench."

Nox gulped. "*Well. I figured out what the cleaning was for.*"

"*What?*" Flint asked.

"*Jurdan.*" A smile curved his lips. "*Looks like I'm finally about to get some answers.*"

Secret Weapon

Violet trailed Guard Captain Gawain into the armory. The drafty room sat inside the tower the Castle Guard called home.

She'd checked on the dragons after Gawain bade her and Ryon to follow him out of the library. They'd left them resting in the moonlight with full bellies and a squad of guards hovering around—for their protection, Gawain had assured her. After all, with so many wedding visitors at the keep, anyone might wander over.

Orry had chosen to stay with them, curling next to the humongous dragons like they were birds in the Aviary. Violet couldn't blame her. It had been a long, eventful day. She was dying to rest, too. But it would have to wait.

Now, she found herself marching into what was likely the most well-stocked armory in all of Dracwood. Torches lit the echoey chamber, and weapons of all shapes and sizes hung from the walls. Even more rested on racks. Boxes overflowed with blunt practice swords, arrows by the hundreds, and so much more that she struggled to catalog it in her mind.

And in the center of it all stood her aunt strapping a knife sheath to her thigh. She'd piled her long red hair into a bun and replaced the charred plum dress for a plain brown tunic and trousers. The dull traveler's gear looked so strange on her aunt Violet bit back a gasp. She couldn't remember ever seeing the queen when she wasn't wearing a dress.

"Violet. Is that you?" Kayda spun toward them, her red eyes not quite connecting with her across the room. "Mena said you were headed inside."

"Yes, it's me." She stopped next to a bin filled with polearms and quirked a brow. "Are we gearing up for war?"

"Better to be prepared for anything," Gawain cut in. He marched to Kayda's side. "My queen. Are you sure—"

"Save your breath, Gawain. I'm going." Kayda waved in his direction. "Find me a proper knife for this sheath, would you?"

Gawain sighed but walked away and began hunting for a knife inside a box propped against the far wall.

"Better grab a few," Kayda added. "You'll be wanting some too, I wager?" She tilted her head in Violet's direction.

Violet nodded. "Please. Make them small. Good for throwing."

Ryon cleared his throat. "I didn't know you could throw knives."

Violet shrugged. She strode along the wall, her fingers drifting across a small bow. "I can. I'm a decent shot with a bow as well."

Not that she'd been granted many opportunities to show off her skills since she'd met Ryon. When the boat she and Nox had sailed across the ocean sank, her weapons sank with it. Since then, she'd rarely had anything to defend herself with, besides her magic and her wits. She plucked the bow off the wall, smiling as the familiar weight settled in her hands. It would be nice to have weapons she was confident wielding at her disposal again.

"Decent?" Kayda scoffed. "Don't let Conall hear you say that. To hear him tell it, Vi could take down a whole army single-handedly after his lessons."

Violet's cheeks warmed. "I don't know about all that."

"And the knives." Kayda leaned closer to Ryon, a mischievous smile on her face. "You should've heard how much she begged for lessons when she was a little tot. She was obsessed with the knife throwers in the Wandering Bards. Wanted to be just like Meital." Kayda chuckled, cocking her head in Violet's direction. "And your mother was all too keen to teach you. I told Ereni you were too young and sure to lose a finger, but she wouldn't listen."

"Good that she didn't." Gawain stopped beside Violet and offered her a handful of small sheathed blades. "You can keep your fool aunt out of trouble." Violet plucked the first, testing the weight before grabbing the rest, along with the knife belt Gawain had slung over his wrist.

"Gawain!" Kayda tutted, hands on her hips. "I could have you demoted for that."

Gawain chuckled dryly, making his large belly jiggle. "You won't. No one else with the seniority to replace me would ever allow you to fly off on a damned rescue mission. They'd lock you away before letting you put yourself in danger. It's what I ought to be doing."

"Don't be ridiculous." Kayda's lips thinned. "Mena will protect me. Besides, if anything goes wrong, we'll use our secret weapon."

"Secret weapon?" Ryon asked. "What's that?"

Kayda grinned. "We have Violet to thank for that as well."

"Me?" Violet squeaked. Aunt Kayda was really laying the compliments on thick. "I don't remember being involved with any secret weapon."

"Of course you were, Vi. It's thanks to you that Lark was saved. When she returned and told me the story of those darts and the sleeping tonic on them, it got me thinking." Kayda's smile turned sly. "There's a creature that secretes a toxin that does something similar."

"There is?" Ryon's brow furrowed.

What creature was she talking about? Violet racked her brain, but it wasn't until she replayed the story of Kayda's time in the Suland Waste that it hit her. "No. You can't mean the tetrela?"

"I knew you'd figure it out." Kayda waved in Gawain's direction. "Show them."

Frowning, Gawain pulled a vial out of his pocket.

Violet gaped at the clear liquid rolling across the bottom of the glass jar. "How did you get that?"

"I'm lost." Ryon scratched his scalp, shaking his dreads. "What is that? And what's a tetrela?"

"They're spiders that live in the Suland Waste. Huge ones," Violet explained.

Kayda shivered. "Nasty, massive creatures. Big enough to lift a full-grown woman and spin her into a cocoon before you can blink."

"Are you serious?" Ryon jerked back, eyes wide.

"Oh, they're real all right. And that"—Kayda's hand shot toward Gawain, who still held the vial—"is how they incapacitate their victims. They shoot out venomous spines that paralyze their prey. Makes your limbs lock up, every muscle taut and stiff as a board."

"Wow." Ryon squinted at the liquid lining the bottom of the jar.

"But how did you get it?" Violet crossed her arms. It couldn't have been more than a few weeks since Lark returned. And the Suland Waste wasn't exactly close.

Kayda shrugged. "I called in a favor. I still have a few cousins out in the waste. How they procured it, I didn't ask, but I imagine there's one less tetrela haunting the sand dunes tonight."

Well, that made sense. She'd noticed a few Suland Warriors at the meal they'd interrupted. It wouldn't have been too much trouble for one of them to bring the toxin with them.

Gawain lifted another jar out of his pocket. Unlike the clear liquid, which only coated the bottom of the first jar, this one was filled to the stopper with a dark crimson fluid. "And what is this red stuff again?"

"Let's just say that's the antidote." A lopsided grin twisted Kayda's lips. "Hopefully we won't be needing any, but I figured it was better to prepare for anything—like you love to tell me, Gawain."

"Yes. That's very shrewd of you, Your Grace," Gawain grumbled.

Violet's gaze caught on the crimson liquid, and her stomach rolled. She remembered the story of her aunt's tetrela hunt all too well. But, no reason to share where they'd obtained the second liquid. It would only make Ryon less likely to drink it if he ever had a need. Frankly, Violet wished she could unlearn its origin herself...

"So, what's the plan? How do we use that stuff?" Ryon asked.

Kayda leaned back on her heels. "You don't need much toxin for the effects to take hold. I propose we each coat the blade of a weapon or two with it. But we need to be careful only to use it if absolutely necessary."

Ryon rubbed his bearded chin. "Why's that?"

"Once we use it, it won't be a secret anymore." Kayda shrugged. "Sure, we can use it again, but the element of surprise might be useful."

"That's smart." Violet smiled. "Maybe it will give us an edge if we get in trouble."

"See?" Kayda spun to Gawain. "I'm not just a useless noble after all." She winked in his direction, earning a scowl.

Violet tuned out the pair as Gawain began lecturing Kayda on safety and pleading for her to reconsider. She walked over to a barrel stuffed full of arrows and lifted one, inspecting it carefully. They were similar in length and weight to the ones her father taught her how to make, but a bit smoother than his handcrafted arrows.

Ryon appeared at her elbow, wearing a frown. Violet glanced at his hands, surprised to find them empty. "Do you need help picking a weapon?"

His frown deepened. "That obvious, huh? I'm out of my depth here, Vi. I never trained with any of this stuff."

"Hey." She set down the arrow and grabbed his hand. "Don't worry. Just take anything. Chances are, we won't need it." She eyed the walls, then pointed at a huge double-sided sword. "What about that one? I bet anyone who sees that thing would be scared off just by looking at it."

Ryon shook his head. "I'm liable to cut my own foot off with that. Or stab one of the dragons in the eye by mistake."

Violet giggled. "Well, we don't want that. Take whatever you're most comfortable with, then."

"So, nothing?" Ryon waggled his brows.

Violet rolled her eyes. The motion made her notice a weapon she'd overlooked last time. She pointed. "What about that one?"

It was a battle axe, about the same size as the pickaxe Ryon wore strapped to his belt when they'd first met. He'd used the old tool expertly while helping Uncle Aren chop trees to build the raft they'd taken out to sea. If it hadn't broken on the day before they sailed to rescue Nox and Lark, he'd likely still be carrying it with him.

"Hm. That might work." Ryon marched to the wall and lifted on his toes. Violet forced herself not to sigh as she admired the lean lines of his legs and the flexing muscles in his back. He pulled it down, finally smiling after he swung it a few times.

"What do you think?" Violet asked.

"You have a good eye. I like it." Ryon turned that smile on her, and for a moment Violet forgot how to breathe.

She broke eye contact and strode toward the box of knives. "It's good for your main weapon, but you'll need another to coat with toxin." Violet dug through the box, thankful that the guards were careful to keep their blades sheathed. "How about this one?" She offered him a blade about the same size as the crafting knife he'd always carried.

Ryon took the knife. It shone in the torchlight as he unsheathed it and flipped it over in his hands. "That'll do, too. Thank you."

Violet looked away, unable to stop the squirming in her gut when she met his gaze. "You know, you don't need to—"

"Nope." Ryon stuffed the knife under his arm and stepped closer, placing a finger over her lips. "You can save your breath, too. You're stuck with me now, whether you like it or not."

Violet wasn't sure if it was the firm lilt of his voice or the light touch of his finger on her lips, but when she met his gaze again, shivers raced up her spine.

The knife clattered to the floor, breaking the tension building between them. Ryon chuckled. "Oops."

Violet cleared her throat. "Let me find you a sheath for your belt." She bent to dig through another box. "And Ryon?"

"Yeah?" He stood with the knife.

"Thank you. I'm glad you're here with me." Violet handed him the leather holder.

"There's nowhere I'd rather be." Ryon smiled.

Violet hurried to the arrow bin before she blurted out anything else. Like how she—No.

There'd be time for that later. She had an uncle to save.

One More Stop

Ryon swung the axe, jitters spreading across his skin. Violet and Kayda seemed so at ease in the armory. So natural selecting weapons and preparing for battle. He couldn't help feeling overwhelmed.

He hadn't been kidding when he'd admitted to being out of his depth. Ryon learned at a young age that hunting would never be his calling. The one time he'd tagged along on a tritusk hunt as a youth, he'd emptied his stomach into the grass while the poor beast drew its last breath.

He only hoped that Violet's assumption would prove true and they wouldn't need the weapons. And if they did, he'd have to overcome his repulsion. He refused to let her walk into danger alone.

He slipped the axe into the new holster on his belt. At least the heft of the weapon was familiar. After long years digging for silver in the hills down below, he certainly had the stamina to swing it. He just had to ignore the fact that he'd be using it on living creatures and not rocks...

"There's one more stop we have to make tonight," Queen Kayda announced. "Then we all need to get some rest. We'll leave first thing in the morning."

Violet nodded. "All right. Ryon and I can stay with the hatchlings. We just need—"

Kayda clicked her tongue. "I will not have my niece sleeping out in the Royal Grounds. The maids are already airing out rooms for you. Gawain will make sure the dragons aren't disturbed, won't you?"

"Of course, Your Grace," Gawain replied smoothly.

"Come." Kayda waved a hand. "Take my arm, Vi. Gawain will lead us to our next stop."

Violet hustled over and linked their arms. The sight of them together piqued his curiosity about their family history. They certainly didn't share much of a likeness. Queen Kayda was tall and willowy, with red curls and freckled light-brown skin. Violet couldn't have been more different. She was shorter than most women he'd met, and her pale skin and white hair looked even more remarkable next to her aunt.

But despite their physical differences, the love they shared shone brightly. Violet carefully dodged the overflowing weapon racks and barrels as they exited the armory, watching diligently to make sure she wasn't leading her aunt astray. Kayda followed her with a small smile, lightly patting Violet's hand.

He couldn't fathom ruling a country while blind. Ryon was certain there must be a tale behind it. He made a mental note to ask Violet about it later.

Gawain led them through the tower halls. The circular stone structure reminded him of the Aviary. It was nearly as tall and the right shape, but instead of being pockmarked with holes and roofless, this building was clearly well maintained. Weapons hung on the walls like prized trophies, and detailed paintings of men in battle decorated the common areas.

They arrived at a curving stair. Gawain plucked a lit torch off the wall and began descending. Ryon's pulse sped as they stopped on the bottom floor. Pained moans bled into the air even before they left the stairwell.

"Where are we?" Violet asked.

"Did you know the tower used to be a prison?" Gawain held open a door and ushered them through. "Before the prison in Southgate was built, this was where criminals were kept. We converted it into the Castle Guard barracks, but there are still a few rooms in the basement we use when the need presents itself."

Ryon gulped as he entered the dreary space. Barred cells lined the walls, all of them empty except for one.

In the cell closest to the stairwell, a bandaged man moaned, his arms and legs strapped down. With so many bandages wrapped around him, it was impossible to be sure, but he suspected that it was Jayan. Ryon's stomach lurched as the familiar charred stench reached his nose, though now the scent mingled with fresh herbs. A woman wearing an apron atop a pale-pink dress hovered over the prisoner, working a mortar and pestle in her hands.

"Lark?" Violet unhooked her arm from Kayda's and launched herself into the cell. Lark looked up from her task in time to throw her arms out to the side.

Lark smiled, linking her arms around Violet and returning her hug. "Watch it, Vi. You almost made me drop my poultice." Ryon returned the smile Lark sent him over Violet's shoulder, his heart lifting. It was good to see she'd made it back to Dracwood in one piece.

"Sorry," Violet replied sheepishly. "I was wondering where you were. Is this why you weren't at the dinner earlier?"

Lark stepped back and began grinding herbs again. "Yes and no. I was assisting with a birth this afternoon." She brushed her long brown curls behind her ear and frowned at Jayan. "When I returned, the guards stopped me and said I was needed here." She leaned in, tears visible in the corners of her hazel eyes. "Is it true, what they're saying? Who this man is?"

"Yes. It's Jayan." Kayda sighed deeply. "How is he?"

"Honestly? Not good. With wounds this extensive, he should be dead." Lark lowered her voice. "He might not make it through the night. The guards told me you want to question him, but I don't know if he'll recover enough to speak. I've given him something for the pain, but keeping him awake like this—it's cruel. I'm not sure what he's done, but what he really needs is sleep."

Kayda's shoulders slumped. "I suppose—"

The queen cut off as a commotion erupted outside. Gawain leaped into action, throwing the stairwell door open. He peered out and yelled, "What's going on out there?"

A black blur darted into the room above his head. Two guards rushed in after it.

"Stupid bird flew in from outside," the first guard explained. "My apologies, Guard Captain. Your Grace. We'll have it out of here—"

"Wait," Violet cut in. "Is that a crow?"

All eyes in the room flicked away from the out-of-breath guards and to the bird. It landed on Jayan's chest and cawed in his face. No one bothered to answer Violet's question; instead they gaped at the crow with slack jaws and widened eyes.

Ryon's heart skipped a beat. The crows were Jurdan's messengers. Was he sending Jayan a message now?

Jayan's fingers twitched inside his bindings. Ryon's gaze locked on the motion. Until now, Jayan had been mostly motionless, content to simply lie there groaning. But now, he began to tear at his bindings. He didn't stop, even when the bandages on his wrists bloomed with red.

Did he want the crow off his chest? Or was something else happening? A memory flashed in his mind. One he'd tried hard to forget.

"What are you waiting for?" Gawain barked at his men. "Get that bird out of here."

"No." Ryon stepped into their path. "I know why that crow is here."

"You can't be serious." Gawain shook his head. "Your Grace?"

Kayda frowned. "Explain."

Ryon glanced at Violet, who nodded encouragingly. He took a deep breath. "I think this has to do with the black aura that Violet's mother saw. This crow is here to heal Jayan."

"Guards. Leave us," Kayda ordered. The pair of guards filed out, shutting the door behind them.

"You need to break that down for me." Lark set aside the mortar and pestle. "What did Ereni see?"

"Ereni watched them fly over Magehaven," Kayda explained. "She spotted the same kind of magic that she encountered during the battle in the Abandoned Lands."

Lark covered her mouth. "That foul magic." She turned to Ryon, staring with widened eyes. "I think you're right. Crow—Jurdan's champion—used it, too. He killed a crow in the ring and healed himself."

"Look at him. He's trying to reach for it." Ryon shuddered. He'd witnessed the same battle Lark had. The crack of that bird's neck still haunted him. And if Crow could heal himself, who was to say Jayan couldn't, too? Blood coated the bandages on Jayan's wrists, yet he still hadn't stopped groping for the bird that sat dutifully on his chest.

"Free one of his wrists," Kayda ordered. Gawain stalked forward.

"Wait!" Violet shook her head. "How can we allow that? He'll kill it."

Gawain paused with his hand on Jayan's bindings.

Kayda's voice softened. "We need to question him. I don't like it any more than you do, Vi, but the things he could tell us..."

Violet nodded gravely. Ryon pulled her into his embrace as Gawain undid Jayan's bindings. No sooner was Jayan's hand free than it sought out the bird's fragile neck. Ryon closed his eyes and wrapped his arms tightly around Violet's head, hoping he muffled the sinister *crack* that echoed so clearly in his ears.

When he braved a peek a heartbeat later, the crow's limp body smacked the cell floor, and Gawain was retying Jayan's wrist to the cot.

Lark rushed forward and carefully loosened the bandage wrapped around Jayan's face. Ryon's arms relaxed, and Violet jerked out of his hold, both of their eyes widening in tandem.

Jayan's flesh healed slowly but surely, the charred red blisters receding, replaced with dark-brown skin.

"It's true," Lark said. "I-I knew they were the same. It's the same magic that the Unseen wielded."

Kayda wandered closer to the cot, her lip curling. "What did Jurdan do to you?"

At the sound of her voice, Jayan lurched up, screaming, a murderous look in his eyes. Gawain rushed in between them, though there was little chance of Jayan breaking free with his arms and legs strapped down.

"Your Grace." Gawain tugged Kayda out of the cell, away from Jayan. Once she was out of his eyesight, Jayan visibly calmed, sinking back on the cot. "You should leave the questioning to the guard."

"Perhaps you're right," Kayda admitted quietly.

Lark returned to Jayan's side, peeling off more bandages. "His wounds are significantly improved, but he's still showing signs of damage. I suspect he'll need a few weeks to heal fully. Unless you want to hunt down another crow?" Her upper lip curled.

"No." Kayda pivoted toward Gawain. "Question him while I'm gone. I expect answers when I return."

"Gone?" Lark stepped out of the cell, wiping her hands on her apron. "Where are you going? What about the wedding?"

"It's been delayed." Kayda sighed. "It's a long story. Why don't you walk with us to the keep and I'll fill you in?"

"Sure. I just need to do one thing first." Lark turned to Gawain. "Will you be waiting until morning to begin his questioning?"

"Yes. I'll need time to—" Gawain began.

"I thought so. No need to fill me in on the particulars." Lark cleared her throat and glanced at each of them in turn. "You'll either want to leave or cover your ears. This won't take long."

Ryon exchanged a knowing look with Violet before shoving his fingers in his ears. Only Gawain gaped in disbelief when Lark began to sing. Jayan's eyelids sluggishly fluttered closed and his breathing evened.

Gawain removed his fingers and shook his head. "What was that?"

Lark smiled. "The best lullaby he's ever heard. I'm sure you'll set one anyway, but you needn't bother with a guard tonight. He'll sleep till dawn." She pushed past Gawain and linked arms with Kayda. The two sisters spoke quietly among themselves as they led the way out of the tower and into the moonlight.

Ryon fell behind with Violet, not bothering to listen closely as Kayda recapped everything that had happened that day. His mind spun, filled with questions by the dozen and a whole heap of fears for what was to come.

How could they hope to defeat Jurdan? He had to assume that if Jayan could heal himself, then the rest of the masked could, too. Facing off against them had seemed daunting before, but now that they knew what power Jurdan's men wielded, how would they ever match up?

Violet's hand slipped into his. "Hey. That was genius back there. You saved Jayan's life."

"Yeah." The snap of bones breaking echoed in his ears. "I hope it was worth it."

Stay Sharp

Nox cursed inwardly as he followed the bear through Thalassia's seemingly endless halls. He kept hunting for a moment to sneak his feather out of the guard's pocket, but so far, he hadn't found the right time. There was always someone watching. From the moment they'd stepped out of the dank washing room, they'd been surrounded.

Bear led him down halls that mimicked the outside. Grass crunched beneath Nox's bare feet, and the blue ceiling glowed in a poor imitation of the sky. The city was so strange. Why fashion an underwater structure to look like the outside? Wouldn't it make more sense to go out there in person? To live a life with the wind in their hair, and the sun's gentle kiss on their faces?

No wonder the people here were half-mad, when they were forced to live in a place that was, at best, a poor imitation of what existed out there. The folk lingering in the halls stared as he passed, likely recognizing him from his last battle in the ring. Though none sought to speak to him, with his boon, he caught a few whispered murmurs.

"So it's not a rumor. I thought he was gone for good," a man said.

"Did you hear what the Supreme is planning?" Another chuckled darkly. "I can't wait to watch."

Nox's heart pounded. That certainly sounded ominous...

Flint's voice rose in his mind. *"Don't let yourself be distracted. You need to get that feather back."*

Nox flinched. *"I'm trying. We haven't been alone yet."*

All the youths of Raimire played at pickpocketing. Some of them could pluck a diquat out of a Mata's hand while her eyes were closed in anticipation of the sweet taste—all without being caught. Nox didn't have quite the same knack for it. Not to mention, it'd been decades since he'd practiced. But perhaps with enough of a distraction, he might slip his feather out without the bear noticing.

Maybe waiting wasn't the smartest plan. He'd been hoping they'd turn a corner and find an empty corridor spread out before them, but people were scattered everywhere. Almost as if word of his return sent them scurrying out to gawk.

Nox scanned the area ahead, seeking something, anything, he could use to his advantage. *"I may need to cause a scene. What can I do, Flint? I'm out of ideas."*

"Funny. I wouldn't think that would be a problem for you."

Nox's lip twitched, but he banished the smile before it spread. *"Usually you'd be right. But I can't afford to have the bear drop me with that rotting pole."* He winced, burying the urge to rub his temples. *"Maybe if my head wasn't already aching from getting hit earlier, I could think of something."*

Flint hummed. *"Is there anyone close by? Trip them."*

"No. They're giving me a wide berth. Hasn't stopped them from staring, though." He bit back a sigh. *"I considered knocking down some*

planters, but I don't think Bear would be too keen to allow that without a little discipline."

"Better think fast. I doubt you'll be walking forever."

"Thanks for the reminder," Nox grumbled.

Just as he'd given up hope that he'd find anything useful, a toddler waddled around the corner at the far end of the long hall they turned down, kicking a round ball about the size of a melon. He couldn't have been more than three, with chubby cheeks and dark curls flopping over his forehead.

Despite himself, a tiny grin tugged the corners of Nox's mouth. The boy was clearly enjoying himself. He chased the ball in the oblivious way that children often did, giggling to himself and not paying a lick of attention to his surroundings. And unlike everyone else they'd passed, the lad was headed straight for them.

"This might be it." Nox's gaze locked on the child.

"What is?" Flint asked.

Nox held his breath as the boy spun gaily in a circle. The ball rolled between his spread legs, making him laugh like it was the funniest thing he'd seen in his entire life. Who knew, maybe it was?

"There's a boy with a ball ahead."

Flint's voice rose. *"That could work! Send it sailing into the planters."*

Nox frowned. *"There aren't any in this stretch of hall."*

"What about Bear? Use it to trip him. Or lob it at his groin."

"With him standing so close? It would be a gamble." Nox shook his head slightly. *"I doubt I'd have the leverage to do anything other than piss him off."*

"There's always the boy. Children crying can be quite the distraction."

Nox's mind raced. It certainly seemed like the only viable option. In the time he'd been talking with Flint, he'd traversed half the corridor. He didn't have long to decide.

"*What are you going to do?*"

"*Shh,*" Nox insisted. "*I need to concentrate.*"

Try as he might, all Nox kept picturing was the ball smacking into the poor kid's forehead and the lad wailing. Sure, that would certainly be distracting, but the thought of purposely whacking the unsuspecting boy had his stomach turning.

Sucking in a deep breath, Nox decided to try it. The ball looked soft and bouncy. It wouldn't hurt much... he hoped.

Suddenly, the boy kicked the ball harder than it appeared even he had expected to. His little jaw dropped, and he squealed with glee, chasing it a few steps before it rolled and landed directly in front of Nox's feet.

Nox froze as the child's gaze lifted and met his. The joy shining in the boy's eyes faded, and he took a wary step back.

Now. Just one little kick.

Bear jerked Nox's arm. "Come on. This way." The force of Bear's tug left Nox with no choice but to step aside. Bear drew him toward a door set into the corridor wall—and away from the ball. The lad raced forward, kicking it up the hall and even further from Nox's reach.

"*Rot and decay.*" Nox's heart fell.

Flint asked warily, "*What happened?*"

"*I couldn't do it...*" If he had more time to think of an alternative, or if he could stomach the thought of hurting the child, he'd have the feather in his hand right now. "*Now Bear's taking me somewhere else.*"

"*Stay sharp. As long as he's there, you still have a chance.*"

Flint was right. He couldn't give up. That feather might be the difference between life and death.

Nox stood by Bear's side as he knocked on the door. He glanced over his shoulder. There weren't any people nearby. This might be it!

Shifting closer, he reached out carefully. Bear's mask was trained forward as he waited for the door to open. If Nox timed it perfectly—just as the door swung—maybe he could snatch it with no one the wiser.

Footsteps echoed behind the door. The knob slowly turned. Nox's fingers itched.

A revolting feeling washed over Nox. Bile rose in his throat and his skin crawled. His fingers curled involuntarily, and he couldn't force them to unbend before the door swung open.

"Well, well. The champion is back. Bring him in." Jurdan the Supreme backed away from the doorway, waving a hand. He looked exactly the same as Nox remembered. His long purple robes swept the floor, and his nose stuck in the air above the cocky smirk on his lips.

Bear snagged Nox's arm again and dragged him inside a richly furnished bedroom. A huge four-poster bed swathed in patterned blankets dominated one half. Jurdan strolled to a plush sofa on the other side and wasted no time reclining upon it. He kicked his feet up on a nearby table and motioned toward the armchair across from him. "Take a seat, Nox."

Bear didn't wait for Nox to comply. He shoved him into the chair before stationing himself behind it with his arms crossed.

Jurdan flicked his wrist at Bear. "Wait outside." The bear crossed the room and ducked into the hall without a backward glance.

"What's happening?" Flint asked. *"I sense trouble."*

"Jurdan's here. We're in a fancy room. It's done up like a bedchamber at Kings Keep."

Jurdan flicked his long black hair over his shoulder. "Why so quiet? *Cat* got your tongue?" A devious grin spread across his lips.

Nox fumed and his fingertips burned. Was that why Jurdan had brought him here? To remind him of the bondmate he'd lost? But if Jurdan was so intent on angering him, then why send the guard away?

"*Tread carefully,*" Flint warned. "*I don't like this.*"

"*Me either.*"

Nox choked down the urge to tear the bastard's throat out of his neck. Flint was right. He'd come here for a reason. Nothing else mattered if he couldn't find Mariun. "Where is she?"

"My daughter is safe." Jurdan clicked his tongue. "That was a dirty trick you pulled, dragging her with you on your little escape."

"She's not yours," Nox hissed. "And I didn't drag Mariun anywhere. She begged me to take her away from this place."

Jurdan shifted on the couch, then had the audacity to yawn. "So I hear."

Nox leaned forward. "Where is she?"

"Learning a lesson."

Nox's blood ran cold. "What lesson? If you hurt her..." He sucked in a breath through clenched teeth. "If you so much as touch her, I will bury you." He kept his tone even somehow, but held Jurdan's gaze, eyes like knives.

Jurdan snickered. "Please. Your threats hold no weight with me. Mariun will be brought to heel as I see fit. And if you want any chance of seeing her again, you'll do exactly what I say."

So this was the true reason for this meeting. And the reason Jurdan was confident enough to meet with him alone. "What do you want from me?"

Jurdan smirked. "What else would I want with my champion?"

Nox's stomach sank. The ring, then. "I thought the champion only battled those who directly challenged him?"

Jurdan chuckled. "You're quite right. But what do you think happened the moment you fled the city?"

Nox's eyes widened.

"I'm afraid you have quite the list of challengers waiting to spill your blood." Jurdan leaned back. "The way I see it, you have two options. Accept my gifts and crush them." He lifted a brow. "Or die."

Again with the gifts. Curiosity burned hotly within Nox. But instinct made him recoil from the offer before he'd even fully turned it over in his mind. "I want nothing of yours."

"No?" Jurdan's lips twisted. "Not even my daughter?"

Nox's fists clenched. "Mariun doesn't belong to you."

Jurdan sneered. "Let me guess, you think because she allowed you to defile her, she's yours instead?" He rolled his eyes. "The delusions of small-minded fools never cease to amuse me."

Nox itched to slap the ugly look off Jurdan's face. His stomach burned. How could Jurdan take a moment that was so perfect and twist it into something sick and wrong? But Nox couldn't lash out. Not when Jurdan had Mariun in his clutches.

He had no choice but to give into his demands. Not about whatever sick gifts he wanted to spread... but the rest. Maybe if he fought long enough, he could buy time for Violet and the dragons to return. After all—Violet had saved him once. He had to believe she would do it again.

"I'll fight. Let anyone who challenges me have a fair match. And I don't need your gifts to win. I'll do it on my own." Nox puffed out his chest, projecting an air of confidence that barely went skin-deep.

Jurdan smirked. "Very well." He stood. "I'm going to enjoy watching you die." He stalked to the door and threw it open. "Take him to the ring and stick him in a cage until the stands fill."

Nox's heart pounded. He had another chance. If everyone in the city was rushing to the fight, then surely he'd have an opportunity to snag the feather from—

"*Oh no,*" Nox blurted in his mind.

"*What's wrong?*" Flint replied, awash with urgency.

"*They're making me fight, Flint. Apparently there's a whole line of challengers waiting to take me out.*" Nox swallowed the lump in his throat as he stared at the masked man striding across the room. "*But that's not the worst part.*"

"*No? Then what is?*"

Nox winced as a man in a shark mask gripped his arm in a punishing hold. "*Bear is gone.*"

For once, Flint didn't reply with any reassurances. Nox sensed they were thinking the same thing. He'd narrowly survived three battles last time, and only one in which he had to truly fight—and back then, he'd had a silver feather to rely on. What chance did he have now?

Nox stared blankly as the spectators leisurely filed in. He was back in the ring. The cavernous, circular fighting pit that lived in his worst nightmares. The awful place where he'd been forced to watch from this same cage while his bondmate fought the last battle of his life.

I should've never come back here. Nox shivered before he shoved the thought aside.

He hadn't even been given a reprieve to prepare. When Shark tossed him in the metal cage and slammed the door closed, the stands had already begun to fill.

Dirt crunched beneath his toes, and the stench of blood invaded his nose until a hawker wandered above him, a basket of sweet bread balanced in his arms. Nox's stomach rumbled, reminding him about the breakfast he'd missed.

How long could he truly expect to last? It'd been days since he'd eaten a proper meal. And not long before that, he'd been injured so badly he'd needed to recuperate under the care of a skilled healer. He wasn't exactly at full strength.

"*You'll win.*" Flint's voice rang out, thick with confidence. "*Call on your boons.*"

Nox sucked in a shaky breath. "*I will.*" It was the only advantage he had left.

Bonding with animals didn't just allow the pair to share their thoughts. They shared certain physical attributes as well. And Nox had racked up quite the assortment of boons over the years. Still, they wouldn't stop his opponent from landing a lucky strike when he was worn down by exhaustion.

"*Maybe Jurdan was exaggerating about how many challengers there are,*" Flint offered.

Nox lifted one shoulder in a halfhearted shrug. "*It's possible. The men locked up with me certainly seemed to fear me. It's strange that so many would want to try their hand at defeating me.*"

It appeared he wouldn't have to wait long to find out. The door that led to the prison level snapped open.

A man wearing a bat mask emerged first. He threw the door open wide and whipped his pole in a circular motion, urging the men following him forward. As the line of prisoners shuffled in, Nox's stomach sank. "*I don't think Jurdan was exaggerating.*"

"*Why not?*"

Nox went silent as he counted each man who exited the door on the far side of the dirt ring. *"Because they just brought up twenty-three men from the prison level."*

The men crossed the ring slowly. A few wore intimidating expressions, their fists clenched at their sides. But most seemed wary—or in a few cases, so frightened they were one step away from wetting their pants.

A skinny teen with a face full of acne blanched as he spotted Nox crouched in his cage. He shook his head so hard Nox wondered if it hurt the boy's neck. "I take it back. Please, send me down below. I-I can't do this..."

Bat shoved the teen cruelly. "Shut it. You knew the consequences when you made your challenge. Deal with them."

The teen grimaced, scrambling away from Bat's blow. "B-but he was gone. I would've never challenged him if I'd known he was coming back."

One of the menacing men spat into the dirt. "You think any of us would have? We were betting on that damn loophole." He sneered, staring directly into Nox's eyes. "What kind of idiot comes back to the place he escaped?"

Nox's brow furrowed.

Bat stalked forward, his pole lifted high. "I said shut it, all of you." The men fell silent, cowering away from the weapon. Then the guard stalked forward and opened the cage beside Nox's. "Get in," he barked. "Move it."

Nox frowned as he watched the prisoners crowd into the small barred box. There were so many they were rubbing elbows and jostling each other constantly. His gaze flicked to the two empty cages beside them. Why didn't they spread them out? A punishment for talking, perhaps?

The bat slammed the door closed and stalked off across the ring. Nox shuffled sideways, getting as close as he could to the packed cage. He spotted the teen shuddering in the far corner. "Hey," he hissed. "What's the loophole?"

The boy met his gaze, but instead of answering, he shifted, giving Nox his back.

Luckily, the menacing man had been listening. "Of course you didn't know. Curse my rotten luck."

Nox nodded to him. "Tell me. Why did you make your challenge?"

"It's the law. The champion has forty days to respond to any challenge. If the champion refuses, the challenger wins by default." The man glared at him through the bars. "We were days away from earning our freedom. But you couldn't stay gone, could you?" He spat into the dirt. "I hope that ice princess' twat was worth it."

Nox slammed a hand on the bars. "Leave Mariun out of this."

The man's eyes narrowed. "Make me." He smiled cruelly, flashing a row of broken yellow teeth.

Nox opened his mouth, but before he blurted out a reply, the door on the other side of the ring slammed open again. He whipped around, and his jaw dropped. Wolf held open the door and ushered another string of men into the ring.

His gaze darted between the new prisoners and the empty cages. How many men was he about to fight? If what that man had said about the law was true, he wouldn't be surprised if all the prisoners had issued a challenge.

Nox's stomach sank. *Flint... I'm in big trouble.*

Worries and Dreams

Ryon rubbed the heels of his palms against his eyes, trying to ease the ache. It was no use. No matter how much he rubbed the damn things or forced the lids closed, he couldn't relax.

Based on the path of the moon in the sky, he guessed it was about an hour before dawn. Even the finest bed he'd ever slept on couldn't lull him back to sleep. He'd rested a little, exhaustion causing him to nod off as soon as he collapsed in the guest room in Kings Keep. But he'd awoken in the night and hadn't been able to fall back asleep, no matter how hard he'd tried.

They were about to embark on a dangerous mission. Violet had tried to ease his mind earlier, but Ryon couldn't help worrying that they would need those weapons.

It was clear that he was the least trained. Did he have any right to leave on such an important quest when he was so woefully unprepared? Maybe it would be better for everyone if he gave up his seat on dragonback to someone who could hold their own in a fight. There was certainly no shortage of soldiers and warriors here for the festival.

If he became a liability, he'd never forgive himself. Still, he couldn't bear the thought of leaving. He'd promised Violet he'd stick with her on her journey. He didn't want to let her down.

But was it truly letting her down if he wasn't properly equipped for the task?

A knock on his bedchamber drew him from the maddening circle of his thoughts. He sat up in bed, his gaze glued to the door. Who could that be at this hour? "Come in."

Moonlight lit Violet's face. She slid inside wearing a sheepish grin and a thin nightgown that made Ryon's heart race and a lump lodge in his throat. "Violet?" he croaked. "Are you all right?"

Violet slowly crossed the room on bare feet. "I had a nightmare. C-could I stay with you until dawn breaks?" She lifted her gaze off the floor as she paused at Ryon's bedside. "Please?"

Ryon threw off the covers. "Get in." A blast of cool air chilled his skin, and then the bed sank as Violet hopped in. Ryon tugged the blankets back up, pulling them to their chins.

"Are you sure this is all right?" Violet asked. "These beds are so big I knew you'd have the room, but I can leave in a little while if you'd like."

Ryon shook his head. "Don't go. I could use the company. I've been lying awake for hours."

Violet scooched a little closer. "Really? You just couldn't sleep?"

Now that she was within arm's reach, the bed quivered slightly. She was shivering. Was she cold? Or was her nightmare so bad she was still feeling its effects?

Ryon rolled closer and reached for her, flattening Violet against his chest. She came easily, wrapping an arm around his stomach and pressing her toes against his leg. The tiny digits were colder than his skin but nowhere near as icy as he'd expect to account for the tremors still wracking her body.

The nightmare, then. Perhaps if he shared a bit of his troubles, it would help take her mind off it. "I haven't been able to quiet my mind," he admitted.

"Do you want to talk about it?" Violet rested her chin on his chest, and the warmth of her breath bled through his nightshirt.

Ryon trailed a hand through her silky locks. "I can't stop worrying that I won't be much help on the rescue mission. That maybe it'd be smarter for me to give my spot to someone who trained—"

Violet lifted her head and met his gaze in the moonlight. "Don't say that. I'm stuck with you, remember? That means you're stuck with me, too. I don't want anyone else." She bit her lip.

Ryon used his thumb to soothe her battered lip. "I don't want to be anywhere else." His brow furrowed. "But I don't want to put you at risk, either."

"You won't. And even if you do, we'll figure something out, together." Her head sank back down on his chest, and she wrapped him tightly in her arms. "I'm not letting go until you agree."

Ryon chuckled as she squeezed him with a death grip. "Fine. I promise I'll go. You don't need to attach yourself to me like a barnacle."

Violet giggled and loosened her hold, but she kept her arms where they were. Ryon sighed, pleased his confession had had its desired effect. But right when the thought crossed his mind, Violet stiffened.

Was she thinking about her nightmare again? Maybe he was going about this all wrong. If distracting her hadn't worked, then perhaps she needed someone to vent to? "Do you want to talk about what's keeping you up?"

Violet shuddered. "I dreamed about the ring again."

Ryon frowned. "That's nothing new, is it?"

Violet shook her head, her chin wobbling on his chest. "No. I've dreamed of it a lot. But the feeling I got tonight was different."

"How so?"

"Before, it was always curiosity driving me. I'd swim and swim, trying so hard to reach it, desperate to find out what's on the other side."

Ryon trailed a hand down her back. "Have you ever made it through? Is there more than just water once you've swam through it?"

Violet's fingers tightened, tangling in his nightshirt. "No. I always woke before I got close. Until tonight." She shuddered again, harder than ever.

"What happened tonight?"

"I still didn't make it through, but I nearly reached it this time. And as soon as I was close enough to touch, the curiosity disappeared. Suddenly, I wanted nothing more than to turn tail and swim away as fast as I could. This sense of dread washed over me. I knew if I passed through that ring, my life would never be the same."

Ryon's palm stilled on her shoulder blades. "And then?"

"And then I woke up and came in here." She planted a hand on his chest and propped her chin on the back of her fist, shifting to look into his eyes. "What do you think it means? It has to mean something, doesn't it?"

Ryon twisted his lips and glanced at the ceiling, giving the dream some thought. But he didn't last long before shaking his head. "I honestly have no clue."

Violet sighed. "Yeah. Me either."

Ryon frowned. He hated the hint of defeat he sensed in her tone. And with his mind weary from lack of sleep, he couldn't think of a single thing to say to comfort her. But there was one thing that might get Violet's mind off her odd dream.

He slid a hand to the nape of Violet's neck and gently tugged her toward him. Her lashes fluttered and her gaze dropped to his mouth. Moving slowly, he lowered his lips to hers.

He hovered there with their mouths a hairsbreadth apart. "I know you just came in here to talk—"

Violet silenced his statement, pressing her lips against his and wrapping her arms around his neck so tightly Ryon bit back a gasp. She kissed him like she was drowning and he was the air she needed to survive. Like she was still running from whatever had frightened her in that dream, and he was the only one who could save her.

He clung tight and met her with equal fervor, trying to say without words what he felt so deeply but couldn't utter. He was there for her. Would always be there for her. Even if he was woefully unprepared.

Whether she was drowning, running, or fighting the darkest enemy the world had ever known. They'd face it all—together.

Before long, daylight bled through the curtains and a warm glow seeped into the room. Ryon hardly noticed until a knock sounded.

"It's time to rise," a man announced.

Violet stiffened in his arms. Ryon lifted a brow and whispered, "Who is that?"

She shrugged.

Bang, bang, bang. "Queen Kayda requested you to awaken at daybreak."

Seems whatever servant had earned that task was not prepared to leave until he knew he'd accomplished it. Ryon cleared his throat and raised his voice. "Yes, I'm up."

Footsteps retreated. Then a weaker knock shook the wall. "Lady Violet, it's time to rise."

Violet's eyes widened, and she covered her mouth when the servant's voice boomed from further down the hall. "He's at my room."

Well... the servant wasn't about to find an answer there. "I'll take care of it." Ryon pressed one last kiss to Violet's lips and hopped out of bed.

His bare feet grew chilled as he strode to the door. He stuck his head into the hall and spotted the servant with his fist raised to knock again. "Hey."

The man whirled around, and Ryon flinched. Guard Captain Gawain marched down the hall, his brow furrowed. "Is something amiss?"

Ryon gulped and lowered his voice. "No. I just wanted to let you know Violet is awake before you knock that door down."

Gawain pursed his lips, his gaze darting between the rooms. Then his eyes bulged and his face reddened. "Oh. Well, then... carry on." And he hustled out of the corridor like he was being chased.

Ryon closed the door and leaned against it. "That wasn't awkward at all." Violet giggled behind her hands. He grinned. "I suppose we should get ready." She nodded and climbed out of the blankets. Before she left, he couldn't resist reaching for her one last time. He dragged her into his arms with a sigh.

Was this the last moment of normalcy they'd have? With all the danger on the horizon, this might be the last time they slept under a roof in a proper bed. Maybe that was what Violet's dream meant. A warning that things were about to change.

But he didn't want to worry Violet when she'd finally shaken off the shivers wracking her. So he kept the thought to himself and held her a little tighter, determined to make the moment last as long as he could.

The Incoming Storm

The sea breeze whipped through Violet's hair and the sun warmed her face. They'd been flying for hours, and though her body ached, she couldn't stop marveling over the experience. "*Is this how it always feels to fly?*"

Orry tilted her long neck sideways from within the cradle of Violet's arms. She'd flown on her own for a short while but had spent most of the flight tucked in her lap atop the blue-scaled dragon. Since Kayda was now bonded to Mena, they'd been paired with Ari for the return voyage.

"*I've found that nothing in life is always the same.*"

Violet grinned. "*You're right.*" Her bondmate seemed to have an uncanny knack for saying the right thing. "*Even so, I doubt I'll ever grow tired of this.*"

Orry sighed. "*I never imagined the ocean would be so calming. The salt in the air. The wind ruffling my feathers. The endless blue stretching out so far you realize how small we all are. Just a little speck in a grand world filled with untold wonders.*"

"Why do you sound so surprised? You lived on an island."

"True. But that doesn't mean your assumption is correct."

Violet didn't even bother to ask the question burning on her tongue. Of course Orry knew what she'd been assuming. Who wouldn't think a bird living on an island flew over the ocean constantly? Instead, she asked, *"Why didn't you?"*

"Mother Orea doesn't leave the Aviary."

Violet's eyes widened. *"Never?"*

Orry twitched her head. *"The world is a dangerous place, and I was the only one of my kind. Until now."*

A pang struck Violet's heart. She couldn't imagine being locked inside one building for her entire life. And to think... all the Mother Oreas who came before her had led the same life without the reprieve Orry got by bonding with Violet. At least Orry would experience a small taste of the world before her inevitable end.

The pang struck again, jerking in her chest so strongly it burned. She didn't want to think about losing Orry. It wasn't fair that they had so little time. A few weeks... maybe a month. And now that she knew what Orry's life had been like for so long, the injustice rankled anew.

"How could you stand it? There's no way I could've stayed cooped up when everyone around me was free to come and go as they pleased." Violet had seen the silvers flitting in and out of the Aviary. She'd met Ryon's friend Quill down below. It would've driven her mad if she were in Orry's place.

"It was my calling. My sacred duty." Orry's voice rang with sincerity.

Violet wrinkled her nose. *"Still, I don't know if I could do it. I'd go stir-crazy."*

Orry turned, meeting her gaze. *"When the fate of the world depends on your actions, there's not much you won't sacrifice."*

Violet's stomach clenched. With her bondmate staring at her so intensely, it was hard not to take her words to heart. It was almost as if Violet heard the silent statement Orry didn't voice when she gazed into her bondmate's black-and-gold-speckled eyes. *You'll see...*

A shiver raced down her spine. It wasn't only her bondmate who had her unsettled. The closer they drew to the ring, the more she felt it. Whatever lived inside her heart linking her to the strange sunken relic hummed louder with every moment.

She'd promised herself one day she'd return. She ought to be relieved she'd accomplished the task so swiftly. But instead, a thousand unspoken worries assailed her. Were they brought on by that dream? Or was she working herself up over nothing?

Mena pivoted suddenly, flying sideways, and Ari followed. Violet gripped tightly with her thighs, her pulse racing. Crys pulled alongside her, and she shared a smile with Ryon. He'd taken to flying as quickly as she had. Every time she caught a glimpse of him, his grin stretched as wide as his eyes.

Violet scanned the water with a furrowed brow until she finally spotted a dot of green on the horizon. *"Look. An island! I bet that's where Gwen is."* She squinted, trying to get a feel for the size of the solitary blip of land resting in the middle of all that blue.

"We'll find out soon enough. No need to strain your eyes." Orry delivered the line in such a motherly tone that it sliced right through Violet's chest. She hadn't realized how much she wanted to see her own mother until Kayda had explained how impossible that would be. Then a burst of homesickness struck her.

Her parents had always been there, the strong cornerstone of her life. She'd almost begged to stop in Magehaven to say hello. But time was of the essence. Who knew what was happening to Nox in that mysterious city under the sea? She'd need to wait a little longer to reunite with her parents.

Soon the island loomed large enough that Violet had no need for squinting. She didn't recognize it, though she doubted she would from this angle. It certainly wasn't Ryon's home, or the little forested island where she'd found her uncle Aren. This island was far too small, barely large enough to hold a stretch of beach and a handful of scraggly trees.

Before they came close to landing, a blur of green burst into the air above the island. The dragons increased their speed, which was surely taxing after such a long flight over the sea. Yet it seemed the sight of their sister elated all of them.

Violet whooped when Gwen reached them. She circled above and then flew alongside, leading her siblings to the little speck of land. Sand sprayed the air as the four dragons glided to the beach with great swoops of their wings. She sputtered and shaded her eyes until the particles resettled.

Ryon appeared at her side, his arms outstretched. Violet reached down, intending to pass Orry to him, but she lifted out of her lap and flew to a nearby branch. *"You all right?"*

"Avoiding the sand shower. If I were you, I'd fall back until they're through."

Out of the corner of her eye, Violet spotted Crys barreling toward Gwen. More sand kicked into the air as the excited dragons rubbed flanks. She grabbed Ryon's hands and let him help her off Ari's back. Ari bolted for Gwen the moment her boots hit the ground. Only Mena held back, content to stand with Kayda on the edge of the ruckus. Violet chuckled at their antics, enjoying the way their colorful scales flashed in the sun, but pinching her mouth closed when the particles threatened to make her cough. She'd nearly decided to hightail it into the trees with her bondmate when the dragons froze.

Gwen slowly approached Kayda and Mena. She lightly bumped flanks with her sister. Then her long, lithe neck wound sideways, and she sniffed, sending a few tendrils of hair blowing across the queen's forehead. Kayda trailed a hand across Gwen's green scales. "Pleased to meet you, Gwenstasia."

With the sand finally settled, Violet cautiously approached. "What's happening, Auntie? Does Gwen know anything that will help us find Nox?"

Kayda's hand fell at her side. "Give me a moment. I'll find out." She pursed her lips as her gaze darted between Mena and Gwen. "There's a boat. Nox didn't know about it when he went down to Thalassia. That's where they're keeping Mariun."

Ryon frowned. "So she's not even down there?"

Kayda sighed. "It seems so. Gwen didn't find it until this morning. There's a storm rolling in from the east that blew it off course. It won't be long until the storm reaches us here as well."

Violet scanned the sky. She couldn't see any sign of the storm yet, but that didn't mean it wasn't out there. She shuddered, recalling the tempest that had ripped across the sea before they'd found the dragon eggs. If the incoming storm was anything like that one, she wasn't looking forward to it.

Unless... "Do dragons have trouble flying in rain?"

Kayda turned to Mena and, after a moment, replied, "No. As long as there's no lightning, they shouldn't have a problem."

Violet chewed on her lip. "What if there is lightning?"

"They can still fly, but it's risky. A strong enough strike might send them careening out of the sky." Kayda narrowed her gaze on the sky.

"Mena doesn't think it would kill them, but they'd be stunned and in for a hard splash."

Violet's heart raced. She didn't even want to imagine what would happen if she were riding a dragon who was struck. Sure, there'd be water to break their fall. But at what height did slamming into water start to feel like you'd smacked into solid rock? And that was if the lightning didn't kill her...

Still, a storm seemed like too good of an opportunity to pass by.

Ryon tilted his head. "What are you thinking?"

Violet crossed her arms. "Well, we can try to swim to Thalassia again and rescue Nox. Take the chance that we'll be able to sneak past whatever got him caught."

"Do you think that's what happened?" Kayda asked.

Violet nodded. "If he wasn't, I don't know why he wouldn't have escaped already when he learned Mariun wasn't there."

Ryon rubbed his chin. "He was definitely set on finding her when he left."

"It might be smarter if we go after Mariun first," Violet said. "We can use the storm as cover. If we fly for the boat when it's dark and storming, there's a chance that whoever's holding Mariun captive won't see us coming."

Kayda's brow furrowed. "But didn't you say she was Jurdan's daughter? What if he's the one holding her?"

Violet shrugged. "Sooner or later, we'll need to face Jurdan. At least now we'll have the dragons for backup if anything goes wrong. I'm hoping it won't come to that. If we're lucky, we can sneak in and out with no one the wiser."

"It could work." Kayda patted Mena's flank. "Dragons have much better night vision than humans. We can have them drop us off on the boat to find your friend."

Ryon chimed in. "Then Mariun can help us rescue Nox. She's bound to know some secrets of that city that will help."

"That's what I was thinking." Violet grinned. "So, are we all in agreement?"

Kayda pursed her lips and fell silent. Violet used the time to quickly fill Orry in. "*What do you think?*"

"*Sounds like you've thought it through,*" Orry replied.

Violet met her bondmate's eyes. Why did it feel like there was something Orry wasn't saying?

Kayda's voice boomed over the softly crashing surf. "The dragons agree to the plan."

Ryon clapped his hands. "Sounds good. Should we get going right away?"

Kayda shook her head, and Mena's gaze darted to the horizon. "Not quite. The storm is still moving in. We have a short while to prepare."

"Good." Violet sighed. "I could use a break to stretch my legs."

Kayda chuckled. "We all could." She frowned when Violet stepped away. "Don't wander far. Mena says we should leave at dusk."

Violet scanned the horizon. The first hints of pinks and purples painted the western sky. They wouldn't have much of a reprieve, but after the long flight from Dracwood, she would be thankful for whatever small break she was given.

Ryon appeared at Violet's elbow. "Would you like some company?"

"Sure." She linked their arms together, and they leisurely strolled down the beach. "Does this remind you of anything?"

He cocked a brow. "Not particularly... Why do you ask?"

Violet smiled softly and waved at the sand. "It's just like when we first met. We walked arm and arm down the beach then, too."

"Huh, we did." A soft chuckle escaped him. "I'm glad my ankle isn't twisted this time."

"That feels like a lifetime ago, doesn't it?" It was surreal looking back. It hadn't been that long. But so much had happened since then, and she'd changed in so many ways.

Ryon halted, tugging Violet to a stop with him. "I don't know about that." He traced her check, tucking an errant strand of pale hair behind her ear. "I remember it like it was yesterday."

"You do?" Violet shivered, enthralled by the soft lilt of his voice and the tender brush of his hand.

Ryon nodded. "I do. You made a big impression on me."

Violet grinned. "Well, I did save you from being trampled to death."

"That was a plus." Ryon leaned in and pressed a sweet kiss to her lips.

Violet sank into the feeling. She'd never expected the man she'd met while on a rescue mission would end up meaning so much to her. That one day, she'd be back on a foreign beach, kissing him while the sun set in the distance. It was enough to make a girl swoon.

As her arms wound around his neck, curiosity prickled her shoulders. She hadn't thought to try using her new talent without reason. But as she stood there wrapped in Ryon's arms, Violet called on her boon.

His heartsong blasted to life so strongly she gasped. He pulled away and met her eyes. "Are you—"

Violet crashed her lips into his and closed her eyes. She had no words... Ryon's heartsong wrapped around her soul, the melody so rich and lovely she nearly wept. But instead, she tugged him closer, kissing him and wishing she could share even a hairsbreadth of the beauty she sensed in his song.

All too soon, she silenced her boon and broke away. The sky was awash with color now, not just the bright pastels of sunset, but tinged with the blacks and grays of an approaching storm. "We should prob-ably head back."

Ryon reached for her, wiggling his fingers. Hand in hand, they returned to the others.

Mena's head spun in their direction and Kayda grinned. "Ready?"

"Yeah. Let's fly," Violet said. They clambered atop the dragons and set off. Soon the sea swirled violently beneath them, the storm's angry influence ratcheting up the further they flew. Then their view of the sea began to fade. As the impending night darkened the sky, great billowing clouds of haze stretched out across the sea in advance of the storm.

Violet's pulse thundered as she spotted something out of the corner of her eye. She jerked her head so sharply Orry looked up from her lap. *"What is it?"*

Squinting, Violet scanned the dark waves beside them. *"I thought I saw a boat. A huge one. Much larger than the ships the masked use."* With the mist shrouding the waves, it was impossible to be sure. *"I don't see it anymore."*

Orry shifted. *"I don't see it either."*

"Maybe it was nothing." Violet considered shouting for the others. They could go and investigate. But then they breached the storm's far edge and rain slapped her skin, the frigid droplets piercing her flesh like little drops of ice.

The contrast between the chilly rain and warm winds was enough to make her tremble. The combination didn't make the ocean any happier. Waves leaped into the air, rolling on huge swells that would surely frighten even the most seasoned of sailors.

All thoughts of turning back fled her mind. It would be enough of a struggle to fly through the storm without adding another stop to the mix. Surely if she *had* seen a boat, whoever was on it would be smart enough to sail away from this nightmarish tempest.

The dragons flew on bravely, even when the first lightning strikes lit the sky. Violet held her breath, praying the strike was merely a fluke.

Flashes rained down in irregular spurts. Ari shuddered beneath Violet's legs but didn't turn aside or slow. The moment stretched out, with nothing for Violet to do but hold tight and pray they'd arrive safely.

Finally, the dragons descended. Full dark had arrived, but when the next flash lit the sky, Violet glimpsed white sails ahead. "*We made it,*" she told Orry.

"*Good.*" Orry shivered and Violet clutched her tightly. Was she a fool to bring her aging bondmate on this mission? Maybe she should've left her behind on the island. Or better yet, at Kings Keep. She buried her regrets. It wouldn't do to dwell on them now. Not when they needed their wits to save Mariun.

The dragons hovered above the boat's deck. Violet's heart leaped in her throat as she prepared to jump. One wrong move and she'd end up drenched in the ocean, forced to endure the roiling waves until someone fished her out.

"*Don't think. Just jump,*" Orry instructed.

Violet sucked in a deep breath and launched herself off Ari's back. Her stomach dropped as the air rushed by her. Then her boots slammed down on the boat deck.

Thump. Thump.

Violet sighed when Kayda and Ryon both landed safely. At least, she thought they had. She couldn't see her own hand waving in front of her face.

They'd need to rely on their bondmates for the next part of the plan. Both Orry and Mena were blessed with enhanced night vision that humans lacked.

Kayda used her bondmate's boon immediately, if the whistle of a blade being thrown, followed by another thump, was anything to judge by. But they wouldn't have Mena to rely on for long. Kayda insisted on sending the dragons to safety if they encountered any lightning.

Violet shifted Orry in her arms. "*What do you see?*"

Orry's head darted back and forth. "*The deck is clear ahead. Move to your left three paces and collect Ryon.*" Violet followed her directions, forcing her feet to move steadily despite the shifting boat.

"Ryon," she hissed under her breath before she took the last step. "Is that you?"

Fingers closed on Violet's forearm, making her gasp until Ryon murmured beside her, "Yes. I'm here."

"*What now?*"

Orry's neck jerked sideways. "*That way, five paces. Kayda.*"

Violet whispered, "Stick with me." Ryon's fingers tightened on her arm. They crossed the deck in tandem until they found Kayda right where Orry had said she'd be. "Auntie. Come."

But Kayda didn't move toward Violet. Her hand darted out just as a flash of lightning illuminated the sky. Violet's eyes widened as she tracked the blade's passage.

A masked clutched his neck, and then the sky blackened.

Thunk.

Orry's voice rang out. "*Above you. Look out!*"

Violet jumped back, throwing her weight into Ryon. They tumbled to the deck in a tangle of flailing arms, legs, and wings. A blade whistled so close to Violet's ear she bit back a scream.

"What's happening?" she shouted in her mind. Grunts and more whistling rent the night, and Violet knew that if she heard it over the roar of the storm, it must be happening right before her.

"Don't worry. Your aunt dispatched him." Another bolt flashed, and Violet finally spotted another body laid out, bleeding, beyond their feet. Kayda stood over the man, her chest heaving. Violet registered nothing else before she was blinded once again.

"Behind you," Orry instructed. *"There's a door."*

Violet's heart raced. There might be anything behind it. More men to fight. Jurdan could be lurking in there for all they knew. But they couldn't leave without searching.

Three bolts of lightning struck in quick succession. Enough light filled the sky that Violet spotted the dragons flying away. Her heart sank. Kayda would be blind again. Whatever fighting happened next would fall to her.

Violet grabbed her aunt's ankle before the light faded completely. She carefully stood, tugged Ryon to his feet, and handed Orry to him. Then she led their shuffling trio to the door. With trembling fingers, she turned the knob. They piled inside the dark chamber. When no one immediately charged out to attack, she sighed. *"What do you see?"*

"The room is empty—no. She's here. In the back."

Violet's stomach dropped. "Mariun?" she called out in the dark.

"Don't bother. She's out cold," Orry said. *"There's a lamp ahead."*

Violet reached out, and by feel in the dark, she found the lamp. "Did anyone bring a tinderbox?"

Kayda chuckled. "I don't leave home without it." Violet's ears pricked with soft scratching. Then the sound of metal striking bounced off the walls and a tiny flicker of flame sparked to life. Within moments, the lamp was lit, washing the tiny cabin in soft light.

Ryon kneeled in the shadowy corner beside Mariun's prone form. "She's alive." He patted her cheek gently. "Wake up."

Violet exhaled, and relief washed over her. She bent next to Ryon and slapped Mariun so hard the crack of skin on skin made her hand sting.

Mariun shot up, groaning and cradling her cheek. "What? Where? I-I..." She blinked, forcing the dazed clouds out of her eyes. "Violet? Ryon?" She gasped. "No. Y-you can't be here! It's exactly what Jurdan wants. You're playing right into...into his h-hands."

Then Mariun's lashes fluttered closed, and she slumped back.

Violet's pulse pounded. She shook Mariun. "Please. You need to wake up. We're here to save you."

Ryon frowned. "What did she mean?"

Kayda shook her head, her red eyes staring up and to the left of the spot where they hovered beside Mariun on the floor. "No clue. Whatever it means, it'll have to wait. The dragons can't return until the storm passes."

Violet sighed. "Maybe by then she'll wake and explain."

Ryon met Violet's gaze. "She will. We'll be all right. I know it."

Violet nodded, but she couldn't help worrying. Had they just stumbled into a trap?

Unwanted Gifts

The crowd roared as another body thudded into the dirt. Nox panted, every muscle in his body aching.

"How many is that now?" He'd charged Flint with keeping track. Once he'd hit double digits, the task had become next to impossible.

"Twenty-nine."

Nox wiped the sweat off his brow. *"Rot and decay."* He'd put a dent in the number of challengers, but the cages were still crowded. And after being forced to battle them, one right after the next, he was beyond exhausted and covered in minor cuts and bruises by the dozen.

A door banged open and four masked emerged. A pair rushed forward and dragged the body backward. The other two hung back, metal tubes lifted to the mouth holes of their masks, the darts aimed at Nox.

After twenty-nine battles, their presence didn't surprise him. It was the same routine each time. The masked dragged away the corpse only for another to replace him. He had a sneaking suspicion if he was ever allowed to rest, he'd watch the pattern repeat in his dreams.

But who knew if they would allow that? So far, he'd been given no break. Not unless you counted the few moments between fights before the next challenger was called into the ring.

"*You can do this, Nox,*" Flint urged. "*You have to. Remember what's at stake.*"

"*Mariun.*" Nox closed his eyes for one fleeting heartbeat and pictured her face. His battered hands longed to sink into the silken depths of her black tresses. His ears ached to hear the sweet melody of her voice.

If only he could see her gray eyes flashing at him with annoyance. Or desire.

She was out there somewhere, enduring whatever cruel lesson Jurdan had arranged for her. He wouldn't allow it. Even if he needed to fight a thousand men to find her.

The masked stopped at the door. One lifted his head and barked, "Get rid of them."

Like each time before, a hidden compartment in the dirt ring slid open. Nox strode to it and dropped his bloodied weapon inside. Then he lifted the poor sod's fallen blade out of the dirt and disposed of that.

The panel slid shut, and the lines in the dirt disappeared completely. Nox had marveled over it the first time. How did it work? He'd never seen such a thing. And for it to meld into the floor like it never existed in the first place... Clearly, there was some magic at play he didn't understand.

But it hadn't been long before he'd shoved the question out of his mind. He had more important things to worry about. Like staying alive.

Nox stared at his hands. His boons had been essential to his survival today, but one of them was suspiciously absent. Those rotting claws he'd first called on when he'd battled Crow wouldn't emerge, no matter how many times he tried to use them.

"Are you sure you don't remember what I said when I made that wish?"

This wasn't the first time he'd asked Flint. After Ryon had told him the wording of a wish was the key to understanding its consequences, they'd both racked their brains, hoping they'd recall the exact phrasing.

Flint's sigh reverberated in Nox's mind. *"No, my friend. I still have no clue."*

Nox cracked his neck as the crowd's roar became deafening. He swung his head back, knowing exactly where to look. There were two times the people screamed like that. The moment a body dropped and whenever *he* approached the edge of his box.

Sure enough, Jurdan perched beside the rail of his private viewing box in the stands. He smirked, seeming to take great pleasure in the noise as he basked in the crowd's adoration. But then he lifted his hands, and silence fell over the ring.

"Who here wishes to challenge our champion?" Jurdan's voice boomed over the stands. "Step forward."

One of the cage doors slid open. A masked darted in and, seemingly at random, plucked a man from within.

Nox's stomach dropped. Not a man at all. It was the same pimple-faced youth who'd tried to rescind his challenge earlier.

"Rot and decay."

"What is it?" Flint asked.

"They want me to fight a lad. The damn kid can't be more than sixteen."

Flint was silent for a moment, and then he said softly, *"Remember what you told me. Don't make my mistake."*

Nox's heart raced. Flint had refused to fight when he'd been stuck in the same situation, no matter how much Nox had begged him to. If Flint had listened, maybe he'd still be alive. *"Since when have you thought that was a mistake?"*

"Regret's a tricky thing. Make sure you're alive to experience it."

The boy's feet dragged in the dirt. He kicked and wailed with tears streaming down his face. That didn't stop the masked from hauling him out of the cell and tossing him to the dirt at Nox's feet.

"Speak your challenge," Jurdan demanded.

The boy trembled, his body racked with tremors so strong he looked like he was freezing. "I-I c-can't."

A sharp kick landed on his ribs. The teen screamed and curled into a ball. Nox tensed, ready to leap at the masked to stop the poor lad's torment.

"Speak it or face the consequences," Jurdan commanded.

Nox's brow furrowed. *"This is strange."*

Flint asked, *"What?"*

"The boy is refusing to talk. To repeat his challenge for the crowd." He'd wondered why each man before now obeyed without question. *"Jurdan is trying to make him."*

"Wonder what happens if he doesn't?"

Jurdan's voice boomed out, filled with menace. "Last chance."

The boy lifted his face from the dirt. Nox expected to see a broken boy. To hear the whispered challenge leave his quivering lips. But the lad's jaw was set in a grim line, and he looked Jurdan dead in the eyes and shouted a single word, clear and ripe with defiance. "No."

Jurdan held the boy's gaze as he motioned with his hand. His fingers flattened, and he sliced his hand across his neck.

Nox gaped at the dark king's box and his heart sank. Then his gaze swung back in front of him.

The masked lurched forward, snagged the lad by his stringy black hair, and jerked his head back, exposing his neck. Nox took a single step forward, but it was a wasted effort. Before his bare foot landed in the dirt, the masked ripped his knife through the lad's tender flesh. Blood spurted out, painting the dirt red.

Nox's stomach lurched, and he turned aside, gritting his teeth. *"Add another to the count, Flint."*

"Ah. So that's what happens..." Flint said sadly. *"That makes thirty."*

The crowd crooned their approval, hooting and hollering like a coop of excited hens. It was sickening to witness the glee flooding their faces. Who took pleasure in watching a youth drained of their life at a villain's sick whims? It was enough to make him queasy.

He stiffened as the door pounded against the wall and the quartet of masked emerged to drag the lad's body off. The teen's feet were still twitching when they hauled him away.

"You've seen what happens to those who refuse." Jurdan's fist slammed on the railing of his box. "On with the next. Step forward and speak your challenge."

The masked shoved his bloodied blade back into his belt and darted to the cages. The same one slid open, and a heartbeat later, the masked reemerged, hauling a new man by the arm. This one came readily, a smirk painting his mouth and revealing the row of yellow teeth Nox recognized from earlier.

"It's the idiot who insulted Mariun." Nox's fist clenched at his side.

"Careful with this one," Flint warned. *"He sounds like a real piece of work."*

Nox couldn't help but agree. The fellow sauntered out, seeming entirely too confident for his liking. He halted in front of Nox and didn't even wait for Jurdan to ask again before lifting his nose and raising his voice. "I challenge the champion."

By now, Nox knew the drill. "I accept."

A weapon rack emerged from the dirt. The prisoner strolled over and took his time selecting, trailing his fingers across a battle axe and a long, curved sword before he finally chose a polearm topped with a short double-edged blade.

Nox was more comfortable with smaller blades that allowed him to dart in close. Growing up in a densely packed jungle, he hadn't bothered to train much with weapons such as these. Still, he strode to the rack and selected a matching polearm from the rack. The one time he'd tried selecting what he wanted instead of what the challenger chose, he'd earned a shock to his feet so strong it rattled his teeth.

Flint asked, "*What did he choose?*"

Nox sighed. "*Polearm.*"

"*It's fine. Remember your training at Kings Keep.*"

He'd taken a handful of lessons with the guard as a teen, which meant he wasn't completely inept with the polearm. Still, the weight felt foreign in his hands as he squared off in front of the man. What's worse, exhaustion weighed heavily on his shoulders. And from the hard glint in his foe's eyes, Nox suspected he'd be in for a hard match.

A chant rose from the stands. "Fight, fight, fight!"

The man bent into a fighting stance and charged, a battle cry ringing from his lips.

As Nox dodged the first blow, he cursed under his breath. "*He's fast. I'll give him that.*"

"*You're faster.*"

The man zigzagged, and his polearm sang.

"Oof." Nox grunted as he blocked the next swing. Shock waves spread up his arms. "*He's strong, too.*"

"*You're stronger,*" Flint insisted.

Nox gritted his teeth, dodging one blow and blocking the next. He retreated across the ring, able to do little more than defend. This couldn't be it. He couldn't meet his end in this ring, at the hands of some random prisoner. Not when Mariun was in danger somewhere.

Sweat dripped down his brow, stinging his eyes. Nox refused to wipe it away, certain the man would use his moment of distraction to land a killing strike. Yet every moment the battle stretched out, the wearier he grew. With each strong blow he turned aside, the more his shoulders and arms ached. He couldn't keep this up forever.

"*Look for an opening,*" Flint instructed. "*A weakness.*"

Nox scanned his opponent. Every other match, he'd pulled through. Against enemies stronger and faster. He'd bested smarter ones who had sought to trick him. But even someone gifted with as many boons as Nox still had limits. And it seemed he'd finally reached his.

When the next blow lashed down on Nox, he spun to block it. His polearm vibrated in his numb grip and slipped out of his fingers.

A hush fell over the crowd.

Nox's eyes widened. He was defenseless.

The prisoner raised his blade, a smirk on his lips.

Buzz.

Nox jerked where he stood as sharp pain rippled through his bare feet and up his legs. His opponent shuddered just as violently, and his weapon dropped into the dirt.

A dozen masked descended on them, whisking the weapons out of sight and pulling Nox and his opponent apart. Jurdan appeared at the edge of his box a heartbeat later. His deep voice boomed out over the stands. "Well, wasn't that the best show we've seen in ages? Too bad we're out of time."

Grumbling rose, and Nox spotted frowns painting the faces of nearly everyone present.

"My friends, don't fret. Our champion isn't done." Jurdan lifted his arms skyward. "We'll have an encore performance first thing tomorrow."

Cheers erupted, and all the disappointment washed away as if it'd never been there. Nox's shoulders slumped. The burning pain in his feet and legs subsided. Thankfully, the sensation wasn't so strong he passed out or lost control of his bowels, like the pole weapons the masked carried, but it still stung enough to make him regret all the decisions that had landed him there.

Sure, he wasn't dead—yet. But how long could he expect to last? If they forced him to battle again in the morning, it wasn't like he'd have much of a chance to rest. And he'd hardly put a dent into the pool of challengers. Judging by the men still left in the cages, he'd have double the number to fight tomorrow, and that was assuming there weren't more men who'd spoken a challenge in his absence being kept elsewhere.

But even worse than the dread that sought to overwhelm him, something more insistent prickled Nox's mind. A burning question that he simply couldn't fathom.

Why?

Jurdan had claimed he couldn't wait to watch Nox fall in the ring. Hadn't he said, 'I'll enjoy watching you die'? If that was the case, why did he step in when Nox was so close to death? Did he merely wish to prolong his suffering, or was there another reason Jurdan had saved his life?

"*What's happening?*" Flint asked.

Wasn't that the ultimate question? "*I'm not sure. I dropped my polearm. I thought I was done for. But Jurdan stopped the fight.*"

"Really? Why?"

"No clue." The masked began dragging Nox across the dirt ring. But instead of heading for the cell he'd been crammed in before the fight, or even toward the door leading to the prison level, they hauled him in a different direction. Toward a lone door just below where Jurdan's box hung. *"Think I'm about to find out. Looks like they're taking me to Jurdan."*

Up they climbed. By the time they reached the top of the tall staircase they found behind the door, Nox was ready to collapse. If not for the masked clasping each of his elbows, he'd have lain on the steps at the halfway mark and rested.

They found Jurdan seated on one of the grand golden chairs in the box. He looked on as the people dispersed. They seemed in high spirits, and a few children even cheered when they spotted Nox emerging.

"Have a seat, Nox." The masked dumped Nox into the fancy chair next to Jurdan, and it took all the strength he could muster not to sink into the plush cushion and close his eyes.

Jurdan waved a hand. "Leave us."

The stairwell door closed with a gentle *click*.

"What do you want?" Nox grumbled.

"Is that how you speak to everyone who saves your life?"

Nox shrugged. "I've never been known for my tact."

Jurdan's lips curved into a smirk. "Funny. I think in another life, you and I might've been good friends."

Nox scoffed. "Sure." What was Jurdan playing at? "Why did you do it? I thought you couldn't wait to watch me die."

"I lied."

That was it. No explanation. No excuse. Just the simple fact laid out like it was nothing unusual.

Nox's brow furrowed. "So you don't want me dead?"

Jurdan lifted a hand to his face and casually examined his nails. "No. Unfortunately, my plans require you to live. For now, at least."

What the hell did that mean? What plans? "Did you mean what you said? If I defeat them all, will you bring me to Mariun? Do you even have her?"

"I will. And I do." He sneered.

"Forgive me for not believing the word of an admitted liar," Nox muttered. "Why even bother with this charade if you don't want me dead?"

"There are rules in this city. The people who've broken them need to see that their actions have consequences. I may need you alive, but I still need you to bring them to heel. And there's nothing wrong with lying when it serves a higher purpose."

"What purpose? I would've fought those battles regardless just for the chance to see her. Would it even matter if I knew you'd be there, ready to jump in and save me from a mortal wound?"

As the words slipped past Nox's lips, the truth seared his soul. What did that make him if he was willing to trade all those men's lives for a single glimpse of the woman he loved?

Perhaps Jurdan wasn't the only villain here... Nox shook off the thought. It wasn't the same. And he refused to feel guilty about fighting for Mariun. He'd known it back in that barn on Avion, just like he knew it now. He'd follow her anywhere. Kill anyone who stood in his way.

Jurdan chuckled. "Consider it a test." He waved at the ring. "These battles are not the only thing that happens in this hallowed space. My masked are made here. Every time a new group is ready to join me, I test their mettle. Their obedience."

Nox shivered. Did he even want to guess what that test looked like?

"Your test was not exactly the same, but it was close enough. Now I know for sure you are truly worthy of my gifts."

Nox gritted his teeth. This again. "I told you already. I don't want them."

Jurdan cocked his head. "No? Not even when you're facing a far harder fight on the morrow?"

Nox stared at him, his glare hard and thick with resolve.

"What happened today, that was a one-time reprieve. If you fall again, I won't step in. It will just be you"—he threw a hand out at the stands—"and all of them baying for your blood."

"Not even then. Keep your foul offerings to yourself."

Jurdan snickered. "As you wish." He rapped three times on the armrest of his golden throne. The door jerked open. "Take him back to his cell."

The masked returned, roughly hauling Nox out of the seat.

"Oh, Nox?" Jurdan's voice reached him right before the men dragged him out the door.

A thousand tiny pains flared to life the moment the guards jerked him out of his chair, and only sheer force of will kept him standing. "What?" Nox bit out through clenched teeth.

A cruel grin split Jurdan's cheeks. "I'll send your goodbyes to Mariun the next time I see her."

Obey or Defy

The storm lasted long into the night. Violet and her companions hunkered down with Mariun in the hold of the masked's ship. But with each passing hour, she grew more unsettled. "Why haven't they come?" she whispered to her aunt.

They'd taken turns stationed beside the door, a poisoned blade held at the ready. Ryon stood there now, one ear pressed to the wood, listening. They'd heard countless footsteps—it was abundantly clear they weren't alone. She'd been expecting someone to come. If not to check on Mariun, then to hunt for them once they'd found the bodies of their slain companions on the deck. But so far, no one had thrown open the door.

Kayda shrugged. "The storm must be keeping them busy. It could've even thrown up a swell big enough to knock the dead into the sea."

"Maybe." Violet's nose wrinkled. Something told her they weren't quite so lucky. She shuddered as a shout echoed somewhere on the deck. She darted a glance at Ryon, but he quickly shook his head.

Still, she wouldn't rest easy until they got off this ship. "I think what's more likely is they're waiting. They're riding out the storm and then they'll deal with us after."

Kayda cocked her head. "Let them. As soon as the storm passes, the dragons will return."

"Are you sure they can't come back now?" As if to punctuate her question, the sky cracked and a massive peel of thunder erupted, making Violet flinch.

"Not safely. And we can't afford to have one of them out of commission. Not if we want to escape with our skins intact," Kayda whispered.

She was right. They'd need all the help they could get flying out of here. The dragons might have grown incredibly fast, but they still weren't full-sized. Who knew how long it would be before they could carry more than one person at a time?

Orry shifted, drawing Violet's attention to where her bondmate sat curled in her lap. "*Hey. You all right?*" Violet asked.

Her golden feathers fluttered, shimmering in the lamplight. Orry pushed to standing and turned, gazing directly into Violet's eyes. "*Do you remember how I told you there would come a time when we would part?*"

"*Yes...*" She'd assumed Orry had been talking about her death.

With a graceful swoop of her neck, Orry plucked a single feather from her chest. "*That time has come.*"

"*No.*" Violet trembled. "*What are you talking about?*"

"Is there a problem?" Kayda spoke softly enough that Violet barely registered the words, but it was enough to make Ryon turn. His jaw dropped.

Violet didn't answer. She was too busy gaping at the feather in Orry's beak. "*I don't understand...*"

"Take it, Violet. And don't forget to listen. You'll know when to use it."

Violet grasped the soft feather with shaking hands.

Orry's voice hardened. *"Hide it. Hurry now."*

Violet scrambled to think of a spot. She settled for stuffing it in the smallest of her belt pouches. Whoever had crafted the belt had included a tiny pocket scarcely big enough to fit a few coins in. She'd laughed when she'd first noticed it, but now she was glad for the silly thing. The pocket blended in with the leather, making it easy to overlook.

Orry watched silently, then lifted into the air. A draft pulsed in the cabin as Orry flapped her wings.

A strand of Kayda's curly red hair lashed across her face. "What's happening?" The demand had just left her lips when a massive wave battered the ship. Ryon tumbled from his spot at the door. Violet gasped and flew into motion. She slammed hard into Kayda's shoulder, shoving her sideways.

The breath flew out of her as Kayda's bones rammed her stomach, and they both landed in a tangle of limbs against the cabin wall.

"What the bloody blazes?" Kayda hissed.

When Violet tore open her eyes and spotted Ryon's poisoned blade sticking out of the wall they'd just been resting against, she let out a sigh. Ryon cradled his head and groaned, and then his gaze snapped to them. "Are you two—"

Crash.

The door slammed open, whipping icy rain into the cabin. "Well, well. Right on time."

Violet stiffened. That voice. She'd heard it before, but this was the first time he'd spoken her language. "Jurdan." A wash of disgust poured over her as he stepped into the cabin. Kayda gagged, and Violet fought to disentangle herself from her aunt.

No sooner had Jurdan's purple robes swept over the threshold than a troop of masked poured in. The masked grabbed them and hauled them to their feet, quickly tossing their weapons aside and binding their arms.

Out of the three of them, only Ryon put up a fight. He bucked and roared, knocking the first two loose and reaching for his axe. But before his fingers connected with the hilt, a masked walloped his head with a metal pole.

"No!" Violet screeched as the resounding *crack* echoed in her ears.

Ryon slumped, dazed by the blow. The masked jerked his arms roughly behind him, and a few heartbeats later all of them were trussed at Jurdan's mercy.

"Ryon!" Violet tried to lurch out of the arms of the masked who held her, but she barely budged.

A pained groan spilled out of Ryon's chest. "I'm fine." He lifted his head, and Violet's heart jolted when she spotted blood seeping out of the gash on his forehead. At least he was conscious.

She scanned the room. "*Orry?*"

"*Hidden in the rafters.*"

Though she wanted to check, Violet kept her eyes trained ahead. If Orry had hidden, then she must have a good reason for it. It wouldn't do to draw attention to her. And it might even be an advantage, though she doubted the aging bird would be much use in a fight. Still, it helped to have one of their number free to move about. It was clear Mariun would be no help. She'd slept through it all—the rolling ship, the icy wind, and the men clambering inside.

Violet's pulse skittered as the man behind her searched her pockets and pouches. Relief rushed through her when his fingers skipped the one she'd stuffed the feather in.

Once they'd been searched and the masked collected their weapons and stuffed them in a sack, Jurdan strolled across the floor. A bolt of lightning flashed behind him through the open doorway. Violet shivered, both from the frigid air pelting her face and the sickening sensation that flooded her from being in Jurdan's presence.

He walked to Kayda, a cruel smirk on his face. "Fancy finding you here. I'd hoped our mutual friend would dispose of you for me." He *tsked*. "You can't rely on anyone these days, can you?"

Kayda sneered. "You'll pay for what you've done to Jayan."

"Will I?" Jurdan snickered. "You foreigners and your useless threats. Such feisty captives."

The mention of captives made her stomach lurch. "Where is Nox?" Violet's skin prickled as Jurdan's gaze swung to her, and she choked down the urge to heave.

"Oh, you mean my champion? He's right where he belongs. Pity you didn't show up sooner. I suspect he won't last much longer against everyone who insisted on taking a crack at him in the ring."

"Let him go," Kayda demanded.

Violet expected Jurdan to balk at that. Maybe laugh in their faces and state an emphatic *no*. But he smiled slyly. "That can be arranged. I just need you to do something for me in exchange."

Her heart pounded. Ryon's brow furrowed, and he split a glance between Kayda and Jurdan. Silence stretched out, and in that moment, she didn't envy Kayda one bit.

"What do you want?" Kayda rolled her shoulders and lifted her nose, somehow managing to look regal despite having her hands bound behind her back.

Jurdan jerked his head toward the door. He turned without a word, and a heartbeat later, Violet gasped when the masked at her back shoved her forward. She had no choice but to follow. Soon they were all out on deck, squinting as the storm pelted their faces.

Violet sighed. At least dawn wasn't far off. The sky was no longer an unrelieved mass of black clouds. Purple and orange tinged the sky off to the east, lighting the boat enough that she could see clearly.

Jurdan halted on the midship deck and waved a hand. The masked halted, lining them in a row before him. "I need you to call the dragons back."

Violet's stomach dropped. When Jurdan had left the dragons and only abducted Mariun, she sensed something was off. She *knew* he wanted them for something. But what?

"Why?" Kayda asked.

Jurdan flicked his long black hair over his shoulder. "They won't be harmed. I only need to borrow their magic. Once they've done what I ask, you'll be free to go."

Ryon shook his head. "I don't like it."

A sneer crossed Jurdan's lips. "But the call isn't yours to make." He paced closer to Kayda. "What say you, Queen?"

A massive bolt of lightning lit the sky. Kayda's brow wrinkled. "Even if I wanted to call them back, I couldn't. Not in this storm."

"Oh, this little thing?" Jurdan grinned and lifted his arms skyward. "Say the word and I'll clear them a path."

Violet gasped as the dark clouds ahead parted. The storm receded, just like how Mariun had stopped it that day when they'd been hunting for the eggs.

"What will it be, Queen?" He spit out the last word like the taste of it was revolting. "Can those beasts spare a few moments of their magic for the life of your brother?"

Kayda closed her eyes. After a long pause, she snapped them open and spoke calmly. "Fine. We'll do it your way." She nodded to the west. "Keep the skies clear."

Violet's heart pounded. Jurdan stepped up to the rail, and within a few moments, the western clouds parted. Dawn sunlight lit the sky, but only in that section. Behind them and on either side, lightning still crackled, and shadowy clouds shrouded the boat in darkness.

Why had Kayda given up so easily? True, Nox was her brother, but she'd barely put up any resistance. Not even a single attempt to barter into a better deal had escaped her lips.

Then again, they were at an enormous disadvantage. Bound and weaponless. If Kayda hadn't conceded, she suspected Jurdan would have no qualms about making them agree—by force, if necessary.

Soon, wings appeared on the horizon. As the quartet of dragons sped closer, Violet couldn't keep the question to herself any longer. "What do you need their magic for?"

Jurdan smirked. "You'll see." He turned to his men. "What are you waiting for?"

The masked at their backs stepped forward. Most of them pulled ranged weapons out of their holsters, aiming them off the railing—at the dragons. "Wait!" Violet cried. "You said they wouldn't be harmed!"

Kayda took a step forward and opened her mouth, only to be silenced with a blade at her neck. A masked in a dog mask halted beside her, a curved sword pointed at her jugular. Roaring carried over the waves, and she sensed Mena was plenty upset at seeing her bondmate in danger.

A humorless chuckle spilled out of Jurdan's lips. "Don't worry. This is merely a precaution. As long as your dragons do as requested, this will be over before you know it." He spun to Kayda. "Tell them everything I say."

Kayda's gaze hovered somewhere above the dragon's heads, though surely by now Mena was close enough for her to see clearly again. A tiny smile fought to spread across her face, but Violet forced it back. Her aunt was no fool. She must be keeping her renewed sight a secret.

Jurdan stood by the rails, his hands lifted toward the clouds like he was pushing them aside with sheer force of will. Yet despite how impossible the feat appeared, it only required a part of his attention. He focused on the dragons as they slowed and circled the ship. "I need but a few moments of your concentration. A small smattering of magic. Obey and see both your bondmates returned to you. Defy me and you'll watch your queen fall and never see Nox again."

Kayda must have translated, because it wasn't long before Gwen swooped lower and sent a rain of pebbles skittering over the deck.

In response, Jurdan waved a hand. The clouds closest to the dragons darkened, and a bolt of lightning darted from one cloud to the next, zigzagging back and forth in a maddening pattern that was clearly unnatural. The dragons shied away, clumping close together.

"Stop," Kayda shouted.

Jurdan's hands stilled, and the lightning stopped instantly.

"What do you want them to do?" Kayda asked.

"Beneath the waters lies a ring."

Violet's heart dropped to her feet. The ring. She'd known it was close. Could feel its call singing through her blood like a siren's song. And the moment she heard the word on his lips, her body revolted.

A slow smile spread on Jurdan's lips. "They must part the waters to reveal it, then sink their magic into it."

Kayda's voice rang out strongly. "And then?"

"And then you'll be freed. We'll go our separate ways." Jurdan's boots thumped on the deck as he stopped in front of Kayda. "Do we have a deal?"

Violet stared straight at Mena and shook her head firmly. But Kayda either didn't catch the hint or ignored it.

"Deal."

The intuition she'd been granted shouted a battle cry in her mind. No matter what else happened, she couldn't allow Jurdan's plan to succeed. Even though she had no clue exactly what he was planning, she sensed the truth deep in her bones. If she allowed him to touch that ring, something terrible would be unleashed on their world.

But her thoughts didn't stop the dragons from moving. They flew out and hovered above the ring. Then Ari and Crys opened their mouths, shooting streams of water and air at the ocean.

Violet's heart raced as the water parted and the top of the ring was revealed. Somehow, the massive upper arch of the ring remained completely free of rust and sand, despite being completely underwater.

"That's enough." Only the top quarter of the ring lay above the water, but Jurdan strolled to the railing and demanded, "Blast it. All at once."

Violet's skin came alive with warring sensations as the dragons summoned. The iciness lingering from the storm intensified, and prickles erupted on her skin. She shifted on her feet as the boat rocked in the sea.

But that wasn't what made her eyes widen and her stomach sink. As the streams of earth, water, air, and fire blasted the ring, a swirling vortex coalesced in its center. It was unlike anything she'd seen. A blur of spinning color stretched across the surface, the hypnotic swirl intensifying as the dragons continued to sink their magic into it.

"What is that?" Ryon whispered beside her.

Her voice quaked. "Trouble."

"Yes!" Jurdan erupted in big throaty chuckles that made her skin crawl. "Keep summoning. It's almost ready."

Lightning flashed behind them, and the dark clouds creeped closer to the dragons. A bolt zinged above Mena's head, but the white dragon was so intent on her task she made no move to protect herself. Kayda called out, "That's it. I'm calling them off."

"No." Jurdan lifted his hands, sending the clouds back. "Don't stop or Nox is dead."

She wanted to demand Kayda put an end to this, but could she really condemn her uncle to death?

The ring pulsed and swirled. She could hardly take her eyes off it. It seemed everyone was just as mesmerized. A few of the masked's weapons dipped as they stared at the incredible sight. Jurdan stationed himself at the railing, arms lifted and his jaw set as he held back the storm.

Violet startled when a warm touch hit her wrist. She darted a quick glance behind her. Mariun!

She kneeled behind Violet, hiding as best she could behind her profile. Sweat dripped down her temples as she lifted one shaking arm to the sky with a furrowed brow. In the other hand, she clutched Ryon's blade. The same one Violet had last seen stuck in the cabin's wall.

Blazes! Mariun didn't know that blade was poisoned. She held deathly still while Mariun slid the knife through the rope binding her wrists. One wrong move and she'd be incapacitated.

For once, luck was on her side. The rope snapped, and Violet jerked her head sideways. Mariun slid to Kayda and sliced through her bindings while Violet tore at Ryon's ties.

The bare moment slowed to a crawl. Would they free themselves before someone noticed? Her heart pounded as her fingers flew, working the rough rope loose.

Jurdan cackled into the wind. "Yes! Keep going. Finally!"

Violet held her breath, certain he would spin around to gloat. But a heartbeat passed. Then another. Jurdan and the masked continued to stare out at the ring, and she used every moment to tear at Ryon's bonds.

She needed to find some way to stop them. But they were badly outnumbered, with only one blade between them. How could they fight back against such odds? Her mind raced as she tried to form a plan—but everything she envisioned ended with them dead.

It seemed Kayda had no such worries. The moment the rope around her wrists hit the deck, she plucked the knife from Mariun's hand and sent it sailing—straight into Jurdan's back.

Jurdan jerked from the blow. He whipped around and cruel laughter spilled out of his lips. "You think a single blade can end me?"

If all the poison had rubbed off when the blade was embedded in the wall, or while Mariun sliced through the ropes, then they were done for. Luckily, the toxin was incredibly potent. They only needed one drop...

Jurdan snapped his fingers, and a crow perched on the mast descended. He flattened his palm, but before the bird landed, his knees locked. Then his arms. It was as if every muscle in his body stiffened all at once. He lost his balance and careened face-first into the deck.

"Now!" Kayda yelled.

The dragons turned, abandoning the ring and pointing their streams of magic at the masked. Chaos erupted. Arrow strings twanged, and grunts and cries of pain lashed the air.

A bolt of lightning shot out, nearly catching Ari. Violet finally pulled Ryon's rope off, and she immediately sought Mariun.

"The storm!" She kneeled beside her and gripped Mariun's shoulder. "Stop it. Protect the dragons."

Mariun blinked at her, and Violet sensed her friend was already drained. She wobbled slightly, and her eyes partly focused before fluttering half-closed.

Kayda and Ryon joined the fight. Her aunt disarmed the dog who'd once held a blade at her throat, and was used it to cut down any masked who were unlucky enough to come within her reach. Ryon picked up a barrel with a grunt and threw it at a masked before he loosed the arrow aimed at Kayda.

She'd lost sight of Jurdan in the madness, but he was the least of her worries now. Another bolt zinged, narrowly missing Gwen's tail.

It had worked once... "Mariun, now. Stop the storm." She pulled her hand back and slapped her hard on the cheek.

Mariun's head jerked back, and she wobbled listlessly. Violet's heart sank. But then Mariun's head snapped up. She tore her shoulder out of Violet's hold and threw both arms skyward.

Violet backed away, the memory of that awful strike still seared on her brain. Would that happen again? Had she just condemned her friend to being struck?

The boat shuddered and Mariun quivered violently. The storm dissipated quickly, the angry clouds lightening from black to gray and then fading completely, leaving the sky a brilliant blue.

"You did it!" Violet grinned and raced forward, only for her smile to evaporate as fast as the clouds when Mariun collapsed. She caught her head before it slammed into the deck. Placing a hand on Mariun's neck, she sighed when the steady thump of her pulse beat against her fingers.

"She all right?" Ryon yelled. He'd stationed himself in front of them with a pile of rocks Gwen had summoned scattered by his feet. Every time a masked got close, he'd send a few sailing at them. By now, the deck was littered with bodies, and Kayda had moved out of eyesight.

She wasn't exactly a healer, but the steady rise of Mariun's chest made her reply confidently, "I think so. Have you seen my aunt?"

"She went that way." He pointed toward the bow.

No sooner had he pointed than Kayda came racing back, the bloodied sword waving at her side. "Jurdan's getting away!"

Violet's breath caught in her throat. She swallowed her dismay and yelled to Ryon, "Can you carry her?"

Ryon nodded and lifted Mariun in his arms. They raced after Kayda to the bow railing. Violet gasped. It seemed not all the masked had fallen. A group of them carried Jurdan's prone form between them. A massive murder of crows hovered above them, protecting the men from the dragons' magic.

A few of those strange oval ships they'd used to escape Thalassia hovered at the water's surface. The masked pulled Jurdan atop one, clearly intending to take him back below the sea.

Ryon gently settled Mariun on the deck and squinted through a gap in the rails. "Wait. What's that?"

Violet tore her eyes off the escaping men and glanced behind them. "I've seen that boat before." It was the same craft she'd glimpsed before they'd crossed into the storm. Who were they? And what were they doing here now?

But the question had barely formed in her mind before she shook it off. Now that she stood at the railing, the ring's pull was impossible to ignore. The water had rushed in to cover it as soon as Ari and

Crys stopped summoning, but she could still see the barest hint of it beneath the dark waves.

"You know what you must do." Her bondmate's voice rang out in her mind.

Violet stiffened. *"Orry? Are you—"*

"I'm safe, child. Go. Answer your calling."

As the words echoed through her mind, Violet sensed the truth in them. This was it. The reason she'd been fated to embark on this journey. "I have to stop him."

Kayda whipped around. "What?" She thrust an arm at the vessel. It was already sinking fast into the sea. "Will you follow him into that city?"

She shook her head. "I need to go to the ring."

Ryon stepped up to her side. "I'm coming with you."

Warmth spread through her heart. "I was hoping you'd say that." She grabbed his hand and twined their fingers together. Then she turned to Kayda. "Will you be all right?"

Kayda nodded. "I'll stay with Mariun. Perhaps when she awakens, she'll tell me how to save Nox."

"Maybe you won't need to." Ryon pointed again to the massive boat in the distance. They'd launched a dinghy into the water. It closed in on one of the vessels still bobbing on the surface. "Is that a dog?"

Mena flew in that direction, and Kayda chuckled. "Not a dog. It's Shadow."

Violet's heart jolted. "Does that mean—"

"Yes." Her voice thrummed with excitement. "Your parents are there, too. They must be going after Nox."

Her pulse raced with that revelation. She'd love nothing more than to join them. But she couldn't ignore the ring's call. It sang in her ears, the same haunting melody she always heard in her dreams. Still, the sight of her family gave her hope. She had to trust they would find a way to free her uncle. Maybe even destroy Jurdan while he was under the effects of the tetrela's toxin.

She spared one last glance at her family and tugged on Ryon's hand. "Are you ready?"

"Let's go." Ryon helped her climb over the railing, then joined her on the other side.

A pang of sadness struck her. She hated to leave Orry. But there was no way the old bird could follow her beneath the sea. *I guess this is goodbye.*

Orry cried out, full of urgency, *"For now. If fate is kind, I'll see you again. Now go!"*

With her bondmate's plea ringing in her ears, she leaped. Cold blasted her body as she shot down into the dark waves, but she resisted the urge to swim to the surface. Ryon clutched her hand, and together they swam for the ring.

They were far closer now than the last time she'd seen the ominous relic. It was just as eerie, with the same luminous, cloud-like fish hovering around it. But now it wasn't lit by only the fish. The ring exuded its own glow from the magic swirling within it. The last time, she'd been able to see the ocean through the vast hole in the center. Now, the glowing magic stretched across the surface, encompassing the entire ring and hiding what lay behind it.

Violet sucked in a deep breath of water, and the sting in her lungs barely registered in her mind. She was too consumed by the ring. Its song wound around her—an invisible thread tugging her forward.

Holding tight to Ryon's hand, she swam faster. Like so many times in her dreams, she watched the ring grow larger. The call hummed in her blood and vibrated her bones. She was almost there. She'd finally learn why she'd been brought here. What she was meant to do.

A tug on her hand stilled her before she reached the ring's edge. She pulled, desperate to reach it. But when Ryon didn't allow her to continue onward, she whipped around. What was he doing? What could be more important than fulfilling her destiny?

Ryon pointed frantically behind him. Violet's jaw dropped when she spotted what had him so rattled, and her heart pounded so hard her chest ached.

Blazes! What were they going to do?

The Key

Nox panted as another body fell into the dirt. *"How many?"*

Flint answered wearily, *"Are you sure you want to know?"*

Chest heaving, he waited for the masked to rush out and grab the body. After a night of restless sleep, they'd dragged him back to the ring. His muscles ached even worse after a few hours lying down. He'd forced himself to move, though his body wanted no part of it.

Every time he thought about giving up, he pictured Mariun's face. It would all be worth it if he survived long enough to find her. Even if he was worn down to blood and bone, he would escape this sunken nightmare and save her.

They'd stuck him back in that cage, and he'd watched the prisoners being led in. And just like he'd feared, there were quite a few fresh faces in the mix. Somehow, they'd managed to cram the cages even fuller than yesterday.

Maybe Flint was right. He might go crazy if he kept track of how many men he'd slain. *"Forget it. I don't need to know."*

The crowd cheered as the masked dragged the latest kill away. A trail of red marked his passage through the dirt. The stands were as packed as ever, with one notable absence. Jurdan had disappeared during his first match and hadn't returned.

He hadn't been kidding last night. Nox was truly on his own. If he fell today, no one would save him. The thought had lit a fire in his belly, driving him to fight like mad. But just like last night, he already sensed his strength fading.

Nox sighed and bent, picking up the short swords the last man had chosen to fight with. He discarded them and faced the cages.

Silence fell over the crowd when the masked walked inside and selected the next challenger. Then the whole place erupted in whispered murmurs. So many on top of each other that even with his advanced hearing, he couldn't make sense of it.

Nox tilted his head, but from where he stood, he saw only the broad back of the masked standing in the cage entrance. "*What now?*"

"*Hm? Something wrong?*" Flint asked.

Nox rolled his shoulders. "*Not sure yet. Something's got the crowd excited.*"

His heart thumped mercilessly against his rib cage. Finally, the masked turned aside, and Nox gritted his teeth. "*Rot and decay.*"

"*What is it?*"

The man who'd almost lobbed his head off swaggered out of the cage, yellow teeth on display as he shot the crowd a cheeky grin. "*The idiot from yesterday. I'm fighting him next.*"

Flint's voice held a hint of a purr when he replied. "*That's good.*"

Nox resisted rolling his eyes. "*What do you mean, that's good? He nearly killed me.*"

"*Exactly. Better you fight him now, while you still have some strength.*"

Flint was right, of course. It would be disastrous to face off against such a strong opponent when he was tired enough to drop. But he wasn't exactly at full strength now, either.

The man pumped his fists in the air, egging the crowd on. Cheers erupted, and Nox did roll his eyes then. *Now the idiot's showing off. Give me a break.*

"Let him have his moment. Just make sure it's his last."

Nox nodded curtly. *"I got this."* He strolled out to meet him as the weapon rack ascended, hoping his confidence would work to boost his performance in the ring.

Flint kept up a steady commentary he only half listened to. *"You're better than him. Look at how many challengers you've dropped already. He couldn't do that. Trust in yourself. Use your boons and what you remember from your last match to cut him down."*

"I know. I will." Nox's heart sank when the man selected his weapon. *"The polearm again."*

"Doesn't matter. You can best him. I believe in you, Nox."

His bondmate's reassurance filled him, buoying his spirits as his hand closed around the wooden shaft of his polearm. Nox backed away, ducking into a fighting stance.

Slam.

A shock wave rippled across his arm as he blocked the first blow. Nox grunted, then spun sideways, sweeping his weapon low at the challenger's feet.

The man dodged the blow easily and countered with a swipe to Nox's head. The metal blade zinged in his ears and nearly chopped off his head before he ducked.

Sweat rolled down Nox's back as he dodged blow after blow. They danced across the ring, a blur of jumping, swinging steel, and cracking wood turning the crowd frenzied.

This time, at least, he was giving the man a workout. After long moments, the challenger began to slow, and Nox's heart lifted. Maybe he would win. He needed to wear him down. Find a weakness.

After exchanging another half-dozen blows, Nox spotted it. *"He's favoring his right leg."* Perhaps an old injury that hadn't healed properly?

"Good," Flint replied, excitement clear in his voice. *"Use it to your advantage."*

Nox darted in and swung for the man's leg. He smiled, sure he was about to tell Flint to add another to the tally.

Crack.

Nox's blade slammed out of his hands into the dirt. The man hopped back on his *bad* leg at the last instant and countered with such a powerful blow he had no chance of holding on. *"It was a trick."* A boot walloped his chest, knocking the air out of his lungs.

"Oof." Nox landed in the dirt, wheezing. *"I'm down."*

"Get up," Flint demanded.

The man kicked Nox's polearm hard, and it thunked into the wall. *"My weapon…"*

He trailed off as a bizarre feeling washed over him. He'd lived this moment once before. The scene was practically identical to his battle with Crow.

As he sat gaping at the man who—just like Crow—raised a fist in the air and soaked up the crowd's cheers, the memory of that last battle washed over him with perfect clarity.

"Get up, Nox!" Flint cried.

Tingles erupted across Nox's spine. Flint had said those exact words when he'd fought Crow. And then he'd said, *"If only I were like you, my friend. Then I could take this anger and make him choke on it."*

Flint gasped. *"That's it! Your wish, Nox. It's anger that's the key!"*

He was right! All the moments when his claws emerged flashed before his eyes. The battle with Crow. When he'd learned of Iggy's betrayal. The moment Jayan was unmasked. Each time, anger had pulsed through him, the molten heat scorching his veins.

If he tapped into that feeling now, he might stand a chance!

Nox drew a deep breath and gave the rage that lived deep in his soul free rein. It wasn't hard. Not when so many things in his life had been taken from him. All his bondmates, torn away before their time. His siblings, ripped apart and scattered so far he'd never known they existed until half his life had passed.

And Mariun. They'd stolen her right when he'd made her his. After he'd stormed out of that barn when she'd confessed her secret. She probably thought he hated her. He'd never even had the chance to tell her it didn't matter. That no secret would ever change the way he felt.

They hadn't just taken her. They might have killed his relationship when it'd barely even started.

His hands tingled, then stung. The jagoth claws he'd first called on in his fight with Crow reappeared on his fingertips. Nox leaped to his feet as the idiot faced him, his blade lifted.

The man's eyes bulged when Nox's claws sliced his skin and sank deep. His blade thwacked into the dirt. Nox twisted his hands, one buried in the soft flesh of the man's gut, and the other in his throat. Blood gushed out, the hot liquid spilling down his wrists and painting his forearms red.

Stunned silence reigned. Long enough that the man's last gurgling breaths played heavily in Nox's ears. But once his limp carcass slammed into the dirt, the crowd's roars made him wince. The cheering was so intense he almost mistook the vibration under his feet as an effect of the spectators' cries rattling the floor. But then the cheers morphed, turning from excited, bloodthirsty shouts to screams of fear.

The floor shuddered, nearly knocking him off balance. In the stands, dozens of people fell, knocking others down and causing a chain reaction of utter chaos.

What in the world? Did they feel that too? *Rot and decay. I think we're moving.* As the anger he'd been holding on to faded, so, too, did the claws. But Nox hardly noticed. Not while the whole city trembled around him.

"*What?*" Flint couldn't hide his surprise. "*Is the fight over? Where are they taking you?*"

Nox winced as a few people in the bottom row tumbled down. An especially unlucky fellow flew over the railing and landed in the ring with a resounding *crack* that made Nox certain he wouldn't be getting up.

"*Not just me. All of us.*" His arms shot out for balance as the floor lurched under his feet. "*The city is moving.*"

All around, people panicked. The masked fought to keep them in line, but the sheer number of spectators was too much for them to control. A group of men trampled a guard in a shark mask. Another masked swung his pole in a circle beside an exit, but it wasn't long before the crazed crowd swallowed him.

What was even better, the door that always opened once he felled a challenger remained closed. Nox's heart pounded. This might be it! His chance to escape. He raced across the ring, snagging his polearm on the way to the cages.

His bare feet kicked up dirt as he skidded to a stop in front of the first cage. "Stand back."

The men inside cowered, slinking to the rear of the cage.

"Why are you coming for us? Leave us alone!" a man cried.

Nox grinned. "I'm not here to fight you." He jabbed the polearm into the lock and tore the cage door open. "You're free. Go!"

"I'm freeing the prisoners. We'll fight our way out," he told Flint.

"You sure that's wise?"

"Dunno. But it's worth a shot."

He moved on to the next cage while the men in the first stared at him with dropped jaws. By the time he tore open the second door, the first prisoner had cautiously creeped out of the cage. Once he'd thrown open the third, they poured out, filling the ring and racing for the doors on the ring wall.

Slam!

The prisoners backed away as the doors flew open and masked carrying poles streamed out. Nox cursed under his breath. It was clear they'd trained for this situation. On each door with only one guard, the masked stationed himself in front of it, striking out at any who came close. Where there was more than one masked, a few broke off, advancing on the unarmed men with brutal swipes of their poles. The air buzzed as they found flesh, and convulsing bodies slammed to the ground.

It wasn't long before the broken men cowered, lumping together in the center of the ring. A few even retreated to the cages, seeking safety in the prison he'd freed them from.

But the masked were so few... The remaining challengers outnumbered them four to one. Surely if they worked together, the prisoners could prevail. They just needed to believe it was possible. That there was strength in numbers. And that what happened in this ring—this disgusting display of violence—could stop if they fought hard enough.

Nox yelled, "We won't go back! Cages can't hold us." He tossed his polearm to a bruiser of a man standing beside him. "We're not players for your bloody show."

He grabbed hold of the anger that rose when he pictured the helpless animals they made fight. All the men he'd been forced to slaughter.

Claws elongated on his fingers, his hands transforming into a weapon worthy of the fiercest predator.

He broke into a jog, heading for the closest masked. "It ends now!" he roared.

Blind rage consumed him as he sliced through black cloth and flesh. And when the body hit the dirt, Nox tore the pole out of the masked's lifeless fingers. "Who's with me?"

The cowering prisoners perked up. A tall lad with curly black hair yelled, "I am."

Nox tossed the boy the pole. "Fight! This is our chance!" He lurched into motion, swinging at the next masked who stepped in his path. The fight consumed him, this masked putting up much more of a fight than the last one he'd caught off guard. It wasn't until he felled the man with a slice to his jugular that he realized the battle had turned.

All around, the masked were flagging. The prisoners fought on, crazed and vicious, even while weaponless. The bruiser he'd tossed the polearm to swung it like a scythe, scattering blood in his wake. A few had managed to disarm the masked, and they used their stolen poles against them.

Nox grinned. "*We might just get out of here after all.*" He stumbled as another lurching motion jerked beneath his feet.

As he righted his balance, he spotted something that made his heart sink. Across the ring, one of the masked rushed toward the covered cages. Those cages hadn't been opened since he started battling challengers, but that didn't stop him from recalling what came out of them the last few times he'd seen those metal doors swing open.

"*I think I spoke too soon.*"

Flint asked, "*What do you mean?*"

The masked banged into the cage door as he raced away from a trio of prisoners chasing him. And from within, a sickening *hiss* bled into the air, making Nox's stomach clench.

"*The fight's not over yet.*"

Not Safe

Heart pounding out of control, Ryon waited for Violet to notice what was happening behind them. She'd been so intent on reaching the underwater ring that he'd barely been able to stop her swimming—but now, they had to.

Her eyes widened, and she froze in place as she finally spotted the huge underwater city purposefully moving toward the ring.

He hadn't thought it possible for something so massive to move. Thalassia was at least as large as his home island, mountains and all. Seeing it creeping closer to the gargantuan ring made him suddenly worried they were about to be squashed in between the two.

But when he tugged frantically on Violet's arm again, urging her to the surface, she shook her head.

Violet's hand shot out at the ring, and though neither of them could talk while underwater, he couldn't mistake the determination in her eyes. She jerked out of his hold and resumed swimming.

Ryon's stomach dropped. With the magic spread taut across the surface, the relic struck fear in his heart. What would happen if they touched it? Or worse, what if Jurdan reached it? He'd seen what magic could do. The power of the elements was so often harnessed as a weapon. Would Jurdan gain some terrible new power by sailing through the ring?

Then again, magic often conjured wonderful things. He'd watched Mariun be healed from the brink of death. But he feared that wouldn't be the case today. And from the frantic way Violet swam, hurrying to reach the ring before the city arrived, he sensed she felt the same.

He had to help her. They needed to stop Jurdan. Whatever he'd been planning with the ring—whatever advantage it was meant to grant him—they couldn't allow it.

As that thought entrenched itself in his bones, Ryon turned. Violet had nearly reached the ring already, her hands outstretched to touch the shining edge. He wouldn't be any help to her there.

But there was one thing he could do. He could buy her time.

Ryon raced through the water, heading for Thalassia. The current aided his strokes. It pulled him closer, sucking him into the wake of the huge city. It had already moved so close that when his hands landed on the smooth surface, he spotted Violet's face clearly through the dark waves.

What was she doing? With the short distance separating them, it merely looked like she was tracing the ring's edge. Did she even know what to do?

Ryon gritted his teeth. She did. Or if she didn't know, she'd figure it out. And he planned to give her the time to discover what had led her to it.

He sucked in a huge breath of water, then, calling on the strength he'd wished for, he shoved with all his might, kicking his legs in tandem.

Thalassia jolted in the water. A slow smile spread across Ryon's face as the city's movement slowed. He hadn't been sure his strength would be a match for the city, but it was working. He was doing it!

Violet's fingers trailed across the ring, eyes closed and her brow furrowed.

The city pushed back, and his wrists burned, pain shooting up his forearms. Still, he kept the pressure constant, fighting to stop the massive structure from advancing.

Guano! Ryon's mouth opened in a silent scream.

They inched closer and closer until he could see the tiny tremble of Violet's lip.

Come on. You got this. I believe in you. He stared at Violet, willing her to soak up his soundless encouragement.

The city pushed him forward, ever closer to the swirling surface of the ring. His muscles quivered and his skin prickled in the cold water.

No! Another few heartbeats and he'd be smashed.

Violet's eyes snapped open and connected with his. She blinked furiously, seeming to notice for the first time what he was doing. How close he was to being pinned.

As Ryon stared into her beautiful violet eyes, a well of untapped strength surged through him. He shoved as hard as he could, ignoring the bones snapping in his wrists, though he couldn't truly ignore the agony that flashed up his arms. Water rushed out of mouth along with a muffled shriek.

Thalassia slammed back in the water from his last-ditch shove at the same moment a blinding light erupted from Violet's hands.

Joy blossomed in Ryon's heart. He knew it! He knew if he just bought her enough—

Eyes widening, he forced his battered body to move, backing away from the swirling surface of the ring. The magic sped up—the lazy vortex whipped into a frenzy in a heartbeat. He reached for Violet, gulping as pain shot up his arm and his hand flopped on his wrist.

But he couldn't spare more than an instant of concentration for his broken body. Not when the worst happened.

Violet took one frantic stroke in the water before the vortex sucked her in.

What was happening? Where did she go?

Ryon's gaze darted across the ring. The magic was already fading at the far edges, revealing the dark ocean behind it. In an instant, she'd be gone. To where?

It didn't matter.

As the swirling vortex shrank to the size of a doorway, he tucked his injured hands close to his torso and dove in headfirst.

Ryon slammed into something hard. He rolled as he landed, instinctively cradling his arms against his chest. Still, pain flashed through him, so intense it made black creep around the edges of his vision.

He retched. Salt water poured out of his lungs. Guano. What did he do? Where was he? Clearly somewhere *not* underwater, if this was the first thing that happened. As he sucked in a breath of moist, pungent air, he finally summoned the strength to lift his head and look around.

"Ryon. Am I glad to see you!" Violet crawled closer, her voice hoarse, leaving behind her own puddle on the grassy hillside they found themselves on.

He coughed. "Where are we?"

"No clue. It's not anywhere I recognize."

Ryon sat up, wincing as the pain in his hands screamed.

"Blazes!" Violet gasped. "What happened?"

Lightning flashed above their heads. "Pretty sure I broke my wrists when I pushed back the city." He sucked in a thready breath. "I'm all right otherwise. How about you? Are you hurt? What happened with that light?"

"I'm fine. As for the light... I'm not entirely sure." Her eyes glazed slightly. "It was the oddest sensation. Like I was being torn apart and pieced back together over and over. But then I blinked and it stopped. And then I was sucked in."

They might never understand exactly how Violet's magic had worked. It hardly seemed to matter now when they were stranded—somewhere. He shifted, attempting to get a better look behind him, and gasped as pain shot up his arms.

"You should heal your wrists." Violet shook her head. "I don't have a knife to use a bloodfeather. Do you?"

"No. We jumped in the water so quick I didn't have time to grab any weapons." He shot a glance at the cloud-covered sky as another bolt shot through the air. Here, at least, no rain drenched them. "Do you think this is the same storm? Did we wash up on an island somehow?"

Violet shrugged. "Maybe." Her gaze trailed along the massive plain of unending grass. Except for a huge hill ahead and a crumbled field of dark rocks behind them, there was nothing of note. "I don't hear the ocean, though. Or—" She gasped again, and her eyes filled with tears.

"What is it?" Ryon's brow creased.

"Orry. I can't hear her." Violet hugged her knees tight to her chest and rocked where she sat on the wet grass. "S-she's just gone."

Ryon started to reach out, wanting to wrap an arm around her, but he abandoned the motion when pain sliced through his arm. "Is she dead?"

"No. If she was, I'd still hear her."

Of course. Just like with Nox and Flint. He still heard Flint's voice in his mind, even after his body had fallen. "I'm sorry, Violet. We'll figure out what's going on." Another flash lit the sky, then a peal of thunder echoed. "Maybe we can—" He groaned again as the ache in his arms intensified.

Violet sighed, and she snagged a stone off the ground. "This looks plenty sharp. We'll slice a feather out so you can heal yourself."

Ryon choked down the wail that wanted out of his throat. "It's not that bad. We should save the feathers. What if we need them for—"

A woman appeared as if out of nowhere, rounding the hillside in front of them. She spotted the pair of them crouched on the grass and began waving frantically and speaking fast.

Violet glanced at him. "Do you understand her?"

"No." She might as well be speaking gibberish. Her words were harsh and clipped, more reminiscent of Thalassian than Violet's tongue, but different all the same.

Violet grinned. "It's my turn to play translator."

"Wh—"

Before the word formed on his lips, Violet dragged the stone down her palm. Then she reached into his hair and began sifting through his dreadlocks before closing her bloody hand on one. His stomach sank, and he regretted showing her exactly which dreadlocks hid feathers before they'd left.

The woman raced toward them, her wary gaze darting all over like she was terrified. More words spilled out of her mouth, and he sensed the exact moment when Violet understood them. She withdrew her hand from his hair and perked up, then answered confidently in kind.

As the woman froze before them, Ryon studied her. She wore pants, like Violet, but these were made of unfamiliar fabric that looked far rougher than the cottons and silks he was used to. The bottoms cut off well above the ankle, revealing sturdy-looking boots.

But what was most curious was the number of pockets and pouches decorating her clothes. Nearly all of them bulged, and an earthy scent emanated from her.

Violet cleared her throat. "This is Helka. She wants us to follow her. Says it's not safe."

Dread pooled in Ryon's belly. "Not safe?" He shifted, and the move must've revealed his crooked wrists to Helka. She hissed softly as her gaze locked on his injury, and then her features softened. She spat out more words to Violet.

Ryon waited impatiently. He was dying to know what Helka had said and could scarcely wait for her to translate. If his hands weren't broken, he'd snag that stone and use a feather of his own. But with his injury, there was no chance of that.

Violet's eyes lit up, and she stood. "Come on. She said she knows where to find a healer. Think you can manage until then?" He nodded and she bent beside him. "I'll help you up, all right?"

Ryon met her gaze. "Are we sure we can trust her?" he asked quietly.

"I think so." She shrugged. "I have a good feeling about her."

"A feeling, huh?" With Violet's intuition, that was as good a reason as any. "If you say so." He got his feet under him and gritted his teeth as Violet's hand slipped under his elbow and she helped him stand. "Thanks."

Helka waved at them and started trekking toward the hill. She spoke as she walked, and Violet listened intently.

"She says she was out here picking mushrooms when she heard a racket outside. That's how she found us."

"Mushrooms..." Guess that explained the smell—and Helka's overstuffed pockets.

"She's bringing us to wait inside. Sounds like someone's coming for her soon to take her home."

Suppose it was good to know they weren't alone out there in the barren wilderness. But the mention of moving elsewhere to find more people made his skin prickle. Sure, Helka seemed friendly, but her friends might not be. And should they really be leaving when they barely understood where they were or how they got there? Shouldn't they be investigating their surroundings so they could figure out how to return?

As they rounded the hillside, a large hole appeared, blocked by a metal door. Helka started toward it, but before she made it two steps, she stiffened.

"Something wrong?" He followed Helka's gaze and his brow lifted. In their path, a red-and-green-spotted lizard reclined, tongue flicking out as if to taste the air.

Helka dug into a pocket with shaking hands.

Ryon bit back a chuckle. It was only a little critter. There were plenty like it down below on his home island of Avion. They were timid, skittish creatures, much more scared of humans than he'd ever been of them. Granted, this one was three times the size of the ones back home, more like a cat than the little palm-sized animals he was used to. But why was Helka staring at it like she'd seen nothing more fearsome?

Suddenly, the lizard sat up straight and hissed. Then it spat at them, an ugly brown sludge that landed in front of their boots. Helka shrieked and tossed a blade haphazardly at the creature. The small knife fell far off its mark, sinking uselessly into the dirt.

"What the blazes?" Violet's eyes widened as the grass sizzled beneath the lizard's spittle.

Ryon jerked backward. "Is it... melting?" The grass disintegrated, followed by the dirt beneath it. He gulped as an image of what would've happened had that spit hit his boots rose to plague him.

Violet thrust out a hand to Helka and barked a few harsh words. Helka rooted in her pocket again. A glint of steel flashed as the lizard reared its head back and opened its mouth.

Metal whizzed through the sky, and this time the blade pierced flesh. The lizard let out an awful screech before it collapsed, the knife sticking out of its abdomen. Ryon's gaze spun from the dead creature to find Violet breathing heavily, her hand outstretched.

Helka laughed and flattened a palm on her heart. She chattered at Violet, smiling. Violet blushed, but before she replied, another screech rent the air.

Skittering footsteps pounded the grass. Helka's smile fell, and she lurched for the doorway set into the hillside. She scrambled with the latch, spinning a dial back and forth in a pattern that made no sense at all.

Ryon's pulse raced as another lizard appeared. Then another. Soon they were surrounded, four that he could see, with more scampering echoing behind them. Had the first animal's dying cries called the rest?

There was no way they could fight them all.

"Come on. Come on!" Ryon stopped beside Helka, desperate to escape into the safety inside. With his hands out of commission, he couldn't do anything else.

Violet kneeled and snagged a blade out of the dirt as Helka spun the door's dial. A lizard that opened its mouth received a blade in the heart. It thumped lifelessly into the grass, but that only infuriated the others.

A spray of sludge flew, but Violet rolled out of the way, lurching toward the dead carcass of the first lizard.

Ryon's stomach revolted when he spotted one rearing back, its ugly mouth aimed straight at Helka. With her attention consumed by the door, she didn't see it. "Look out!" he cried, but Helka didn't glance up from her task.

Stupid language barrier.

He raced for Helka. As the spittle flew, he barreled into her. They went airborne, and he landed half atop her with his injured wrists wedged in between them. Agony burst to life so intensely he couldn't hold back his scream. Grass sizzled beside his ears just before the pain consumed him.

In Sync

How in the blazes did she get herself into this? One moment she'd been praying for some miracle to make her magic work, and the next she'd been sucked into a strange place where lizards as big as cats wanted to kill her with their toxic spit.

Ryon screamed and her head whipped sideways while she jumped in midair, dodging another sizzling shot. She registered Ryon's body crumpled in the grass, half atop Helka, before she forced her attention back to the beasts. If they were down, that meant she was the only thing standing between them and these awful creatures.

She landed on her feet, but her shoulder blades hit the hillside, making her slip. Regaining her balance, she jerked sideways, avoiding a glob of brown that immediately started sizzling and sinking into the dirt beside her arm.

Violet panted. Her throat, already sore from spewing ocean water, protested every deep breath she drew. But she ignored her aching throat and pushed her body to move. She had to keep going. If she drew the lizards away from the others, they might stand a chance.

Her eyes caught a flash of silver. She raced for the knife sticking out of the heart of the beast she'd downed earlier.

A blast of brown sailed under her arm. Her panicked heart slammed to life when a telltale sizzle started—far too close for comfort. Eyes widening, she stared in horror at the little speck of brown on her sleeve.

She kept running and dodging, but she whipped the shirt off her head, thankful the borrowed garment was a few sizes too big. The wet fabric slapped onto the grass as she skidded to a stop behind the carcass.

Her fingers closed around the hilt as her gaze rose. Three pairs of beady black eyes tracked her movements, their mouths open.

Violet's stomach plummeted to her toes, and the world slowed around her. What was she going to do? She couldn't kill them all. And if they all spit at once, she'd likely not even escape their foul spray.

This couldn't be the end. She'd never learn where she was. Never discover if what she did had saved the world like Orry had claimed. Hell, she'd never even hear Orry again, or discover what made her voice disappear from her mind.

And Ryon. Had she saved him? Would he crawl from that door and find her wasted away under a barrage of toxic sludge?

Just when she thought all hope was lost, a rain of rocks fell from the sky. Two of the lizards were crushed in a heartbeat, and the last met its end on the blade she flung between its eyes.

More rocks fell, slamming into the grass with such force she covered her head and crouched low. But then darkness blanketed her, the ground trembled faintly, and a blast of air caressed her bare back.

Violet's gaze lifted. She kneeled in the grass as a massive green dragon flew overhead, the wind from its enormous wings sending her hair flying in every direction.

"Gwen?" Even as the word left her lips, she knew it for a lie. This was not the same hatchling her uncle had bonded. There was simply no way.

This beautiful beast was fully grown, as large as a small house, at the very least. What's more, she noticed the slight differences between Gwen and her brothers, only much more pronounced. This unknown dragon was thicker and stronger than Gwen would ever be. Definitely a male.

And so was her rider.

Violet's gaze caught on the man perched atop the dragon's back. His keen eyes took in the scene, watching carefully as the rocks found their marks, hitting several lizards who'd hung back instead of coming close enough to strike. Finally, the last beast either fell or skittered off, racing away from the enormous dragon.

That was when the rider's gaze landed on her. Violet shivered, instantly aware of her lack of attire. With the long, flowing top still sizzling on the ground, she was left with only a thin chemise covering her chest, leaving her arms, neck, and most of her torso bare.

The rider's eyes narrowed, and he delivered a swift kick to the dragon's haunches. A heartbeat later, the ground thumped as they landed.

Violet scrambled into motion. She tore the knife out of the nearest downed lizard and grabbed her discarded top. Then, careful not to touch the spot that still sizzled and decayed, she sliced the sleeve off.

By the time she crammed the garment over her head and rounded the hilltop, the rider had hopped off. Violet's heart stuttered as she spotted Ryon unmoving on the ground, with Helka standing nervously next to him. She raced over and crouched beside him.

"Ryon?" She shook his shoulder. "Blazes! Ryon, are you all right?"

He didn't budge, but his chest rose and fell in a steady rhythm that made her certain he still lived.

"What is the meaning of this, Helka?" a masculine voice grumbled. "Why are you out here? Especially *now*? Don't you know better?"

Violet trembled, not liking how this man was berating the woman who'd been so swift to aid her. But then again—hadn't the rider done much the same? She tamped down the urge to butt in as Orry's parting words rose in her mind. *Don't forget to listen.*

She needed to use her boon—and not only when she was in immediate danger. Now that the dragon stood watch, blocking the hillside with the door, it seemed they were safer than they'd been since arriving in this mystifying place.

Violet shifted, angling herself to watch Helka and the rider as they argued. Their clothes were similar enough she was certain they must hail from the same town. Pants and long-sleeved tops decorated with more pockets than probably necessary. Yet they were an odd pair, to be sure.

Helka was a twig of a woman, skinny and tall, though her face possessed a lovely softness that appeared at odds with the sharp angles of her limbs. The rider was all muscle and was taller than Helka by a head. They both had dark-brown hair, but Helka's fell in soft curls to her shoulders. The rider wore his straight hair pulled away from his face, drawing attention to a scar on his forehead that faded into his hairline. Violet shivered as she traced it with her gaze. If she had to guess, she'd wager it was the claw mark of a massive three-fingered beast.

She brushed off the thought. She was allowing herself to be distracted. It was time to listen.

Drawing a deep breath, she called on her boon. Their songs played in her mind almost instantly. The melodies rang out clearly, and her brow furrowed. Strange instruments she didn't recognize filled both songs.

Still, their songs played in concert, twining together much like Kayda and Jayan's had, only with one difference. There was nothing off. No single note out of tune. The two melodies were so in sync she knew they cared for each other deeply.

No matter the harsh timbre of the rider's voice, he was in love with Helka. Violet's brows lifted as she heard something faint but unmistakable in the mix. A third melody—this one a gorgeous mix of the rider and Helka, yet unique all at once.

"You're pregnant." The words slipped off her tongue before she could snatch them back.

The rider and Helka stopped mid-conversation. The rider's arm shot out. "Who the flash are they?"

Helka's eyes widened. "H-how?" Her hands fell to her flat stomach. "No one knows. We haven't told anyone."

The rider dragged a hand through his dark hair, mussing the tail he wore it in. "Helka. Who. Are. They?"

Each word slammed into her, thick with malice. Violet shrank back in the face of the man's rage.

But Helka rolled her eyes and patted the hulking rider's chest. "Give your bluster a rest, Kai." She took a step closer, only for Kai to snatch her around the waist and haul her back. "Please! Hasn't Roc told you yet they aren't a threat?" She jerked out of his arms.

"How can we know that?" he growled.

Helka stacked her fists on her hips. "She took out a bunch of disanders with my knives. And he knocked me out of the way when I was in the path of their acid. Even when saving me made him land on his injury and pass out from the pain."

Violet cleared her throat. "I'm Violet, and this is Ryon." She met the rider's gaze with pleading eyes. "Can you help him, please? Will you take us to the healer? Helka said there was a healer."

Kai glared at Helka. "Did she now?"

Helka snagged his hands in hers and met his eyes. "They saved me. It wouldn't be right not to return the favor."

Kai stared at Helka with a set jaw long enough that Violet began to internally despair.

What if he said no? What if he jumped on his dragon, plucked Helka off the ground, and disappeared into the air? There'd be nothing Violet could do to stop them. She and Ryon would be stuck there alone, with no help and more of those awful creatures out there somewhere.

"Fine." Kai tugged his hands free from Helka's. He stalked toward Violet and kneeled on the other side of Ryon.

Violet's breath caught when he pulled a sprig of green leaves out of one of his many pockets. "Of course. You're the healer! You'll use his boon." She grinned at the earth dragon as it began to summon, and the ground beneath her trembled slightly.

But Kai froze, his shrewd gaze scanning her face. "Don't think I've forgotten you." He jabbed a finger in her face. "I expect answers as soon as I'm through." Then he bent to his task. He carefully turned Ryon, staring first at his bent wrists, then sifting through his dreads, looking for whatever caused one to be bloody, no doubt.

"I think his head is fine." The cut he'd earned from the blow to the head on the boat had wound up being a tiny thing, and it'd already stopped bleeding. And as for the blood in his hair... Violet winced as she stretched out her hand. Without adrenaline pumping through her, the pain from the jagged slice in her palm made itself known. "I touched his hair with this."

Kai's brows dipped. He frowned at Ryon's broken wrists and carefully straightened the bones, laying his hands flat on his chest. Then he pulled a few more small items out of his pockets that Violet didn't get a clear view of. "All right. Give it here." He wiggled his fingers and glanced pointedly at her hand.

"It's nothing." She started to pull her palm away, but Kai snagged it. A gasp spilled out of her lips.

He pulled her hand forward and placed it gently atop Ryon's. "I'll heal you together." Then Kai's huge palm landed atop both of theirs. The crinkle of leaves, along with something round and squishy, pressed into her skin.

Kai closed his eyes, and within moments a gentle warmth bloomed on Violet's flesh. Her jaw dropped as the pain in her palm completely faded.

She braced herself, ready for Kai to crumple the way Nox had when he'd healed Mariun. But when the rider's blue eyes snapped open, not a drop of dizziness shadowed their depths. He removed the plants and lifted Violet's hand, a tiny smile tugging at the corner of his lips as he examined the reformed flesh.

Violet pulled free and cupped Ryon's cheek. "Hey." His wrists looked normal again, but his eyes remained closed. "You're all right now."

"He might take a while to wake. That wasn't a mere scratch I just healed."

Violet's gaze snapped to Kai. "Shouldn't we wake him? What if more of those *things* come back?"

Kai shoved the plants back into his pockets and stood. "They won't. Not with a dragon here."

"She's right," Helka said. "The disanders might be gone, but that doesn't mean there aren't worse out there. And he might fall off Roc if we try to fly back while he's out of it. We should drag him inside before anything else shows."

"Not so fast." Kai threw out a hand to still Helka when she bent beside Ryon's feet. He faced Violet, scowling. "I told you I have questions. I need answers before we help them any more than we have."

Violet got up and brushed the dirt off her knees. As much as she hated standing there like a sitting sparling, it was clear that Kai was as stubborn as they came. "I owe you as much. What do you want to know?"

Kai blew out a huge breath, then started spitting questions rapid-fire. "Who the flash *are* you? Where did you come from? What are you doing out here, of all places? How did he get those injuries? What are you doing here with my wife?"

Violet sighed. "I doubt you'll believe me."

"Try me." Kai crossed his arms.

"Ryon and I"—she pointed at her chest—"Violet, we were"—she paused, trying to think of the simplest explanation that wouldn't make her sound like a lunatic—"swimming, and the next thing we knew, we ended up in that field of rocks, wondering where we were."

She still wasn't sure where that *was*, but she refrained from asking. She could tell by his permanent scowl Kai wasn't in the mood to answer her questions.

"Ryon was hurt while we swam. Something in the water tried to crush us, but he held it back. He saved us both."

Kai rubbed his temples. "Let me get this straight. You were *swimming*"—he spat that out like it was the most unbelievable part of her story—"when something tried to squash you. Then you just dropped into a field an hours' flight from any water safe enough to swim?"

"Pretty much." She shook her head. "I knew you wouldn't believe me."

Helka pursed her lips. "Look at the state of their clothes, Kai. They're still sodden. How do you explain that?"

Kai's gaze flicked over Violet, and she buried the urge to squirm. "Caught in a freak shower, I bet."

"Maybe. But look at the clothes themselves. Have you ever seen a weave so fine? I certainly haven't. And landing out *there*, of all places." Helka's arm shot out, pointing toward the rock-strewn plain they'd landed on. "I believe her. You know what the stories say. What those rocks used—"

"Violet's telling the truth."

Violet gasped and spun to Ryon. "You're awake?" She fell to her knees beside him, her brow scrunching when she realized what he'd just said.

What *language* he'd spoken.

His right hand was clenched in a fist, and she knew if he untangled his fingers, she'd see a cut on his palm. "I thought we were saving those?" Violet's softly spoken question in her own tongue made Ryon's gaze flick to hers.

He responded in kind, and she didn't miss the way their use of another language made Helka and Kai stiffen. "I didn't like the way he was talking to you." Ryon's lip curled. "Or looking at you."

Violet had the sudden urge to shove Ryon down into the dirt. She resisted it—barely. "Seriously? I would've handled it."

Ryon's expression softened. "I-I—"

"And if you'd just waited until I talked to you, you'd learn that they're married. Kai was questioning me about how we got here. Of course it was a little tense."

"Sorry." Ryon cringed. "What's done is done now."

"Are you two through?" Kai's deep voice boomed.

Ryon sat up a little straighter, his stare wary and one step away from a glare.

Violet swapped languages. "Yes. Can we go inside now?"

"No." Kai's voice was hard, brooking no argument.

Violet's heart fell. Was he turning them out? Had that short private conversation convinced him they couldn't be trusted?

Helka spoke before Violet had a chance to plead their case. "You can't mean that? Don't you think the oracle—"

"Flashes, Helka. Relax. They're coming with us." He whistled sharply, which was clearly some signal for the dragon. It twisted sideways, and with its immense body no longer blocking the way, Violet gasped.

Six dragons hovered in the air. Each was as massive as Kai's, their scales shimmering despite the overcast sky. They thudded into the grass beyond the hillside.

Violet's stomach churned. Where did they come from? Finding one adult dragon when the rest of the world thought them extinct was unbelievable enough... Now there were six?

Kai jerked his head. "Come on. We'll talk more in the village, where it's safe." His scowl fell away, and Violet finally spotted a full smile cross his face. "Ready, Roc?" He patted his dragon's neck and vaulted atop his back. Then he reached for Helka and told them, "Take your pick of the lone riders."

Ryon hissed in Violet's ear, "Are we following them to their village?"

Violet trudged away from the hillside. "What other choice do we have? Maybe once we get there, we'll find some answers." Helka, at least, appeared willing to help. If she talked to her again, she might work out where they were.

Ryon trailed her to a massive white dragon carrying a female rider. The woman reached down, and Violet clasped her hand. Still, it was a much harder task mounting a house-sized dragon versus the smaller hatchlings she was used to. Her scrambling attempts earned a few chuckles before Ryon pushed her up from below.

"See you there," Violet called.

Ryon waved and jogged to a black dragon waiting in the grass. Soon all the dragons lifted off, flying together in a loose formation, with her and Ryon in the center.

Violet squinted, doing her best to examine the other riders. Curiously, it seemed they liked to mount their dragons in pairs. There was always one rider up front who paid close attention to the land they flew over and the dragon. The riders in the rear kept a vigilant watch on the skies, their hands tightly clenching ranged weapons.

Violet shuddered. Why would they need those? Her gaze darted through the clouds, but no matter how hard she looked, she saw nothing.

After long moments of searching, some of the tension in her frame faded. She relaxed into the joy of the flight. The wind in her hair. The sensation of being weightless.

But then the wind shifted. A break in the cloud cover drew her attention. And when she spotted what lay through it, Violet's pulse skyrocketed and her jaw dropped.

Not one, but *three* moons hung on the horizon.

She blinked until her eyes hurt. But the vision didn't fade away like she'd expected. Three bright ovals seared themselves on her mind until the clouds obscured them once more, leaving a ghostly glow in their wake.

The ring didn't just send them to another island. It sent them to another world. What in the blazes were they going to do?

Suicidal

All around Nox, the battle raged. Grunts and pained cries abounded. Bodies slammed into the ring, kicking up dirt. And all of it happened while the city lurched and trembled. But Nox wasn't focused on any of it. Not with that awful *hiss* ringing in his ears.

"I don't like the sound of that..." Nox's stomach revolted as one masked backed into the cage on the ring's far side. A group of challengers chased the masked, attacking him relentlessly, though the black-clad man kept flinging them aside.

The guard couldn't be planning to let any of the caged creatures loose... could he? It would be idiotic at best. More likely suicidal. The starved beasts in those cages wouldn't care if they attacked prisoners or masked. They'd tear through the ring, killing indiscriminately.

"What is it?" Flint asked.

He couldn't answer. Fear paralyzed him as the masked reached up and did the unthinkable.

"The masked are setting free the caged beasts," he yelled in his mind. His momentary paralysis shattered the moment he noticed the guard reach for the lock. "We'll all be slaughtered!"

Anger surged up, burning his chest and making his hands ache. The spectators weren't paying attention. And Jurdan wasn't even there... Why send all these men to their deaths?

Nox raced for the cage, dodging fighters and praying for a miracle. One of the challengers could knock the masked's hand off target. Tackle him. Something...

No! His eyes bulged and his feet halted of their own volition. It was too late. Nox's pulse raced as the cage door swung open.

Quick as a lightning strike, a serpent darted out. It slammed into the masked, embedding its teeth into the man's thigh. The sand-colored snake looked just like the one who'd felled Flint.

The challengers scattered, finally backing off. One landed a parting gift to the guard, knocking his black-and-white mask askew and giving Nox a perfect view of the man's bizarre expression. It was clear he was hurting. He howled, fingers busy trying to pry the snake's head off his leg, but despite the pain, a grim smile painted his face between screams.

Was the fool pleased he'd loosed that awful predator into their midst?

The snake released the masked after a few heartbeats, only to leap to another—a prisoner this time, clamping on his shoulder. With the deadly venom at its disposal, it didn't even need to stick around to make a kill.

He had to be careful not to end up on the wrong side of those fangs. They all did.

A quick glance confirmed that the doors were still guarded. If he didn't do something, there was no hope. Not with them pinned in like cattle.

"Look out!" Nox shouted, hoping to spare the others the slow, painful death Flint had endured. "Get those doors open *now*."

But the warning was all he could spare. Someone had to stop more beasts from being freed.

The bizarrely smiling man slipped his mask back on and hobbled toward the next cage. Nox raced after him, weaving through the mad scramble of men trying to escape the snake.

He couldn't allow another animal to be freed. The serpent would be hard enough to kill. Whatever mystery beast waited inside needed to stay caged if he wanted to escape with his life intact.

With his heartbeat thrashing in his ears, Nox finally broke free from the crowd. Darting around the snake, who'd moved on to a third man, he closed in on the masked. "Stop!"

A manic chuckle spilled out of the masked. Twin puncture wounds in his thigh wept blood, but he kept hobbling on—and he was going to make it!

Nox took a running step, then leaped, landing in a slide that swept out the masked's feet right as he was about to unlatch the next cage.

He would've been elated if the brute hadn't landed atop him. Nox grunted, his leg crushed beneath the full body weight of the guard. Realizing he wouldn't get his feet under him immediately, Nox sat up and stabbed out with his claws, slashing the fool until he stopped moving.

One problem down. But another emerged, sending a jolt of terror through his heart. The snake dropped the man in his clutches and swiveled his head directly at Nox.

By now, all the challengers had crammed along the far wall. Many still fought the guards, attempting to overpower them and open the doors. Others cowered in clumps, their terrified gazes trained on the snake as they tried to move as far away from the beast as possible.

The two unlucky prisoners the snake had already poisoned convulsed in the dirt, clutching their wounds and moaning.

There were only two other things moving on Nox's side of the ring. The snake... and him.

"Rot and decay," he muttered. He shoved at the masked's body, trying to roll the dead weight off his leg.

The snake slithered closer, eyes narrowed and tracing his movements. His skin grew clammy, and Nox lost hold of his anger as terror overwhelmed him. His claws receded, leaving him not only stuck but completely defenseless.

Still, he shoved, desperate to free himself. His mind raced as he fought to call forth some memory that would reignite his rage.

Hiss.

The snake reared up just out of reach, readying to strike.

An arrow sank into the snake's eye. Then a flash of gray pounced, darting out from behind the cages and tangling with the snake.

Nox kept shoving while his mind screamed. Had another beast been set free? And where did that arrow come from?

The blur of scales and fur stopped moving as Nox wrenched his legs free. He scrambled to his feet and his jaw dropped. "Shadow?"

The wolf's tail wagged, even as his jaws clamped tight to the serpent's neck and he shook his head violently.

Nox's heart lifted. If Shadow was here, then that meant—

A familiar voice spoke behind him. "Good kill, Brother."

Nox whipped around. "Conall." His half-brother stood within the shadows of the massive cage. His bow was drawn, and his hazel eyes hadn't stopped moving, tracking the men in the ring.

"C'mon," Conall hissed. "This way, quickly. We need to move."

Shadow dropped the snake's lifeless carcass and bounded after Conall. Nox followed, a million questions flooding his mind. How had his brother arrived just in time to save him? The last time he'd talked to Conall, he'd been laid up in bed with a broken leg.

Nox pushed the questions aside. There'd be time for them later. They had to go.

"*What's happening?*" Flint asked, a hint of panic in his tone.

"*I'm all right,*" Nox assured him quickly. "*Conall and Shadow saved me. Looks like I might make it out of this in one piece after all.*"

"*You're joking.*"

Nox grinned as he spotted a slim feminine profile topped with a brown ponytail holding open a door behind the cages. "*No. Ereni's here, too.*"

Two downed masked were sprawled beside the wall. It seemed his brother and sister-in-law had accomplished what the dozens of challengers couldn't. Nox almost yelled for the prisoners to follow until an enormous lurch nearly knocked him off his feet. "What *is* that?"

Conall caught him, gripping his elbow and stopping him from tumbling face-first into the dirt. "The city's moving. We need to get out of here—fast."

"Moving?" Nox's voice rose, incredulous. "To where?" He followed Conall, Ereni, and Shadow as they ducked through the door into a dimly lit stairwell. Relief pulsed through him as the door closed behind them, muffling the clamor in the ring.

"You don't want to know." Conall shouldered his bow and detached a knife belt from his waist. "You might need this."

Nox grinned crookedly and took it. "Thanks." His hands quivered as he attempted to put it on while scanning his saviors. Their homespun traveler's attire was decorated with so many weapons it was clear they'd come prepared for a fight.

"Here." Ereni pulled the belt out of his shaking fingers. "Let me help you."

"T-thanks." Nox's teeth chattered. Cold from the stone stair seeped into his bare soles. Without adrenaline pumping through him, every ache and pain in his body made itself known. Once that compounded with the bone-deep weariness he'd tamped down while fighting, Nox wobbled on his feet.

Conall gripped his elbow again. "You all right?"

Nox blinked repeatedly, ignoring his body's cries for rest. "Yeah. I will be when we escape." He met Conall's gaze. "How did you even find me?"

Conall grinned. "Hitched a ride with a witch."

Nox's brows screwed up.

Ereni finished fastening the belt and shot her husband a sharp glare. "It's not important. What matters is getting out of here." Her gaze trailed away, lingering on the walls until she shuddered.

"Something wrong?" Nox didn't like the look in her eyes. Being a seer, Ereni sensed more than most.

Ereni backed away, nodding. "I don't know if I'd say wrong. Certainly unusual."

"Can you tell us while we walk?" Conall mounted the first step. "We need to move."

Their footsteps slapped the stairs, and Nox didn't miss the way Ereni shied away from the walls, even when the city trembled again. She climbed nimbly, despite the shifting stairs. "You remember how I can see auras? I see different types of magic as colors."

"Yeah." Nox struggled to keep up. Shadow stayed behind him, guarding their rear.

"Well, this place—" She shuddered again. "I've seen nothing like it in all my years."

A thread of unease unraveled in his chest, coiling around his pounding heart. "What do you mean?"

Ereni paused on the stair above him and turned, her blue eyes wide. "Everything in here—the walls, the floors, that fighting ring—is giving off a yellow glow. This city has an aura. I-I think it's alive."

Ride's Over

They flew for so long the sky dimmed, darkening the ever-present clouds to a dull blue black. Violet craned her neck, one eye on the sky, searching for another glimpse of the moons she'd spotted earlier. But the clouds were annoyingly uncooperative.

Finally, they slowed in the sky. Violet tore her gaze off the clouds and looked down, her eyes widening at all the lights. Then she squinted. From so far up and with nightfall close, it was hard to make out any details. Still, she wagered they flew toward a large village about half the size of Flamesmoat.

It was clear the two cities were far different. This one rested on a flat plain, surrounded by waterlogged fields sprouting stalks of greenery. Hut-like structures spread out in a grid pattern, lined on neat roads. And ringing everything, strange spindly towers stood sentinel, poking out of the ground like shining tree stalks.

Violet's heart skipped a beat. She'd never seen a city like this. Never heard of one either.

Her stomach sank, and she fought to choke down her panic. Surely they might still be on some island. Though while they'd flown, she hadn't spotted a hair of blue on the horizon. Maybe if she'd been looking at something other than the sky...

Had she dreamed it? Was she overwrought from battling and seeing what wasn't there? It seemed too bizarre to be believed. Were they really on another world?

With each new fact she turned over, the odd revelation made more sense. There were the people who spoke a language she didn't recognize. Talking about bizarre things that made no sense. Then there were the creatures that had tried to kill them.

And of course, the dragons. They were nearly extinct back home. She'd traveled half the world to track down the last eggs. But here six massive adults flew right before her eyes.

The evidence piling up certainly appeared damning. Would they ever find their way home? What if they were stuck here for good?

She clenched her thighs as the dragon beneath her spun in a circle. "Is this where we're headed?" she shouted to the rider in front of her.

The woman ignored her, her attention trained on the lead dragon.

Violet sighed. Maybe she would've spent her flight more wisely chatting up the rider instead of worrying over her impending doom. But it wasn't every day she was transported to another world.

A gasp spilled past her lips. What were the riders doing?

The passenger on the lead dragon pulled out an arrow topped with a bulky-looking tube. She sent it sailing as the black dragon opened its mouth and spat a gout of flame at it.

The arrow ignited, sizzling and glowing like an ember in a hearth, only a hundred times brighter. Violet instinctively averted her eyes, shying away from the light.

What was that? What purpose did it serve? They weren't attacking the town, were they?

The arrow careened down, falling toward the village and leaving a dim trail of sparks in its wake. It made it halfway to the ground before sputtering out and fading away to nothing.

Violet's pulse drummed in her ears. She held tight to the dragon, waiting.

While flying on dragonback, she hadn't noticed the low-level hum in the air until it disappeared. The quiet sound had been constant as they hovered over the city, but so unobtrusive that it wasn't worth noting, in the same way a distant waterfall or blowing wind faded into the background.

It appeared that was what the dragons had been waiting for. As soon as the sound cut off, they descended, flying to the city center and landing in a massive square.

Violet's jaw dropped. More dragons. They lounged in the square, a few dozen at least. People flitted around them, tending to their needs like groomers back home with their prized mounts.

The rider ahead of her flipped around and barked, "Off. Ride's over."

Violet swung her leg over the side, doing her best to slide off the massive white dragon without landing on her ass. As her feet hit the ground, the hum started again. "What is that?" she muttered under her breath.

Ryon appeared at her elbow. "Hey, you all right?"

"Hm? Yeah. I'm fine. You?" She scanned him up and down, lingering on his wrists.

"Good as new." He grinned and twisted his hands. "I hear I have Kai to thank for healing me." Ryon's smile fell as he nodded to the scowling rider who was currently helping Helka slide off Roc.

Violet's brows shot up. "Where'd you hear that?" There hadn't been time for her to explain how Ryon's injuries were healed before they'd hopped on the dragons.

"Had a little chat with my rider on the way back."

"Of course you did." Violet smiled crookedly.

Ryon had a way about him. Talking came easily to him, and he made new friends effortlessly. She wished she could say the same for herself, but when you looked different from everyone else, that wasn't always the case.

Violet leaned in. "Did you learn anything else?"

He opened his mouth, but a booming voice interrupted him before he spoke. "You two. With me." They both turned and spotted Kai hustling across the square in their direction. He waved a hand. "C'mon. This way."

Violet met Ryon's eyes and shrugged. They didn't have much choice. Not if they wanted to stay on these people's good side and uncover some answers.

Sidestepping around puddles, Violet followed Kai to a building on the far side of the square. He threw open the thick wooden door and stood waiting for her and Ryon to enter. Helka raced over and linked her arm around Violet's before they crossed the threshold, earning a huff from Kai.

"What?" Helka lifted a brow. "I found them. I'm coming, too."

Kai grumbled, "Fine. Just let me do the talking."

Helka chuckled. "If you say so," she sing-songed back to him, and Violet got the clear impression that she had no intention of keeping her word.

"Where are we?" Ryon asked as they slipped into a bustling hall lined with oblong tables filled with dark-haired people wearing pocketed garb. Neither Kai nor Helka answered. Instead, they set off at a fast pace through the room, weaving between tables and not making eye contact with any of the people who gaped at them.

The room was awash with unusual scents and sounds. Roasting food cooked somewhere within, but Violet's nose wrinkled at the musky aroma, redolent with spices she couldn't pinpoint. A few villagers shoveled stew into their mouths and sipped out of massive mugs, occasionally spinning circular stands on the tabletops and plucking jars of seasonings off to sprinkle over their dishes.

The music playing made the skin on her neck prickle. She recognized some of those strange foreign notes from Helka's and Kai's heartsongs playing in this room. Her gaze caught on a man in the back cradling an odd stringed instrument between his knees. It reminded her of Uncle Aren's lute, but it was much larger, with a triangular base instead of an oval.

She hardly had a moment to linger over the curious sight before Helka tugged her away. They crossed the room, earning enough stares and whispers that her limbs quivered with tension by the time they made it to a closed door in the back.

Kai pounded on the frame.

"Come in," a man called from within.

Kai shoved open the door, revealing a lone table with seven people sitting around it. "Elders. We found strangers on our watch."

Violet's stomach fluttered as she stepped inside. She smiled politely at the ring of old men and women who stared at her from their seats. "Hello. It's nice to meet you." She waved, feeling incredibly awkward but determined not to stand idly by and let the others talk for her. "I'm Vio—"

"Silence," a man at the head of the table barked. "You'll speak when spoken to, understood?"

Violet flinched and inched closer to Ryon. Kai closed the door behind them and remained standing. She took that as a sign to stay standing as well.

One of them whistled and muttered, "Flashes."

"Strangers, you say?" An old woman wearing a midnight-blue tunic squinted at them both. "How curious."

"Who are they?" another asked.

"Where did you find them?" demanded the rude one on the end.

Violet opened her mouth, but Helka nudged her roughly with her elbow. Violet clamped her mouth shut.

Kai explained, "This is Violet and Ryon. I found them at the old ruins, being attacked by disanders."

"The old ruins?" The blue-shirted woman gasped, her eyes widening. "What were you doing there?"

"Helka begged a ride from one of the trainees to harvest mushrooms there this afternoon." Kai spared a glare for his wife. "When I returned from my watch and heard where she was, I left to fetch her."

The rude man *tsked*. "As you should."

Helka's cheeks reddened, but she kept silent.

Kai's lips twisted. "They say they were *swimming* before they appeared in the ruins."

Murmurs broke out, and the elders bent their heads, whispering quietly behind their hands. Finally, they leaned back in their chairs, seeming to have come to some agreement.

The rude man cleared his throat and stared at Ryon. "We'll hear the story from your own lips, boy."

Violet bristled. Was she being dismissed because she was female? But why, when they had female elders at their table, and female riders for their dragons?

Ryon's Adam's apple bobbed in his throat. "Well, what Kai said is true. I'm not sure how it all happened. One moment we were underwater swimming through an enormous ring—"

The word set off a flurry of chaos. Hands flew up. A chair scraped back. One elder even yelped.

The rude fellow's face paled, but he frantically shushed his companions. "Go on now."

Ryon continued. "Yes... I guess you could say we were sucked in. And then the next thing I knew, we were here."

An ancient man who hadn't said a word until now spoke up, his voice wobbling and thick with doom. "The oracle. They must be brought to the oracle at once."

The woman who'd spoken before clicked her tongue. "You know the oracle will only speak to riders."

Ryon met Violet's gaze as the elders began arguing among themselves, and shrugged. An ominous chill spread through her chest. If these elders were here to decide their fate, then she couldn't just stand here and do nothing. Say nothing.

"Excuse me." She raised a hand, and silence fell over the room. "May I please speak?" Her heart pounded as she waited for an answer. If they wouldn't allow her to talk, she might scream.

The rude man eyed her coolly. "Say your piece, girl."

Violet's stomach churned. "I noticed something strange as we flew here. The clouds parted, and I glimpsed three moons hanging in the sky."

Ryon stiffened beside her, but the elders only looked at her like she was mad.

"Why is she wasting our time with this foolishness?" the rude man grumbled. "Of course there were, girl. What did you expect?" He chuckled cruelly, but the sound cut off sharply when Violet replied.

"I expected only one." A hush fell over the room. "Where we come from, there's only one moon."

The elders began talking at once, a mixture of shock, horror, and undisguised excitement punctuating their conversations. Violet could barely make heads or tails of what they said, except for one word that kept being repeated—again and again.

"I'd like to see this oracle," Violet declared, pitching her voice loud enough to be heard over the elder's chatter. "Please, if they can help us find a way home, then I must see them."

"Impossible. The oracle only speaks to riders," the blue-shirted woman insisted.

The eldest man rubbed his wrinkly chin. "Though I wager it's the only place you'll find your answers. The oracle is said to know the true story of the ruins. And back when I was a young rider, the oracle told me a tale about rings. Seems there is more than one, on this world and others." He smacked his lips together, and then his brow furrowed fiercely. "Can't say I remember much more than that, though. I suppose you could ask again."

Violet's heart pounded. This might be it! If there were more rings, then surely they'd find a way home, wouldn't they?

Ryon puffed out his chest and inclined his head toward Violet. "We've both ridden on dragons many times."

Kai scoffed. "Merely riding on dragonback doesn't make you a rider."

Violet turned to Kai. "Can you ask the oracle for us?"

He shook his head. "It doesn't work like that. If you want the honor of speaking with the oracle, you must prove your worth."

Violet crossed her arms. "If that's what's needed to see the oracle, then we'll do it." She grabbed Ryon's hand. "We'll become riders."

Ryon squeezed her fingers, and his silent support calmed her raging nerves.

Kai burst out laughing. The melodious sound filled the room and made Violet's skin prickle. "You think you have what it takes?" He threw an arm toward the door. "The riders out there train from birth for the honor."

Helka cleared her throat. "They deserve a chance to try."

The rude man frowned. "How can you be so sure?"

"They saved me." Helka lifted her chin. "Ryon kept me out of danger even though it worsened his injury. And Violet took down a bunch of disanders with a pair of knives before Kai arrived."

Her words washed over the elders, causing most of them to stare openly or scan Violet and Ryon with narrowed eyes.

"Did they now?" The rude elder directed the question to Kai.

Kai nodded curtly. "It's true."

"That certainly sounds like the heroism and bravery we expect all riders to display." A new woman spoke up, her keen gaze almost as sharp as the nails she rapped on the tabletop. "Let them be tested. If they pass, then allow them to train with the fresh recruits."

"Mother, I—"

The woman cut off Kai. "I've made my decision."

Kai bowed his head and fell silent, accepting the decision, though from the hard set of his jaw, Violet suspected he wasn't thrilled with his mother's ruling.

So, not all women were looked down on here. Curiosity filled her, but Violet flung it aside. There would be time to ponder over these people and their ways later. Another question demanded answering.

"What test?" she asked.

But it seemed the elders weren't in the mood for more talk. The rude fellow stood and shooed them away with a few deft flicks of his wrists. "Go, then. Find them proper lodgings for the night and have them ready upon the morrow." He met Helka's eyes. "Since you're so keen to stick up for the strangers, you shouldn't have any problem taking them under your wing, yes?"

"Of course. I'll see to it, elders. Thank you." Helka grabbed Violet's arm again and hauled her out of the room. Then she hurried across the crowded hall and back into the square.

Kai peeled off as they exited, heading to his dragon. Helka paid him no mind and began leading her and Ryon down a side road.

"Where are we going?" Violet asked.

"I'm taking you to your lodgings, like the elders requested." Helka grinned. "Don't worry. It's quite nice in the women's boarding house." She frowned. "Unless—are you two wedded?"

"Wedded? No." The words escaped without thought, and she instantly cursed her quick reply. If there were women's houses, then that must mean there were men's as well. Her stomach clenched. They must be planning to make them sleep apart.

Ryon caught on quickly, too. "Can't we stay together? I can't leave Violet alone."

Helka shook her head firmly. "Oh, no. That simply won't do, I'm afraid. Out in the wild, the rules might be different, but here in Lanwell, unwedded couples do *not* sleep in the same house."

Lanwell. That must be the name of the village. Violet slotted away the fact for later. "Are you sure you can't make an exception this once?"

Ryon slung an arm around her shoulder. "Or just call for a priest."

"Ryon!" Violet's eyes bulged, and she stopped in her tracks.

"What?" He pulled her close. "We're just speeding up the inevitable." He winked, and Violet's heart fluttered.

Was that a joke? The wink meant he was joking, didn't it?

Helka chuckled and shoved her hands between them, forcing them to each take a step back. "Not happening. At least, not tonight. And if you pass the test, then it won't be happening while you're training, either. Riders in training are expected to concentrate solely on their lessons."

"What is this test all about?" Violet allowed Helka to drag her away from the square, down a side road dotted with identical homes. Most of the buildings were small, made out of black logs with some kind of gray cement pasted in between.

"There are two types of riders. The ones in the front we call bonded, and they always share a mental link with a dragon." Helka glanced at her. "I don't suppose either of you can bond a dragon?"

Violet and Ryon both shook their heads.

"Then you'll need to test to be a defender," Helka replied matter-of-factly.

Violet's stomach churned, but she bit back the question on the tip of her tongue. She was dying to learn what dragons needed help defending against. More dragons? Or was it something worse? But she honestly couldn't handle any more terrifying revelations, so she kept her mouth shut.

Ryon cocked his head. "Are they the ones in the back?"

Helka smiled. "Yes. You'll need to prove your skill with ranged weapons if you'd like a chance to be taught. You don't need to be an expert yet. Just good enough that it wouldn't be a waste of time training you." She chuckled and nudged Violet's side gently. "After watching you throw those knives today, I don't think you'll have any trouble convincing them of your skill."

Warmth spread through Violet's belly. Ranged weapons happened to be her specialty. But then she heard Ryon mutter beside her.

"Guano."

She gulped. What would they do if Ryon didn't pass? He'd never trained with weapons. She was already being forced to spend her nights away from him. Was she about to be torn apart from him during the day, too?

Helka stopped in front of a house that was longer than those around it. "Here's where women training to be riders stay." She pointed across the street to an even larger house with a wide porch and bench seating ringed around the front. "The men are over there."

Violet's shoulders slumped. At least they wouldn't be far from each other. Still, she'd been dying for a chance to talk to Ryon privately. There was so much she needed to say. "Can we have a few moments alone before we head inside?"

Helka pursed her lips. "Alone? I'm afraid not. But if you'd like to talk while I'm here with you, that would be fine." She glanced at the darkening sky. "I can't stay long. It's almost full night. Kai will come looking if I'm not home soon."

The last thing she needed was to end up on the prickly rider's bad side when she was about to try to join their ranks. She'd have to take what she could get. But at least they had one way to ensure their conversation stayed between the two of them.

She switched to her own language. "Did you see the moons?"

Ryon swapped to her tongue as well. "No. But I believe you. This place is so strange. It makes sense that we're on another world."

Violet wrung her hands. "How can it be? I-I don't know what to do, Ryon. What about everyone back home? Jurdan was after them. We have to get back. We need to help them."

Ryon sifted his fingers through his hair. "I still have the feathers. We can wish ourselves back. Be done with all this nonsense right now."

Violet's pulse sped up. But something about his suggestion felt wrong. "What if we're here for a reason?" She met his gaze in the fading light. "Orry said my journey was fated. Maybe we're meant to talk to that oracle of theirs. What if something we learn here is the key to defeating Jurdan back home?"

Ryon sighed. "You might be right. So what do you want to do?"

"I guess we play along. Learn how to be defenders and find another ring." Violet wrinkled her nose. "If anything goes wrong, then we have the bloodfeathers to fall back on."

"All right. Sounds like a plan." Ryon edged closer and lifted a hand, aiming for Violet's cheek. Before his palm cradled her face, a voice cleared loudly, and he dropped his hand at his side.

"You two finished?" Helka asked.

Violet nodded stiffly. "Yes."

Helka smiled. "Head on in. There ought to be stew boiling in the kitchen. Help yourselves to some food and grab an empty bed. If anyone asks, say the elders approved your petition. I'll come round to collect you in the morning."

Violet shared a look with Ryon. He shrugged once and turned, heading across the road. "I'm not going anywhere," he called over his shoulder in their language. "See you in the morning," he added, swapping back to Helka's tongue.

Helka waved at Ryon, then frowned at Violet. "Go on, then. What are you waiting for?"

A pang struck Violet's heart as she watched Ryon disappear into the house across the street. Then she shuffled in the opposite direction, praying she hadn't just made a terrible mistake.

The Test

R yon slipped into the kitchen of the men's boarding house the next morning, shifting his borrowed trousers across his legs with a frown. Didn't anyone appreciate the benefits of a skirt these days?

He sighed. Guess it made sense. People who rode on horseback—or dragonback, for that matter—wouldn't be as comfortable in them as the people in his hometown, who rarely did more than walk.

A pang of homesickness struck him as he scooped a bowl of stew out of the massive communal pot for breakfast. He'd spoken to a few men last night and learned that the stew was a staple here. They kept it continuously cooking, adding more broth, vegetables, and meat as it dwindled throughout the day.

And mushrooms. His nose wrinkled as he spooned a sizable chunk atop his spoon. Apparently they grew dozens of varieties, many of which were considered a delicacy. Luckily, the texture of these wasn't as spongy as the ones he avoided back home, or he wouldn't be able to stomach them.

Thoughts of home hounded him that morning. What was Rovan up to? Had he pledged himself to the Aviary yet? Was his mother doing well on her own, or was she lonely?

Would he ever see his family again?

His heart twisted as he shoved a bite of stew into his mouth. They *would* find a way back. If that elder could be believed, there were more rings. And if not, the feathers would take them home. Surely if they could change one thing about a person, they'd be able to change their location.

Some of the tension lingering behind his temples eased. Having a backup plan was certainly a relief.

Still, he couldn't shake the fear that Violet had been right. With his plan foiled, Jurdan was bound to be angry. He was undoubtedly back home, terrorizing their friends. And from what Mariun had told them, he had no qualms about destroying anyone who'd wronged him.

Had the actions they'd taken to stall him started a war?

But perhaps they'd gain an advantage. If this oracle knew so much, maybe they'd know what to do about Jurdan. After all, he'd been about to use the ring when Violet forced it to close. Was he intending to travel here? Or did he have something more sinister in mind?

A knock at the back door drew him from his thoughts. Helka poked her head in. She spotted him scooping the last of his stew out of his bowl and grinned. "Good. You're awake. Come on. The test starts soon."

His stomach gurgled, and he couldn't even blame it on indigestion. He was beyond nervous. He boasted no skill with ranged weapons. Still, he had to try. Being a defender was bound to be dangerous. If Violet made it without him, then no one would be there to watch her back. He had to figure out some way to pass, too.

Ryon placed his bowl in a washbasin and followed Helka outside. A cool breeze greeted him, blowing thick clouds across the overcast sky. He was suddenly glad for the thick pocketed clothes he'd been given after washing up last night. The garb was much warmer than what they'd had on yesterday and would be a blessing in this dreary climate.

After Helka knocked for Violet, she emerged wearing borrowed clothes as well. She'd plaited her long silvery-white hair into a single braid, and a few loose strands framed the beautiful smile on her face. "Good morning. Did you sleep well?"

Her gaze trailed down his outfit, and Ryon resisted the urge to spin around, even though he knew it would make her laugh. "I did. How about you?" She certainly looked well rested. And far more ready than he was for whatever trials awaited them.

Violet nodded. "No dreams, for once."

Suppose that made sense, now that she'd returned to the ring. But what did that say about her journey? Did no more dreams mean the part she'd been fated to play had ended?

He shoved the depressing thought aside. "So, where is this test happening?"

Helka waved them forward. "It's not far. Follow me." She led them down the same streets they'd traveled last night.

It wasn't long before Ryon guessed where they were headed. "Back to the square?"

Helka grinned. "All riders train there. The dragons enjoy watching."

"Great. We'll have an audience."

Violet patted his arm. "It will be fine. If you need help with anything, just ask." She squeezed gently and lowered her voice. "We're in this together, remember?"

"Thanks. I'm sure I'll need all the help I can get." He flashed a lopsided smile as they turned a corner and approached the square. The area had been impressive last night, even though shadows obscured much of the space in the dwindling twilight. But now... he gulped, awed by the size of the enormous clearing.

It had to be huge to fit all the dragons that lazed around it. A few dozen house-sized dragons reclined along the edges. Many appeared to still be sleeping, but a handful were up and about. As they entered the square, a green-scaled dragon ambled over to a rock pile and bent its head.

Crunch.

His eyes widened. "Did that dragon just eat a rock?"

Helka casually lifted a shoulder. "Yes. Earth dragons eat rocks occasionally."

Violet brightened. "That's right! My aunt told me a story about that once. Dragons need to consume the elements they summon to keep up their strength."

His brow furrowed. "I didn't realize that. Funny that I never saw the hatchlings eating any."

"From what Kai tells me, it's not like eating food. It has more to do with how much they've been summoning. If they haven't used much magic, they won't need to replenish anything." Helka dragged a hand through her dark-brown curls. "There are dragons where you come from, too?"

"Not nearly as many as there are here." Violet frowned. "For a long while, we thought they'd been wiped out, until we found a clutch of dragon eggs."

An amused grin spread across Helka's lips. "I'd like to hear more about this world of yours."

Violet shrugged. "Sure. I'll tell you whatever you'd like. And maybe you can tell me more about Lanwell?"

It was good to see Violet making a friend. Helka seemed like a good sort. Perhaps she could help them navigate this new village and settle into her people's way of life while they became riders.

"I'd like that." Helka's smile fell. "Later. Looks like they're ready for your test." She pointed to a group of riders chatting next to a bin overflowing with weaponry. They'd set up two beams a short distance away from each other and balanced objects atop them. Chipped mugs and cracked plates, mostly.

His heart sank. How many of them did they expect him to break?

Helka led them over, and the crowd parted, revealing Kai. Ryon frowned when he recognized him. Something about the gruff man rubbed him the wrong way.

Yeah, he'd saved their asses out by the ruins, but then Ryon had woken and heard the way he'd been talking to Violet. When he'd spotted the suspicion in the rider's body language, and the way he'd dragged his gaze over her...

It had been pure instinct that made him snag a rock off the ground and jab his palm. He *had* to know what they were saying. Maybe one day he'd live to regret it if they ran out of bloodfeathers, but he wasn't sorry about it now.

"Morning." Kai nodded to them both. "Are you ready?"

Ryon bristled. "Can we at least hear what we'll be doing? No one's explained what this test is, exactly."

Kai walked to the bin. "You may choose any weapon you'd like. Then you need to down the targets over there." He pointed to the beams.

Violet's nose wrinkled. "That's all?"

"Yep." Kai crossed his arms. "But if you miss more than three, you fail."

Ryon's spirit shriveled as he mentally tallied the targets at the other end. Twenty. Could he knock over sixteen targets with an unfamiliar weapon? "What happens if we fail? Can we take the test again?"

A chorus of chuckles erupted from the riders.

"Sure." Kai grinned. "In a year."

"A year?" Violet blinked repeatedly. "Are you serious?"

Kai's expression turned stonelike. "Does it look like I'm joking?" He gestured to the riders. "Ask any of them. They all faced the same challenge. There's a reason riders train from birth."

Violet pushed her shoulders back and strolled to the bin. "I guess I'll fit right in." She lifted on her tiptoes and began shuffling through the weapons.

Ryon's feet froze in place. There was no way he would pass.

Miraculously, the voice escaping his throat didn't waver. "Are we allowed any practice shots?"

One rider yelled, "He wants to practice?" He punctuated the question with a cruel snort. "No such thing as practice when death gets the drop on you."

Those ominous words spread ice through his veins, chilling him to the core. What was out there these people were so afraid of?

"The time for practice is over," Kai confirmed, his deep voice ringing through the square. "Will you take the test or not?"

Ryon forced his feet to move. He joined Violet at the bin, swallowing heavily.

"It's all right," she whispered beside him. "I think I can do this. As long as one of us makes it, then we'll get to talk to the oracle."

Ryon glanced her way as she grabbed a slim bow, hefting the weight in her hands. She lifted it to eye level and scrutinized it before discarding it and selecting another.

She was prepared to go it alone. She might even be fine in the long run. She was certainly skilled enough, both physically and mentally. Maybe he should stand aside and find another way to help. He could scour the city for clues about the world they'd been stuck in. Make allies with the common folk. That might prove just as useful.

Yet a tiny voice in the deepest corner of his mind screamed, *No.* Violet was *his* to protect. If she became a rider on her own and she was hurt while he cowered in the village, safe and protected... Just, no.

"I'm taking that test." Ryon spoke firmly, and he reached into the bin, sifting through javelins, spears, and bows by the dozen.

Violet tucked the bow she'd been examining under her arm. "Good. You can do this, Ryon. I believe in you." She smiled at him warmly, then glanced into the bin. "What weapon are you—"

"Have you chosen, Violet?" Kai asked.

Violet spun around and hefted the bow. "This will do."

"All right." Kai jerked his head to the first beam. "Let's get started."

Violet gave Ryon's shoulder a squeeze and walked to Kai. He pointed to a line painted on the ground and spoke softly to Violet. Ryon frowned and abandoned his riffling to watch as she planted her toes on the line and raised her bow.

The distance from where she stood to the targets was not so vast. It would only take him a handful of strides to cross the space. Still, when they could only miss three shots out of twenty, it was bound to be challenging, no matter how close it was.

Kai handed Violet an arrow and said something to her so softly Ryon couldn't hear it. Whatever it was made her eyes widen briefly.

He had half a mind to demand Kai repeat it. But he refused to break her concentration with so much riding on this test. The fate of their world might hinge on Violet smashing those ugly old dishes.

Whatever had been said, she shook it off quickly. She closed her eyes and shifted her face into the wind. Then her eyes popped open, and she took aim and let loose.

Smash.

The satisfying sound of broken pottery rang out, and Ryon whooped.

Violet shot a grin at him over her shoulder, her cheeks pinking adorably. Until Kai thrust another arrow in her face.

She plucked it out of his hands and fired.

Smash. Crash. Thud.

She dropped three more swiftly. And when Kai passed her the fifth arrow, a tiny grin lifted the corner of his mouth.

His stomach churned, and his fingers itched to slap the bastard. He ground his teeth instead, keeping the wayward thought to himself.

Violet aimed again. But when her arrow whistled through the air, no crash followed. His heart sank.

It was only one. She was still doing well. If she kept hitting four out of every five... He gulped as the math came up wanting. Still, if anyone could do it, Violet could.

He kept his gaze trained on her while she aimed again. Smashes rained down again and again. He flinched every time the arrow string twanged until the reassuring clatter filled his ears.

On the twelfth shot, Violet missed again. She heaved out a huge breath and her shoulders slumped.

"That was nothing, Vi," Ryon called. "You've got this."

Violet swiveled around and met his eyes. She blinked a few times, then straightened her stance. Though she didn't reply, she winked at him before she turned.

Her hand shot out to Kai, who slapped another arrow onto her palm. Ryon held his breath while her arrows sang. She broke the next six dishes so quickly it was like she'd hardly paused to aim.

Then another miss.

The air caught in his lungs. Violet had no chances left. If she missed another shot, it was all over.

All the riders had gathered by now, craning their necks for the best view. They'd spent most of the time chattering among themselves, dissecting Violet's stance and complimenting her aim.

Now that she was on her last try, a hush fell over the square. Kai held the last remaining arrow in his hand. Violet's lip quivered as she stared at it.

Once again, Kai spoke softly, and Ryon cursed his decision to hang back by the weapon bin. This time, at least, his words appeared to bolster Violet's spirits. A wry smile curved her lips. She leaned in and muttered something before snatching the arrow out of his hands.

What was *that* all about?

A heartbeat later, the question shattered like the remaining dish. The riders cheered. Violet dropped the bow and bent at the waist, grasping her knees and heaving out huge breaths the way a runner might after they'd jogged far and fast.

He abandoned the bin at last and sped across the square. He arrived as Violet straightened, and he grabbed her under the arms, scooping her off the ground and swinging her in a circle. "You did it! I knew you'd do it!"

Giggles erupting, Violet's arms clamped around his neck at the same time her legs flew out wildly behind her. "I did it!"

The glee pouring out of her was so palpable he wished he could bask in it forever. But all too soon, she cried out between giggles, "All right, enough spinning, you loon."

He slowly lowered her, sliding his hands down to her hips to hold her steady. Violet grinned at him sweetly, and it took all the control he could muster to stop his lips from crashing into hers.

Kai cleared his throat. "Congratulations, Violet. You begin training this afternoon."

She stepped back and dipped her head. "Thank you."

Kai turned to him. "Your turn. Have you chosen a weapon?"

Ryon jolted, and suddenly it felt like the world ground to a halt. Could he do that? Did he even have a chance when Violet barely managed it?

The answer slammed into him like a tritusk stampede.

Ryon leaned in. "Sorry, but would it be all right if I took a break first? Too much stew for breakfast, if you know what I mean."

Kai sighed wearily and pointed to a nearby building. "There's an outhouse behind that storehouse. Don't keep us waiting all day."

Violet frowned as he stepped toward it. "You all right?"

"Yep." Ryon grinned. "I'll be right back."

He locked himself in the tiny, stinking room with a sigh. He sat without bothering to remove his pants and cradled his head in his hands. Truth was, he'd lied. He didn't need to relieve his bladder. What he needed was a moment to think.

There was no way he was hitting those targets. But he couldn't stomach the thought of leaving Violet alone. That left him with only one choice.

Ryon worked out a tiny sewing needle he'd nicked from a closet in the men's boarding house and stashed in the inner hem of his pants.

The tiny thing wasn't much of a blade, but it was blessedly sharp. Besides, he only needed a single drop of blood.

He hadn't shared his plan with Violet. If he had, he was sure she'd caution him against it. Since she'd already passed, it wasn't that dire of a need that he passed, too.

But some things were more important than holding on to a wish for a rainy day. And this was one of them. The truth of it thrummed through his bones. Violet was his one. And he'd be damned if he didn't do everything in his power to protect her.

Ryon worked a bloodfeather out of his hair and pricked his finger. As warmth spread up his arm, he closed his eyes and whispered, "I wish for perfect aim."

The outhouse door slammed behind him as he cleared out. He rounded the storehouse and marched straight to the bin. Violet was there to greet him, leaning nonchalantly on it with her arms crossed. "You ready for this?"

"I think so." Ryon bent over the edge, pursing his lips as he considered his options.

"Is there something like your pickaxe in there?" she asked.

Ryon's eyes narrowed on a tiny weapon in the corner. He bent and plucked it out. "This will do."

Violet gaped at the slingshot in his hands. "You're sure?" She stepped closer and whispered, "Have you used one of those before?"

A smirk danced on his lips. "Nope." Ryon left Violet standing there with a dropped jaw and strode to Kai's side.

Kai lifted a single brow. "Interesting choice. Are you ready?"

"Yes." He listened with half an ear as Kai explained where to stand and reiterated the rules. And then he took the first rock the gruff rider passed him and hefted its weight in his hands.

The round stone had been polished to a smooth shine. He smiled as the rock slid along his fingers.

Ryon dropped the slingshot.

Kai frowned as it smacked into a puddle. "Your weapon."

Sucking in a deep breath, Ryon trained his gaze on the first plate. "I am the weapon."

Crash.

Ryon waggled his fingers for another rock. The next plate fell just as easily. And the next. It seemed making a wish for perfect aim and combining it with the enhanced strength he'd gained while helping the hatchlings were exactly what he needed to pass this test.

Soon every dish smashed on the ground. The riders stood in silence, eyes wide with disbelief.

Ryon clapped his hands together and surveyed the wreckage with a smile. But when he spotted Kai, his smile fell.

"How?" Kai backed away, shaking his head, his brows pinched together.

Violet collided into his chest the next instant. "You did it. I knew you would." She reached up and tousled his dreadlocks with a mischievous grin. The pride shining in her eyes made his head swim and his heart expand.

Kai shook off his surprise and clapped Ryon on the back. "Looks like you're both in."

Congratulations erupted from the other riders, along with plenty of whistles and whoops.

Ryon grinned. "So what's first?" He turned as the crowd died down, eyeing the dragons, most of whom had awakened by now and watched their group with undisguised interest. "Will we be assigned to a dragon?"

Kai chuckled. "As a brand-new recruit?" Guffaws exploded as the rest of the riders joined in. "Yeah. Not even close." He reached out, spinning Ryon so he was pointed toward a small group of bald-headed teenagers. "You're with them. But not just yet." Kai whistled three times, and a woman approached, her pockets bursting with many familiar things. Since he'd grown up with a hairstylist for a mother, it didn't take him long to put it together.

Ryon's gaze darted from the bald-headed youths to the woman while his stomach sank.

"I hope you're willing to part with that unique hairstyle of yours." Kai laughed.

Ryon blinked. "What? Why?"

Kai shrugged. "Better not to have anything flying behind you while you're still learning."

Guano. What was he going to do? He couldn't cut his dreadlocks. Not when they were the only thing keeping his remaining feathers safe and hidden.

Violet must've sensed his panic. She wrapped an arm around his waist and squeezed. "I'll take care of them," she whispered against his chest.

Ryon nodded curtly. "All right. I'm ready."

One of the riders chuckled. "Look at who's eager now. Are you gonna let the lady go first?"

Ryon's eyes widened. They made female riders cut their hair too? He sighed. Hopefully this wasn't just the first surprise of many...

What a strange, strange world they'd landed in.

Alive

Nox gaped at Ereni as shock reverberated through his heart. "Alive..." He blinked, forcing his tired legs to scramble up the stairs behind his half-brother and sister-in-law. "Are you certain? How is that even possible?"

Ereni shook her head. "Honestly? I have no idea. If you'd asked me before today, I would've sworn it wasn't possible for a place to emit an aura. I've certainly never seen it before." She eyed the stairwell walls warily. "But I was wrong."

Conall paused on the landing ahead of them, waiting for them to catch up. "It makes sense to me. Lark told us this place was unlike any she'd seen, with odd magic she'd never encountered before."

Nox heaved out a labored breath. "That's true." How many times had he thought something in Thalassia was unnatural but come up with no way to explain it? What if this was why? What if—He gasped.

"What is it?" Ereni asked.

"I can't hear Gwen right now. And Lark couldn't communicate with Muse while she was trapped in here." Nox's brow creased. "If this place really is alive, maybe that's why..."

They stood in stunned silence, digesting Nox's words. Until Shadow whipped around with his ears perked and let out a high-pitched whine. The hair on Nox's neck stood on end.

Conall raised his voice. "Move!" he barked, full of urgency.

Nox's heart slammed against his ribs. He faced forward and lurched up a few steps as the door to the ring crashed open.

A bloodcurdling roar rattled the stairwell walls. Nox fought the urge to turn around. As much as he wanted to know what was chasing him, he couldn't spare the energy. Not when his body was barely hanging on and he needed all the strength he could summon to scramble up the steps. His foot slapped the cold stair.

Conall wrenched the landing door open. His jaw dropped as he turned and held the door against his back. He waved frantically, urging them up.

Another step down. The brush of fur on his ankle almost made Nox yelp. But it was only Shadow overtaking him. Fear shot prickles down Nox's spine, yet still he refused to look, even though he was holding up the rear now.

He lurched up another step. A roar echoed behind him, and the stairwell trembled. Was that the city rocking again? Or had the beast mounted the stairs?

On his next step, Ereni disappeared through the opening. Then Shadow darted in, fast on her heels.

Nox had two more to go. His breath sawed out of his lungs. The taste of metal lingered in the back of his throat. And his nose twitched as the putrid stench of soiled fur wafted up behind him.

Another step. Conall lifted his bow and aimed over Nox's shoulder.

Nox took the last step on a leap. The arrow string twanged and a chilling howl pierced his ears.

"Go!" Conall shouted as Nox scrambled through the doorway.

He burst into a brightly lit hall and spun as his brother jumped out and dragged the door closed. They'd emerged into a tiny corridor that looked much like the stairwell.

"What was that?" Nox blurted on a gasp.

Conall winced when the door rattled. "No clue. But I don't want to be here when that creature breaks down the door."

"Good call." Nox hurried after Conall. Luckily, it seemed whatever beast had followed them was having trouble with the knob. But the animal's brute strength would undoubtedly triumph if given enough time.

His brother had nearly caught up to Ereni and Shadow a few paces ahead. She'd paused at an opening in the corridor and flattened herself against the wall. Her arm darted out, and she snagged Conall's sleeve, lifting a finger to her lips.

Conall followed her lead, wearing an uneasy expression that made Nox's stomach churn.

Were guards ahead? Or something worse? His pulse pounded. They couldn't turn back. The only thing behind them was the stairwell and that beast. Nox caught up and slowed, tilting his head to peek around the bend.

"*Nox?*" Flint's voice soothed some of the panic thrumming through his chest. "*Are you all right?*"

"*Mostly.*" Nox still couldn't see around the bend. "*I'll fill you in later.*" He cautiously inched out a little further.

His breath caught at the first glimpse of black cloth ahead. Masked hustled down the long, curved walkway beyond their corridor, carrying something between them. But stranger still, a few dozen crows flitted around the men, their flapping wings obscuring his sight of whatever they were hauling. The churning in his gut increased, and he wasn't sure if he should keep blaming it on the sickening way the city heaved and swayed.

A muffled roar reached his ears, along with enough scratching and pounding that he was certain the animal was still trying to break free. Yet they couldn't continue onward. Not as long as the masked were out there.

Nox chanced a glance back. The door vibrated but blessedly held. For now... Would it hold long enough for the masked to pass?

He gulped and peeked into the hall again. The masked had nearly traversed the entire length. A few more moments and they'd round the far bend, out of sight. Then they could slip into that corridor and head in the opposite direction.

Just as Nox was ready to rejoice, he finally spotted what the men carried. A wash of disgust poured over him, spreading out from his stomach and making him shudder. They balanced a stretcher between them, with a motionless man lying stiffly upon it. Birds sat dutifully on his chest and hovered around his head, obscuring Nox's view.

As they turned, a crow shifted a little too slowly in the air. Nox's jaw dropped. "It's Jurdan."

Conall stiffened. "Where?"

Nox pointed to where the men had disappeared. "With them. Lying on a stretcher." He rushed forward, but Ereni darted in front of him.

"Wait. We came to rescue you, not get you killed."

Nox sidestepped around her. "But he's injured. Come on. This might be our best chance to kill him."

He didn't give her time to argue. Racing down the corridor, he followed the masked, not looking back to see if his family followed.

Conall caught up as they rounded the corner. A crow flew straight toward Nox, claws raised and aimed at his eyes. His brother whacked the bird with his bow, sending it careening into the wall.

Squawk!

The crow's angry cawing alerted the rest of the flock. They came at them in force, leaving the masked to scurry faster than ever down the hall.

"Blazes!" Ereni exclaimed, but Nox couldn't spare the concentration to see what had her so excited. Not with a murder of crows descending.

Whipping the knife off his borrowed belt, Nox slashed and stabbed like mad. Squawks and grunts pierced his ears as they all joined in, battling the birds. Conall felled several with arrows, and metal flashed as Ereni threw her knives. Even Shadow joined in, leaping up and crunching into low-flying birds with his powerful jaws.

Nox's arms stung from countless scratches by the time the last bird fell. Worse, the masked were gone.

Wiping the sweat from his eyes, Nox heaved a heavy sigh. "Come on. We still might catch—"

Crash!

The words snagged in his throat, and terror seized him.

"The stairwell." Conall shoved open a side door. "In here. Hide!"

He hated the thought of slinking away like some frightened child. But when the unseen beast roared and its footsteps rattled the floor, he followed. He was in no shape to take on some enormous predator. Not when he was still winded from killing those crows and exhausted from the ring.

They piled inside the room, and Conall slammed the door. Not a moment too soon. Snuffling echoed beyond the door. Then the crunch of bone and tearing of flesh.

The beast had discovered the dead birds. It was no surprise it stopped to feast. Jurdan kept the animals on the brink of starvation so they would be ravenous when it was their turn in the ring. Still, his heart sank. They'd been so close.

"*What's wrong?*" Flint asked.

"*We almost had Jurdan, but we lost him.*" He'd actually had a chance to confront Jurdan—when he was injured, no less. But now they were cut off. Stuck in another endless hall.

Flint scoffed. "*So find him.*"

Was it really that simple? But surely in a city this large, there was more than one hall that led in the same direction...

"We need to go after him," Nox whispered urgently.

Conall clapped a hand on his shoulder. "I know." He nodded to Shadow.

It seemed Shadow had the same idea as his bondmate. The gray wolf's snout was raised, taking huge sniffs of the air. Then his tail wagged once, and he loped forward.

"Shadow thinks he caught their scent." Conall strode after him. "Come on."

They followed Shadow through the hallway. The inner corridor they'd emerged in was one of the ones that mimicked the outside. By now, Nox was used to the place, and he hardly noticed the grass crunching beneath his feet. He couldn't say the same for the others. Conall stared at the unnaturally lit sky-blue ceiling, and Ereni trailed her fingers through some herbs overflowing from a wall planter, her eyes lit with wonder.

At least there were no crowds strolling through the space and staring at him like his last walk through the city. Perhaps they'd hunkered down in their homes when Thalassia began to move?

His aching body started to protest again. Most of the crows' scratches were shallow, but a few still bled, sending trickles down his arms. And it wasn't only his wounds dragging him down. He'd endured so much in the last few days. How much longer could he push himself before he dropped from sheer exhaustion?

After a few turns, Shadow stopped in front of a closed door that looked the same as all the rest they'd passed.

His heart pounded. Was this it? Were they really about to find Jurdan?

They burst inside. Nox frowned. There were no men. No stretcher. Just a mysterious room filled with oblong containers full of liquid.

Conall scratched the side of his neck. "I guess Shadow got off track." He shrugged. "He must've been following an older trail."

"What is this place?" Nox's brow wrinkled.

"No idea." Ereni strolled to one of the enormous containers filled with yellow fluid and set her hand on the vessel. "But for some reason, these are glowing more strongly than the rest of the city."

Nox approached another and squinted at the cloudy glass. He lifted his arm and used a bit of his sleeve to scrub the layer of grime preventing him from getting a clear view inside. The stubborn dirt barely budged, making him wonder how long these tubes had been there, slowly collecting dust.

He put a little more elbow grease into the task until finally he'd cleared a small spot. Then he bent, gazing into the clear glass. Thick, viscous-looking yellow fluid stared back at him. His eyes narrowed as he spotted something hovering within it. But try as he might, he couldn't see clearly what it—

Crash!

"Not again." Conall grabbed Nox's arm, tugging him behind the container he'd been examining and out of view of the door that'd smashed open.

Nox held his breath, all thought of the fluid forgotten as the giant beast roared in the doorway. From his vantage, all he spotted was a small window of the hall outside the door.

Had the beast tracked them down? Was it about to cram its massive body through the door, smash the glass vessels to pieces, and discover where they were hiding?

But then black cloth flashed in the corner of the doorway. A familiar *buzz* tickled his ears. Then another. And another.

A huge crash made the floor shudder beneath his feet. And then voices rose, speaking Thalassian.

"Lucky we caught him before he made it inside," one man said.

Another slightly higher-pitched voice replied, "You're right. The Supreme would've been livid if anything happened in there."

Movement across the room caught Nox's eyes. Ereni jerked her head toward a side door.

Conall started toward it, rushing from one container to the next to keep hidden from the masked in the hall.

Nerves skittering, Nox followed. Soon they'd made it to the door and slipped out of the room into another corridor. Grunting and cursing rang out. Enough for Nox to guess what was happening nearby. The masked must be carting the beast away while he was stunned.

They creeped silently away from the noise. Nox didn't dare speak until he was sure they'd traveled out of earshot. "Where to now?" He waved at Shadow. "Has he found another trail?"

Conall shook his head. "No, nothing. I hate to admit it, but we've lost them."

Nox's stomach sank. But there still might be a chance...

Voices rose, coming from ahead. Ereni threw open a door and ducked inside.

A child's whimper made Nox's blood run cold as he followed her in, closing the door quietly behind him.

Eyes widening, he spotted Conall with his bow drawn and pointed at a cowering man on the floor of a small dwelling. Ereni clasped a quivering woman in her arms, a knife at her neck. A child who appeared to be about twelve sat on the floor, frozen, with silent tears dripping down her cheeks as she gawked at Shadow.

"Shh," Ereni insisted. "We don't want to hurt you. Please, stay quiet."

Nox's stomach lurched. They'd finally found where some of the Thalass were hiding. He couldn't say he was happy about how they'd found them, or how his family was keeping them quiet, but desperate times...

Out in the hall, the voices grew louder, then tapered off. Nox eased open the door and peeked through the crack. "They're gone."

"Sorry." Ereni released the woman, and Conall dropped his bow.

They piled back into the hall, but they'd only made it a few steps before the man who'd just looked like he was about to soil himself stuck his head out of his door and screeched, "They're here! Invaders are here!"

The door slammed closed the next instant. Nox almost shoved it back open and strangled the rotting big mouth, but boot falls were already echoing, their pounding steadily growing louder as the masked who'd just passed whipped around and gave chase.

"Run!" Ereni yelled.

They raced away in the opposite direction. Nox's heart pounded in his throat.

As soon as they rounded a corner, Conall's hand shot out, forcing them to halt. He lifted his bow again. Ereni drew a knife.

When a trio of masked rounded the corner, they were ready for them. Conall dropped the first easily, one of his arrows sinking into his chest. Ereni darted in and slashed, once, twice, three times, felling the second.

Nox's fingers closed around his knife hilt, but he didn't need to bother. Shadow clamped on the poor fellow's thigh, and before the man could do more than yelp, Conall had drawn another arrow and sent it sailing into the man's throat. He thunked to the ground, his hands flailing as he drew in a few gurgling breaths, then stilled.

"Come on." Conall spun on his heel. "We have to get out of here."

Nox turned, yet he couldn't help objecting. "But Jurdan—"

Ereni cut him off as she bent, retrieving her dagger from the belly of the man she'd dropped. "No. There are too many of them. We don't know where to go. Too many things might go wrong." She shook her head as she stood. "We need to escape this city while we still can."

"She's right," Conall insisted. "Trust me, Brother. I want to defeat that fiend as much as you do. But there are only four of us and far too many of them. We have to regroup. We'll come back as soon as we summon a large enough force to end this once and for all."

As more shouting echoed behind them, he had to agree. It would be foolish to stay. He just hoped that retreating now wouldn't cost them their only chance at defeating Jurdan.

Lost Chances

R yon dragged a hand across the prickly scruff on his head and sighed as a damp chill caressed his neck. He still woke every morning expecting to feel the long length of his dreadlocks dragging across his shoulders. It was bound to take a while to get used to. After all, he'd been eleven when he'd begun his petition at the Aviary and started growing his hair out.

Still, it'd served its purpose. After allowing their hair to be shorn, he and Violet were admitted into the training group. Violet ignored the strange looks and whispers of the villagers as she collected his fallen locks. Then she fashioned his remaining feathers into a necklace.

He patted his chest, as had become his habit lately. When his fingers encountered the string holding his precious silver feathers, he let out a sigh.

Violet peeked at him. "You all right?"

"Yeah." He dropped his hand and grinned as they walked to the village square. "Just thinking."

"About what?" She cocked her head. Though she'd been forced to cut her hair as well, the look didn't detract from her beauty. Honestly, he doubted much ever would. Not in his eyes.

"About what we'll be doing today." He pursed his lips. "What do you think it will be? More weapons practice?"

They'd trained with ranged weapons practically every waking moment of the last few days. Once they'd proved their accuracy with stationary targets, they'd graduated to moving ones. And to make it even more difficult, the trainers thought up countless ways to break their concentration during their training.

He had to wonder what it was all for. Still, he couldn't complain much. Not when he got to spend every day with Violet.

Of course, the lingering worry about what was happening at home continued to nag at him. How long would they train before becoming full riders? When he'd asked, they would only tell him it was different for each rider.

Guess he had no choice but to go with the flow.

They arrived at the square, and Ryon resigned himself to another long day of target practice. But as soon as he stepped into the space, his skin prickled. The atmosphere was off.

Normally, the dragons lazed about in the mornings. Some watched their training with interest. Others would ignore them in favor of snoozing. Today, they were awake and alert. Full riders hustled around them, and they appeared to be preparing for something.

"What's going on?" he wondered aloud.

Violet shrugged. "Dunno. Let's find out." She sauntered over to one of the trainees with a warm smile. "Binn. Good morning."

The excited teen hurried to greet her with a flick of her hand. The riders had an elaborate system of hand signals they'd been tasked with learning. Apparently they needed more than one way to communicate when they were in the sky. It was ingenious, really. So ingenious that their trainers insisted it be the only method of communication they used while training.

Binn's gaze skimmed the square—making sure no trainers were lurking nearby to scold her for speaking, no doubt. "Have you heard? They're taking us up today." Binn bounced on her toes, looking excited enough to burst. "And we're getting our rider assignments, too!"

"Really?" Violet's grin widened. "That's fantastic."

His stomach sank. Sure, he was glad to be moving on from the constant target practice. After his wishes, he barely needed it. But going up there might mean flying into danger. He couldn't stand the thought of anything happening to Violet.

He'd tried discovering exactly what threats were waiting for them, but except for a few vague mentions of monsters, his instructors hadn't been too keen to share any details. And since he could only talk with hand signals, he hadn't found the right question to get them to elaborate. Now, he'd see them with his own eyes.

A deep voice cleared behind them. Ryon whipped around, frowning.

"It is a momentous day for our new brothers and sisters. Your instructors have sung your praises. But what you'll face today will be far more dangerous than moving targets that don't strike back." Kai strolled through the square, his boots ringing out on the cobbles as everyone fell silent. "It's not too late to back out. No one will think any less of you for it."

Kai ran his gaze along the trainees. No one spoke after his offer. "Good." A slow smile spread across his face. "Gather round for your assignments."

Ryon and Violet joined Kai in the center of the square. The rest of the teens in their group eagerly lined up beside them, scanning the dragons with obvious curiosity. He couldn't help wondering who he'd be chosen to accompany as well.

Though he wasn't sure exactly how the selections were made, he'd noticed a pattern from observing the bonded riders who already had defenders flying with them. If the bonded was slim or of a smaller stature, their defender was usually on the taller or heavier side, and vice versa. He assumed they made their pairings based on weight. It made sense. If they wanted the dragons to fly long distances together without tiring, they wouldn't want one carrying more than the others.

A plump trainer wearing a pocketed skirt walked forward, her sharp brown eyes tracing across a list. "Binn, you're with Asten."

The slim teen headed over to one of the biggest bonded riders. The muscled man waved at Binn and led her to a white-scaled dragon.

"Ryon." He jolted when the lead trainer called his name. "You're with Tora."

He gulped, swinging his gaze across the square until he spotted a petite brunette standing next to a black dragon, waving at him. Sparing a glance at Violet, he crossed the square.

He listened with half an ear as the instructor began giving out more assignments. He'd just reached Tora's side when the last name made him freeze.

"Violet. You're flying with Kai."

Great… He couldn't say exactly what it was about the guy, but hearing Kai's name made Ryon's stomach sink. He was self-aware enough to realize some of it was jealousy. Kai was the leader here. As powerful as he was attractive. And he couldn't help worrying that Violet might fall for his gruff charm. Ryon's heart clenched when she smiled at the scarred rider as she stopped beside him.

He couldn't even be fully appeased by the fact that Kai and Helka were married. Not when he recalled one of the strangest things about

Lanwell they'd learned since arriving here. Tora clapped Ryon's shoulder, breaking his train of thought. "Don't worry. Your girl will be safe with Kai."

"Thanks." Ryon shot her a lopsided grin. Hearing her call Violet *his* calmed a bit of the wild clawing in his gut.

Belatedly, he remembered his instructions to sign, but when he moved his hands to say thank you, she waved him off. "Save the signs for when we're in the skies," Tora said.

He had to admit, he couldn't have asked for a more capable partner to keep Violet safe. If it was a choice between seeing her snuggled up on dragonback with another man or putting her in danger, it was an easy decision. He'd just need to learn to swallow his discomfort when they had their flying lessons.

"You ready to do some flying?"

"Sure."

"Good." Tora grinned, and Ryon smiled at her.

They'd chatted once or twice during training, though never more than exchanging pleasantries, yet she had a pleasant way about her that set him at ease. Tora was one of the smallest bonded, but her short stature didn't detract from her capability or her kindness. The younger riders deferred to her and sought her help when they had problems.

"I've watched you training." Tora leaned in conspiratorially, a twinkle in her light-brown eyes. "Some say you must've struck a deal with the Maker to be blessed with an aim that never misses."

Ryon chuckled helplessly. "They say that?" He'd never even hinted as much to anyone here, but the truth wasn't much further from their guesses.

"Flashes, you should see your face!" She laughed heartily. "I know it's only a wild rumor. I'm sure you'll miss plenty when we take to the sky." She clapped him on the shoulder again, then gathered her long brown curls in her hands and began twisting them into a tight bun. "All the same, Legon and I will be glad to have you watching our backs."

"Legon?"

Tora nodded to the massive black dragon at her back. "This is Legon. He's pleased to meet you."

He strolled closer, admiring the shimmering flecks of purple and green in Legon's scales. The dragon lazily turned his head, using one massive red eye to scan Ryon from head to toe. "He's a fire dragon, right?"

"You're quite right. In fact, it's why I think we'll be well suited having you defend us."

"Oh?" He lifted a brow. "Why is that?"

Tora strolled to a metal bunker on the outskirts of the square, and Ryon kept pace with her. "I noticed you favor throwing rocks during target practice. You have a powerful throwing arm."

He'd become quite adept at smashing dishes with rocks. When his instructors forced him to train with something else, he missed half as often as he hit a target. Perfect aim could only account for so much when using an unfamiliar weapon. But if they let him throw the stones with his hands, he struck his mark every time.

"I asked for you specifically."

"You did?" He couldn't imagine why.

"Yep." She rocked on her heels. "I've been working on something that I need your help with. I think it will give us an edge up there."

He rubbed his chin. "What do you need from me?"

Tora squeezed his biceps. "That throwing arm of yours. How far can you fling these?" She threw open the bunker's lid.

He lifted a small cloth ball about the size of a fruit pit. He rolled the curious thing between his fingers. "What's inside this? Sand?"

"Not quite." Tora crossed her arms. "I have a friend who works in the mines. He stumbled across a rock that fizzled into white flames when he tossed it into a fire. He brought a bunch here, and we broke out all the little specks mixed into the regular rock. I'm hoping by packing them together, we'll get a nice big flash."

He lifted the ball to eye level. "Hm. I see."

"So, how far can you throw it?"

He hefted it in his hands, testing the weight. "How far do you need it to go?"

She pointed to a building on the far side of the square, about thirty paces away. "Can you hit that wall?"

He grinned. "Easy."

She lifted a brow. "Great. Stuff a few of those in your pockets, will you? If we get a chance, we'll test my theory out today. Load up on your rocks, too."

He shrugged and slipped a handful of the cloth balls into his pocket. Then he hurried to the weapons station and stuffed his pockets with as many rocks as he could carry. With his borrowed clothes covered in pockets, that was a lot. He felt twice as heavy as usual when he hobbled back to Tora.

She'd mounted Legon in his absence, and she reached down to help him clamber up. Ryon spun around once he'd mounted the dragon, preparing to strap in backward the way his instructors had taught them. The dragons were all fitted with rope harnesses their riders used to help avoid falling off in midair.

"You need to face forward for this run."

He frowned. "I thought I was supposed to protect your rear?" Still, he shifted, following her instructions.

"Not this time. Watch this." She lifted her hand, swinging her raised pinky in a tight circle before shooting her arm out.

He watched the movement carefully. "The instructors didn't teach me that signal."

"I made it up. That will be your signal to try out the new stuff. Throw it where I point and then Legon will light it up."

"Oh…" Understanding dawned on him. *That* was why he had to face forward. "Got it."

Shouts filled the air, and riders whooped and whistled. Ryon tensed as he glimpsed Violet strapped in backward on Roc, Kai's enormous green dragon. She waved before Roc turned, blocking his view.

"Ready?" Tora asked.

He swallowed thickly. The scratchy rope brushed his fingers as he double-checked that he'd secured it around his thighs. "Yeah." Though he tried to swallow his fears, he must've let some of them show.

Tora patted his thigh as Legon stood and stretched out his wings. "Don't worry. You'll do fine." Before he replied, Legon took three running steps and leaped. Ryon held his breath as they lifted into the cloud-strewn sky.

The underlying buzz he'd grown so used to hearing inside the city cut off as they rose higher. He wanted to ask about it. Dozens of questions swirled in his mind. But without knowing exactly what they'd be facing, would it really be wise to break Tora's concentration midflight?

He kept quiet instead and watched the sky vigilantly. They flew in a loose V formation, away from Lanwell and toward a string of mountains to the east. Legon hovered just behind the lead rider, off to the right. Roc flew in the same spot on the left, giving Ryon a perfect view of Violet.

Finally, the curiosity became too much to bear. "Where are we headed?" he yelled in Tora's ear. With the wind whipping around them, he was sure none of the other riders heard his question.

Tora glanced back before pointing ahead. "The mines. They live underground. Work in shifts. We ferry them to Lanwell."

He'd wondered where all the metal in the city came from. They clearly spent a lot of time and resources to mine it. A pang of homesickness struck him. Wasn't so long ago that he'd spent his days digging for metal too. He'd let nothing stop him from his task, even stampedes from enormous beasts. Would the creatures here be as fearsome? Would they be worse?

"About the monsters..." Ryon began. "I still don't know what they are. Can you—"

The words snagged in his throat as the lead rider lifted both arms above his head and formed an X with his raised fists.

His stomach dropped. He recognized that signal. It was the first one his instructors had taught him. Danger.

Tora stiffened. "Be careful what you wish for." She lifted her chin, her gaze on the thick cloud cover overhead. "Get ready. They're coming."

Heart pounding, he dug two rocks out of his pocket, one for each hand. He followed Tora's gaze, but he saw nothing unusual. Just endless gray clouds stretching out in all directions.

Wait... He squinted, positive he'd seen something.

It appeared again. The flick of a wing breaking through the cloud cover. The dragons increased speed while simultaneously moving into a tighter formation.

He shouldn't have taken his eyes off the clouds, but he couldn't resist seeking out Violet. She clutched her bow firmly, an arrow nocked.

Legon tilted suddenly, the move so unexpected it made his head spin. He tore his eyes off Violet, and they instantly widened as he spotted a monster barreling toward him. A golden-furred beast with leathery wings bared its knife-like teeth and swiped its leonine paws at the lead rider.

"Look out!" Tora shoved him sideways, and something whizzed past his ear.

He dropped the rocks in his haste to hang on. He grappled with the rope, certain he was about to tumble off Legon and fall to his death. The rope held and the beast darted back into the clouds before he'd fully righted his balance.

"What *is* that thing?" He forced the disorientation to the back of his mind.

"Manticore," Tora hissed. "Don't you know anything?"

"Manti-what?" There was definitely nothing like *that* back home.

"Stay sharp. There's bound to be more."

The words had scarcely passed her lips before a dozen of the beasts descended. This time, he got a clear enough view to spot the sinuous tails lined with spines. That must be what almost impaled him. The creatures' bright yellow eyes were set into faces that looked eerily human, sending shivers across his skin.

The dragons ducked and weaved in the air, shooting blasts of magic in all directions. Arrows sang and blades flashed.

He could hardly track anything in the madness. His stomach clenched, but he let his training take over. Rocks flew from his hands, and he was thankful for Legon's erratic path so that he didn't see when his targets hit their mark.

Shrieking cries pierced his ears, making his stomach roll. He forced himself to shove the sickening wash of disgust to the recesses of his mind. It worked long enough for the crowd of beasts to thin.

A cry rang out just behind him. Ryon shifted, turning as best as he could while strapped facing forward.

He reacted a heartbeat too slowly. A clawed foot sliced the back of his shirt and tore his flesh.

"Ahh!" He kicked Legon's side hard, signaling the black dragon to turn.

Legon rolled, spinning sideways so swiftly Ryon's stomach heaved and buckled. But it got the manticore off his back.

It happened so fast he hardly had time to blink. Then Tora swung her pinky and pointed, aiming just ahead of the manticore.

His fingers darted in his pocket and plucked out one of the cloth balls. With a deft flick of his arm, Ryon sent it sailing. A gout of flame erupted from Legon's jaws.

Time seemed to slow as he watched the projectile and fireball sail toward each other. They collided and the cloth burst into flames. The manticore shrieked, unable to avoid flying into it.

The beast writhed from being singed. But where was the—

He shielded his eyes as a bright burst of white light erupted. Heat pulsed in the air, and the manticore squealed, a preternatural screech that made his skin crawl.

Then he made a terrible mistake. He lowered his hand and sought out the dying beast. The charred monster's wings still flapped, keeping it aloft even as the skin and flesh melted before his eyes.

As the beast's wings finally stopped and it plummeted to the ground, Ryon leaned over Legon's side and gave into the nausea he'd fought off while the battle raged. His throat burned after he finished emptying his stomach into the sky.

The rest of the flight passed in a blur. Before he knew it, they'd touched down outside a small mountain outpost ringed with a few long metal poles. Once the familiar hum of static filled his ears, Ryon's tense muscles finally relaxed.

He took his time detaching the rope around his thighs and sliding off Legon onto shaky legs.

Kai's voice boomed. "Good work out there. You all did well."

Violet appeared at his side. "Ryon? Are you all right?"

He sent her a wobbly smile, though he had to admit, he still felt a little out of sorts. "I think so. Are you?" He cringed internally. He'd barely spared her a glance after the battle while he'd tried to tamp down the disgust raging through him.

He still couldn't believe he'd done that. He'd helped *kill* that thing. Bile stung his throat, and he pushed the thought aside before he heaved again.

"I'm all right," Violet insisted. "I'm more worried about you." She ducked behind him, and he frowned.

"What are you doing back there?" He tried to spin to face her, but the glare she pinned him with stopped him.

"Shh, stay still. You're bleeding."

"Oh." That was right. The scratch. He'd hardly noticed once his stomach started acting up. Now that she mentioned it, he registered a little sting between his shoulder blades. "Is it bad?"

"No. It's not deep. I think you'll be fine once we clean it—" She gasped.

"What? Is it worse than you thought?" He did spin then, and when he spotted Violet's widened eyes, his heart jolted. "What is it, Vi?"

"Your necklace."

He froze, and his heart disintegrated, like he was the one caught in that awful explosion of light. "No." He tore off his shirt, sending rocks flinging out of his pockets. His pulse drummed so loudly in his ears he hardly heard the whistles and laughter that rained down on him from the other riders.

"Is there a problem?" Tora approached, her brow furrowed.

"My necklace." He clenched the fabric in his hands before dropping it when he didn't see any silver stuck to it. "Have you seen it?"

Tora shook her head. Ryon raced to Legon, scanning the black dragon all over.

The other riders must have overheard. One of them said snidely, "Pretty boy lost his necklace, did he?" Guffaws and snorts followed.

"Shut it, Teek." Kai slapped the smirking rider on the back of the head.

Compassion filled Tora's eyes. "We can put the word out to the other riders to search for it."

A wave of devastation crashed into him, threatening to grab hold and pull him under. "I-I..."

"It's nothing," Violet cut in. "A family heirloom. He can live without it."

Ryon stiffened, instantly understanding why she wanted to downplay the significance of the bloodfeathers. "She's right. It's just all I have left from back home." He sighed and forced a smile. "I'll be all right."

Violet snagged his shirt off the ground and dragged him aside. As they fell silent, the riders stopped paying attention to them in favor of tending to their dragons. She lowered her voice. "I'm sorry. I should've made it with a thicker string."

"It's not your fault. Neither of us saw this coming. Maybe we'll find it while we're out training." He tugged the shirt back on.

"I doubt it."

He couldn't help but agree. The land they'd flown over was vast. It would be like hunting for a lone rock in the ocean.

She worried her lower lip between her teeth. "We can take Tora up on her offer."

"No. Then we'd need to explain why they're so important. Better to keep it to ourselves, don't you think?"

"You're probably right." She patted her belt. "We still have my feather to fall back on."

His stomach clenched. Sure, that was true. Still, it wasn't the same. "Remember what Orry said? You only get one wish on a golden bloodfeather. I used mine already." And since a wish on a golden feather only changed one thing about someone else, it didn't leave them with many options.

Violet stared at her boots. "I know. But it's better than nothing." She met his gaze and smiled sadly.

"I'm not leaving here without you, Violet."

A sharp whistle blared, silencing whatever response she might've made. "Everyone inside." Kai dropped his fingers from his mouth and waved at the tunnel entrance.

"Come on. Let's clean that cut." Violet grabbed his hand, pulling him along in her wake.

Ryon's heart sank as they followed the rest of the riders. Violet may be putting on a brave face, but he knew he'd screwed up. Massively.

He just lost the best chance they had of returning home.

Spinning Gaily

Violet stared into her cup with a sigh. She'd just finished another long day of training with no end in sight. She dragged a hand through the short scruff covering her head.

The seat beside her scraped loudly. She glanced up, shooting a grin at Helka as she settled on the bar stool. "Hey. Glad you could make it."

Helka pursed her lips. "Wouldn't miss it. Though it looks like you started without me. Rough day?"

Violet quirked a half-smile. "You could say that." She nodded to the barmaid. "What are you having?" She could likely guess. It had become her ritual to grab a drink at the local inn after training ended, and Helka joined her more often than not.

Helka grabbed Violet's mug and gave the contents a sniff. "Not what you're drinking." She coughed dramatically. "You've grown a taste for the strong stuff, haven't you?"

"I'm only having one." She shrugged and took a small sip after Helka slid the cup back to her. The sour brew made her mouth pucker and her head buzz. She'd been warned more than once to take it easy on the stuff, but she preferred the taste to the yeasty ale most of the folk here favored.

Helka raised a brow and turned to the barmaid. "Tea, please." She leaned back in her chair and rubbed her rounded belly with a sigh.

"Wow. You're really starting to show."

"I know." Helka grinned. "Not that you needed to be told. Still not sure how you figured it out when we first met."

Violet shrugged and took another sip.

"Back then, the only way I knew was because of Legon," Helka admitted.

She nearly choked on her drink. "Really?" Her cup clinked atop the bar. "How did a dragon know you were pregnant?"

With a smile, Helka accepted the steaming cup the barmaid offered her. "Seems he has a knack for sniffing it out, like you."

"Strange." Violet sighed, then cocked her head at a loud ruckus across the bar. Truth was, a dragon that could predict pregnancy wasn't the only thing strange about Lanwell.

Violet spotted a pretty brunette rider laughing while her two companions sat very close, taking every opportunity to grab her hand or lean in close and whisper in her ear.

They'd barely been in Lanwell a day before they'd learned it was common for couples to pair up in threes and even fours. The good folk back in Flamesmoat would be positively scandalized. Ryon had agreed those types of relationships weren't common in Avion, either. Where her uncle Nox hailed from in Raimire, on the other hand—

"What's wrong?" Helka asked, interrupting Violet's musings.

She tore her attention off the young woman and her flirtatious dates. "Nothing." She lowered her head. "Well... not exactly nothing."

Helka nudged her gently. "You want to talk about it?"

"It feels like training is taking forever. I need to become a full rider. I *have* to talk to the oracle."

"Don't fret." Helka patted her arm. "You will. It just takes time."

Time... the one thing she couldn't afford to waste. What was happening back in her world? What about Orry? Her family and friends? Her stomach churned, and she was certain her drink wasn't causing the sinking sensation. It had been so long. Anything might be happening to them. Were they already embroiled in a full-out war?

Helka spun her teacup on the bar. "There is one way to speed up the process."

Her face lit up. "What is it? I'll do anything."

"You need to really impress them. If you prove you're dedicated and go above and beyond what the average defender does, they'll let you in faster."

"You think so?" Violet rested her bent elbow on the bar and leaned her chin against her fist.

"Yep. I've seen it happen a time or two."

She wrinkled her nose. "But what more can I do? I haven't missed a single day. I've been showing up early and staying late. Isn't that enough?"

"Sorry, Vi." She blew on her tea before sipping. "I wish I knew what to tell you."

Violet hung her head and lifted her glass. Squealing across the bar made her pause before the mug reached her lips.

It was the girl again. Only this time, her lovers weren't content to keep their affections contained. One of them had lifted the smiling beauty out of her chair and plopped her atop a spinning table topper. The bar used them on large tables to hold spices for easy passing, but someone had shoved all the jars off. Giggles erupted as the two men spun the girl between them, and they each took turns planting kisses on her blushing cheeks.

"Ah... to be young and in love again," Helka mused with a dreamy smile.

"You say that like you're older than dirt." Then again, she couldn't picture Kai ever spinning Helka like that. She had the distinct impression he wasn't the sharing type.

Helka chuckled. "I suppose. I certainly don't feel very young these days. Not like them."

Violet could relate. Had she ever been so carefree as that young beauty across the bar? They might be close in age, but with the weight of responsibility hanging over her, she knew she wouldn't be spinning gaily anytime soon.

Unless...

Violet sat up straight. "Helka. I have to go." She pushed her half-empty mug toward the barmaid, not bothering to drain it.

Without another word, she strode out of the inn and into the road. Twilight painted the gray clouds a murky purplish black. She really ought to head to her room—but first she had an idea that might be the answer to her problems.

She scanned the stores lined up near the inn, looking for one in particular. A bell chimed as she walked inside.

"Hello." An old man in worn overalls greeted her with a smile. "Can I help you?"

Violet paused inside the entryway and sneezed twice in quick succession.

"You all right?" the man handed her a handkerchief.

She took it gratefully. "Thanks. Sorry about that."

"Not a problem." The man leaned on a workbench scattered with tools and chunks of wood. "It gets a bit dusty in here."

She gave him the handkerchief back. "I have a project I hope you can help me with."

Violet hurried to the boarding house with a smile on her face. The carpenter had assured her he'd be able to convert one of his existing pieces into what she'd been picturing within a few hours. And since riders—even trainee riders like her—were highly respected in Lanwell, he even offered to set aside what he was working on.

Her steps felt lighter than they had in ages when she made her last turn. But before she arrived at the women's boarding house, a voice rose across the street.

"Hey."

She spun, a huge smile lighting her face when she spotted Ryon sitting on the porch of the men's boarding house. She crossed the road quickly.

"I thought you'd be sleeping by now." He'd been worn out when their training session ended late that afternoon. Instead of accompanying her to the inn for drinks, he'd gone back to rest—or so he'd said.

He patted the bench beside him. "Couldn't sleep."

She gazed around the empty street before taking him up on his invitation, though she stayed far enough away on the bench that any passersby wouldn't be angered by finding an unwed couple together... she hoped.

It was baffling getting used to the courting rituals here. Lanwellians didn't want two—or more—lovers meeting privately, but public displays like the one she'd witnessed in the inn were celebrated. It was an odd dichotomy that she didn't quite understand.

"I have some good news." Violet grinned. "I had a great idea tonight. I think it will help us become recognized as full riders faster."

Ryon's face lit up. "Really? That's incredible." After a heartbeat, his smile fell.

"Hey. What's wrong?" She glanced around again, and after confirming they were alone, she grabbed his hand.

He squeezed her hand back gently. "Sorry. I didn't mean to dampen your excitement. I'm just feeling a little homesick."

Violet scooted closer. "I am too. I keep wondering about what's happening. How are my parents faring? What if Orry... It's been so long already. What if she's..." Her voice broke, and she couldn't bear to finish.

"Oh, Violet." He wrapped an arm around her waist and cupped her cheek. "It'll be all right. We'll find a way back home. I promise."

Violet stared into his eyes, blinking back tears. "I-I hope you're right."

A voice cleared loudly in the street. Violet jerked away, her heart racing.

"Violet. Ryon. Getting late, isn't it?" Kai stood in the road, his hands in his pockets.

Violet gulped, thankful it was Kai who'd spotted them. She wouldn't say they were friends, exactly. Even after weeks of training together, he still treated her like any other trainee. But she'd gotten to know him well enough that she doubted he would say anything about finding them sitting so close.

Violet stood. "I was just heading in." She sent Ryon a final smile before hopping off the porch. "See you both in the morning."

She woke early the next morning and snagged a piece of dry toast in the kitchen. Normally she waited around for Ryon and the other trainees. They'd head into the square together and start training first thing.

Though none of the teens had as much on the line as she and Ryon, they were all as eager to become full riders. No other member of the community was as respected. It certainly lit a fire under the trainees and ensured they worked hard to achieve the lauded position.

This morning, she didn't have time to stick around. She managed a quick word to Binn before leaving. Once she knew the girl would pass on her intentions to Ryon, she darted out the door.

The sky had just begun to brighten. A dim glow painted the clouds on the horizon as she made her way through town to the carpentry shop she'd visited the day before.

Chiming rang in her ears as she entered. The same old man stood at the workbench, and he grinned when he spotted her. "Good morning. I see you weren't kidding about coming in first thing." A yawn spilled out of his lips.

A pang of regret struck her. "Did you stay up all night working, Demi?" She'd stuck around long enough last night to learn the carpenter's name. She'd also learned he was a family man who lived in the attached house with his wife and two children. She didn't enjoy knowing she was the cause of a sleepless night he could've spent with his family.

He shook his head hastily. "No, don't be silly. It was a simple enough task. I'm not much of an early riser, that's all."

"Good." She approached slowly, peering this way and that. "Where is it?"

He chuckled lightly. "Here. I bagged it for you. You still have a bit of a walk to the square."

With a huge grin, she took the sack he offered. "Thank you." She dug into her pocket for some of the metal chits Lanwellians used as currency, but he backed away.

"Keep it. If that idea of yours works as well as I think it will, I'll be swimming in orders thanks to you."

With a parting wave, she left the shop. This early, the streets were mostly empty. Her boots clapped loudly on the cobblestones as she made her way to the square.

Here she found several people awake already. Besides their riders, the dragons had a fleet of attendants who saw to their every need. There were always a few people about, even in the dead of night, to make sure the majestic beasts wanted for nothing.

Violet nodded to a few of the attendants as she passed, but she didn't stop until she'd reached Roc's side. He opened one massive eye and watched as she approached, but made no move to shift out of his reclined position.

The huge green dragon lounged on his belly in a pile of fragrant hay. She halted next to his head and lifted the bag. "Hey, Roc. I have some new equipment I'd like to show Kai today. Mind if I hop on your back and strap it on you?"

Roc lazily lifted his head and nosed the bag.

"You want to see it?" She opened the sack and pulled out the odd-looking creation. Roc cocked his head at it, seeming confused, but Violet couldn't stop a grin from spreading across her lips. It was even better than she'd imagined it. And it looked more comfortable, too. Demi hadn't been kidding when he'd boasted about being the best man for the job.

"What you got there?" Kai's deep voice boomed behind her.

Violet fumbled with her things, nearly dropping them. She whipped around, shooting Kai a scowl. "Didn't anyone ever tell you not to sneak up on people?"

Kai's expression remained flat. "What is that?"

"It's something new I had Demi whip up. I think you're going to like it." She twisted the creation in her hands. Demi had padded both sides of the wooden base and attached a number of hooks and straps to the bottom portion.

"Am I?" Kai leaned against Roc's flank. "Roc said you want to try it on him? How's that supposed to work?"

She brightened. "I'll show you." She turned to Roc. "If you don't mind?"

Roc nodded and shifted slightly, lowering himself closer to the ground. "Mind handing this to me once I'm up?" Violet gave her creation to Kai and mounted Roc's back.

It took a few moments of shuffling and reattaching the ropes, but soon she'd finished. Demi's project sat flat on Roc's back, in the same spot she usually strapped herself in backward while protecting Kai in the sky.

Kai frowned. "Well... what is it?"

Violet smiled. "The idea came to me last night at the inn. Have you seen those spinners they use for spices?" She crawled forward and settled her weight atop the creation like she would a saddle on a horse.

"Yes." His brow furrowed.

Violet grabbed the straps and secured her thighs. "It got me thinking, what if we didn't have to only strap ourselves in backward? What if we could spin in any direction?" The moment of truth. She held her breath, then lifted her legs, bent them tightly against her chest, and spun.

The seat easily whirled her around in a circle. She planted her legs once it circled back to her original position. Slightly dizzy, she gazed down at Kai, who stood with his arms crossed and an unreadable expression on his face.

"What do you think?" She unstrapped her thighs. "Demi said he could make more. As many as we need." She slipped off Roc's back and landed beside Kai. "Do you think it will help?"

She peered at him, desperate for some kind of reply. Was he about to laugh at her for being an idiot? Or praise her for thinking of something ingenious?

After a moment of tense silence, Kai spun on his heel, crossed the square, then disappeared inside a building.

Violet's heart sank. Why would he walk away? Did she do something wrong?

"Violet!" Ryon waved and peeled off from the group of trainees who arrived in the square. "Hey, what's going on? I forgot to ask exactly what you had in mind for today when we talked last night."

"Oh." She forced a smile. "It's up there on Roc."

Ryon narrowed his eyes on the seat. "What's it do?"

"It spins around so we won't have to be forced to strap in facing one direction any longer."

Ryon grinned. "That's genius!"

Violet toed at the ground with her boot. "I thought so too. But when I showed it to Kai, he didn't say anything. He just... left."

"Seriously?" Ryon shook his head. "Can't say I'm surprised. I bet he doesn't have an imaginative bone in his body. I mean, what kind of name is Roc for a dragon? It's a little on the nose for an earth dragon, don't you think?"

Violet stifled a giggle.

"His full name is Rocodolphan," Kai announced as he rounded Roc's flank. "And I didn't name him. His mother did."

An eerie familiarity struck her at the name. It was like something a dragon in her realm might choose. But with a gulp, she shoved the thought aside.

Kai hadn't returned alone. A dozen riders—at least—crowded behind him.

"Would you mind climbing back on Roc, Violet?" Kai asked.

She glanced at Ryon. His cheeks were rosy, but he nodded encouragingly despite his embarrassment.

"Sure." She climbed again, and it was a much simpler matter to perch atop the seat now that it'd been strapped in already. Wind tickled her scalp as she spun. She completed a full circle in one direction, then reversed, only dropping her legs after she'd completed both.

When her head cleared from the momentary dizziness, she found everyone staring. Slack jaws and wide eyes scanned the seat with undisguised curiosity. And dare she say... delight?

Kai's flat expression had even lifted. A small smile pulled at the corners of his lips before he motioned for the other riders to gather around him. They conversed quietly with their heads bent together.

Violet took that as her cue to slide off. Ryon helped steady her as she landed on solid ground. "That was incredible. You're amazing."

She lowered her head, wishing she had her long hair back to hide her heated cheeks. "Thanks." If only the rest of the riders were so quick with their praise... As Kai and the others continued to converse, her stomach filled with knots.

Finally, they broke apart. Kai turned to her, flashing the first genuine smile she'd seen on his face in weeks. But it was gone so fast she wondered if she'd imagined it. He opened his mouth, speaking with an air of professionalism. "Good work, Violet. We're all in agreement.

This idea has great potential. In light of that, we'd like to make you an official rider today. What do you say?"

Her heart took flight. "Yes. Of course."

By now, all the trainees had crowded nearby. A chorus of whoops sounded, and before she knew what was happening, they'd surrounded her, clapping her on the shoulder and showering her with congratulations. But among the crowd, she sought one familiar face.

Ryon wrapped her in a tight hug and whispered in her ears. "I knew you could do it."

The riders swooped in, each of them with a word of welcome or a warm smile. She answered them all on autopilot while her mind raced and her pulse pounded furiously. She'd really done it. She was a rider now.

Kai strode to her with a warm smile. "I meant what I said earlier. Well done."

The others had broken off by now. Many of them, including Ryon, gathered around his bonded, Tora. She'd climbed atop Roc and untied the seat. Tora wore an awed smile as she fiddled with it before passing it around for the others to check out more closely.

Violet grinned. "You had me worried when you tore off without saying anything."

"Sorry about that." Kai shot a quick glance at Roc before meeting her gaze, chagrined. "I had someone talking at me nonstop at the time."

"That right?" She patted Roc's scaly side fondly. In the weeks they'd spent training, she'd become very comfortable around the fierce dragon.

"He insisted I bring the others to see your invention. That it would revolutionize the way we do things around here."

Warmth spread through her chest and pooled in her limbs. "Did he really say that?"

"Sure did." Kai leaned back on his heels. "So, I guess you'll be wanting to see the oracle now."

Violet blinked back her surprise. She'd been certain she'd need to broach the topic. "Can we go now?"

"I don't see why not."

She clapped her hands. "I'll get Ryon."

"You can't." Kai's brow furrowed. "He's still not a rider, remember?"

"Oh." Violet's stomach clenched. "Can I at least tell him where I'm going?"

Kai nodded. "Sure. Say your goodbyes. I'll take you to the oracle as soon as you're through."

She grabbed Ryon's elbow and tugged him away from the crowd. "Kai's taking me to see the oracle."

Ryon brightened. "Already?" His face fell when he examined her expression more closely. "That's what we wanted, isn't it? Why do you look upset?"

She bit her lip. "I can't take you with me."

He rubbed her upper arms a few times. She scanned his face, and though he looked calm, she sensed the decision bothered him. "It's fine. Go. I'll be right here waiting when you return."

Violet sighed. "See you soon." She walked away, returning to Kai's side.

"Ready?" he asked.

She nodded forcefully. "Of course. I've been dying to meet the oracle since the first day we arrived."

Kai chuckled. "Yeah. I remember."

Violet's breath sped as Kai led her away from Roc. She'd been certain the oracle would live far away. Maybe in a cave somewhere like the miners. Or some other out of the way spot they needed to arrive at on dragonback.

Instead, he opened a door she'd passed by hundreds of times on the outskirts of the training square. She'd never been inside, but had watched full riders go in and out occasionally. To think, the oracle had been here all along, right under her nose. She shook her head before she laughed at the absurdity of it all.

The small log cabin appeared much the same as the others in town from the outside. Even the interior didn't seem abnormal. A row of tables and chairs filled the space, and she suspected they used the building for meetings, or perhaps to share a meal. There was enough seating that a few-dozen riders could gather comfortably.

Kai strode to the rear of the room and shoved open another door. Violet wrinkled her nose at the pungent scent that escaped. "What's in there? Manure?"

"How did you guess?" He shuffled sideways into the tiny storage room. Shelves packed with boxes and bins overflowed, leaving little space for the muscular rider. But he went in anyway and turned back to stare at her. "You coming?"

She drew in a deep breath—through her mouth—and followed. Her heart pounded against her rib cage as she crammed herself inside, so close to Kai they were practically touching.

What were they doing? There was no way out. Was Kai tricking her?

"Close the door," he stated gruffly.

Her stomach churned. "What? Why? We won't be able to see." Panic clawed at her mind, and she was a heartbeat away from running, when Kai's hand landed on her elbow.

"Violet. Relax." He squeezed her arm softly and gentled his tone. "Trust me."

In the last few weeks, she'd learned how to do just that. Riding together on dragonback, they had to work as a team. And although she still didn't know him very well, she trusted he wouldn't hurt her. Kai wasn't that kind of man.

"All right." She reached behind her and dragged the door closed. *Click.*

She held her breath as darkness descended. The black was so complete she couldn't see the barest shadow before her eyes. "What are we doing in here, Kai?" The voice that escaped her was far shakier than she'd intended.

"Just a moment."

Soft rattling echoed in her ears. A heartbeat later, the back wall of the storage room slid aside, and she gasped. "A secret passage." Light spilled into the storeroom, coming from somewhere below. She peered around Kai's bulky frame and spotted a stairwell.

"Come on." Kai jerked his head down as he set his boot on the first step. "The oracle is down here."

The old wooden stairs creaked with every step they took. Before long, the air cooled and the musty aroma of moist earth filled the air.

"What is this place?" She trailed a hand along the wall, keeping her balance as they descended.

"Old tunnels. They found them not long after the city was founded."

"Found them?" Her brow furrowed. "Your people didn't dig them?"

"No. They were here already."

"I never knew there were others here before you."

Kai finally reached the bottom of the stairs. He turned and met her gaze as she trailed down the last few steps. "There's a lot you don't know. But now you have the perfect opportunity to ask."

She gulped. "Can the oracle really answer any question?"

He shrugged. "That's what I hear." He pursed his lips. "Just... be polite. The oracle doesn't care for riders with attitude."

"I'll be on my best behavior." She followed Kai down a long dirt tunnel lined with oil lamps. A few metal doors were set into the walls, but all of them were closed. They stopped in front of a door at the end of the tunnel. Kai knocked three times, waited a beat, and shoved the door open.

"Hello." A woman in a long, flowing dress covered in pockets rose from an armchair as they entered. "Kai. I wasn't expecting you." Her eyes widened as she noticed Violet behind him. "Who do we have here?"

Violet strode forward, certain she didn't recognize the woman. Her bright-red curls and freckled face certainly stood out from the typical dark-haired Lanwellians she passed every day in the streets. "I'm Violet." She nodded her head slowly—the preferred greeting of the people here—and silently swallowed her surprise when she lifted her eyes.

An enormous smile painted the woman's face. Was she pleased to see her, then?

"I have much I need to ask you, great oracle," Violet blurted.

Tinkling laughter spilled out of the woman's lips. "Oh, I'm not the oracle."

"You're not? I'm sorry, I—"

She waved off Violet's explanation. "No need to explain. You're not the first to make that mistake. I'm Shandra, the oracle's attendant. Come. I'll take you to the oracle."

Her skin prickled with goose bumps. This was it. Her questions were about to be answered.

She followed Shandra but paused when Kai remained in the same spot. "Aren't you coming?"

He shook his head. "No. The oracle will only speak to one rider at a time."

"Oh." Violet steadied her racing nerves.

"Go on. You'll be fine. Just remember to be polite."

She straightened her shoulders and followed Shandra through a dimly lit corridor. The tunnel twisted and turned before finally brightening.

Violet gasped as Shandra stepped aside, revealing an enormous chamber. Firelight danced in the space from a central hearth, illuminating tiny shining gemstones set into the walls. But that wasn't what made her breath catch and her heart beat like mad.

Shandra smiled and extended her arm, pointing to the room's lone occupant. "Violet, meet the oracle."

A pair of red eyes narrowed on her before the enormous black dragon inclined her head. The oracle was a dragon! A female, too, from the look of her.

Her surprise wore off quickly. Disappointment rose to take its place. All this time, she'd placed her hopes on the word of a creature she couldn't even speak to. Who knew what might be lost in translation?

Shandra stiffened, and her demeanor changed in the blink of an eye. "Don't look so forlorn, girl." Her voice was a full octave lower, and her eyes were glazed.

"What's going on?" Violet backed away a pace, her gaze darting between Shandra's stiff figure and the oracle.

"Isn't it obvious? Shandra is lending me her voice."

She gasped. "I didn't think that was possible…" Then again, her aunt could see through Mena's eyes. It didn't seem like that much of a stretch when she considered that.

"There's much you wouldn't believe possible. So much your little mind could barely grasp." Shandra's voice boomed, and from the menacing stare the dragon leveled on her, Violet got the distinct impression she wasn't pleased.

Polite. She had to be polite. "My apologies. I didn't mean to doubt you. Please, great oracle. I need your help."

The black dragon relaxed, folding her wings and sitting solidly on the chamber floor. "I know you do, girl. Now come closer. I'll tell you everything you need to know."

Violet hesitated. Would it really be that easy?

Shandra chuckled darkly. "Don't you want to learn how to destroy the vermin plaguing your world?" The oracle tilted her head, staring at Violet intently. "Its ship has a weakness. And I can tell you exactly how to end it. For good—this time."

Violet's heart jolted. How did the oracle know? "I'd like that very much." She smiled and walked closer.

Time Taken

Ryon's heart pounded as he stopped in front of a metal door underground. He'd spent a short while training after Violet and Kai had left until Tora asked him to follow her. She'd been all smiles, chatting away about nothing in particular and setting him at ease. But once she'd opened the door to a secret passage, he'd caught on to the gravity of the situation, and every speck of ease fled his body.

"Where are we?" he asked for the dozenth time.

"Shh. You'll see." She shot him another massive grin after answering with another non-answer—like every other time he asked.

Knock, knock.

Tora rubbed her knuckles and waited.

"Come in," a deep voice called.

Tora pushed open the door but made no move to enter. "This is where I leave you." She leaned in and lowered her voice. "Take your time. I don't want to see you till morning." She winked, then turned on her heel and jogged back to the stairwell.

With a slack jaw, Ryon watched her go. Then he straightened his spine and stepped through the doorway.

"Kai. What's going on?" His eyes widened as he took in the modest bedchamber. A lone cot occupied most of the space, with the muscular dragon rider standing in front of it. But if he was here... "Where is Violet?"

"She's the reason I asked you to be brought here."

Panic flared, bright and hot, making him dizzy. "Is she all right? Did something happen?"

"No, nothing like that," Kai insisted. "She's with the oracle now."

"Oh." He pressed a hand to his heart.

"I have no fears for Violet's safety, but meeting with the oracle can be... challenging." He smiled wryly. "It certainly was for me. It helps to have someone you trust to talk over things once you're through. That's what you're here for."

Ryon frowned. "You brought me here to talk to Violet?"

"Is that so hard to imagine?" Kai crossed the room and clasped his shoulder. "I've seen the way you two act. And Helka told me what you said when she mentioned being wed. You wanted to call for a priest, right?"

He nodded. "That's right."

"You love her, don't you?"

Ryon met Kai's gaze. He hadn't admitted it yet... Not aloud, at least. But the truth of those words hummed through his ears and settled in his bones. "I do. I love her with all my heart."

"Then it should be you." Kai squeezed his shoulder. "I know she'd want you here, too. They'll bring Violet to this room once she's through with the oracle. Listen to her and help her come to terms with the truths she's learned. Take all the time you need." He strode to the door.

"I thought I didn't belong down here... not until I'm a full rider."

Kai paused in the doorway. "Just speeding up the inevitable."

Ryon grinned as the head rider's footsteps faded away to nothing. He'd been so worried Kai was interested in Violet, but maybe he'd misjudged him. Either way, he couldn't contain the excitement spreading through his chest.

Despite spending every day together, he'd never felt further apart from Violet. There was always someone around during training. And with Violet striving to do her best, he hadn't wanted to break the rules to force the issue. Now, they'd be alone—really, truly alone—for the first time since they'd arrived in this strange place. There was so much he needed to say. He kept putting it off, hoping to find the perfect time. Fact was, there'd never be a perfect time. And he was sick of waiting.

Footsteps echoed outside. Ryon's stomach fluttered and his mind raced, swirling with everything he wanted to tell her. Then the door opened, and when he spotted Violet's blank gaze, he knew his confession would need to wait a little longer.

"Violet?" he asked. "What's wrong?"

A young woman with long red hair held open the door, and Violet shuffled inside with unfocused eyes and a tiny crease between her brows.

The woman met his gaze from the doorway. "Take as long as you need." She sent Violet a sympathetic smile and quietly shut the door.

Violet strode right past him, looking disturbed. "What's wrong? I honestly don't even know where to start." She sank onto the edge of the bed.

Ryon sat beside her and gathered her into his arms.

She sighed and wrapped her arms around his waist. They sat in silence until she peeked up at him. "Wait... How did you get here?"

He grinned. "Sounds like they're used to the oracle sharing some harsh truths. Tora and Kai arranged for me to be here so you'd have someone to speak with when you were through."

"Oh. Good." She snuggled more firmly against his chest.

"Do you want to talk?" He loosened his arms. "Not that this isn't nice, too."

She sighed again. "It is." All too soon, she pulled away, breathing rapidly. "The oracle is a dragon, Ryon."

He blinked, doing a decent job of containing his shock. "Huh. I didn't see that coming."

"She told me so much..." Violet shivered.

"Take your time." He rubbed her back softly, and her fingers tangled in his shirt.

Violet chuckled halfheartedly. "At least you're already sitting down." She blew out a deep breath. "Dragons built the rings eons ago. And not only here and on our world. They explored dozens of worlds."

Ryon frowned. "Well, I suppose that explains why dragon magic was needed to open the ring."

"Oh, that's not all. They discovered all kinds of things."

"Like what?"

"More than just us and them. The oracle said there are as many creatures as there are stars in the sky."

"Wow. That's incredible." His face brightened. "Then they must know how to send us home."

Violet's voice wobbled. "Not anymore."

His stomach sank. "Why not?"

"According to the oracle, one day they stumbled upon a new world that changed everything. Back then, the dragons traveled with people whose understanding of magic was much more advanced than ours, or even the dragons', called the Hilfolk. They crafted a special ship the size of a city that saw to all their needs while they traveled."

"A ship the size of a city." His brow furrowed. "You don't mean..."

She nodded. "Thalassisa. That's where it came from."

"So, what happened next?"

She stiffened. "They encountered a new creature during their travels they called murkborn. At first, they thought they were just like us. Thinking beings with a few lucky members who could connect with us through bonding—sharing our thoughts and lives."

"Like you and Orry, or the dragons and their bonded."

"Yes. But it wasn't long before they realized these creatures were different. When they bonded with someone, it wasn't the same. They'd take over and use their bonded's magic for their own ends."

"What ends?"

Violet's gaze turned downcast. "Power. Control. They won't stop until they have it. Everywhere. On all worlds."

"No..." Horror filled him. "And that's what we're dealing with back home?"

She nodded gravely. "When the dragons realized what they'd unleashed by finding the murkborn, they put an end to their travels. By then, a few of the murkborn had slipped through the rings. And the Hilfolk people had been destroyed."

"They were destroyed? How did that happen?"

"The same way it did with the dragons back on our world. The murkborn used their dark magic to take over the Hilfolk. Then they siphoned their magic out of them and into the ship." She rubbed her temples. "The oracle said that's the key."

"The key to what?"

"Destroying Jurdan. If we kill the ship, then we'll remove his power. She told me exactly how to do it."

"Really?" His heart sped up. "That's great news." But when her expression didn't match the elation he felt, his stomach sank. "What's wrong?"

"*We* can't go back." She met his gaze with misty eyes. "You have to."

"No." Bile rose in the back of his throat. "I'm not leaving you here, Violet. Why can't we both go?"

"They destroyed all the rings on this world. That field of rocks we landed in used to be one of them."

His eyes stung. "Can't they build another?"

She shook her head. "The oracle said it's a lost art. If the dragons could even be convinced to try, they'd have no way of knowing where it would take us. That leaves us with only one option." Her hand fell to her belt—right on the pocket that hid the single golden feather she possessed. "I'll wish you back."

"Violet, you can't." He grabbed her hand and squeezed. Her eyes shot to his, and this time they weren't just misty. They brimmed with unshed tears, making his heart clench. "The consequences. You haven't suffered enough to make a wish freely, have you?"

A tear slid down her cheek, and she swiped it away with her free hand. "It doesn't matter. I can't sit here knowing what I do—certain that it's the key to helping everyone I love back home—and do nothing." She squeezed his hand back and sent him a wobbly smile. "When the fate of the world depends on your actions, there's not much you won't sacrifice."

Ryon's stomach churned. He opened his mouth, trying to think of something—anything—to convince her to reconsider. She'd heard what Orry said about the bloodfeathers, same as him. She knew, likely better than anyone, that she wasn't prepared for this. Anything might happen after she made her wish to ensure she'd paid the price for it. But as he stared into her eyes, he knew he'd be wasting his breath.

Violet was determined to do this—no matter the consequences.

"What's your plan?" he reluctantly asked.

Violet drew back, and her brows lifted as she examined his face. "You're agreeing to it?"

Ryon sighed. "I don't want to. Believe me, Violet—leaving you here, all on your own, is the absolute last thing I want to do." Hadn't he been ready to confess his feelings a few moments ago? And now she was telling him to leave. To abandon her on a world filled with dangerous beasts far stronger than what they faced back home. He pressed his quivering lips into a firm line. "Just tell me what you're planning, would you?"

Her chest heaved as she sucked in a deep breath. "I'll use the golden feather. Then I'll stay here and learn everything I can while you're gone. The oracle's promised to meet with me again and answer anything I'd like." Her brows screwed up. "I just have to discover the right questions."

He leaned forward. "And what about you? How will you return?"

"You'll find Orry. Have her give you another feather and find someone to wish me back. I'll keep looking for the silver feathers here." She shrugged. "One of us will find a feather eventually."

Disappointment curdled his blood. None of this would be happening if he hadn't lost those silver feathers. This was all his fault. And he might not even be able to accomplish what she wanted back home. "It took me years to earn my first feather. Not just years. Decades."

"Then I'll wait," Violet replied quietly. "But I doubt it will come to that. If you go quickly, Orry will offer you one right away. I know she will. Then you'll just need to find someone who's never made a wish."

He didn't say a word despite the fears brimming in his mind. Orry had told them when they'd first met she didn't have long left to live.

Would she still be alive when he returned? He sensed from the silence that followed Violet was worrying about the same thing.

She chewed on her lip. "You might not even need Orry. Nox has a feather already—and I've heard his heartsong. If he hasn't used it yet, then he can wish me back."

"So, I return. Find Orry or Nox and get someone to wish you back," he stated blankly. No way it would be that easy. He sensed it deep in his bones. But at least when he laid it out like that, it sounded possible. *I can do this, can't I?*

"Exactly." Violet shifted, kneeling on the bed and bringing their faces level. "I know you can do it, Ryon. And I'll wait for you. For years, if I have to."

He cupped her cheek. "I don't know if I can wait that long to see you again." He closed his eyes as the words he'd been dying to say rose to the tip of his tongue. Was it right to tell her when he might not see her again for weeks—or worse, years? Maybe even forever if something went wrong.

No. If this was the last chance he ever had to tell her how he felt, he was damned sure going to take it. He opened his eyes with his pulse hammering painfully in his chest. "Violet, I need to tell you something."

Her lips curled up. "So tell me."

"You're amazing and so brave. The way you stopped at nothing to follow your destiny... I'm so glad I got to be part of your journey. And I've never met anyone with a kinder heart. Violet... I love you."

The soft smile she'd been wearing disappeared. "Y-you do?"

He nodded and barreled on, ignoring the slice of pain in his ribs when she didn't say it back. "I do. More than anything. I don't want to leave you here. I don't want to leave you *ever*. What if something goes terribly wrong? What if—"

Violet's lips crashed into his, interrupting his rant. He kissed her back, taking solace in her touch until a thought broke through the utter bliss he felt with her in his arms. *Is this goodbye?*

He stiffened, and Violet pulled back, gasping. She met his gaze and smiled so beautifully it made his soul ache. "I love you too, Ryon."

A weight lifted off his shoulders, and a giddy lightness filled his body. If she hadn't been holding on to him, he'd have likely lifted off and shot to the stars. But it wasn't long before the euphoria faded, tainted with the knowledge of what needed to happen next. "How am I supposed to leave you now?"

"Don't." She wrapped her arms around his neck and threw a leg over his, settling firmly on his lap. "If we're about to save the world, then I think the least we deserve is one night alone, don't you?"

"That's definitely not too much to ask." His heart started pounding for an entirely different reason. "Good news is, I think they were serious about taking as long as we need down here." Tora, Kai, and that redhead had all said something along those lines.

Violet's arms tightened. "Perfect. Then tonight, you're all mine."

"Not just tonight. Always." He sighed and dragged her lips back to his. If one night was all they had, then he'd make the most of it.

Hours later, Ryon rested with a warm weight on his bare chest. Violet's eyelashes fluttered as she slept, tickling his skin. He'd never been so content. So completely satisfied, body and soul.

After long hours spent sharing their love in the most intimate way, Violet fell into a deep sleep, but sleep had eluded him. The worries that he'd pushed aside came flooding back, and no matter how hard he tried to bury them and live in the moment—they kept bursting back to the surface.

Was he foolish to think he might pull this off? That they could save the world—that he could save Violet—and bring her home where she belonged?

Violet stirred, and her eyes popped open. "Hey," she said groggily. "How long was I asleep?"

"Not long." He cupped her cheek as she propped herself up on his chest.

Her nose wrinkled. "What's wrong?"

"Nothing." He shook his head. "Everything."

"I know. I wish—"

"Not yet." Ryon pulled her close. "Let me hold you a little longer first."

Violet chuckled. "I don't even have the feather yet." She wrapped her arms around his chest and squeezed. "I don't want you to go."

"Me either." He held her tighter, his heart breaking as her warm tears splattered his skin. "I'll bring you home. I swear it."

"I know you will." Her voice trembled, but he couldn't mistake her certainty.

They dressed in silence, picking their discarded clothes off the floor and donning them one by one until a single article remained. Violet's fingers quaked as she cradled her belt in her hands.

Ryon handed her the new crafting blade he'd purchased at a local shop with the chits he'd earned during training. "It's clean."

"Thanks." She lifted her tear-stained face to his. "Are you ready?"

He nodded. "No. Wait." He closed the space between them in a few sure strides. Then he dragged her into his arms. Violet's cheeks were damp and her lips tasted of salt, but he'd never regret stealing one last kiss.

When he pulled back, they were both panting, and he had half a mind to drag her back to bed. Instead, he murmured, "Now I'm ready."

Tears filled her eyes as Violet pulled the shining golden feather free. She winced as the blade nicked her flesh. He took the hilt when she offered it and slid it back in his belt.

Violet's fingers trembled. She stared at the tiny pool of red growing larger in her palm but made no move to place the feather into it. "I-I… Ryon—"

He tipped up her chin, forcing her to meet his gaze. "You're doing the right thing. I believe in you, Violet."

She sucked in a shaky breath. "I'm sorry." She dropped the feather onto her palm and whispered, "I wish Ryon would safely return to our world." She hissed and her eyes screwed shut.

Oh no. He remembered that burning pain. When he'd made his wish for Rovan, the agony had been so intense he'd thought he'd made a terrible mistake. But when he reached out to comfort her, he couldn't grasp her. Fast as a blink, a force greater than anything he'd ever felt ripped him away.

His eyes closed instinctively, and he screamed, more in terror than in pain, though the experience was extremely unpleasant—like when he'd spin as a child for so long his stomach hated him.

And yet, quick as it started, the sensation disappeared. He opened his eyes as his body plunged into dark water.

It was lucky he'd already wished to breathe water as well as air. The cool wet flooded his lungs until he finally slowed. He treaded water while the world spun, and he fought to overcome the disorientation.

Where am I? Did it work?

He blinked, staring past the black water enveloping him and into the distance. Then a smile spread across his face. The ring! It hovered underwater a few strokes away, shrouded in the light of glowing fish. Violet's wish had returned him to the spot he'd left from.

Guano. That wasn't good. He'd been gone for weeks, and the ring was in the middle of the ocean. How was he supposed to get back to dry land?

What's worse, the strange travel had sapped his strength. His limbs were flagging in the water, and sleep weighed heavily on his eyelids.

Perhaps there would still be some debris from the battle on the surface? He could climb atop it and hope to be washed onshore.

It was as good a plan as any. He used his remaining strength to breach the top of the waves. Water gushed out of his lungs. By the time he'd finished hacking, he was so weary it took everything he had left to keep his head above water.

It didn't help that a storm raged off in the distance, making the surf choppy. At least the late-morning sun had broken free of the clouds, and the storm was moving away. But it would make his plan to swim—or float—to safety more difficult. He cursed his luck, until the massive wave he'd surfaced beneath shifted, raising him atop the swell and giving him a glimpse of the chaos beyond it.

A battle raged, striking more fear in his heart than the storm did. Especially when he spotted four dragons flying around the charred remnants of a boat. One that he recognized.

He gasped as a thought crashed into him with utter clarity. That wasn't just some storm. And that battle wasn't just any battle. It was the same storm. The same battle.

How was it possible? *How long have I been gone?*

Death or Forever

Nox's pulse raced as the tiny craft's roof slid open. They'd stolen one of the same peculiar vessels they'd used last time to escape Thalassia. Sunlight burst in, making him squint. "At least that storm has moved elsewhere."

Conall set a foot on the bottom stair with a furrowed brow, like he wasn't sure if they'd collapse. Shadow had no such qualms. The large gray wolf bounded up the stairs and leaped out of the vessel.

"Come on." Ereni mounted the stairs next. "Let's see how the others are faring."

"Others?" Nox followed them up, shielding his eyes as he emerged. "Who's here?"

Conall spoke behind him. "Kayda, for one. And Violet. I'm not sure who else."

Nox frowned as the boat rocked wildly beneath him, though he had little trouble keeping his balance. The storm wasn't as far off as he'd originally thought. Dark clouds still blanketed the sky in the distance. Debris and black-clothed bodies floated everywhere, slamming around in the vicious surf.

Conall might be clueless, but Nox could ask someone who might know who else was around. "*Gwen?*" As soon as he emerged in the fresh air, he sensed his bondmate was nearby. "*Where are you?*"

"*Here! I sure am glad to hear your voice!*" Gwen replied cheerily. "*Just never disappear like that again. Be there soon. We're picking off stragglers.*"

He spun, hunting through the wreckage for anything that had survived. Squinting, he finally made out the shape of wings in the distance. Smoke obscured much of his vision, most of it coming from an enormous ruined ship sitting low in the water. He stared at the vessel as a black-clothed man plummeted off the edge.

His gaze tracked upward, and he spotted a flash of long black hair dangling over the railing. "Mariun."

Splash!

Cold water enveloped him as he dove without thought. Using his boons, he sliced through waves, spanning the distance as fast as a fish. Within moments, he shoved the dead body aside and clambered up the sinking ship.

Ereni yelled, "Nox? Where are you going?"

He didn't bother answering. Not when one thought kept playing on a loop in his mind over and over. *She's here!*

"*Get away from that burning boat!*" Gwen shrieked.

Flint's panicked voice rose in his mind. "*Aren't you tired of being rescued?*"

"*I saw Mariun. She's here!*" Nox leaped over the railing and immediately started coughing.

"*Don't worry. We're coming,*" Gwen insisted.

Nox waved his hands, willing the smoke to clear. He'd just seen her, hadn't he? Where was she?

"Nox?"

He whipped around. "Mariun." A gout of flame separated them. He was a heartbeat away from jumping through it when a blast of water splashed down, extinguishing the fire. Nox spluttered and blinked, saying a silent thank you when he spotted dragon wings above him.

Nox raced forward at the same time Mariun did. They collided and clasped their arms around each other. "Mariun. Thank the Mother!" He breathed in deeply, surprised that a hint of flowers still lingered in her hair beneath all the smoke.

"I'm so sorry, Nox. It's all my fault." Mariun gripped him so tightly he worried she'd never let go.

Nox frowned. Her fault? Didn't she realize this was all Jurdan's doing?

Before he could think of something to reassure her, the boat sank and water sloshed over Nox's bare feet. He looked over Mariun's shoulder and smiled at Gwen as she landed. She'd grown so much in the few days he'd been gone.

"Hop on. Hurry! This boat won't stay afloat much longer."

Nox reluctantly pulled away from Mariun's arms. "Come on. We have to leave now." He raced across the smoldering deck and leaped onto Gwen's back. Then he reached down, helping Mariun climb up after him.

"Can you carry us both?"

"I hope so," Gwen replied.

Nox gulped. He hated putting a strain on his bondmate. But it couldn't be helped. As they lifted off, he spotted Kayda flying atop Mena. Ari hovered beside the small vessel as Conall climbed on his back with Shadow. And Crys flew nearby, carrying Ereni. His bondmate wouldn't be the only dragon burdened with more than one passenger.

Mariun wrapped her arms around his waist as Gwen began flapping furiously, and shouted, "Wait! What about the others? Violet and Ryon were here. We can't leave without them!"

Nox nodded. "I'll tell Gwen." He spoke in his mind, *"Gwen. Fly low and look for Violet and Ryon."*

Gwen shook her head sadly as she lifted into the air. *"They're gone."*

"What do you mean, gone?"

"Water dragons can see underwater as well as you can see at night. My brother watched Violet and Ryon get sucked into that ring. They... disappeared."

Nox's heart sank. "No!" What did that even mean? He had no clue, but he wouldn't rest until he found out. After everything Violet had done for him, she deserved as much.

Mariun's arms tightened around his waist. "What is it?"

"They're gone. Sucked into the ring."

Mariun gasped and buried her face against his back.

Gwen pivoted, flying away from the wreckage. *"Mena says Kayda suggests we regroup on a nearby island."*

"Kayda?" Nox turned his bewildered gaze to his half-sister, the blind queen. He'd barely had time to consider the implications of her presence, but it was rather peculiar finding her here. *"What is she even doing here? Isn't she supposed to be getting married right now?"*

Gwen chuckled. *"There's a lot you missed."*

Flint replied drolly, *"Clearly. Why don't you fill us in?"*

Nox sighed, feeling calm for the first time in days with both his bondmates' voices in his mind, and Mariun's arms wrapped securely around him. He spent the short flight listening to Gwen and absent-mindedly rubbing the back of Mariun's wrist with his thumb.

"So, Kayda called off her wedding after bonding to Mena?" he asked as Gwen wrapped up her explanation.

Flint purred thoughtfully. *"Sounds like she just postponed it."*

"That's right," Gwen added. *"And she can see now, through Mena's eyes."*

"Huh. Guess we did miss a lot." Nox sucked in a deep breath as the first hint of green rose on the horizon. *"Hopefully we can set up a plan once we land. We need to find Violet. I refuse to accept that she's gone for good."*

"I hope so, too," Flint agreed.

Gwen thumped down on the beach, kicking up a cloud of sand. The other dragons followed suit, and everyone slid off. Nox helped Mariun off Gwen, frowning when she avoided looking him directly in the eyes.

"Brother!" Kayda called behind him.

Nox faced her, smiling widely. "Kayda. It's good to see you."

Kayda strolled over with tears in her eyes. "And I, you." And unlike in the past, her hands didn't fall off to the side when she reached for him. She wrapped her arms around him perfectly the first time and drew him in for a hug.

Tears rose to Nox's eyes too, but he blinked them back. As thrilled as he was for his sister's returned sight, he was just as determined to find his niece. "I hear the dragons saw Violet and Ryon disappear. We have any idea where?"

Ereni gasped. "She... disappeared?" She clasped a hand over her heart and wobbled where she stood.

Conall grabbed his wife's arm, steadying her in the sand.

Mariun spoke up, her voice grave. "There is a story my people tell about that ring. It is said to lead to another world."

"This is it!" Ereni's voice rose until she was practically hysterical. "My vision all those years ago. My father said Violet would travel far beyond the lands I've tread. I thought it was just those islands… but it's not. It's so much more."

Conall wrapped his arms around Ereni while she silently shuddered, clearly taking the news hard. Nox couldn't blame her. It had to be hard to hear their only daughter was beyond their reach.

Kayda broke in. "Listen. We don't know for sure if she's on another world. Violet could be anywhere. I'd like to return and search for survivors with the dragons. If I find Violet and Ryon, we'll bring them back." She frowned as Mena's gaze trailed over everyone. "You know—we're missing Orry as well."

Nox's stomach sank. "Violet's bondmate was there?" He glanced at Gwen. *"Did Ari see Orry go through the ring, too?"*

Gwen was silent for a moment, and then she shook her head gravely. *"No. Crys remembers spotting Orry on the boat after the ring closed. Then… we all lost track of her."*

Nox turned to Kayda. "I think searching is a wise plan. Do you want me to go with you?"

Kayda pursed her lips. "No. We'll have more room for survivors if the dragons don't need to carry us both." She waved at the mostly barren island. "Why don't you set up shelter for the night while we're gone? If anything goes wrong, Gwen will tell you right away."

Nox sighed and rubbed the back of his neck. "All right. We'll—"

Ereni chose that moment to break out of Conall's arms. She narrowed her eyes and strode across the sand, straight to Mariun. "You know what I want to know?" She jabbed a finger at Mariun. "What *are* you?"

Mariun blanched. "What are you talking about?"

Nox stepped in between them. "Calm down, Ereni. Please."

Conall inched closer, but Ereni didn't back down. She crossed her arms and scanned Mariun closely. "I've never seen a yellow aura until today. You have it. And so did that city."

Mariun's brows creased. "Yellow?" She took a step back.

Conall explained, "My wife is a seer. She can see what magic someone possesses by looking at them. It manifests as different colors."

Kayda chimed in. "Yellow. That is curious."

Nox rubbed his chin. "Mariun can summon lightning. Didn't you say the city runs on the same magic?"

Mariun nodded.

Kayda paced in the sand, stopping next to Ereni. "Did you say the city had an aura as well?"

"It did." Ereni rubbed her temples. "Yellow just like her. But I saw him too. Jurdan."

Nox's heart sped up. Could Ereni's seer sight give them a new insight into exactly what made that villain tick?

Ereni's nose wrinkled. "I've never seen anything like him, either. His aura wasn't only one color. It was a blend of black, yellow"—she sucked in a deep breath—"and green."

"Green." Conall stepped back and covered his mouth. "But I thought there was only one person with a green aura."

"The Winter Witch." Ereni blinked furiously. "Don't you see what it means? Jurdan must be using the dream elixir. He can glimpse the future."

Mariun gasped. "He knew. Jurdan knew I would betray him." She twisted her hands in the hem of her shirt. "And he knew Nox would come for me. He planned for it. He even knew that the first attempt to kill Kayda would fail. He told me so himself." She lifted red-rimmed eyes to meet Nox's. "How can we fight someone who's always two steps ahead?"

Nox wrapped an arm around Mariun's shoulders as part of her statement stuck in his mind. "So Jurdan did try to kill you, Kayda? I guess, since you're here, at least Violet arrived in time to warn you."

Kayda sighed. "He did. Twice. First with poison in my wine. Then he used Jayan to attack me."

Nox's stomach sank. "Jayan attacked you?" He'd heard the sincerity in Jayan's voice when he'd insisted on returning with Violet. Jayan was set on warning Kayda about the attack Jurdan had planned during her wedding. Nox never would've let the man live if he thought Jayan intended to harm his sister.

"It was the strangest thing." Kayda's brows pinched together. "One moment we were reminiscing about the past, and the next his hands were wrapped around my throat. I never thought Jayan would ever hurt me... I'm sure Jurdan was behind it somehow."

"It's just like with Chumy." His eyes widened as the parallels clicked into place. "I never thought my bondmate would attack me, either."

Ereni turned to Kayda. "Maybe you shouldn't be hunting for survivors. At least, not any masked. What if they turn on us, too?"

Kayda's lips thinned. "That's a good point. But they could be useful if interrogated..." She clasped Ereni's shoulder. "Either way, daylight is wasting. I'm going back to search for Violet."

Nox nodded. "Good luck, Sister. Be careful."

Kayda returned hours later as the sky began to darken. By then, Nox had helped the others set up a few rudimentary lean-tos. As far as shelters went, they weren't much, but they'd have to do for the night.

The dragons thumped down on the beach, and it didn't take long for his heart to sink. Kayda slid off Mena's back and shook her head sadly as she strode toward them—alone.

"You didn't find anyone?" Conall asked.

"No. By the time I made it back, there weren't even any masked." She frowned at her boots. "Perhaps they surfaced in those crafts to collect their dead and injured?"

Ereni's lips pinched closed. "What if they found Violet? She might be trapped in that blazing underwater city, like you were, Nox."

"I suppose it's possible," Nox admitted, though he doubted that was what Ereni wanted to hear.

"Let's not jump to any conclusions." Conall's face brightened. "I haven't seen Halynn since we got here. What if she scooped them up?"

"Halynn?" Nox lifted a brow. "Who's that?"

Ereni waved a hand. "The Winter Witch. She met us in Magehaven and insisted we come with her on a voyage out to sea."

"Ah." Nox grinned. "Guess that's what you meant when you told me you hitched a ride with a witch."

Conall smiled wryly, but it didn't quite reach his eyes. "Yes. We docked at a different island. One a lot bigger than this one, with some helpful locals."

Kayda cleared her throat. "We should head there tomorrow. I bet she went back there after the battle. We can ask if she's seen any sign of Violet, Ryon, or Orry."

Everyone quickly agreed and began preparing for bed. Nox was more than ready to rest, but it didn't take him long to notice one person was absent from their camp. His pulse kicked up, and he tamped down the urge to panic.

"*Have you seen Mariun?*" he asked Gwen.

His bondmate replied immediately. "*Yep. She wandered off into the woods.*" Gwen jerked her head toward a thick clump of trees. "*I figured she just needed a moment of privacy...*"

"*All right.*" Nox's heart slowed marginally. But after waiting for a few moments without her return, he headed after her. "Mariun?" he called as he ducked behind the first tree. The last thing he wanted was to intrude on her privacy, but if she wasn't taking a quick break to relieve her bladder, then he had to go after her.

The sky grew darker with every passing moment. He had little trouble navigating through the trees with his boon, but Mariun would surely struggle to find her way back. He couldn't lose her again when he'd just found her.

"Mariun? Are you here?" With each step, his pulse pounded harder until its intensity matched the thrashing surf. What if Jurdan found her again? What if he—

"I'm here." Her sweet voice rose in the distance, and calmness stole over him.

Nox emerged on a deserted beach. Mariun stood on the shore, watching the tide go out. He slowly approached, marveling at her beauty. Bathed in the dim glow of the setting sun's rays, she looked ethereal—and more than a little lost. "Something wrong?" he asked softly as he stopped beside her.

Mariun lowered her head. "Of course there is." She wrapped her arms tightly around her middle. "I overheard Conall and Ereni telling Kayda what happened when they found you." She lifted her bleary gray eyes, and his heart tore in two at the pain he glimpsed within them. "He made you fight for me, didn't he?"

Nox took a step closer. "I'd do it all again. A thousand times, if I had to."

She rubbed her wrists. "Don't." Her lip quivered. "I'll be the death of you, Nox." She turned away, giving him her back.

His heart sank. After everything he'd gone through, didn't she see how much he cared for her? Shouldn't she be leaping into his arms and spewing thanks? He almost stomped into the woods, livid that everything he'd sacrificed had been for nothing.

But he didn't miss the way her shoulders trembled. And he couldn't help remembering her tragic past. Mariun had never been given the love she deserved. She'd grown up with a caretaker who thought of her as a job, and she was abandoned by her mother and thrust into the care of a father who only wanted her around to serve his own ends.

He had to show Mariun that she was worthy of love. And that no matter what happened, he'd always be there for her.

Nox circled her and gathered her hands gently in his. "Look at me."

After what felt like an eternity, she finally lifted her gaze.

He gulped, knowing this would be the most important conversation he'd ever have. "The moment I learned you were missing, it felt like a dagger sliced through my heart. I followed you, and I never regretted it. Not for an instant. I've killed for you, and I won't hesitate to do it again. You and me? We're meant to be." He pressed her palm against his chest. "I can feel it. I know you feel it too."

Mariun's lips trembled and tears spilled down her cheeks. "I-I..."

Nox wrapped a hand around the back of her neck, dragging her so close her thready breath kissed his lips. "You won't be my death, Mariun. You're my forever." He pressed his mouth softly—so softly—against hers.

She stiffened.

Panic flared, and he was certain she would tear away and run into the trees. After so long being abandoned by the people who ought to hold her close, would she ever be ready to let love in?

But then her hands threaded through his hair, and she dragged him closer. He kissed her with a furious longing unlike anything he'd experienced. He'd been so worried. Terrified that he'd never find her. When she sank into his embrace, it felt like the greatest gift he'd ever experienced—until it didn't.

As Mariun's nails trailed down his back, she caught one of the many wounds he'd earned in the ring. He hissed, unable to contain the soft cry that erupted from his throat.

Mariun gasped. "Nox? Did I hurt you?"

He shook his head vehemently. "It's just a scratch." In fact, hearing the concern in her voice was more than enough to take his mind off the pain. "Maybe you could look at it for me back at the campsite? Gwen told me Kayda packed some healing balms."

She clicked her tongue. "Of course I will. I can't believe you hid it this long."

"Sorry. Slipped my mind." He grinned crookedly and offered her his hand. "Walk back with me?"

Mariun's hand slid into his. He clasped it firmly and led her into the darkened trees. They quietly traversed the small stretch of forest and emerged in the silent campsite. Thankfully, everyone was already asleep, or at least, no one sought to talk to them upon their return.

Nox made sure Mariun was settled under the lean-to they'd built together and snagged a jar of healing balm and some bandages. Then he sat beside her and eased off his shirt, trying not to wince as the fabric tugged on the cuts littering his abdomen and back.

She gasped. "Nox." Her voice quivered but her hands worked methodically, gently cleaning his injuries like a woman who'd tended much worse. "Can I ask you something?" she asked softly once she'd patched up the deepest wound on his back.

Nox nodded. "You can ask me anything."

"Did you ever doubt me?"

He shifted, making sure she met his eyes when he answered. "Never."

Mariun pressed her lips together. "Why not?"

He cupped her cheek. "I've been betrayed before. When I look back on that time, even before it happened, there were signs. I ignored them, and I almost paid the price with my life. But it's different with you. When I look into your eyes, I know you feel it too, even if you're not ready to say it yet." He dropped his hand and smiled softly.

He expected her to ask how he knew. How could he be so sure about Mariun's feelings—or his own? But the next question she asked threw him for a loop.

"What was it like back then? I could barely handle having my own voice in my head when I was a teen. I still can't believe you had four voices talking in your head at such a young age." She giggled softly, and the sound was music to his ears. "Did they all gang up on you?"

Nox chuckled, surprised at the turn of conversation but eager to indulge her if the topic set her at ease. "Not quite." He frowned as Mariun continued tending to him, moving on to a cut on his chest. "My bondmates back then couldn't hear each other. Not like Flint and Gwen can. I'm not sure why..."

"Huh. That's strange." She spread balm on his rib cage.

He shrugged. He'd often wondered why some animals communicated with each other in his mind, while others were deaf to each other. "There's so much I don't know. I wager we'll never learn the whole of it. Magic has always been... mysterious."

"Maybe for you." Mariun sighed. "For me, it's more like a curse. I'd be glad to be rid of it."

Nox frowned. "Let's get through this mess, and then I'll take you back with me to Raimire. You'll never have to use your magic ever again if you don't want to."

She flashed a lopsided smile. "Is that a promise?"

"Yep." Nox grinned and stared at the stars. "The first of many. And I intend to keep all of them."

Mariun scoffed, and he sensed that she didn't believe him. Not truly. But he didn't hold it against her.

I'll just have to show her, won't I?

A Little Mouthy

Violet sat cross-legged in the cave. She'd begged for another visit with the oracle after her training session ended. Anything to take her mind off Ryon's disappearance.

The thought of him was enough to send a pang of longing through her. He'd only been gone half a day, and she already missed him so much it was painful.

His absence had certainly been fun to explain... She'd shared the truth with Kai and a few others, but she wasn't sure if they believed her. And it hadn't taken long for rumors to spread that he'd been killed out in the field.

She'd been livid when she'd first heard, but Kai counseled her to ignore the gossip. Quelling it would only make the common folk ask questions they didn't want them asking. It was better if they thought Ryon died—and as much as the idea sickened her, she could see the benefit to letting them believe it was true.

"Are you paying attention, girl?" Shandra asked caustically.

"Sorry." Violet cringed. "My mind wandered for a moment. It won't happen again."

The large black dragon lifted her head lazily and aimed a pointed glare in her direction.

"See that you don't," Shandra said in a rich tenor. "Now, where was I?"

Violet's gaze darted between the dragon and her attendant. It was strange hearing the oracle speak through her human caretaker... but she'd seen stranger. She'd put up with anything if it meant finding answers. "You were telling me about the rings."

"Ah, that's right. The rings may come in all shapes and sizes, but they always come in fours—one for each element. You'll find them on each world in a place where that element plays a significant role."

Violet's eyes lit up. "That's fascinating. And it makes a lot of sense, too."

"Why do you say so?"

"Well, the ring Ryon and I traveled through was in the middle of the ocean, so it certainly fits."

Shandra chuckled. "That's clearly the water ring. Any clue where the rest are?"

Violet racked her brain. "Hm. I bet the fire ring was in the caves under Dracwood, where my father found the Unseen." She leaned in. "Remind me to tell you the story behind his defeat one day."

"You've told me enough." Violet had shared the short version of her family's role in the war with the Unseen during their first meeting. "They defeated the murkborn by tossing it in boiling lava, isn't that right?"

Violet grinned. "You have an excellent memory."

Shandra's voice thrummed with amusement. "What kind of oracle would I be if I didn't?" A grumbly rumble erupted from the dragon's chest.

Wonder if that's what passes for a dragon chuckle? Violet cocked her head thoughtfully.

"Well? What of the rest? Air and earth. Do you have any idea where those are on your world?"

She wrinkled her nose. "I'm not sure." Something tickled the back of her mind, but she couldn't quite grasp it.

"You likely won't find the air ring. Not without wings," Shandra said. "As I understand it, most of those are placed in the clouds on their respective worlds."

"I suppose that makes sense."

"As for earth, it might be anywhere on land. The scattered rocks you landed among were once our earth ring. The dragons of old placed it there because of the rich fertility in that soil. There are half a dozen species of mushrooms that will only grow in that small stretch of fields."

The explanation struck a chord in her heart. "That's it! I think I know exactly where the earth ring is!"

It made perfect sense—to her, at least. And when she thought back to the time she'd spent in front of the mysterious circular relic on her homeworld, she could even recall a feeling washing over her. One that she hadn't quite known what to make of at the time—but in retrospect, she must've sensed on some level that she was standing before a powerful artifact.

Violet's veins pulsed with excitement. She opened her mouth to share her theory, but before she choked out a single word, the air in the cave shifted.

"Get out!" Shandra barked.

Violet flinched, stunned by the venom in her tone.

"I said, out! Now!"

Violet scrambled to her feet and raced out of the drafty chamber with her heart in her throat. Footsteps pounded the stone behind her. She whipped around as she emerged in the attendant's chamber and found Shandra following fast on her heels.

"Blazes! What was that for?" Violet bent at the waist and sucked in a few quick breaths, trying to calm her speeding pulse.

Shandra closed the door firmly behind her, but the thick stone wasn't dense enough to block out a roar that made Violet's blood run cold.

"The oracle becomes... troubled... from time to time." Shandra's voice softened, returning to the sweeter tone she spoke with when not lending the oracle her voice. "It's nothing you need worry about."

Violet shuddered as another roar split through the silence. "What's wrong? Maybe I can help." It was the least she could do after all the knowledge the oracle was sharing with her.

Shandra shook her head. "I'm afraid there's nothing to be done. It's an unfortunate consequence of the oracle's long life and many bondmates."

"Oh." Understanding dawned on her. "Is she... going mad?"

A soft smile quirked Shandra's lips. "I promise you she's still in control—most of the time. But imagine having dozens of voices in your mind. It can be a little much."

"How many bondmates has she had?"

Shandra shrugged. "Like I said, dozens. Each one a human, lengthening her lifespan."

Violet's eyes bulged. "So, she's ancient..."

"Exactly." Shandra patted Violet's shoulder. "There's a reason she remembers so much. The oracle is like a living history book. If there's ever a question about the past she can't answer, one of her bondmates likely can."

"Wow." Violet rocked back on her heels. "But how does she stand it? All the voices."

Shandra shrugged. "She's had a lot of practice, I suppose." Shandra led her toward the stairwell. "Don't worry. Come back tomorrow. She'll have calmed down by then. She always does."

Violet nodded absently, but her heart wouldn't stop pounding. *Will the oracle be all right? Or will she succumb to madness before I learn all I need to know?*

She sighed as she emerged on the surface. The dreary weather was enough to make her shiver, but at least it was a match for her melancholy mood.

"Violet!" a voice called behind her.

She spun around and sent a halfhearted smile to Helka. "Funny meeting you here."

Helka caught up to her and looped her arm around Violet's shoulders. "Come on. I'm buying you a drink."

Violet nudged her shoulder lightly. "You don't need to do that." Helka had been with Kai that morning when she'd shared the true story of Ryon's disappearance. "He'll find a way to bring me home. I know he will."

Helka's brows pinched together before she plastered a bright smile on her face. "I'm not worried at all. Just thirsty."

Violet rolled her eyes. "Sure you are."

Still, she appreciated the invitation more than she cared to say. The last thing she wanted to do was return to her lonely room in the women's boarding house to sit alone with her thoughts. Especially not when the mere thought of lying in bed without Ryon felt like the worse kind of torture.

"So, how did your chat with the oracle go?" Helka waggled her brows.

"All right, I guess."

Helka chuckled. "After hearing about Kai's first meeting with her, I would've thought no one would be willing to request a second meeting."

Violet lifted a brow. "Really? Why's that?"

Helka leaned in conspiratorially. "I suspect he may have gotten a little mouthy with her."

"So that's why he insisted I be polite." She met Helka's gaze, and they both burst into giggles.

But the light moment didn't last long. Helka clutched her belly and stumbled. Violet darted forward, steadying her friend before she took a spill on the cobbles.

"Are you all right?"

"Fine," Helka said hastily. "Just lost my step."

Violet scanned Helka more closely, noticing an odd pallor to her skin. "Are you sure?"

"Yes." Helka patted her arm and resumed walking to the tavern. "I'm perfectly fine. I swear."

As silence washed over them, broken only by the rhythmic tap of their boots on the road, Violet called on her boon.

She'd practiced with it often since arriving in Lanwell. Violet had taken Orry's advice to heart and looked for every opportunity to listen to the heartsongs of the people around her. And with Helka meeting frequently with her for evening drinks, she was more familiar with her friend's song than anyone else's in the village.

So it didn't take Violet long to notice something off. A lone note twanged loudly in her ears, ominous and sharp. Shivers raced down her spine.

Did that odd note mean something was wrong with Helka? As the question formed in her mind, Helka turned back, a smile painting her face and the pallor from before lifted.

Violet pursed her lips. Maybe she was wrong. Was it even worth mentioning?

Helka's brows dipped. "Anything bothering you?"

She shook her head, deciding not to trouble her. "No. Let's grab that drink."

They rounded a corner, and the inn appeared in the distance. Violet smiled, already anticipating the first taste of the sour brew on her tongue.

"Hey, Vi." A young man stepped out of the tavern's doorway. She recognized him as one of the defenders she'd been training with that afternoon. He sported the muscular physique most riders shared, along with piercing brown eyes and shaggy black hair.

He stumbled forward and hiccupped loudly. "I heard the news about pretty boy." The drunken fool at least had the sense to wipe the grin off his face before he stopped before them, but she suspected his act of remorse was just for show. "Dreadful, isn't it?"

Violet gritted her teeth. "Yeah."

"Can I buy you a drink to take your mind off things?" he asked.

Kai's voice boomed from inside. "Helka. Violet. I saved you a seat."

Helka patted the defender's shoulder and smiled apologetically. "Another time, Teek. Violet's drinking with us tonight."

Teek's face fell as she followed Helka into the noisy tavern. Kai pulled out a stool for Helka, but she ignored it in favor of trying to gain the barmaid's attention.

Kai pulled out another stool for her. "Thanks." Violet sat with a sigh.

Her breath caught as Kai leaned close to her ear. "Be careful with Teek."

She glanced across the bar and spotted the young man with a cup in his hand. He noticed her looking and lifted his drink in a wordless toast.

Violet averted her eyes. "He seems harmless enough." Though he clearly didn't understand that it wasn't wise to ask someone for drinks when their lover just disappeared.

"He might seem harmless here, in Lanwell, but the rules are different in the field," Kai explained. "Now that you're a full rider, we'll be spending time away from civilization. You have to watch your back, in more ways than one."

Violet spun on her stool and met his gaze. "What rules are you talking about?"

Kai took a deep pull of his mug. "Out there, no one bats an eye if you keep what you kill. Or if you use what you claim."

Violet's pulse pounded. What fresh hazard had she stumbled into?

Something Useful

Mariun's arms tightened around Nox's waist as they flew over a tree-covered island. His brow creased when something in the lush greenery tickled his memory. *"Where have I heard about an island with a river cutting it in two?"* he asked his bondmates.

"Not sure," Gwen replied. *"Should I ask the others?"*

Flint spoke up. *"No need. I remember."*

Nox scanned the wide channel as they descended. The river mouth emptied into the ocean, creating an inlet bordered by narrow sandy beaches on both sides that were quickly swallowed by thick forest.

"This must be the place where Violet found Aren," Flint explained. *"She told you about it before you parted ways to hunt for the dragon eggs."*

"Ah, that's right." Violet had described the island and its inhabitants to calm the young woman they'd picked up on Jolit Isle, and Nox had relayed the info to Flint. *"I wonder if Zoma is still there?"*

"No idea," Flint admitted. *"But looks like we'll find out soon enough."*

It felt like so long ago that they'd stolen those ships and set off to hunt down the eggs. It was strange to realize it had only been a few weeks. And now it seemed they were heading to the same island that Aren and Lark had stopped at on their way back to Dracwood.

The dragons thumped down on the beach. Nox slid off Gwen's back, but it didn't take long for a chill to spread down his spine. "That noise... I've heard it before." An animal's whooping call echoed through the woods.

Mariun cocked her head. "I recognize it too. It sounds like those apes Jurdan kept in the cells. I bet this is where he found them."

Nox's heart stalled as the memory of one of his first matches washed over him. They'd wanted him to kill then, too. All those voices in the stands had cried out, baying for blood. But he'd looked into that tortured creature's eyes and known that it was a prisoner—same as he was. And he'd resisted, using his boon to calm the gentle giant.

If only he'd been able to stop all his matches so easily... He stared at his hands as another call echoed through the trees.

Mariun's boots thudded into the sand beside him. "Hey." She peered at him, concern in her eyes. "You all right?"

Nox forced a smile. "Yeah. Let's find the locals, shall we?"

He glanced at Gwen. "*Are you guys going to be fine waiting on the beach?*" Probably smarter not to show up to the island village with mythical creatures in tow. They already had a wolf traveling with them, who was bound to be fearsome enough.

Gwen stretched out her wings, and he spotted Ari and Crys already posed in the same position. "*Yep. We'll soak up some sun while you're off exploring.*"

Conall waved them forward, nodding to a break in the trees. "There's a path over here that will lead us to the village."

Nox ducked onto the shaded trail. "Hey, did you know this is the same island that Aren stayed on when Lark was missing?"

"We know." Ereni peered around Kayda, whom she'd been helping navigate down the dirt-covered path. "Aren drew us a map before we left Dracwood. Said the people here were friendly, even though they spoke a different language. How did you figure it out?"

"The river down the middle." He shrugged. "If there's anything you've been dying to ask them when we arrive, I can translate."

Kayda chuckled, clearly thinking he was joking. "Can you now? How did you manage to learn their tongue?"

Nox grinned. "A bloodfeather. You're no stranger to those, are you, Sister?"

"Ah, I see." Kayda shuffled carefully down the trail. "Sorry I doubted you."

"I can help translate as well," Mariun offered.

"Thank you." Ereni flicked her long brown ponytail over her shoulder. "Though I'm not sure if it will matter. I didn't see any boats moored offshore. It doesn't look like Halynn returned."

Nox's stomach sank. If the Winter Witch sailed her boat back to the Northern Depths, then they'd have a long journey on their hands to question her.

Shadow gamboled ahead, his tongue lolling out the side of his mouth. Conall titled his head as he watched his bondmate lead the way. "Let's worry about that once it's confirmed. Maybe they're out for the day fishing."

"You're right, Brother," Kayda said brightly. "Besides, even if Halynn hasn't returned, the villagers might tell us something useful."

Silence fell over their party as they continued onward, and Nox passed the time picking out sounds in the forest. The ape's hooting calls were near constant, but beneath them, insects buzzed and birds warbled in a chorus that reminded him vaguely of the jungles back home.

Soon, he picked out the undeniable murmur of voices on the breeze. "I think we're almost there."

"You're right." Conall grinned, lifting his nose and breathing deeply. "And I smell bread."

"Are you joking?" Mariun sighed. "I'd kill for some bread right now"—her brow furrowed—"but I can't smell anything."

"Conall's been blessed with an enhanced sense of smell," he explained, nodding to Shadow. "It's a boon that wolves bring to their bondmates."

"Oh..." Mariun scratched the side of her head. "I see." Her nose wrinkled, and she fell back from Conall, looking uneasy as she lagged on the trail.

Nox slowed and kept pace with her until they were a few lengths behind the others. "What's wrong?" he whispered.

Her cheeks reddened. "It's just that I can't remember the last time I bathed..."

He tried to hold back the laughter brimming in his chest—and failed miserably.

"Hey! It wasn't by choice!" She shoved his side and scowled as he fought to control his snickers.

He rubbed his eyes and slung an arm around her shoulders. "I'm sure I don't smell like a spoolwood blossom, either."

She shot him a sidelong glance. "Now that you mention it..."

He roared with laughter again and squeezed her tightly to his side. Once his chuckles subsided, he said, "Well, guess the first thing I'm asking the villagers for is a washcloth."

"Maybe not the first..." She grinned crookedly. "I am dying for some of that bread."

Nox grinned at Mariun, and as their eyes met, lightness spread through his limbs and warmth pooled around his heart. *I'm so lucky I found her.*

Hours later, Nox's belly was full and he'd washed—scrubbing extra hard to appease the discerning noses in their party. The villagers had been very hospitable, lending them supplies, sharing their food—flatbread included—and offering them lodgings in the wooden cabins they'd built in the forest.

Nox smiled at the old man sitting next to him at the fire. "Thank you for all your help, Balun."

They'd spent the last few hours chatting, eating, and being gawked at by the villagers. The people dressed strangely, in furred tops and loincloths that left their abdomens bare, and they were endlessly curious. Nox answered what felt like a thousand questions for every one they asked.

"It's no trouble." The weathered skin crinkled around Balun's eyes when he smiled back. "I'm sorry about your friend, though. I wish we had better news to give you."

Kayda asked, "What did he say?"

Nox leaned close to Kayda and switched tongues. "He's apologizing again for not seeing Halynn after the storm."

He sighed. Frankly, he was getting a little sick of playing translator. But they wouldn't be here much longer. They'd decided to do another sweep with the dragons over the ocean above Thalassia. He'd insisted on it. He had to quell the nagging voice in his head screaming that they'd missed something.

Mariun met his gaze across the fire and flashed a tired grin. She'd spent as long chatting with the village women as he had with the elders.

Nox had been pleased to find Zoma among them. He wasn't sure if she'd find a home here, but the young woman seemed far happier here than where they'd met her—seeing to Jurdan's men's base desires on Jolit Isle.

He was about to stand and save Mariun from the endless giggling, when Gwen spoke in his mind, full of urgency. *"Hurry, Nox! Get back to the beach."*

"What is it?" Nox bolted up and waved at his friends.

"Sails on the horizon. They're too far away to make out who—hold on. I'll take a closer look."

"What is it?" Conall demanded as he stood.

"Sails. Gwen is flying closer."

Ereni's eyes lit up. "Is it Halynn?"

Nox's brow furrowed. "We'll know in a moment." He swapped to Thalassian. "Balun. There's a boat approaching the shore."

"Go on." The old man frantically shooed them away. "See if it's friend or foe."

Murmurs erupted from the villagers, and a few gathered their things hastily like they were prepared to run and hide. He didn't blame them. The people here were used to the raiding parties Jurdan occasionally sent out. When they'd arrived in the village that morning, the place had looked deserted, despite the fresh bread cooling by the fire. The people hadn't come out until someone recognized Conall and Ereni from their hiding place.

His boots slapped the worn dirt path through the trees. But before he'd taken more than a dozen steps, Gwen spoke again. *"It's the witch's ship. I recognize it."*

"Thanks, Gwen." Relief rushed through him, and his steps slowed. He spun around. "It's all right. It's her. Gwen says it's Halynn's ship."

Mariun turned to share the news with the villagers, and then they resumed their hike to the beach at a slower pace. Now that they knew they weren't about to face Jurdan's men, his nerves settled a little. Still, a thread of excitement wound around his chest.

What if Violet was on board? If his niece had returned from her journey safe and sound, that would be the best news he could ask for.

And even if Violet wasn't there, at least he could hope for more answers. To hear Conall and Ereni tell it, Halynn was privy to more than most. He wouldn't mind having a glimpse of his own future right about now.

By the time they arrived at the beach, the boat was fully visible, floating slowly closer to the coast. The massive-sailed vessel was far too large to park on the shore. He shaded his eyes from the midday sun, looking for Gwen's green wings in the sky. *"Can you drop us off on board?"* he asked.

At the same time, Ereni said, "We'll be waiting another hour for them to drop anchor and ferry ashore."

"Yes," Gwen answered. *"Back up so I can land."*

"No, we won't." Nox waved the others into the tree line. "Give Gwen some space to land. The dragons will fly us to them."

Conall grinned. "Genius." He turned to Shadow, who cocked his head before taking off into the trees. "Shadow will do a little hunting while we're talking so we can repay the villagers' hospitality."

"All right." He couldn't imagine the wolf enjoyed traveling by dragonback much. His lips tipped up, and he buried a chuckle.

Gwen spotted his face as she descended. "*What's so funny?*"

"*I just had the silliest image pop into my head—Flint flying on your back.*"

A light hiss echoed in his ears. "*Silly? Surely you mean majestic.*"

Nox rolled his eyes. "*And what about your fear of heights?*" Everyone who traveled in the Raimish jungles packed a hammock with them, since the best way to avoid the nocturnal predators was sleeping high in the trees.

"*You got over yours,*" Flint replied. "*I would've too.*"

Nox's stomach shook a little as he climbed atop Gwen. "*True...*" The first time he'd flown on Gwen had been nerve-wracking, and he still tried not to look down more than necessary, but he'd adapted swiftly when it had been the only way to save Mariun.

"*I'm sure you'd both look like heroes of legend.*" Gwen twisted her long neck and glared at him, sounding impatient. "*Come on. I've never seen a witch before.*"

Nox settled on Gwen's back and stretched out a hand to help Mariun up. Soon they were airborne, and within moments, they hovered above a gigantic ship with *Laumarle's Triumph* emblazoned on the side. The ship was built for hunting enormous ocean creatures in the Northern Depths, so the dragons had no problem finding space to land on deck. The boat scarcely even sank in the water with their weight.

A curly-haired blonde stood by the railing, her simple black dress swirling around her legs in the ocean breeze. "Good day." Her bright-blue eyes landed on Ereni. "Your daughter isn't here."

Nox flinched. How did she know exactly what they wanted to ask? He slid off Gwen's back and stretched out his arms to help Mariun down.

Ereni's voice cracked. "She's really gone, isn't she?"

Conall dragged her into his arms. "Vi will be fine. She's tough. You taught her well."

"I did find something of hers floating in the sea." Halynn's boots tapped loudly on the deck as she strode closer. "Follow me. I'll show you."

Nox's heart skipped a beat. Orry. It had to be. Perhaps he could convince Violet's bondmate to gift him another feather to replace the one he'd lost. After all, Jurdan was still out there. Once he'd licked his wounds, he'd be back, eager to recapture Mariun and settle the score. They'd need every advantage they could get before that happened.

She led the way to a door in the mid-deck. Nox cleared his throat, realizing Ereni and Conall were likely too distraught to make introductions. "You're Halynn, I presume? I'm—"

"Nox. Yes, I know." Halynn glanced at the beauty walking beside him. "And you're Mariun. It's lovely to meet you in the flesh."

A chill ran up his spine. Halynn possessed an ethereal allure that he'd have to be blind not to notice, but her instant familiarity was unsettling. They followed her below deck, and his nose twitched, the lingering aroma of fish doing nothing to calm his stomach. Lamplight lit the hall, a straight off-white corridor lined with doors on each side, most of them closed.

Halynn ushered them through an open doorway and Nox gasped. "Ryon?"

Ryon rested on a cot in the small chamber, unconscious, wearing a sickly pallor. His chest rose and fell softly beneath a thin sheet.

"What happened to him?" Mariun rushed into the room and sank onto the bed beside him. Even when her weight made the bed springs squeal and the surface sink, he remained sleeping. She covered her mouth with her hands. "Look... his hair."

Nox frowned and spun to Halynn. "Did you cut his hair?" His long dreadlocks were missing, replaced with a neatly trimmed style that was surprisingly even.

"No. He was like that when we fished him out of the sea as the battle was ending." Halynn marched to the closet and threw open the door. "And he was wearing this."

Ereni arrived at the tiny closet first, bringing Kayda along since their elbows were linked. She wasted no time grabbing the garb and lifting it for everyone to see. Kayda reached out, fingering the fabric with a furrowed brow. "I've never felt anything like this. What does it look like?"

Nox cleared his throat again. "It's brown and covered with pockets. The pants too." He shook his head. "I don't recognize it."

Conall rubbed his temples. "You found him—and him alone?"

Halynn nodded. "I'm afraid so. We hung back and scoured the waters to be sure."

Nox's stomach sank. What did that mean for Violet and Orry? Were they both lost... maybe even dead? He swept away the worrying thought, refusing to believe it.

"Has he woken?" Ereni asked.

"Not yet." Halynn stepped closer to the bed. "I thought it wise to let him rest. But now that you're here..." She pulled a small vial out of her skirt pocket.

"What's that?" Conall asked.

"Smelling salts." She bent beside Ryon's prone form, and something snapped loudly. Then she waved the salt below Ryon's nose.

Ryon jerked awake, his wild eyes scanning the room in a panic. "Wh-where am I? What's happening?" He grabbed the sheet, wrenching it up his bare chest. "Who..." Then his gaze landed on Nox, and his words flew out in a maddening rush. "Nox! Violet sent me back. I have to tell you how to defeat them. She figured it out!"

"Relax." Nox strode to the bed and grabbed Ryon's hand. "One thing at a time." Even as the words left Nox's lips, he sensed Ryon's strength flagging.

As his first burst of speech ended, Ryon fell back on the bed, his eyelids drooping and his breath labored. "Find the Hilfolk. Set them free." He grabbed Nox's sleeve. "That's how you'll defeat Jurdan. How you..." His eyes slid closed and his hand flopped bonelessly to the mattress. "H-how you destroy the... city."

"Rot and decay." Nox grabbed Ryon's shoulder and shook him. "Stay with us, man. Where is she? Where's Violet?"

It seemed his niece's name was enough to rouse Ryon again, though he was far from completely lucid. "Violet. She's s-stuck." His lashes twitched, but from the way they barely budged, he knew it wouldn't be long before Ryon fell asleep once more. "Orry... W-wish... She needs..."

Ryon fell silent, and no amount of shaking was enough to wake him. Nox thrust out a hand and snapped his fingers. "The salt. We need more. He has to explain."

Halynn stood stubbornly behind him with her arms crossed. "No. He can't handle it. Look at him."

Nox bit back a curse when he examined Ryon closely. Yes, he was unconscious again, but you could hardly tell by the way his chest heaved and his breath skittered out of his lungs.

He stood, his jaw clenched. "Did any of you have the slightest clue what he was talking about?"

Mariun shook her head, and Kayda's forehead creased deeply enough that she needn't confirm her confusion. But Conall and Ereni stared at each other, wearing shocked expressions. And Halynn leaned casually against the wall, a knowing glint in her eyes.

"What is it?" Nox walked to his half-brother's side. "Do you know what he meant?"

Conall nodded. "I think so. When Halynn met us off the coast of Magehaven, we dreamed together. Our shared vision was... strange. So strange that I thought it was a waste of time. But now..." He trailed off, blinking repeatedly like he wasn't sure if he could believe his own story.

Halynn continued, "We watched the tragic history of an ancient people play out before our eyes. Ages of their existence as they explored lands far beyond our world." She pushed off the wall. "I don't blame Conall for his doubts. Even I wasn't sure what to make of it. Until now."

Mariun pursed her lips. "I don't understand..."

"Hilfolk," Ereni blurted. "That's what he said, wasn't it?" She peered at Ryon's prone form and shuddered. "That's what the people in the vision were called too." She spun, facing Mariun. "I said I'd never seen a yellow aura before, but that wasn't entirely true. I'd seen it in my dreams. The Hilfolk had it too."

"You can't mean..." Mariun's hand rose, resting on her chest. "I'm one of them? But how?"

Ereni lifted a shoulder. "I don't know. Perhaps you descended from them. Or by some twist of fate, you gained their power by living in such close proximity to the last of their kind."

Mariun's brows dipped. "What are you talking about? I've spent my whole life in Thalassia. If there were people called Hilfolk living there, I'd know about it."

"No, you don't understand." Conall's voice softened. "They aren't alive... exactly."

"I'm lost," Nox admitted.

Conall explained, "From what I can gather, the Hilfolk possessed a greater understanding of magic than we do. The dream was... hard to parse, but I think at some point they used that magic to put their people into a type of sleep."

Ereni nodded. "I think it was like hibernation. They wanted to preserve their people until it was safe for them to wake."

"Hibernation?" Mariun asked. "What's that?"

"One of my bondmates had the same ability," Nox said. "Animals sometimes sleep far longer than normal to conserve their strength when their prey is sparse."

"All right..." Mariun gathered her long black hair to one side, her fingers tangling nervously in the silky strands. "But what does that have to do with me?"

"They're in there," Ereni stated firmly. "It's the only explanation that makes sense."

Conall's lips thinned. "The vision cut off before we saw what the Hilfolk had crafted with their magic to preserve their people. But I think Ereni is right. They must be in Thalassia somewhere. And if what Ryon said is true... then by setting them free, we can destroy Jurdan, too."

"We have to go back," Nox replied flatly as the second part of Ryon's warning rang in his ears. "Before the city falls, I need to find the feather I lost. If Orry truly is missing, it might be our only chance to wish Violet back."

"I agree." Kayda nodded curtly. "But this time, we need to be better prepared. We'll need more fighters and supplies. Lots more weapons as well. Along with a plan that ensures our people are protected."

His sister was apparently a good deal wiser than he'd been, rushing in with a plan that was foiled before he'd taken more than five steps inside the city. "I'm sure the dragons can help gather supplies."

"Yes." Kayda reached out blindly, and Ereni grabbed her hand. "We have a lot of work to do. Shall we meet onshore and get started?"

Conall cocked his head to Ryon. "What about him?"

Kayda replied, "Bring him if he's well enough to sail ashore. When he wakes again, we'll question him more."

They split up, and he got to work preparing Ryon for the trip ashore. As he pulled the unusual clothes out of the closet, a million questions flooded his mind.

Where did Ryon get these clothes?

Was Violet truly stuck on another world?

Would they be able to pull off yet another rescue—one much more complex than any they'd attempted so far?

He wasn't sure he'd like the answers... but he was determined to find them, no matter what they might be.

Not a Chance

V iolet sighed as she climbed the stairs out of the oracle's chambers. She'd taken to visiting frequently, as much to take her mind off Ryon's absence as to ask more questions.

A sinister thought took root in her mind. *Did I send him to his death? Is that why he hasn't wished me back yet?*

"Vi, there you are." Kai's deep voice made her flinch as she walked into the square. "Visiting the oracle... again?"

She nodded and stared at her boots. "Did you need me for something?"

Kai waved her over to Roc's side. "I do. We're making a run to the wilds this afternoon. I need your help strapping down supplies." He hopped on Roc's back and held a hand out expectantly, clearly wanting her to pass up the items he'd stacked nearby.

"Oh. Sorry, I didn't realize..." Her cheeks warmed, and she hurried over, pulling an oblong sack off the top of the pile. "What's this?" She huffed as she lifted it and handed it to him.

Kai grabbed the blazing thing one-handed without even breaking a sweat. "Overnight pack. Don't worry. I packed enough food for both of us."

"We're sleeping out in the wilds?" Her heart sped. She'd known it would happen eventually, but the thought of spending a night beyond the safety of the village conductor fields still sent a shiver down her spine.

"Maybe not. Will depend on how long it takes to dig through the wreckage."

"What wreckage?" she asked.

Kai's jaw stiffened, and she nearly apologized again for asking too many questions.

"It's at the site of a city that belonged to the ancients. No one is sure what happened, but the city was destroyed long ago. And since the ground there is prone to quakes, new wreckage is unearthed every so often. A scout spotted something out there the other day, so we're heading over to investigate."

Her brow furrowed. "I'm surprised the oracle doesn't know what happened."

He shrugged. "Guess it happened so long ago even she wasn't around."

"Oh." She hefted another bag up. This one, at least, she recognized as a folded tent. Some of the tension in her frame evaporated when she spotted a second tent in the pile. At least they weren't expected to share...

"Can I ask you something?" The scar on Kai's face twitched as he lifted a brow. "What do you talk about when you meet with her?"

"Who, the oracle?" She handed up a bedroll.

He nodded. "Most riders are happy enough to speak with her once, if at all."

She pursed her lips as she lifted another bedroll. "They aren't trying to discover a way to return to their homeworld."

Kai's lips turned down in a frown. "Huh. Has she been any help so far?"

Her heart sank at the reminder. "Not exactly. But she told me a lot about the rings. Did you know each one led to a single destination?"

He carefully strapped down the stacked supplies. "Did they?"

"Yep. Oh, and she told me how the dragons decided where to settle when they stopped traveling between worlds."

Kai glanced at her, and though his face stayed impassive, she sensed the curiosity lingering in his eyes. "Which was?"

She leaned against Roc's hide. "They split into groups and settled on three worlds. The first—I think, at least—was my homeworld. The oracle said that was where the peaceful dragons settled. At the time, there were only a few humans there, and the land was considered safe, with no big predators they'd need to worry about battling."

Kai grunted as he tugged the rope tight.

"And of course, some stayed here. The oracle said only the fiercest dragons chose to stay here. Those who boasted a great desire to fight for glory and honor."

"That sounds familiar." He chuckled as he slid off Roc's back and landed beside her. "Roc is always going on and on about honor and glory." He smiled fondly and patted the green-scaled dragon's hide. "What of the last world?"

She crossed her arms. "She didn't say much about that one. Only that it was largely unexplored and brimming with magic. Apparently that's where the adventurous dragons went."

"I see." Kai's brow furrowed. "I wonder why they picked only three to settle on?"

"I asked the same thing. Evidently those three were the best-suited for dragons. One was overrun with humans. Another was the home-world of the murkborn." She shuddered.

"But why—" Kai's words died on his lips as a piercing ring blared through the square.

"What's that?" Violet's heart raced.

Kai leaped up on Roc's back. "Manticore sighting. Come on." He leaned down and grasped her hand. "Duty calls."

Violet quickly strapped herself into her new spinning seat behind Kai. Demi had built a handful of the creations so far, and they'd doled them out to the defenders using a lottery system. Luckily, Violet was given first dibs, seeing as it was her idea.

She blew out a deep breath as she settled her quiver on her back and clasped the bow in her hands. She started facing backward. Even with the ability to spin forward, it made sense to have someone watching their back.

They lifted into the air with a few others and quickly settled in a V formation. Violet counted the pairs of wings. "Ten," she whispered under her breath. Tingles ran down her spine. They wouldn't send such a large group without an equally large force of manticores to deal with.

She wanted to ask Kai for more details, but wisely kept her mouth shut. He was bound to be busy communicating with Roc, who shared his orders with the other dragons in their group. She'd quickly learned not to interrupt him while they were in flight with others. As the leader, everyone relied on him, and the last thing he needed was his defender chattering in his ear.

The unending hum of the conductor fields cut off, and she tensed as they rose past their range. But before she spotted anything, Kai called over his shoulder. "False alarm. They're retreating." She spun to face him as he pointed ahead. She squinted, catching the tip of a barbed tail as it disappeared into the cloud cover.

Not for the first time, she wondered what was up there. Why did the manticores always come from above and retreat there as well? And what of the beauty she glimpsed on the rare occasions the clouds parted?

"Shouldn't we follow them?" she ventured.

"No." Kai fell silent, and when he spoke again a few moments later, he'd let the subject drop like she'd never mentioned it at all. "We're going ahead with our original plans. Look lively."

Violet sighed and swiveled back around. She'd never been to the wilds before, but she'd heard it was a long trip—thus the need for overnight supplies.

When they began their descent over an hour later, she was ready for a break. It was hard to remain vigilant for so long, but luckily, no monsters had dropped on them during the flight.

They flew low over a massive stretch of hills and valleys. At first, it was difficult to picture a city ever stood there. The wilds clearly had had time to retake the spot, but she glimpsed something unnatural inside a few of the larger hills as they drew closer. They touched down beside one such hillside that'd split down the middle, exposing the innards of a crumbled ancient building.

Violet stared in awe. Kai chuckled as he noticed her slack jaw when he smacked down on the ground. "Nothing like this back home?"

"Definitely not." She grasped the hand he offered and hopped off Roc. "What are we looking for here again?"

He tugged a long rod out of one of his pockets. "These, for one. Or anything else that might be useful."

Violet stared curiously at the strange item. "What is it?"

"Here." He passed it to her. "Be careful not to bend it." The stick looked stiff at first glance, but she quickly realized it was flexible, the hollow inside filled with a clear liquid. "It's a glow rod," Kai explained. "If you snap it and shake it, the liquid inside glows."

"Really?" She carefully handed it back. "How does it work?"

Kai shrugged. "No idea. They belonged to the ancients." He gestured to their surroundings. "All of this did. We make use of what we can scavenge, but no one truly understands how the relics work or how to recreate them."

"Interesting." Violet shifted her bow on her shoulder. "So, how can I help with the search?"

Kai led her closer to the wreckage. "We riders will sift through the wreckage. You hang back with the rest of the defenders and keep watch."

"Oh." Guess she wasn't in for much of a break after all. "Got it." She took a spot close to where Kai disappeared into the wreckage and tried not to look too bored while she waited for him and the other riders to finish their search.

Time passed slowly, but she kept a vigilant watch, aware that any slip could be deadly out here so far from civilization. Even so, she struggled to stay in the moment, especially when her mind wanted to linger over the worries she'd been so keen to bury.

When one of the other defenders wandered over for a chat, she was happy about the interruption, until she spotted who it was.

"Hi, Violet."

"Teek. Hey." She offered him a small smile and shifted, pretending great interest in the barren landscape.

He chuckled lightly. "So serious." He stopped at her elbow. "The riders won't care if you relax for a moment."

"What about the manticores?" She edged away from him. "Will they take it easy on me, too?"

He smirked and waved an arm around. "I don't see any, do you?"

She fell silent, hoping he'd take a hint when she failed to strike up a conversation.

"Are you heading out for drinks when we get back?"

No such luck. Violet groaned internally. "Yep. With Helka." Truthfully, they hadn't nailed down any firm plans.

Maybe she was being too quick to refuse. Teek might be perfectly nice deep down. He might even make some Lanwellian a decent husband. But that woman would never be her.

He leaned closer. "Do I need to wait for Helka to whelp her brat before you'll have a drink with me?"

Her eyes narrowed, and she made no effort to hide the disgust in her tone. "No. You'll have to wait a lot longer than that."

Teek drew back and shot her a shocked grin. "Really? Don't tell me you're holding out hope pretty boy will be back..."

Violet's chest ached at the reminder. That was exactly what she was doing... And who knew if her wait would ever be rewarded? No. She shoved aside the doubt and spun to face him.

"Flashes, Teek." Kai strode back from the ruins with his pockets stuffed and a loaded sack in his arms. "Can't you take a hint? She's not interested."

Teek backed away. "Oh... I see what's happening." He spat on the ground, narrowly missing Kai's boots. "Didn't think you were the type to take a third."

Kai barreled forward, not stopping until he reached Violet. By then, Teek had jogged a good distance away, out of earshot. "You all right?"

"Yeah. Thanks, but I could've handled him on my own."

"Sure." Kai rubbed the back of his neck. "Listen, I know things are different where you're from." He set the bag on the ground and huddled closer, lowering his voice. "If you want to make sure no one bothers you like that again, the solution is simple."

She cocked a brow. "What are you talking about?"

He sighed. "Take yourself out of the running."

"Huh?"

Kai's brow furrowed, and he looked pained all of a sudden. "No one will try to bed you if you're already sharing someone else's bed. Someone they respect."

She shook her head. "That's not happening."

He clasped a hand on her shoulder. "Just... think about it." He smiled. "You know, Teek is dumber than rocks, but he might be right about one thing."

"What's that?"

He lifted a brow. "You'd fit in as a third with Helka and me."

He couldn't be serious... Sure, she'd become close with Helka. And she'd even learned to tolerate Kai and his mercurial moods. But what he was asking... just no.

Violet crossed her arms. "You know how I feel about Ryon."

"I do. But I understand how these things work." He hefted the bag back into his arms. "I'm sure Helka would appreciate having another set of hands when the baby comes. You'd get to move out of the women's boarding house. And I wouldn't have to worry about chasing off every idiot who sets his sights on you. It'd only be temporary—until Ryon finds a way to bring you home."

"Sure..." She twisted her lips. "It's the whole bed-sharing thing I'm not interested in."

Kai barked out a laugh. "You think I want to lie with a scrawny thing like you?"

"Hey!" She shoved his shoulder—and of course, the bastard didn't budge. He only laughed harder, attracting the attention of a few of the riders returning from the wreckage. Violet scowled and her cheeks burned.

His chuckles finally subsided. "Don't look so insulted. You want nothing to do with me either, right?"

She rolled her eyes. He was right, of course. After what she and Ryon shared, nothing would ever compare. The thought of lying with someone else—even someone as handsome as Kai—made her skin crawl.

Kai started heading back to Roc's side. "At least we don't need to sleep out here tonight. Search went quicker than expected."

"That's good." As the words slipped off her lips, the dark clouds above parted, revealing a small glimpse of blue sky and sunshine. But just like every other time, the momentary bright spot disappeared swiftly, swallowed by the thick clouds around it. "Have you ever been up there?"

Kai stopped and turned to face her. "Where?"

"Above the clouds." She couldn't tamp down the curiosity burning inside her.

"I have."

"Will you show me?"

"Not a chance."

"Why not? It seems so... beautiful."

"I got this up there." He tilted his head and gestured to his scar. "It might be beautiful, but it's dangerous."

"So it's dangerous." She twisted her lips. "What if I'm not scared?"

He dumped the sack in her hands, then climbed onto Roc. "You should be."

Violet shuddered as that statement settled in her marrow. She had plenty to be frightened of here. And she suspected that whatever hid above the clouds would be the least of her worries.

Heroes

Heart pounding, Nox turned to the others as the stolen vessel docked within Thalassia. "Be ready. Masked were waiting for me last time."

Conall nocked an arrow. Shadow bared his teeth. Ereni unsheathed two knives, one for each hand. Mariun didn't reach for a blade, but with the magic she possessed, she hardly needed to.

She'd already proven her worth on this mission, turning what he thought would be the most difficult part—finding a way into the underwater city—into child's play. Her knowledge of Jurdan's schedule gave them an enormous advantage. They'd arrived just as one of the boats surfaced, releasing a few crows. After the dragons dispatched the birds, Kayda dropped them off and retreated to Halynn's boat, knowing her sight would be a hindrance below the sea.

Now it was up to them to slip inside and destroy the city. If they could sneak past the guards stationed at the entrance...

"How many masked were there when you snuck in?" Ereni asked.

"Too many." Nox shook his head. "At least a dozen, likely more. I thought I'd be able to breeze right in with Spider's mask, but they saw through my disguise instantly."

Mariun pursed her lips. "I'm not surprised. Jurdan was planning on you coming to save me. They were expecting you."

His stomach sank. "Guess we're about to find out if they're waiting for us now." It didn't seem too far-fetched to assume if Jurdan was using the dream elixir.

The vessel clanged loudly, and then a great *whoosh* filled his ears, which he knew signaled the water draining. Once the boat finally settled, Mariun whispered, "Ready?"

Nox's nerves kicked into high gear as the door swung open. They burst into the room, weapons raised.

"Where is everyone?" Conall asked.

Mariun shrugged as she circled the vessel and stared down the long rows of identical, oblong ships in the massive chamber. "Not here. Guess Jurdan wasn't expecting us after all."

"I don't know..." Ereni sheathed one of her knives. "He might still be up to something."

Nox couldn't help agreeing. It felt too easy. But they had a job to do. "Let's get this done."

Their boots echoed loudly in the chamber. Mariun strode to a bank of cabinets lined along the wall. "Oh no." She threw open the doors, one after the other. "They're empty."

They were planning to use the masked's clothing to sneak in. "Guess all our luck couldn't hold out," Nox said.

"It's fine." Conall patted Shadow's head. "Not like we could've hidden all of us. We'll have to take our chances."

They'd planned to tie a lead on Shadow and pass him off as a new addition to the ring if asked. Without the disguises, it hardly mattered. Just one more complication they weren't expecting.

"He's right." Mariun straightened. "Let's go for plan B."

Nox sheathed his knives. "Lead the way."

They followed Mariun into the hall with their weapons holstered. They'd prepared a second plan in the event they couldn't find the masked's clothing. The hope was, if they marched through the halls like they had every right to be there, no one would question them until it was too late. Mariun was Jurdan's daughter, after all. It was the main reason they'd decided not to return with a huge force of men. A few people walking calmly with the ruler's daughter wouldn't raise much suspicion. An entire army would definitely be cause for alarm.

Sure, word would spread. That was a given. But they had to try something...

Kayda had given them a few hours to sneak in and finish the job quietly. If they didn't report back by noon, the dragons would part the sea so the fighters on Halynn's boat could take the city by force.

Hopefully it wouldn't come to that. He wished he could check in with Gwen and learn what was happening outside, but like every other time, he'd lost touch with her as soon as he'd entered Thalassia.

With her head held high, Mariun led the way into the city. He swallowed thickly, half expecting a troop of masked to be waiting outside. Yet, it appeared they still had a few shreds of luck lingering. They exited into the brightly lit corridors that mimicked the outside, and except for a few commonfolk who stared at them with wide eyes, they didn't encounter anyone.

The plan appeared to be working, but it didn't take long for him to notice something strange. Nox cleared his throat and asked quietly, "Where are all the masked?"

Mariun shook her head. "No idea... It seems quieter than usual." They turned down another corridor and spotted a lone woman watering the plants in the hall. "Let me try asking."

"Wait—" Nox clenched his hand into a fist at his side when Mariun ignored him.

She strode to the woman and raised her voice, speaking in Thalassian, her tone thick with command. "Where is the closest masked? I need to find my father."

The woman lowered her dark eyes to the floor and cowered. "I-I don't know. F-forgive me."

"What do you mean, you don't know?" Mariun stopped in front of the woman. "Did you break your fast already?"

"Yes." She peeked up nervously before returning her gaze to the floor. "B-but you won't find the masked there. There weren't any this morn."

Mariun frowned and clasped a hand on the worker's shoulder. "Thank you. Return to work." She jerked her head and headed for the far end of the corridor. Once they turned down a new hall, she lowered her voice and switched tongues. "I don't like this. Masked are always there at meals, keeping the commoners in line..."

"What do you think is happening?" Ereni's brow furrowed.

Nox shrugged. "Who cares? That just makes our task easier."

Conall suggested, "Maybe they're on the surface, preparing to attack."

Mariun halted. "Wait... If the masked aren't even here, then maybe we don't need to destroy the city. Think of all the people."

Before they left, Nox had hardened his heart to the casualties they needed to inflict. It seemed a fair price to pay to take out Jurdan once and for all. After watching the bloodlust in these people's eyes when he'd battled in the ring, he wasn't too sorry about it.

"We decided it had to be done," Nox reminded her.

Mariun twisted her hands together. "I remember. But think of all the innocent lives that will be lost. All the children."

A little boy's face flashed in his mind. It wasn't so long ago he couldn't even bring himself to kick a child in the face with a ball. Had all the killing made him so jaded that he was prepared to sentence that boy to death? "No. You're right." He rolled his neck. "What do you suggest we do?"

Some of the stiffness in Mariun's posture vanished. "I'll spread the word for everyone to meet us in the ship room. If we send them up to the surface, we can save them."

"All right." Nox sighed. "We'll have to split up. What about the animals and the men in the cells?"

Mariun twisted her lips. "The prisoners can come with us. But the animals... I don't think we'll have time to move them safely."

A pang of regret jabbed him square in the chest. "You're probably right."

He didn't like it. Fact was, those animals were more innocent than the people who lived here. But they were starved to the point of madness. It would take planning and a massive amount of manpower to return them to their homes safely—and they couldn't handle that right now. Especially not if Jurdan was out there, readying an attack. At least if they wrecked the city, the fighting would stop. As much as he longed to save the animals trapped here now, he'd have to settle for saving the ones destined to be snatched from their homes in the future.

"I'll release the prisoners." He had to hope that some guards were still down there. Then maybe he'd find the idiot who stole his feather. Or at the very least, someone to question so he could track down his room and search his belongings. He glanced at Mariun. "You spread the word to the people." He turned to the others. "Do you think you three can find the Hilfolk?"

Ereni grinned. "That's what we're here for." Her smile fell. "The way Jurdan is using them for his own gain is sickening. We'll do whatever it takes to set them free."

Conall grabbed her hand. "She's right. Some lines should never be crossed."

Nox shifted uneasily. "But where are they? We don't have time to search the entire city."

"I know where you should look first." Mariun pointed down the hall. "If you follow this corridor until it dead-ends, you'll be close to the city center. There was one room there Jurdan never allowed me to enter."

"Are you sure that's where they'll be?" Nox asked.

Mariun shook her head. "No. But I got a peek inside once. There were these tubes filled with liquid that gave me the creeps."

Ereni gasped. "Of course! We hid in there when we helped Nox escape. I thought at the time it was just part of the city's glow... Those tubes glowed yellow, too. I think she's right." She covered her mouth with a hand. "The Hilfolk were in there."

Conall nodded sharply. "If that's the case, then we'll find it. Shadow can sniff out anywhere we've already been."

"All right." Nox clasped his brother's shoulder. "Then we'll all meet where we came in and escape this place before it's destroyed."

"Sounds like a plan." Conall, Ereni, and Shadow took off without delay, an eager bounce in their gait.

He stepped close to Mariun before she split off. "Are you sure you're up for this?" His heart sped, and he nearly insisted on going with her—prisoners be damned. If not for the possibility of finding the lost feather, he might have. "I can't believe I'm letting you out of my sight when I just found you."

She planted her hands on her hips. "Letting me?" She lifted a brow. "I can handle myself. And I refuse to be—"

"I'm sorry." Nox cringed, belatedly realizing how terrible that sounded. She'd just escaped a man who'd kept her sealed away from the world. And he knew exactly how it felt to be locked up. He'd never cage her like that. "I swear, I trust you to take care of yourself. I only meant"—he pulled her close, resting his forehead on hers—"I don't want to lose you again."

"Never." She rose on her tiptoes and planted a peck on his lips. "You found me. I'll find you too. Promise."

With that, she twirled on her heel and darted off. Nox sighed and headed for the prison level, filling in Flint while he walked. It didn't take him long to find it. Soon the stench of excrement and the pitiful moans of men and animals in pain rose to greet him.

With his heart pumping furiously, he slowly eased the door open.

Flint spoke up. *"Careful. There's bound to be masked guards stationed at each end of the hall."*

Nox replied, *"I know. I'll dispatch them quickly but leave one alive for questioning."*

Except this time, there were no guards. The skin on his arms prickled as he shuffled down the corridor.

"Nox?" A familiar voice rose from one of the cells. "That you?"

He whipped around, frowning when he spotted the voice's owner. "Iggy."

"You've gotta help us!" A pair of scabby hands closed around the cell bars. Iggy's twin-braided beard wobbled on his chin, and his dark eyes flitted around nervously before settling on him, full of terror. "No one came to feed us today—or yesterday. There hasn't been a peep from the guards for ages." His voice faltered. "I-I think they've abandoned us. They're gonna leave us to starve to death."

He shook his head and nearly left the blabbermouth to his fate. But then his gaze caught on the scared-looking men huddled in the cell behind him. "You're right. The guards are gone."

As the words escaped his lips, his stomach sank. If that were the case for the whole level, then his plan to find his lost feather might be doomed.

"Gone?" Iggy's Adam's apple bobbed, and tears filled his eyes.

"Don't worry. I won't let you rot." Nox paused. "Even if you deserve it."

Iggy's face brightened. "You won't? Oh, bless you! I knew we would be friends."

"Hardly." Nox scoffed as he scanned the hall for the keys the guards used to lock the cells. "I just don't want to be responsible for the lot of you drowning when we sink this city."

Iggy's eyes bulged. "You're going to do what?"

He snagged the keys off a hook on the far wall. "Truth be told, I'm not sure if it will sink. Maybe it will explode." He shrugged as he jingled the keys in his hand. "But either way, this city won't be around much longer."

"Can't say I'm sorry to hear that... as long as we aren't going down with it."

Nox chuckled humorlessly. "Always looking out for yourself, aren't you, Iggy?"

Iggy lowered his head. "Can't fault a man for wanting to live, can you?"

Nox raised his voice as he slid the key into the cage's lock. "You need to head up the stairwell and find the exit. By now, all the city folk will be heading there too. There are vessels inside that can take you safely to the surface." He threw open the door and waved for the men to depart. "Go! Hurry! There's no time to waste."

Iggy patted his shoulder as he stepped into the hall. Nox drew in a deep breath, fighting the urge to slap the delighted smile off the old man's face. "Thank you, Nox. You don't realize how much this means to me. I thought I'd die in that cell."

As much as he wanted to say something cutting, he couldn't bring himself to. Not after he'd just sworn he'd never allow Mariun to be caged. These men didn't deserve that fate, either. Even if their crimes were real and not invented like the ones that had landed him in the cell, they'd already suffered plenty for their crimes by being forced to perform in the ring.

A haunting wail pierced the quiet. His stomach clenched, and he wished he could free them, too.

Iggy halted and carefully scanned Nox's face. "You always had a soft spot for the beasties, haven't you?" A massive smile spread across his face. "And I might have the perfect way to pay you back..."

Nox emerged into the upper halls with a spring in his step. He clasped Iggy's shoulder and offered him a tight smile. "I appreciate what you did back there."

"You might not if you hang around here much longer." Iggy met his eyes as they hurried down the corridor. "The ring won't hold them forever." A piercing howl split the air, as if to punctuate the old Jorian's words.

Before they'd left the prison level, Iggy had showed Nox a switch that opened a tunnel the guards used to haul the unconscious animals up to the ring. Of course, he couldn't resist using it and opening all the animals' cage doors. He might not be able to transport them to safety like he wanted, but at least now they wouldn't die locked up like criminals.

They might even have a chance to swim to safety when Thalassia fell—if they didn't kill each other first. He cringed as he pictured the battle happening in the ring right now. Put all those starved animals together, and there was bound to be some bloodshed. A pang of regret struck him that he shoved aside. It couldn't be helped. At least they were free...

Another howl reached his ears, and Nox froze. "Wait... that's not coming from the ring." He spun, sprinting down the hall toward the center of the ship.

"Nox!" Iggy called out behind him. "You're going the wrong way!"

Nox ignored him, racing toward the animal's cries. It wasn't just any animal... It was a wolf. And from the pitiful sound of its whine, it was injured.

Shadow... It had to be. None of the animals from the prison level would've had the time to escape the ring and make it this far inside the city.

His stomach dropped. If Shadow was injured, then what about Conall and Ereni? Were they all hurt? He had to find them—fast. Luckily, the stairwell he'd climbed let him out close to Thalassia's center. He wasn't even short of breath by the time he found them.

"Rot and decay." Nox crouched at Shadow's side. The huge gray wolf panted on the ground and whimpered miserably. His fur was matted with blood, and a knife slash wept fresh blood down his neck.

Nox's hands trembled as he tore a strip of cloth from his shirt and wound it around Shadow's cheek. That cut seemed shallow, at least, but from the pain in his golden eyes, it was clear the single wound wasn't his only injury. "What happened?" he muttered.

He sensed a presence approaching and lifted his head in time to see Conall perched in the doorway with one of the masked's dart tubes pressed to his lips.

Nox jolted as a dart flew, impaling Shadow in the side. He blinked repeatedly, trying to make sense of what he'd witnessed. "Y-you... What did you do that for?" He gaped at his brother. Why would one bondmate turn on another? They wouldn't, unless... Nox scrambled away, certain another dart was about to hit him. The only reason Conall would turn on Shadow was if his brother was under the control of that vile creature—

But then Conall dropped the dart tube and fell to his knees at Shadow's side. "I'm sorry, brother," he whispered with tears running down his cheeks. He cradled Shadow's head on his lap as the wolf's eyelids fluttered. "I need you to protect Violet. I'll talk to you soon."

Shadow's breathing settled and his eyes closed. Conall petted Shadow once more, then lifted his tear-stained face. "Take him and go."

Nox shook his head. "What? I don't understand..."

"You have to." Conall placed Shadow's head gently on the ground and stood. "It's the only way."

Nox followed Conall through the doorway. He bit back a gasp at the scene he found within. Dozens of masked lay dead, scattered around the chamber with liquid-filled tubes.

Then his gaze found Ereni, and he did gasp. "N-no." He rushed to her and kneeled beside her. She held a bloodstained cloth to her gut. Red dripped down her legs and pooled beneath her. "We need to get her out of here. I'll use Gwen's boon."

"It's no use." Ereni's voice was firm despite the pallor in her cheeks. "I'll bleed out before I make it to the surface."

Conall lowered his head. "They were hiding when we got here. There were so many."

Nox's stomach churned. "I should've come with you. Mariun too."

"Don't blame yourself, Brother." Conall clasped his shoulder. "I smelled their sweat before I opened the door. We could've gone back for you. We could've waited. It's not important now."

Ereni coughed. "Wouldn't have mattered, anyway." She kicked a downed masked with her boot. "One was alive long enough to talk. He pleaded for his life in our tongue. Begged us not to smash the glass. Said the city would break apart as soon as we did... before we could escape."

Conall squeezed his shoulder. "Someone was always going to need to stay behind."

"No." Nox met Conall's kind hazel eyes. "I'll do it. I can swim free. You take Ereni and Shadow, and—"

"Brother." Conall's grip turned crushing. "Ereni and I are staying. We both swore we'd finish this. We've been fighting this evil our whole lives." His lips wobbled as he looked at his bleeding wife before he forced his mouth into a grim line. He lowered his voice. "She's the love of my life. You understand?"

A few weeks ago, he would have no clue what Conall was hinting at. But now he knew all too well. If their roles were reversed and Mariun was about to bleed out in a strange place, he wouldn't want to leave her either.

Nox's heart shattered as he met his brother's gaze and nodded.

"Take Shadow. His injuries can be healed." Conall drew in a deep breath through his nose. "And promise me that when you find Violet, you'll look out for her. Bring Shadow to her so part of me can be with her through him." His eyes flooded with tears again. "Tell her we love her. We'll always love her."

Ereni chimed in. "And we're proud of her. So damn proud..." Her throat was thick with emotion.

"I will." Nox blinked back tears of his own. "I promise."

Conall pushed him weakly toward the door. "Go. We'll give you a head start. Get out of here."

Nox turned, but before he walked out the door, he spun back and clasped Conall in a tight hug. "You've always been my hero, big brother," he whispered in his ear.

As Conall's arms closed around him, the tears he'd been holding back finally fell. He meant every word. Sure, he'd spent a lot of time feeling jealous of his older siblings when he first met them. He'd yearned to prove that he was just as important as they were. To leave his own mark on the world—like his big brother already had.

He never imagined that he'd lead his hero brother to his death... Regret washed over him, so dark and deep he worried it might drown him where he stood.

Conall pulled back and stared into his eyes. "You're the real hero, little brother." He clasped his cheek and smiled sadly. "Go prove to the world what I already know."

Nox sent one last wobbly smile to Ereni and strode through the doorway.

Determination fueling him, he scrubbed his cheeks with his sleeve and stared at the massive gray wolf passed out in the hall. He refused to let Conall down, but how was he supposed to carry Shadow that far? It wasn't like he had superhuman strength as one of his boons...

He almost returned to ask Conall for advice, when a clatter rose down the hall. Nox tensed, and his hand fell to his knife hilt.

"Iggy?" He squinted as the old man hustled closer, dragging a wheelbarrow behind him. Nox jogged to him and helped roll it to Shadow.

"I caught up to you. Heard you and your brother talking." Iggy sniffled. "What I wouldn't give to see my brother one last time... Thought you could use some more help."

Nox couldn't quite dredge up a smile, but he managed a quick, "Thanks." Then he got to work, dragging Shadow's heavy weight into the wheelbarrow.

One way or another, he'd prove his brother's last words true. Conall and Ereni's sacrifice wouldn't be in vain.

Special

V iolet's knuckles stung as she pounded on the hard wooden
door. She stared at the pink skin on the back of her hand as
shuffling footsteps inched closer. For a moment, she wished she'd
knocked harder. Then maybe the sting in her fist would detract from
the pain piercing her heart.

Helka cleared her throat. "Violet? Shouldn't you be training?"

Sliding sideways to avoid Helka's huge belly, she slipped past her.
The cheery interior of Helka and Kai's cabin usually brought a smile
to her face—Helka had eclectic tastes and stacked unusual knick-
knacks over every surface. Yet today, even her friend's quirky design
sense couldn't lighten her mood. "I just came from the oracle," she
announced grimly.

Helka frowned and waddled past her. "Sounds like I'll want to be
sitting down for this." She sank into a worn wicker rocking chair with
a massive sigh.

Violet wrung her hands. "She told me something awful, Helka. In
hindsight, it makes a lot of sense. If I'd only known before I sent him

away…" Her voice wavered, and she fought the urge to cry. "Blazes, what did I do?"

Helka snagged her arm as she paced in front of the rocker. "Slow down." She jerked Violet's arm and nodded to the couch across from her. "Sit. Tell me from the beginning. What did you ask the oracle?"

She sat but didn't lean back. She perched on the cushion's edge while worrying her lip between her teeth. "I didn't even mean to ask it. I was just so frustrated… We were sitting there, and the oracle was droning on about nothing in particular, when a thought struck me. I blurted it out under my breath. And she heard me. I said… What in the world is taking him so long to wish me back?"

"And she… answered you?"

Violet's eyelids pinched closed, and a wave of devastation washed over her again. "She said I'd wager that's because it's only been a few days for him."

Helka's eyes bulged. "What?"

"That's exactly what I said." She shook her head. "She told me that time doesn't always pass at the same rate on different worlds. It's one of the first things the dragons discovered when they began their travels."

"Oh no…" Helka flattened a palm to her chest. "Violet, I'm so sorry."

She blinked furiously, fighting to maintain her composure. "How long will I have to wait? It's already been months. Will I age years? Will he even wish me back before I…" Her throat tightened, and she couldn't bear to finish the sentence.

If months here truly only equaled days on her world, she might never see her home again. Especially if it took Ryon years to earn a feather. What would a year on her world equal here? A decade? A century?

"Come here. You look like you need a hug." Helka huffed, struggling to pull herself out of the rocker.

Violet waved. "No. Don't get up. I'll be all right."

"Nonsense." Helka shifted again, determination on her face, but then her hand shot to her middle and she gasped.

"Helka!" Violet jerked forward, landing at her friend's side as she settled back in the rocker with a hiss, rubbing her belly.

"It's nothing." Helka grimaced. "The midwife said I'll have some pains here and there between now and the birth. Nothing to worry over."

"Are you sure?" Violet backed away. "Can I grab you anything? Some water?"

"Do you mind?" Helka chuckled softly as Violet headed into the kitchen. "You've seen what happens when I try to get up."

Violet pulled a pitcher off the table and grabbed a mug out of the cabinet. "Are you sure I shouldn't fetch the midwife?"

"No. Don't bother. I've had these pains off and on for days now. She said it was to be expected."

Her cheery voice was clearly meant to set her at ease, but Violet couldn't escape the sinking sensation dragging her down. As the water trickled into Helka's mug, she called on her boon.

The bright melody of her friend's heartsong rose in her mind almost instantly. Helka's heartsong was usually guaranteed to make her smile. But today a single note rose above all the rest, strumming so loudly it made her gasp.

Water splashed her fingers. Violet cut off the song. Her fingers trembled as she mopped up the puddle on the table.

That note. She'd heard it once before. Back then, she'd brushed it aside, not knowing what to make of it—even though the sound had chilled her bones. She couldn't brush it off any longer. Before, it had been a quiet curiosity playing in the background. A mere footnote woven within the sweet melody of her dear friend's song. Just now it had been cacophonous. Impossible to ignore.

She left the kitchen, forcing her hands not to wobble as she carried the mug.

Helka glanced up with a smile. "Thanks." As she examined Violet's expression, her smile fell. "Oh, don't fret. I'm sure Ryon will find the feather he needs swiftly."

Violet shook her head. "No... It's not that." She returned to the sofa and twisted her hands in her lap. "You remember what I told you about my boon?"

Helka sipped from her mug. "Yes. It's how you knew I was pregnant, right?"

"It is..." After months of friendship, there wasn't much she hadn't shared with Helka—including how her boon worked. "This is hard to say, but I heard something else in your song, Helka. Something... off."

"Off?" Helka's brow furrowed. "What do you mean?"

"I'm not entirely sure, but it gave me chills. I-I don't know what to make of it, but I had to say something. To warn you." A tiny weight lifted from her shoulders with the confession. Maybe nothing would come of it. Maybe she was wrong. But she couldn't rest easy keeping the information to herself.

Helka sipped her water again and rocked lazily. "Have you heard this sound before?"

"Just once."

"And what happened after?"

Violet's brows pinched together. "Nothing of note. But it wasn't this loud before." She rubbed her temples. "It was so loud, Helka. Practically deafening."

Helka stopped rocking. "Hm. Well, if I promise to be extra careful, will that make you feel better?" She tilted her head and sent her a smile.

She let out a big sigh. Was Helka even taking this seriously? "I suppose..." It wasn't like she knew what to expect. It was just a feeling. A terrible one that spread through her veins and made her sick to her stomach.

"Well, then. That's what I'll do." Helka's smile brightened, and she resumed rocking.

Violet opened her mouth, yet before she convinced her friend any further, an alarm pealed, ringing through the village so loudly she flinched.

Helka waved a hand. "Don't mind me. I'm used to being abandoned when the riders' alarm goes off."

"Be back later." Violet leaped off the couch and raced for the door. As her boots slapped the cobbles, the anxiety for her friend morphed, turning into fears for the battle to come.

By now, she'd been in dozens of air skirmishes. They were adamant about protecting the skies around the village. Without the dragons to protect the city, they'd be forced to remain underground for fear of attack.

Even the conductor field couldn't be counted on to keep them safe at all times. It was another relic of the ancients. When the scavenged parts occasionally wore out, beasts were known to swoop down and tear unsuspecting folk off the ground.

She arrived at the square just as Kai mounted Roc. He waved her over, pointing at the weapon rack. "Your bow! Hurry."

Breath sawed out of her lungs. She snagged her weapon and vaulted atop Roc as dragons began lifting off the ground.

"You're late," Kai barked. "Where were you?"

Violet gritted her teeth. "I'm here, aren't I?"

"Barely." Kai twisted around, his knuckles white on the ropes. When his eyes glazed, she bit back another retort.

It didn't matter. Not now. She had a job to do.

A blast of wind blew her short fringe across her forehead. This was what she needed. A chance to escape the fear for her friend. To rage at fate for sending her to this awful world and tearing her away from the man she loved.

"Ready?" Kai yelled as the conductors cut off. "They're close."

She smiled and nocked an arrow. "Good. Let them come."

Roc ascended as the first set of wings breached the dark skies. She met the inhuman eyes of the first manticore as her arrow clipped the beast's thigh.

A pained shriek drew more. She spied the excitement glimmering in their bloodthirsty gazes as they poured down from the clouds en masse. She sank another arrow into a wing, and a third in a shoulder.

Kai yelled, "Go for the kill!"

Roc spun, scorching one of the monsters she'd wounded.

Violet sucked in a breath. He was right. She'd been playing with them, eager to inflict pain on the beasts so it lessened the devastation tainting her soul. But this wasn't her fight alone.

She swiveled in her seat, landing a hit in the next manticore's eye.

The dying beast shrieked, spinning in midair and flicking its tail. Her stomach dropped as she ducked, dodging the venomous spines headed her way. Time seemed to slow as the projectiles flew, spread out in a wave.

Her heart stopped. She couldn't dodge them all. She—

Roc dove, plummeting so fast she grew queasy. The spines whizzed past, one so close to her ear the ominous buzz sent tingles down her spine.

"Get your head on straight!" Kai shouted.

Violet shook off her shock as more wings dropped from the clouds. A sudden thought struck, ringing through her head and seeping into her marrow.

This was life or death. Playtime was over. She didn't have the luxury any longer. She needed to survive and not only for a few more days. For as long as it took. Years. Decades.

Roc reversed course with a few big flaps of his wings. Kai glanced back over his shoulder. "Get ready."

She met his eyes as she nocked a new arrow. "I am."

Violet took another swig from her mug in the makeshift camp out in the wilds. The battle had lasted long into the evening. They'd spent all of it leading the beasts away from Lanwell. When nightfall arrived, the monsters stopped coming, but they were too far from home to make it back without resting the dragons.

She'd hardly spoken to Kai while setting up her tent beside his. And she couldn't muster the same enthusiasm as the other riders while they recounted their successes that afternoon. She'd joined them by a campfire for a meal and celebratory drink, though she wasn't exactly in the mood for celebrating.

Sure, they'd chased off the beasts. None of them had been seriously injured or killed. But the worries she'd bottled up earlier refused to stay buried. The oracle's morose revelations kept filling her mind. Was this the price she had to pay for making that wish?

A warm arm slung around her shoulders. Violet flinched.

"Hey, did you all see what happened just before dark?" Teek declared loudly. He squeezed her shoulder roughly. "Ya know, when Vi saved our dear leader from getting his head torn off?"

Violet's cheeks warmed as she shrugged his arm off. "That's what I'm here for." She'd gotten her head back in the fight like Kai had demanded. The moment Teek brought up wasn't the only time she'd saved her bonded from being harmed.

"Pfft." Teek waved lazily. "Listen to this one... No big deal, was it?" He smirked and leaned over with a bottle of her favorite brew. "I saw that shot. You moved faster than I could blink. That was some real talent."

"Thanks." Violet held out her cup and let him refill it.

She shifted in place, looking for Kai. He'd scarfed down his meal and disappeared without saying much. She chugged from her cup, enjoying the way her mouth puckered.

"Can you teach me to shoot like that?" Teek swigged from his own mug. "I could use some work on my timing."

She had to admit, it was nice to be appreciated for a change. She shrugged. "Sure. I might have a trick or two I can show you."

Tora cleared her throat when Teek lifted the bottle to Violet's cup again. "Take it easy on that stuff. We have a long flight back tomorrow. You don't want to make it with a sour stomach."

"You're probably right." She pulled her mug back.

Teek scowled and topped off his own cup. "More for me, then." His scowl shifted to a playful smile.

Tora stood and brushed off her pants. "I'm heading to my tent. See you tomorrow."

Violet nodded goodbye. Most of the older riders had already settled down to rest. A handful of the newer recruits lingered by the fire.

She knew she should probably sleep too, but she couldn't stand the thought of being left alone with her thoughts. Instead, she sat and stared at the fire, letting the chatter of the other riders spread around her like a balm. She continued to sip from her mug, blankly staring at the dancing flames. It wasn't until the voices faded that she blinked and rose on wobbly legs.

"Hey."

She staggered sideways. "Oh, Teek. I didn't realize anyone was still awake."

"Just finishing my last drink." He knocked the empty bottle over as he shuffled around the fire to her side. "I'll walk you to your tent."

She shook her head, wincing when the action made her woozy. "No. I'm fine."

"Really?" He chuckled. "Why can't you walk straight, then?"

"You're one to talk. More for me, wasn't that what you said?" She glared at him, frowning when she watched him stroll along without a single wobble. "Wh—How?"

He sniggered. "You never asked where your favorite drink came from, did you?"

"What's that got to do with anything?" She wobbled toward her tent.

Teek followed her with a smile. "My uncle brews it. I've been sneaking that stuff since I was a little lad. Built up quite the tolerance."

"Well, good for you." She giggled. What an odd boast.

"I can get you as much as you want, you know." He waggled his brows.

She hiccupped. "Oh. That's nice." She brushed past him, wanting nothing more than to lie down. She reached her tent and bent to open it, losing her center of gravity.

"Hey, easy now." He caught her arm. "Let me help you." He steadied her and pulled open the flap.

The world spun as the dizziness of too much drink compounded with her lingering emotions. "Thanks. I-I'm all right. Just need to sleep." She sniffled, fighting the urge to cry.

"Sure." His brow furrowed. "Hey? What's wrong?"

She sat heavily on her bedroll. "Nothing. Just go." Her voice choked up, and the despair she'd been tamping down all night rose with a vengeance.

"Come on, Vi. You can't tell me to leave when you're crying." He sat beside her, speaking so tenderly it made everything that much worse.

Tears spilled down her cheeks. As hopelessness washed over her, she reached out, seeking solace in Teek's arms. He held her while she wept, and even though they were the wrong arms—the wrong man—she took the comfort he offered, sinking into his embrace.

Teek rubbed her back with long, soothing strokes. Violet closed her eyes. It had been months since anyone had held her. Since Ryon had left. She had no idea how long it would be before they met again. Still, she knew it was selfish of her to accept Teek's care, but at the moment, she couldn't bring herself to refuse it.

As she started to settle down, the mood in her tent shifted. Teek's soothing strokes wandered lower. She pulled away instantly. "I-I think you should go now, Teek."

He licked his lips. "I don't want to leave." His face smashed into hers.

Violet froze. She sat there like a stone while his vile mouth moved across her lips. A terrible thought rose to plague her. What if this was what she needed to get home faster? If she allowed it to happen... If she *suffered* through it... could she return to the arms of the man she loved?

No. Her mind might be thick with drink, and she certainly felt lower than she'd ever had, but she didn't want this. She didn't want *him*, and she never would.

"Let me go." She pushed Teek off and scrambled through the tent flap. "I'm sorry. I don't want this, Teek. You need to leave."

She kept her voice low, not wanting to disrupt the sleeping camp. Even if she'd shouted, she might not have attracted much attention. Kai's tent was close by, but most of the other riders were far enough away they might not wake.

Teek followed her into the dark night. "You're kidding... right?"

"No." She shook her head and thrust out an arm. "Go." Out of the corner of her eye, she spotted Roc's head lift from the spot where he rested between Kai's tent and hers.

Teek stalked toward her and hissed, "You kissed me and now you want to play innocent?"

Violet crossed her arms. "I'm not playing at anything."

"Flashes, Vi." His hands clenched into fists. "I thought we were getting along. What did I do wrong?" The touch of hurt in his voice sliced through her chest.

"Nothing." She took a step back to her tent. "Goodnig—"

He snagged her wrist and tugged, slamming her against his hard chest. Then his lips collided with hers again.

She shoved at his chest, feeling sick. How did she ever think she could suffer through this? It was worse now, with his hard grip unyielding. One hand clamped around her wrist so tightly she felt it in her bones. An arm banded around her back, pressing her tightly against him. If she didn't do something fast, he would drag her back into that tent with no one the wiser.

Kai's warning about the wilds flashed in her mind, and panic clawed at her belly. *No one bats an eye if you keep what you kill. Or if you use what you claim.*

Was that what was happening? If she screamed, would anyone help her?

She jerked and pushed, desperate to shove him off. But Teek was far stronger. He pressed his mouth on hers so firmly she tasted blood. You couldn't even call it a kiss any longer. It was all bite, and though his lips on hers stopped her from crying out, they did nothing to disguise the sounds of distress rising from deep in her chest.

And yet, her panic only grew, rising to swamp her. If she couldn't even break free from his kiss, what chance did she have?

Suddenly, the horrid pressure lifted from her face, and Teek's arms unclamped from her body. Violet gasped and fell to the ground.

Snap.

Eyes widening, she stared at Teek's head dangling limply off his neck. A shadowy form caught his body before it thumped against the dirt. Green wings flapped, sending a tremendous gust of wind into her face. Violet blinked, her heart hammering as her cloudy mind tried to come to terms with what she just witnessed.

Then Teek was gone, and Kai kneeled beside her, scowling. He scanned her from head to toe before whispering, "Do you trust me, Violet?"

"Wh-what?" She began to stand up, but Kai's hand clamped on her shoulder, holding her down in the dirt.

"Scream," he demanded.

Her brow furrowed. "Wh—"

"Now." His tone hardened. "Like you're afraid for your life. Keep it up until you wake everyone. Do it."

Her muddled mind couldn't grasp why that was necessary. But when she met his eyes in the dying campfire light, she opened her mouth and unleashed a bloodcurdling scream.

It didn't take long for the others to shuffle out of their tents. When they arrived, Kai was pacing in front of her, his hands tugging at his hair.

"What's wrong?" Tora fell beside Violet and shook her shoulder, stopping her screams.

Kai blurted, "Roc saw it happen. A manticore snatched Teek off the ground."

"A manticore?" Tora's brow pinched. "At this hour?"

Violet's stomach churned. They all knew how rare it was for a manticore to attack at night. It was a poor excuse. But what else was Kai meant to say?

"I saw it," she forced out. "He was walking me back to my tent, and... and it came out of nowhere. I screamed..."

"Roc flew after them." Kai shook his head. "Teek's gone. His neck snapped."

Well, that much was true...

Tora helped Violet to her feet. "All right." Her eyes went cloudy. "The dragons will double their guard. We should all get under cover." She turned to the crowd of riders who had gathered and shooed them back to their tents.

Kai cocked his head at Violet and pulled back the flap on his tent. "Come on. You're with me tonight."

She hung her head and climbed inside without complaint. Kai disappeared, only to return with her bedroll a moment later.

"Thank you," she whispered into the dark once they'd both lain down.

"That will be the last rider I kill because of you." Kai shifted, rolling away from her. "I'm done asking, Vi. You're moving in with me and Helka when we get back."

Violet's heart sank. "I—"

Kai grumbled, "It's not up for debate. You protect me up there. I'm protecting you down here." He sighed wearily. "Don't worry. It will only be for show. Got it?"

"But..."

"No." Kai's tone hardened. "Get some sleep. You're not in any shape to talk about this now, anyway."

She sniffled, fighting back tears for the second time that night. But this time she didn't seek comfort in another's arms. She'd never make that mistake again.

The next morning, Violet woke with a pounding head and an aching heart. A man was dead because of her. Sure, Teek had been far from perfect—after what he did last night, she knew that intimately—but did he deserve to die?

She flipped over in the tent and stared at Kai as he slept. He certainly didn't deserve to have one of his friends' blood on his hands. Maybe he was right. It would be easier to just pretend.

Kai stirred. His eyes fluttered open and focused on her. "Feeling better?" he asked gruffly.

She lowered her gaze. "Yes. Can we talk?"

"'Bout what?" He sat up, scratching his chest.

"Why did you do it?" She lifted her gaze off her bedroll. "I thought—"

"It's done." He tossed his blanket off his legs. "Let's move on." He grabbed his pack and began digging through it. Like this was a normal day. Like he hadn't killed a man in cold blood last night—and gotten away with it.

Would he get away with it? Her stomach churned. "What if someone saw—"

"They didn't."

"How can you know that?" She threw off her own blanket. "Roc was awake. There were dragons on watch."

He pulled out a toothbrush. "Not a problem. Roc took care of it." He opened his mouth.

"Took care of it? How?"

Kai's hand dropped. "Dragons take special care of their bonded." He shrugged. "Teek was only a defender."

Violet's heart pounded. "So am I."

"No, you're not. You're special, Vi. I knew it from the moment I first saw you, and so did Roc. That's why we protected you." His eyes grew unfocused before he turned aside and stuffed the toothbrush back into his bag, unused. "Pack up. Storm's coming. We need to leave."

She rushed out of the tent into the gloomy morning. Lightning flashed far off on the horizon. Yet it wouldn't be long before the storm rolled through. Out here, storms were no joke. They tended to be far larger and last twice as long as the squalls back home—with lightning that killed faster than any monster.

Heart pumping, she quickly packed her tent and gathered her things. The whole time, she couldn't stop turning over Kai's words. What did he mean? He thought she was special. Why? Because he watched her take out a few lizards with a couple tiny knives? Or had he seen something else when they'd first met—sensed something deeper...

They flew in silence that morning, barely beating the storm back to Lanwell. They landed in the square with the wind whipping at their skin and the tang of rain thick on the breeze. As she slid off Roc's back, a heavy weight settled on her shoulders. The somber mood was reflected in all the riders' faces. Losing a rider was never easy.

Someone needed to share the grim news with Teek's family. Normally, they wanted to speak to whoever was with them in their last moments. Frankly, she wasn't sure if she could bear it... Could she look Teek's parents in the eyes and lie? Tell them he'd met an honorable death?

She'd just decided to beg Kai to stand in her stead, when he stiffened. "Mother. What are you doing here?"

Violet spun and spotted the older woman she'd met on the elder's council standing in the square, cradling a blanket-wrapped bundle. The wind kicked up, and a sharp cry rose with the gust.

"Your daughter." Kai's mother stepped forward. "Helka named her Aylia."

"Helka had her while I was away?" Kai's face lit up, and he stopped at his mother's side. Tears filled his eyes as he stared at the wailing infant.

Violet hung back beside Roc. She couldn't wait to meet little Aylia. But Kai would want a private moment with his family first. It was probably best if she returned to the boarding house. She'd collect her things. Give them time to bask in the new life they'd created.

But his mother's next words froze her in place and shattered her heart.

"Helka didn't make it."

Kai's outstretched hands fell at his sides. "What?"

"The birth was too hard on her." His mother stood solidly even as the wind whipped, sending her long robes and loose white curls lashing around her. "I'm sorry, Son."

Kai shook his head. "No."

"It's true."

Violet covered her mouth, praying the howling breeze disguised the sound of her gasping breath.

Helka... Blazes.

She'd known something was off. That awful note. Was this what Helka's bloodsong had been warning her about? Had she discovered a *death* note?

Violet's lips quivered. She should've tried harder. Should've been there... done something. Now her best friend was just... gone.

Kai's mother cleared her throat. "I can take Aylia. Give you some time to—"

"No!" Kai practically roared. He wheeled around, swinging his fist at the thing closest to him, a wooden stall door.

Violet winced as the resounding crack jarred her ears.

His mother backed away and hissed, "Well, I can't hand her to you with you acting like that, now can I?"

"You don't have to," he forced out through clenched teeth. Blood dripped down his fingers and stained the cobbles. Then his gaze spun to her, and Violet flinched from the rancor in his tone. "Vi. Take her."

Instinct made her lurch forward while her mind screamed at her to run. Should she help a man who growled at his mother in a crowded square? Who barked orders at her... Who looked a heartbeat away from snapping? Really, what business did she have inserting herself into these people's lives? She shouldn't even *be* here.

But there was no question. Kai needed someone. And she needed a distraction from the shambles her life had become. So, she marched to his mother and plucked the crying child out of her arms.

"Come on," Kai barked. "We're leaving."

With her heart breaking, Violet followed him out of the square as the storm broke and drenched them to the bone.

No Small Feat

Ryon jolted up, gasping. "Where am I?" Haziness clouded his vision. He rubbed his eyes, trying to remember... "Violet!" He swung his legs over the edge of the simple cot he'd awakened on.

"Hey, easy there!" A weathered old man brushed aside a beaded curtain and shuffled through the doorway of the long log cabin.

Ryon blinked, his brow furrowing. "Balun? Is that you?" If Balun was here, he must be back on the island a half day's sail from his home. How did he get here?

"Got your wits about you, I see." His wrinkled face creased in a dozen places as the old man hurried over to the cot. "The healer was worried you wouldn't be the same when you woke, seeing you slept so long."

"How long?" His toes hit the floorboards, but before he pushed to his feet, Balun's hand closed on his shoulder and pressed him back with surprising strength. Or was it just that he was weaker than a newborn chick?

"I said easy! You've been lying in that bed for days with nothing to eat or drink. You can't expect to jump up and dance round the fire straightaway."

Ryon's head spun. "Days?" he croaked. "How many?"

Balun frowned and reached for a jug of water. "Three since you arrived. And I hear it took them a day to bring you here after they plucked you out of the water half-dead."

That statement unlocked a hazy memory. Being pulled onto a massive boat. A blonde woman with kind eyes. Nox... Was he there too?

"Four days..." Water trickled into a cup while Ryon reeled, trying to gather the scattered remnants of his memories.

Balun attempted to hand him the cup, and he swatted it aside. "Thick-headed fool," Balun grumbled.

Ryon jumped to his feet. "I have to get—" The words died on his tongue as he collapsed backward onto the cot.

Balun clicked his tongue. "What did I tell ya?" He thrust the cup at Ryon again. "Now drink."

Seemed newborn chick was the right guess... This time, Ryon drained the cup. When he slowly rose after, he actually managed to keep his feet beneath him.

"Where you going?" Balun called.

Ryon stumbled toward the exit. "Have to find Nox."

"You won't find him out there."

He spun and lifted a brow. "Why not?"

"They set sail while you slept."

Ryon's heart sank. Had they left him for dead? What could be more important than finding Violet? Hadn't he told Nox she was lost... or was that a dream conjured out of his deepest desires?

He had to find her. The thought whirred through his mind over and over, even while everything else was a muddled mess.

"Where did they go?" He had to go after them. No matter the distance. No matter the obstacles. He wouldn't rest until she was back here where she belonged, just like he'd promised. With two long strides, he stopped in front of Balun and glared at him. "Tell me!"

"They went to the city under the sea." Balun's lids drooped, his gaze downcast. "I warned them it was suicide, but they didn't listen. I'm sorry, lad. They've been gone for days... I can't imagine they were successful."

He was supposed to return and tell them how to defeat Jurdan. What would Violet say when she learned he'd failed? How would she grapple with the loss of all the people she held dear? Was Nox dead? Mariun? Would he ever see them again?

Ryon's knees wobbled, and he was a heartbeat away from sinking down on the cot again, when a commotion rose outside. "What's that?"

Balun's eyes widened. "No idea. Let's take a looksee." He shuffled to the doorway and shouted at someone outside. "Hey, what's the ruckus?"

A voice yelled, "Lelano's back from the beach! He spotted sails on the horizon and wings in the sky!"

"Well." Balun spun back, a huge smile painting his wrinkled face. "Seems it's your lucky day."

Pulse hammering, Ryon shoved past him. He ignored the old man's cries to wait and followed the crowd of curious villagers through the trees. In the back of his mind, he realized his guess had been true. He was back on the island neighboring his own. But he barely noted the pungent fruit and piercing howls. Not when he had to use all of his waning strength to endure the hike.

He should be resting in that bed. Clearly it was foolish to tramp through the jungle after being out cold for so long. But he couldn't bear to stay away. Not when there was a single shred of a chance that she might be out there.

He knew it was a long shot. He couldn't recall sharing more than the barest details of her plight with her uncle... but all the same, hope sprang to life in his soul. Maybe they'd saved her. Four days was a long time. They could've found a way.

And if Violet was still trapped on the hellish world where he'd left her, then maybe Nox had that feather. Or Orry might be there. They could wish her back right away.

He stumbled out of the jungle path as a cascade of boots thumped into the sand.

"Ryon?" Mariun rushed forward. "Am I glad to see you!"

He endured her embrace, trying not to wobble sideways. "And I you. What's happening? Where were you? Violet—"

"Slow down." Nox clamped a hand on his shoulder. "We just got back." His eyes narrowed. "And from the looks of it, you don't seem too—"

"I don't care how I look!" Ryon shouted. "Violet's in danger!" His breath, still harsh from the trek, caught painfully in his chest. Dizziness made the world spin.

"Whoa..." Nox grabbed both his shoulders and helped him sink into the sand. Mariun crowded him, staring into his eyes and placing a hand on his forehead while he fought to catch his breath.

"I think he'll be all right." Mariun pulled a pack off her back and thrust a waterskin at his chest. "Drink. You need to calm down."

He gulped a few hurried sips. "I'll calm down when you tell me what's happening."

Nox's brow furrowed. "We heard what you said on the boat." He shook his head sadly. "Orry's been missing since the battle. I lost my feather when I was captured... We looked for it when we returned to Thalassia, but it was gone."

Ryon's stomach churned. "No. W-we need a feather. We have to bring her back. Now."

"Is it true, then?" Nox sounded hopeful. "Mariun said the ring may have brought you to another world."

He nodded while his body shuddered, his insides left... hollow. If he couldn't find a feather, he'd never bring her back. He couldn't bear the thought of never seeing her again.

She'd trusted him, and he'd failed. Why didn't he demand to stay with her?

"We'll get one." Mariun rubbed his back comfortingly. "Your island's not too far from here, right? We can head there next. We'll have Violet back in a matter of days." She glanced at the dragons. "We just need to wait until they're rested enough to fly in the morning."

He listened numbly as she talked, while inside his soul felt like it was imploding.

"What is it?" Nox asked.

"It's just... When I came back..." He closed his eyes, trying to make the strange facts make sense. "How many days has it been since Violet and I went through that ring?"

Nox's brows pinched together. "Hm... Four."

Guano... That was what he'd been afraid of.

"What is it?" Mariun demanded.

Ryon rubbed his temples. "It doesn't add up. Violet and I spent weeks in Lanwell." He lifted his tortured gaze to the sky. "We were sucked through the ring just after dawn broke. And when I came back, I landed right where I started. I-I saw the sun before I passed out. It was nearly midday."

Nox leaned back on his heels. "What are you saying?"

"Either Violet's wish sent me back in time... or a few hours in this world equals a few weeks where Violet is."

Mariun's jaw dropped. "Is that even possible?"

Ryon pursed his lips. "I didn't think traveling to another world was possible until now. If that can be true, then why not this?"

Nox scrubbed his face, heedless of the sand he dragged in his wake. "If that's true... then how long has passed for her now?"

Ryon thrust the waterskin toward Mariun. "I don't know. But every moment matters. I have to find her."

Nox helped him to his feet. "*We'll* find her. I promised her parents before they..." He choked up.

Ryon blanched. "What happened to Violet's parents?"

Mariun stared ahead flatly. "Someone had to stay to destroy the ship. There was no other way."

His stomach dropped to his feet, and only sheer force of will kept him from sinking onto the sand and cradling his head between his knees. Poor Violet. She loved her parents. She'd be devastated when she learned they died while she was too far away to save them.

How was he going to tell her when he brought her back? Would he even manage it in time?

Another sinister thought snagged in his mind, refusing to shake off. What if this was part of the price she had to pay to wish him back? Had saving him doomed Violet's parents to die?

Ryon woke with the dawn and stumbled out into the village square. An old woman greeted him by the fire, pushing food at him so insistently he finally relented and choked down a few mouthfuls of yesterday's flatbread smothered with ploomfruit jam.

The fruit's unique flavor coated his tongue and brought back memories of his first moments on this island. Violet staring up at him so sweetly as she offered him a bite. The surprise in her expressive eyes when he bent close to sample it rather than pluck the messy thing out of her hands.

A nostalgic smile spread across his lips before his worries chased it away. Would the new Mother Orea grant him the feather he so desperately needed?

They'd made a plan last night before heading to bed. Gwen volunteered to take him to Avion, and Nox insisted on tagging along. Mariun would stay behind to help the hundreds of displaced survivors sitting on Halynn's boat whom they'd rescued from Thalassia before it went down. She'd help... while questioning them.

Crys and Ari agreed to leave before daybreak to scan the seas and nearby islands, collecting more survivors. They'd volunteered to ferry the Thalass to the boat, hoping someone they saved might have information about Jurdan's whereabouts. So far... nothing.

Kayda was already gone. She'd insisted on heading back to Dracwood last night without even allowing Mena a proper rest. The queen had been so distraught from the loss of her beloved brother Conall that Mena was willing to chance a long journey across the sea to allow her bondmate the solitude she required to handle her grief. Nox had tried to talk her out of it, but in the end, Kayda couldn't be swayed.

The dragons remained in communication through their separation, which settled his nerves slightly. He honestly couldn't blame her. He knew like few others how tight the bonds of siblings could be.

Ryon stared into the flames as he chewed the last bite of his breakfast. Then he sighed and stood, wondering if it was still too early to wake the others. He hated to disturb Mariun and Nox when they'd clearly been through so much. Mariun had lost her home. Not only that, but she'd taken part in destroying it. That had to be weighing on her.

And though Nox tried to adopt a brave façade, he had to be struggling as well. Conall wasn't just Kayda's brother, he was Nox's too.

Ryon couldn't imagine what was running through his mind right now... If Rovan had been the one to sacrifice himself to take down that vile fiend, he wasn't sure if he could handle it with half as much strength as Nox.

But they had so much to do. And wasted time was a luxury they couldn't afford. Nox had insisted on resting Gwen since she'd be carrying two full-grown men today. And it wasn't like he could leave any earlier without a boat, so he'd been forced to wait. Surely by now he'd waited long enough.

He stalked through the forest toward their cabin and straightened his shoulders, but as he lifted his fist to knock, an impossibly lovely voice sang in his ears. One he recognized instantly. "I never imagined you were the sort to disturb a love nest."

His gaze lifted just as a beautiful gull-sized golden bird landed on the rooftop. "Orry! Where have you been?" He backed away, a smile stretching from ear to ear.

"Here and there," Orry trilled. "Until one of your dragon friends found me this morning."

His smile fell. She didn't sound quite the same. A weariness in her voice made his heart clench. "Are you... Are you well?"

"What's going on out here?" Beads clacked as Nox shoved through the doorway. Mariun padded out on his heels, along with a gray wolf, his posture slumped but his golden eyes alert as anyone else's.

Ryon nodded to the roof. "Orry's back."

Shadow whimpered, and Nox explained, "Violet's bondmate."

The wolf whimpered again, a low, mournful sound that spoke of the ultimate pain.

"I think he already knows." Mariun stopped at his side and reached out, but Shadow tromped off to a nearby tree and sat heavily without ever taking his sorrowful eyes off Orry.

"Grief will weigh heavy on us all before long," Orry trilled.

Nox lifted a brow. "What'd she say? Will she give us a feather? I can wish Violet back right now."

"Wait. I didn't get that far yet." Ryon turned to Orry and started whistling. Soon, he'd shared the whole strange tale with her, whistling so long his throat ached. "So, we need a feather to bring her back. Will you give one to Nox?" he finished.

Orry tilted her head, her beak bobbing as she gave Nox a cool once-over. "No."

"What?" Ryon tore at his scalp. "Why not?"

Nox snapped his fingers. "What is it? Translate."

"She won't give you a feather," Ryon blurted.

"What? Why rotting not?"

He spun to Nox and barked. "I'm getting to that!" His eyelids pinched closed as he fought to tamp down his annoyance at being made to play translator. But when Orry speared Nox with a hard glare and spoke as if to him, Ryon knew his job wasn't over yet. He listened carefully and translated as she spoke.

"You were entrusted with a golden feather and lost it—you can't have another. And even if I gave you one—you haven't suffered enough for this. I can hear it in your heartsong. There will be consequences."

"Damn the consequences!" Nox shouted. "Violet would save me if I were in her place. She *has* saved me." He thrust out a hand. "Let me save her."

"Weren't you listening, boy?" Orry puffed out her chest. "You can't have another. One wish is all you'll ever get."

Ryon's heart sank. If that was the case... "Then we'll find someone else. Surely there must be someone here who's suffered enough to wish Violet back."

Mariun shifted, her gaze landing on the wolf at the fireside. "What about Shadow?"

Nox shook his head. "How would we ask him? Without Conall, no one can talk to him."

The seed of hope blooming in his chest withered. "Rovan... He lived for so long trapped in his mind." Even as the words spilled out of his lips, they felt wrong. How could he ask his brother to suffer more after everything he'd been through?

Orry cocked her head, her golden feathers gleaming in the morning sunshine. "Rovan would face dire consequences. This is no small feat."

A new voice rose from the jungle path. From so far away, it seemed unlikely she'd have overheard their conversation. Yet she slipped into it seamlessly with nary a pause. "The queen must do it." Halynn strolled out of the trees, her golden curls shining almost as brightly as Orry's feathers.

"Yes." Orry's sharp gaze landed on the Winter Witch. "I've listened to her heartsong. Kayda can bring Violet back."

Nox sucked in a sharp breath. "It's true... Kayda lost her entire family in the first war. She lost her sight. She lost a bondmate. If anyone has suffered enough, it's her." He closed his eyes briefly. Then they snapped open and focused on Ryon. "Gwen will take you and

Orry to Kayda. Go to Dracwood. Talk to Kayda. She'll bring Violet back to us."

Ryon nodded, and the withered bud in his chest blossomed anew. Kayda was the answer. Violet's aunt would save her... wouldn't she?

Into the Ether

Delighted giggles rang out in the training square. Violet grinned as Aylia wobbled back and forth, using Roc's tail to help balance on her knobby little knees. "That's it, baby girl. You've almost got it!"

She'd been helping coax Aylia to walk on her own for the last few weeks. Helka's daughter was big for her age, like her daddy. She was Kai's spitting image, with beautiful blue eyes and dark curls, but she hadn't inherited his daring—at least, not yet. She was content to stick close to Roc for support, no matter what Violet dangled just out of reach.

"Come on, Lia. You can do it." She held out a toy ball, Aylia's favorite.

Kai stuffed supplies in his pack, watching with an amused smile. She nearly sighed at the faint hint of pleasure on his face—Kai's smiles had been few and far between in the last year.

In all fairness, she couldn't blame him. He'd lost the love of his life and had to learn how to juggle being a father while still bossing the riders around each day. It certainly hadn't been easy… She'd been there to help, moving in like she'd promised. And Kai had kept his word, never seeking to strike up anything physical between them.

It was strange, raising a child with a friend. But she didn't question it too much. Not when the distraction of taking care of Aylia was exactly what she needed to keep her mind off her own troubles. She crawled into bed exhausted every night and fell a bit more in love with the beautiful little girl each day.

Aylia cooed, "Ba." She stretched out one chubby hand, and her eyes narrowed on the soft toy ball.

"Let go of Roc and come get it, baby girl." She kneeled, holding it a few paces out of reach.

Violet held her breath as Aylia stepped as close as she could while still gripping Roc's tail. She paused there before finally letting go. She took one step… Two.

"That's it." Violet scooted back a little further. "Get your ball."

Aylia waddled over, planting one wobbly leg in front of the other until she snagged the toy with a giggle. "Ba!"

"Yay! You did it!" She lifted Aylia in her arms and squeezed, feeling so excited she could scream. "Look at you! You're walking." Proud tears filled her eyes.

Aylia lifted the ball triumphantly. "Ba, Mama."

Violet's heart sank. "Vi-lit," she corrected. Her gaze lifted just in time to watch Kai turn away.

"What is it?" Kai barked at a man in overalls who'd wandered over.

"Sir, there's a small problem with the conductor field…" He glanced over Kai's shoulder, smiling when he spotted Aylia giggling. "It can wait if you need more time with your family."

Kai stiffened. "No need. I'll look at it now."

She sighed as the two men stalked off, their footsteps ringing loudly on the cobbles.

Tora strolled over. "Hey, Aylia. Did you just walk?" Aylia drew her ball close to her belly and hid her face in Violet's neck. "Still a little shy, hm?" Tora asked with a kindly smile.

"Everyone tells me she'll grow out of it eventually." She rubbed Aylia's back, not really minding how the little girl clung to her. It was nice to have someone to hold, even though she still longed to be wrapped in another's arms.

Tora leaned back on her heels. "He'll grow out of it eventually too, you know."

She followed Tora's line of sight and frowned at Kai's retreating back. "I'm not so sure."

"I know he's been unsettled lately... I can't imagine he's much more fun to be around at home."

Violet shrugged. "I'm used to it."

"He had it rougher than most growing up." Tora leaned in and whispered, "Ever wonder why he doesn't talk to his mother?"

Her heart twinged. Honestly... yeah. Especially after he reacted so strongly to his mother taking Aylia after her birth. "What happened?" She felt a little slimy asking, but Tora wasn't wrong about Kai. He'd been a challenge to live with as he navigated his grief. She wasn't sure if she should ask him about his past... or if he'd be willing to share.

"Kai comes from a long line of bonded. It was no secret his mother expected him to follow in the family tradition, even though she'd chosen a different path. Rumor has it she took his training very seriously, without sparing punishment when he stepped out of line."

Her eyes widened, and she clutched Aylia a little tighter. "That sounds awful."

"Kai couldn't move out fast enough. He tested to be a rider the first day they let him." Tora sighed. "I'm not surprised he doesn't want Granny having any part in raising little Lia."

"Me either." She'd thought his mother seemed cold. But if what Tora said was true, it went much deeper than that. Now Kai's efforts to dodge his mother made a lot more sense.

"You're doing them both a kindness, stepping into Helka's place. I wanted you to know that. And maybe... give you a little hope that it won't always be like this."

Her brows pinched together. "It's all right. You don't—"

"No. I do." Tora patted her shoulder. "Kai loved Helka so much. It's going to take him time to work through his grief. But he will... And he'll be worth the wait."

Violet lowered her gaze. *Great.* She'd thought no one had noticed the tension between her and Kai. Guess everyone realized things weren't exactly normal between them. "Thanks..." Not that she wanted to wait... She was already waiting for someone else.

Still, she knew all too well what it was like to be separated from the person she loved. They were kindred in that. But would that be enough to hold their fragile alliance together?

Violet brushed shoulder-length silvery strands behind her ear. "Thanks again, Shandra. I realize this must be a little unusual for you." Hope bloomed in her heart as she clutched the old book against her chest.

"Not at all." Shandra chuckled. "It's been fun getting a glimpse at the past. Same time tomorrow?"

"Sure." She set the book down and left with a wave, heading to the surface.

She'd found the remarkably well-preserved book in the ruins a few weeks ago, only to discover no one in Lanwell could read the centuries-old dialect. Luckily, the oracle had a bondmate from that era who was happy to help.

After days of sifting through the personal journal of an ancient woman, they'd encountered something incredible. A story that might be the key to defeating Jurdan. If she ever returned home to share it...

Her nose wrinkled as she passed through the storage closet. All these years and she was still waiting. This was her challenge. Her price for making that wish. Each day, she woke wondering if she'd ever see her home again. And each night, she went to bed plagued with worry.

Had something gone wrong? Did Ryon make it back? What was taking him so long to wish her back? Hadn't she suffered enough already... or was something awful coming? Some terrible calamity she'd be helpless to escape?

"Violet!" A high-pitched voice drew her out of her thoughts as she exited into the square. "There you are. I thought you were gonna braid my hair before class?"

Violet winced, turning. "Sorry, Lia." She stood there with a pout on her lips and her arms crossed... and two adorable pigtails bobbing on the sides of her head.

"It's okay. Binn did it for me."

Violet met the young rider's eyes across the square and sent her a nod of thanks. Aylia was always hanging around, and thankfully, the other riders had gotten into the habit of helping when she or Kai were busy. "Looks like she did a better job than I would have."

"She tugged less too." Aylia giggled.

"Hey!" She feigned distress. "Are you replacing me as your stylist?"

Aylia's giggles increased before she smacked into her torso, wrapping her arms around Violet's back and squeezing tight. "Never. Love you, Violet."

Violet's heart pulsed with warmth. "Love you too, baby girl. Have a good day at class."

"I will!" Aylia released her and jogged off, heading into town.

As Violet watched her retreating form, she sucked in a deep breath and called on her boon like she did every morning. Some might say she'd become a little obsessed with the habit. But she had to know...

She breathed a sigh when Aylia's jaunty melody hummed in her ears. Another day, and no death note. She lived in perpetual fear that one day she'd hear it, and just like with Helka, she'd be unable to stop Aylia from dying.

"Something wrong with Lia?" Kai appeared at her elbow with a furrowed brow. He'd clearly spotted where she'd been looking and noticed the distress on her face.

She didn't want to worry him. Not when her weird obsession had nothing to do with Aylia and everything to do with her own insecurities. But what could she say to explain her odd behavior? Thinking fast, she blurted, "I found a story in that book that might be the key to—everything back home." She sighed deeply. "But I doubt I'll ever get to tell them."

"I know it's taking a lot longer than you expected." Kai inched closer. His hand hovered in the space between them before he shoved it into one of his many pockets. He frowned for a moment before his face brightened. "Hey, I might know something that'll cheer you up."

Violet lifted a brow. "You do?"

"Yep. Come with me." He jerked his head to Roc, and she followed, her curiosity piqued. Soon they were perched atop him, and Roc lifted into the sky.

"Where we going?" she asked as the conductor field's buzz momentarily shut off.

Kai turned, flashing a sly smile. "Are you ready to see the other side?"

"Really?" Violet's pulse skittered. She'd given up badgering Kai for a peek above the clouds after her first year here. "I thought you said it was too dangerous?"

"It is. Beautiful and dangerous." He shrugged. "Now that I know you better, I think you'll fit right in." He winked and spun back around.

Violet's heart jolted. *Huh? Was that a... compliment?* She buried the thought as they lifted higher in the sky.

"Don't worry. It'll be less dangerous than usual," Kai said loudly over his shoulder. "Since we've been seeing so few manticores lately, I sent up a scout. Seems they're occupied right now. Breeding season."

Tingles spread down her spine as they lifted higher than she'd ever gone before. Dark clouds enveloped her, and a cool mist tickled her cheeks. They climbed slowly, basking in the dim glow of the bright sun shining above.

Roc creeped out of the cloud cover, just enough to allow their heads to pop up while still keeping his body shrouded in the clouds.

Violet squinted as her eyes adjusted. Then a gasp spilled out of her lips. "Blazes! It's like a whole different world up here."

Bright sunshine bathed the upper clouds, turning them bright yellow and white. The lower layer glowed in phosphorescent shades of green and blue. Everything glittered and gleamed like a billion stars scattered across the horizon.

She'd never seen anything so utterly gorgeous. The beauty stretched out endlessly in all directions, with no one to see it—except for them.

Scattered yowls broke the illusion they were alone. Kai lifted a finger and pointed at one of the upper clouds.

Violet's eyes widened as she spotted a pair of manticores rolling through the clouds. The fluffy layer of gas lifted, exposing a rocky-looking floating platform that was quickly shrouded again.

She swallowed the urge to beg to stay when they began descending. Her body still buzzed with delight from the stolen peek as they landed on a hill outside the conductor field, with Lanwell off in the distance.

"That was incredible!" She slid off Roc's back with a grin. "Thank you, Kai."

He thumped down beside her. "Thought you'd like that."

She glanced around. "What are we doing here?"

"I just—" Kai gulped. "I didn't only show you that to cheer you up." He grabbed her hand. "I know you're dying to go home, Vi. But I want you to know you have a home here. You fit in here, with us. Aylia sees it—and so do I."

Violet sucked in a thready breath. "Oh." Her fingers trembled. Her mind screamed at her to pull them back. But she couldn't deny how lovely it felt to allow herself that simple pleasure. Sure, Aylia held her hand plenty. But Kai's calloused palm sent a spark into her belly she hadn't experienced in a very long time.

"I know I don't say it much." He met her gaze. "Thank you."

Her eyes widened. "For what?"

"If you hadn't stepped in when Helka passed, I would've never recovered. You've been my rock, Vi." He stepped closer. "When you first moved in, I said it would only be for show, but now... I want more." He softly brushed a strand of hair behind her ear and added gruffly, "I want to be your man for real."

She tugged her hand free and backed away. "I can't, Kai. Ryon... I still love him." She tensed, wondering how he'd react. Would he yell at her like Teek had when she'd rejected him? Like he'd screamed at his mother in the square?

He stuffed his hands into his pockets and smiled. "I know. It's all right if you do."

She gaped at him. "What?"

"I still love Helka. I always will. But my heart can handle more. It doesn't have to be either or, Vi." He gazed at her with so much sincerity shining in his eyes her heart clenched.

And she just stood there, reeling. Maybe for Kai, this was normal. But it wasn't normal for her. And she'd told Ryon she'd wait for him... She had to respect that, didn't she?

Kai sighed. "You don't need to say anything now. Just think about it, all right?" He strode back to Roc's side. "And if your answer is still no, I'll respect it. Promise."

Violet nodded numbly and climbed atop Roc. As they lifted into the sky, her head swirled with questions, doubts... and desires.

She wasn't so blind that she'd missed how her heart thudded a little faster when Kai was around, more and more often as the years passed. A certain amount of attraction was bound to happen when they lived and worked together for so long. She'd always ignored it. Locked it away in a silent corner of her mind, unexplored.

Kai's confession made it spring forth with a vengeance. Was he right? Was it normal for her heart to make room for more than one love? *Am I a horrible person for wishing that it was?*

Another voice cautioned her against it. She'd be a fool to allow it. Look what happened to Helka. Look how worried she was for Aylia's safety. If she let herself get close to Kai, she'd be endangering him, too.

Was it wrong for her to be part of their lives? To let Aylia see her as a mother? To let Kai develop these feelings for her... Deep down, she knew she was asking for trouble by surrounding herself with people she cared for, who might fall prey to the awful consequences she needed to pay for that wish.

Why did it have to be like this? What in the blazes was she going to do?

The wind whipped through Violet's long hair. Her tense fingers loosened around her bow as Lanwell grew large on the horizon. Kai kicked Roc's side, and the dragon turned, banking sharply before descending.

Violet gazed at Kai's broad back, and her heart squeezed. He'd been much quieter lately. She often wondered if she'd made a mistake when he'd admitted his feelings for her.

They had gone on with life as they'd been. Living and working together. Raising Aylia. But the haunting attraction she'd tamped down so successfully in their early years refused to stay silent in the wake of his confession.

Still, she held back. Every time she caught Kai glancing at her with longing, or his hand lingered a hair too long on hers when he helped her mount Roc, she reminded herself of her promise to Ryon.

I'll wait for you. For years, if I have to. Who knew she'd *actually* need to live up to that bargain?

Was she a fool for holding on to hope after so long? Was she driving away a man who loved her—here and now—to honor a ghost?

They descended above town as the ever-present hum faded. She sighed as Roc touched down in the square, feeling like she could sleep for a hundred years. They'd just wrapped up a long, drawn-out battle, felling dozens of monsters. Their attacks had exploded lately. Kai explained that it was always a problem when their young came of age.

"Violet!" Aylia barreled across the cobbles, waving like mad.

Prickles spread across her arms. Something was off... but what? As she spun to face Aylia, it clicked. The hum... The conductor's hum hadn't restarted.

She called on her boon as a breeze tickled her neck.

The death note crashed in a maddening crescendo, overpowering Aylia's heartsong. "Lia!" she screamed, snagging the bow off her back.

Snap!

Aylia's feet lifted off the ground, her blue eyes round and unblinking.

Twang!

Violet's arrow sang, sinking into the manticore's eye. The beast sank instantly, dropping Aylia, then slamming into the ground.

In the space of a heartbeat, her world shattered. Roc's wing shot out, providing a soft landing for Aylia's still form. But no matter how gently he set her down, her baby girl would never get back up. She knew it even before the healer rushed over and shook her head sadly. The moment that awful snap rang out—Aylia's heartsong was forever silenced.

Kai ran to his daughter's side and roared with anguish as the conductor's hum kicked back on.

No. She didn't just see that... Aylia wasn't gone. She—

Violet sank to the cobbles with tears spilling down her cheeks. "Lia! Lia... No!"

She wasn't sure how long she sat there crying. Cursing fate. Screaming and weeping. Pushing away every hand that sought to comfort her.

At some point, arms closed around her that refused to let go, no matter how hard she shoved. She blinked back her tears and glanced up, meeting eyes that looked just like *hers*.

She shoved Kai's chest before her fists clamped on the fabric of his shirt. "Lia. I c-can't. I-I..."

He ignored her rambling, pulling her close. Weightlessness stole over her, and then she was moving, carried away in Kai's strong arms. She buried her face in his neck, not glancing up again until he set her down inside their home.

He dropped her on the sofa and headed into the kitchen. She listened to the quiet sounds of him puttering around and gazed at the scattered things Aylia had left behind. She was a collector like her mother, finding tiny trinkets to cherish and display everywhere.

She couldn't do it. Couldn't sit there surrounded by her things.

More tears fell as Violet came to a grim decision. She stood and stiffly charged into her room.

Kai appeared in the doorway. "What are you doing?" he asked flatly, a cup clenched so tightly in his fist his knuckles were white.

She searched his face and nearly screamed again when she was met with a stoic mask. "I can't be here. I can't be surrounded by everything Lia left behind." Her lips wobbled. "All the memories." She stuffed some clothes into her pack. "I'm going to stay at the women's boarding house."

Kai nodded blankly. "All right." He followed her to the front door, staring at his feet all the while.

She paused in the doorway. "I'm sorry," she whispered.

Kai's gaze lifted to hers. He blinked. "Me too."

She turned and strode out the door, refusing to look back. She knew if she did, she'd crumble. Kai would have to pick up the shattered shards of her heart and stitch them back together one piece at a time.

He didn't deserve that. Not after everything she'd already put him through. Deep down, she *knew* Aylia would still be here if it weren't for her.

All these years, she'd been selfish to stay with them. To let herself fall in love with Aylia. To fall in love with them both.

So, she marched off, alone. It was better this way. She would nurse her broken heart back to some semblance of normal—without Kai.

Kai was wrong. She didn't fit in here. She didn't belong here *at all.*

Ryon, have you forgotten me? I need to come home… I need you. I can't do this anymore. She wheezed as she sent the thought into the ether. But just like every other time—no one was listening.

Born to Serve

A throat cleared loudly behind Nox at the fireside. He glanced over as the stranger settled beside him. "Good evening," Nox muttered.

The man nodded. "Evening."

Nox's skin prickled. That voice... where had he heard it before? He eyed the man up and down, but he looked no different from any other Thalass they'd saved.

A few dozen refugees asked to settle in the jungle village. The people here had agreed happily. There were plans to build a new settlement on the other side of the river. He guessed this fellow was probably one of the refugees... But why had he sought his company when his people were gathered on the far side of the fire?

"Have we met?" he asked finally when the curiosity became too much to bear.

"Yeah..." The man shrugged. "Not that I expect you to remember."

A fresh wave of familiarity tickled his spine. He definitely recognized that voice... but try as he might, he couldn't place it.

"I have something that belongs to you." The man reached into his shirt and tugged out a string.

Nox's eyes bulged. His lost feather! "You were the bear."

Bear lifted the necklace off his head. "I slipped my mask off when the order came for all masked to leave. Blended in." He shrugged as he handed the golden feather to Nox. "Guess you could say I lost my stomach for violence."

He took the necklace, and his shoulders slumped as the soft feather slid across his fingers. A million questions flooded his mind. "Why give this back?" He clasped his fist around the precious treasure.

Bear cocked his head, staring at his people across the fire. Wood crackled and sparks flashed, one rising on an updraft and fluttering a short distance before sputtering into ash. Silence reigned so long Nox almost lost his patience and demanded an answer.

"I saw what you did for our people." Bear's gaze shot to Mariun, who sat chatting with a few of the islanders. "What she did. All the help you've given everyone who lost everything when Thalassia went down. Jurdan abandoned us in the end, but she didn't. Least I can do is return what I stole."

Nox's heart lifted. "Hm." He wasn't about to thank Bear. Not when he shouldn't have taken his feather in the first place. But it set him at ease knowing the others saw what he did. Mariun was the real hero, standing up for what was right. Saving all those people when he would've let them drown.

He'd make up for that error in judgment. And he could start by finding out what the bear knew. "Tell me. What is Jurdan planning?"

"No clue. I wasn't one of his trusted advisors." Bear leaned in. "I only know we were supposed to meet at Jolit Isle if there was ever an emergency."

Nox's lips pursed. "That all?"

"If I knew anything else, I'd tell you." Silence stretched out again. "Well, goodnight." Bear brushed off his pants and left.

Mariun sank into the seat he'd vacated. "Who was that?"

"An old acquaintance of mine." With a smile, Nox opened his fist, flashing a glimpse of gold in the firelight.

Her eyes widened. "Is that the one you lost?"

"Yep."

"Are you going to do it?" Mariun's gaze flashed with worry. "You said you'd wish her back..."

He probably should, shouldn't he? They owed it to Conall and Ereni to bring their daughter back. More than that, he wanted his niece back. He missed her quick wit and her determination. He even missed the way she sneezed a dozen times a day and scowled whenever he called her squirt. But what about Kayda? "I-I don't know. Let me talk to Gwen."

Mariun nodded and snuggled against his side.

Nox reached out with his thoughts. "*Hey, you there, Gwen?*"

"*Yep.*" Gwen's cheery voice sounded a little labored. "*Flying over Dracwood still. I just spotted Mena ahead hovering over Flamesmoat. Looks like I'll be landing just before sunset.*"

"*The sun set here already,*" Nox muttered before shaking his head. "*Never mind that. I have some news.*"

Flint chimed in, "*What is it?*"

"*I found my lost feather.*"

"*Really?*" Gwen's voice was thick with glee. "*That's fantastic news!*"

"*How'd you manage that?*" Flint asked.

"*Bear was here. He gave it back, but that's not important.*" He sucked in a deep breath. "*I'm... I should wish Vi back now that I have it.*"

"*No!*" Gwen shouted.

Flint said, "*But the consequences...*"

His brow furrowed. "*She'd do it for me... You know she would.*"

"*True,*" Flint conceded.

Gwen added, "*You don't need to. I'm so close to Queenie. You said yourself Goldie told you Queenie can wish the little one back freely...*"

Nox rubbed his temples. Gwen and her nicknames... "*I just feel like I should be doing more to help.*"

"*You are,*" Flint insisted. "*Don't let your desire to play the hero stop you from doing what's wise.*"

Was that what he was doing? "*Since when did you get so smart?*"

"*Please.*" Flint scoffed. "*I've always been* highly *intelligent. Don't worry. One day, my smarts will rub off on you.*"

Nox chuckled.

Mariun shifted, peeking up at him. "What is it?"

"Gwen's almost to Kayda." He shook his fist. "I should probably save this."

She sighed. "Good."

"Bear said the masked were supposed to gather at Jolit Isle if anything bad ever happened."

Her brows dipped. "I never was privy to their comings and goings... but it makes sense. That's where they kept most of the boats docked."

He rubbed his chin. "I think we should check it out tomorrow. Do a little scouting with the dragons."

"Sounds like a smart plan. Ari and Crys ought to be back by morning." She stood, then grabbed his elbow and tugged until he rose with her. "Come to bed with me, Nox."

"All right." He grinned and followed her easily. She didn't have to make that request twice...

Nox woke to a sharp pain stabbing his chest. Instinctually, he curled into a ball, but it didn't stop the blows from raining on him—over and over.

"Stop it!" Mariun screeched. "You'll kill him! I'll never forgive you if—oof!"

He rolled away from the blows, hopping to his feet as Mariun's cry of distress roared in his ears.

Nox's eyes fought to focus in the dimly lit cabin. A blow to the head cut him off from saying anything else. Rage ignited, and the telltale ache in his fingertips signaled his claws emerging. Someone wrenched his arms behind his back before he recovered enough from his ringing head to use them.

"Love the place you have here." The familiar voice sent a chill down his spine at the same time a wash of disgust nearly made him heave.

The villagers had given them a small hut usually reserved for newly paired couples, far enough away from the main camp they could expect a little privacy. When he'd accepted, he'd been keen for a place to spend some quality time with Mariun. Now he cursed his own stupidity.

Jurdan's voice blared out, full of menace. "So... cozy. Let's keep it that way, shall we? Leave your dragon friends out of this."

Mariun shrieked, and Nox stiffened. He'd been about to reach out to Gwen before his head was rattled. Not now. He stayed quiet, heeding Jurdan's silent threat. It wouldn't likely do him much good, anyway. Jurdan picked the perfect time to strike, when all the dragons were away—Gwen and Mena in Dracwood, and their brothers dropping refugees at one of the northern islands.

Jurdan stood in the doorway. Masked crammed into the tiny hut, taking up nearly the entire floor. A storm raged outside, flashes of lightning brightly illuminating the dark forest—the howling wind and thunder disguising the sound of their struggle.

Had Jurdan cast a storm to sneak up on them unawares? Why hadn't he suspected it? He should've known it wouldn't be the end. That Jurdan wouldn't stop until he stole Mariun back.

"Mariun," he choked out when he caught his breath. Blood trickled into his eyes, making everything blurry.

"Nox!" She struggled against the man holding her, and the air inside the cabin crackled.

"Use your power and he dies," Jurdan stated flatly.

Mariun's head hung limply. "Please. Leave him alone. I'll go with you."

"Mariun—no!" Pain exploded in his rib cage as a masked landed a hit to his side.

"Father, please!"

Jurdan turned to face her. "If I leave him alive, you'll go quietly?"

She nodded. "Yes. I swear."

"Mar—" A hand clamped on his mouth, muffling his words.

"Take her to the ship." Jurdan waved lazily and stepped out of the doorway into the room.

Nox's stomach sank. Not again! He struggled against his attackers, dislodging the hand covering his mouth just before they dragged her out the door. "I'll find you. I swear it, Mariun!" Her big gray eyes locked with his as lightning flashed, illuminating the myriad emotions writ on her face. Then she was gone. Torn away into the storm.

Jurdan crossed the room slowly. With Mariun gone, Nox focused solely on him, tamping down the desolation churning in his soul.

He'd meant what he'd said. There was nothing that would stop him from going after her. Even the twisted villain who'd tear her out of sound sleep in the middle of the night. Who made her chose between her freedom—and his life.

"Why can't you just let her go?" Nox forced out through gritted teeth.

"It's simple." Jurdan stopped before him. "Mariun belongs to me. She was born to serve a purpose. *My* purpose."

"You're sick," he spat. "She's a person—not a game piece."

Jurdan sneered. "You know, I thought I'd have a bit of fun watching you get slaughtered in the ring. But looks like that's not an option anymore, is it?"

His gaze hardened. "What a loss. Whatever will you do without all those death matches to keep you entertained?"

"Frankly, I'm getting a little tired of your opinions." Jurdan leaned in, and a slow smirk stretched across his face. "What was it you said at our last meeting? That laughable little threat... Oh, I remember. You wanted to bury me, didn't you?"

Nox's heart hammered as Jurdan spun on his heel and led the way outside, signaling his men to follow. They dragged him out between them, forcing his legs to move. Slick leaves and mud squished between his toes, and rain pelted his face, drenching him quickly.

As they hauled him into the dark forest, he reached out with his thoughts. "*Flint? Gwen? I need you to wake up. Now!*"

"*What is it?*" Flint asked, sounding alert.

"*Huh? I'm up,*" Gwen groggily replied a moment later. After he quickly explained what had happened, she cried out, "*I'm coming!*"

"*You'll never reach him in time...*" Flint warned.

"*Doesn't matter. I'm still coming. Hang in there, Nox. Do whatever it takes.*"

With Gwen's voice ringing in his ears, he drew in a deep breath, more determined than ever. Whatever Jurdan was planning, if he could just brave it for a day, Gwen would save him. Then he'd find Mariun. It wasn't much of a plan... but at least it was something.

Jurdan stopped in a clearing beside the river, next to a freshly dug mound of dirt with a pair of shovels sticking out of it. And—a hole. Nox's heartbeat thrashed in his ears and his knees buckled.

"You wanted to drown me beneath the sea. I'm going to bury you instead." Jurdan stepped close and patted Nox's cheek gaily. "Don't worry. I'll leave you alive like she wanted. Got to keep my word."

Nox wrenched his face away from Jurdan's touch, his stomach roiling. "How is that leaving me alive? You sick—"

The masked holding him chose that instant to clobber the back of his head and toss him into the hole. Pain exploded, sending spots of light across the backs of his eyelids. Nox groaned and sputtered as rain poured down on him and the musty, wet earth suctioned to his tunic and pants.

Then, like a sign from the heavens, lightning exploded in a ring around the clearing and a voice rang out, clear and full of panic. "Nox! The necklace! Use it now!"

He lifted his ringing head out of the muck long enough to spot Mariun running out of the trees. His bleary mind could scarcely grasp what she'd said.

"Nox!" she shrieked, her eyes widening as she spotted him laid out, bleeding in the hole. Her gaze narrowed on Jurdan and thunder boomed. She lifted her arms.

A dart sank into her neck right when the meaning of her words registered.

"No!" Nox cried out. Mariun wobbled, taking another step. A masked appeared from the trees, catching her as she crumpled before she smacked into the forest floor.

"I thought I told you to take her to the ship?" Jurdan scolded.

Nox listened with half an ear while his gaze darted around the hole. He needed blood to make his wish... Was there a sharp rock? Wait—he cursed his muddled thoughts. He was bleeding plenty already from the blows to his skull.

"She downed most of us and ran off. Won't happen again, Supreme."

Nox's fingers slipped into his tunic and closed around the bloodfeather as a pair of boots slapped into the muck. A heavy weight settled atop him, knocking the wind out of his chest. More thuds slammed into the ground, and powerful hands gripped his wrists before he lashed out and landed a single strike.

"What do we have here?" Jurdan tugged mercilessly, tearing the necklace off his neck and slamming Nox's head back into the mud. A wicked smirk curved his lips as the golden feather disappeared into his fist. "Looks like my daughter served a purpose here, after all. What should I wish for?"

Nox hissed, "Give that back!"

"And let it waste away in your grave?" Jurdan chuckled and climbed out of the pit.

He lurched up, fighting to follow. He had to save Mariun. Defeat Jurdan. Get that rotting feather back before Jurdan used it for something terrible...

But the action only earned him more blows. They pummeled him relentlessly until he could hardly move, and his entire body screamed in agony.

Jurdan's voice broke through the haze of pain. "Leave him alive. She might not have held up her end of the bargain, but I won't renege on my word."

From the sick hint of enjoyment in Jurdan's tone, it was clear he wasn't doing it out of the kindness of his heart. He wanted Nox to suffer. To see the pain in Mariun's eyes when she realized he'd fulfilled her demand and her lover *still* ended up dead.

The masked climbed out, and two of them took up shovels. Jurdan's caustic laughter cackled around him, fading away as muck smacked down on Nox from above, clogging his ears.

Digging deep, Nox summoned his last dregs of strength. Just enough to twist sideways and cover his head, creating a tiny pocket of air beneath his arms.

This wasn't the end. He refused to let it be.

Another shovelful of mud landed, and darkness enveloped him. *"Gwen... Hurry. You have to find me."*

Repeat After Me

Ryon paced in the tower room while Orry sat on the window ledge, watching the steady thump of his boots crossing the stone floor over and over. "What's taking them so long?" Ryon whistled.

They'd arrived just as night fell. Gwen had descended on the grounds in Kings Keep, and like last time, they'd been surrounded by guardsmen. Only this time, there'd been no helpful Guard Captain to usher him straight to the queen's side. His befuddled underlings left Gwen on the lawn with Mena and forced Ryon and Orry into one of the drafty tower rooms.

They'd been waiting for ages while the guards decided whether to listen to their pleas. He'd demanded to see Kayda. Insisted that she'd want to hear what he had to say. But so far... they'd done nothing but wait.

"Grief." Orry answered finally. "I wager that's what's plaguing the queen. Don't fret. We'll meet with her exactly when we're meant to."

"What's that supposed to mean? We need to bring Violet back now." His voice warbled, choked with desperation. "Don't you understand? It's already been so long. And that world is *not* safe."

"Violet *will* survive it. She must." Orry's song echoed with certainty.

Footsteps sounded in the hall. Ryon jerked around, staring at the door.

Guard Captain Gawain rubbed sweat from his forehead with a handkerchief. "Blazing stairs. Why they stuffed you up here, I don't understand."

He lurched forward. "Gawain, please. We need to speak to the queen. It's urgent!"

Gawain sucked in an agitated breath. "Yes, of course. She sent me to fetch you." He gestured to the door with his hanky. "Come along. Can't keep Her Grace waiting."

Ryon choked down a retort. He certainly wasn't the one who'd made the waiting necessary...

It didn't matter. No sense in starting an argument when he was finally getting what he wanted. He strode to the sill, lifted Orry in his arms, and followed Gawain into the hall.

They passed countless tapestries and murals of men at battle on the walk through the tower. Guardsmen stopped what they were doing to let them pass, all of them bowing their heads in deference to Gawain.

Ryon's pulse sped as they descended to the lowest level of the tower. What was Kayda doing down there? Had she been there all along?

Gawain shoved open a door. Kayda stood with Lark outside Jayan's cell. Both wore black dresses, though Lark's was covered with a stained apron. Their eyes were red-rimmed, their posture defeated. Something told him he'd interrupted a painful conversation.

Kayda jerked her head toward the door, her eyes not quite lining up with Ryon's. "I hear you want me to make a wish."

He almost asked how she already knew, but then he remembered the dragons. No doubt Gwen had filled in Mena, who had spoken to Kayda. Either way, it saved him time. Time he desperately needed.

"Yes." Stepping further into the room, he spotted Jayan laid out in the same spot he'd seen him last. "Is he... all right?"

Lark shook her head. "He's taken a turn for the worse. I've done all I can to keep him alive, but it's not looking good. We even tried bringing him another crow—nothing."

"Jurdan abandoned him." Kayda's flinty tone sent a shiver down his neck. "At least insofar as healing goes. Who knows if their connection has been severed completely?"

Lark rubbed Kayda's back and sniffled. "It'll be all right. You remember how I saved Nox and broke his connection to the Unseen? We can do it again."

"Didn't you bring him back from the brink of death?" Kayda asked. "How will we ever manage that when you can't heal him with magic now?"

Ryon's stomach churned. This wasn't good. Not in the slightest. Because Kayda couldn't be forced to wish Violet back. Orry could give her a feather, and she might decide to wish her old friend back instead. She'd personally sent him on a mission that ended with him captured for two decades. Then she'd put him on that cot by burning him with her own magic...

"Gwen and Nox!" Ryon blurted. "Nox used Gwen's boon to bring Mariun back. I saw it happen. He can save Jayan too."

Kayda pressed a hand to her chest. "Her boon..." She shook her head forcefully. "No. I can't ask him to do that. I could've died when I called on Druturion's boon."

"Maybe it's different with healing. Nox survived it once already." Ryon's voice rose in pitch as he fought to convince her. "I thought Mariun was done for... until she wasn't. If he did it once, surely he can do it again."

"It couldn't hurt to ask." Lark tilted her head. "Have Mena talk to Gwen. She can ask Nox about it."

Kayda nodded and fell silent. Then her eyes widened. "Gwen's gone. Nox is in danger..." She gasped. "Jurdan."

His heart skipped a beat. "No. What happened?"

Kayda closed her eyes. "Jurdan came for Mariun in the night. He took her and left Nox behind. He's hurt... Gwen's racing back to save him."

Lark sank into a chair, tears spilling down her cheeks. "First Conall and Ereni—now Nox, too?"

"He might be all right. Gwen says he's still alive." Kayda's lips pursed. "She just can't hear him right now..."

"So Jurdan knocked him out?" Lark wrung her hands. "I don't like this at all."

"Don't you see?" Ryon's fingers tightened around the bird in his arms. "We *have* to bring Violet back. When I left, she was searching for a way to defeat Jurdan. She's bound to have learned more by now. It could be the key to defeating him once and for all."

Jayan groaned, and the pained noise made the queen flinch.

Gawain cleared his throat. "I hate to interrupt, Your Grace. But don't forget that he might be sitting on a treasure trove of inside information as well."

Kayda's brows dipped like she was weighing his words. Ryon glared at the Guard Captain, fighting the urge to throttle him.

He thought he'd found the perfect solution by suggesting Gwen and Nox heal Jayan... but with Nox's safety in question, it would be a gamble. Gwen would need time to fly back to the islands. Kayda might insist they wait even longer before she decided.

Would she choose to save her old friend? Or her niece?

Kayda leaned against the wall. She stood there in silence for what felt like ages. Then her head snapped up. "You're right."

His heart slammed against his ribs. Gawain had spoken last... Did that mean—

Kayda swung to face Ryon. "I'm bringing Violet back."

He exhaled, the breath escaping in an enormous whoosh.

"I'm doing this for my brother." Kayda straightened, pushing off the wall and adjusting her posture until she looked every inch the queen she was. "Conall saved us from the Unseen. He sacrificed years of his life back then to do it. And now..." Her voice broke. "Now, I'm bringing his daughter back. I have to believe that she'll hold the key to defeating Jurdan."

"Thank you!" Hope bloomed in Ryon's heart. "You won't regret this." He swapped to whistling. "She's agreed to wish Violet back. Give her a feather!"

Orry opened her mouth and whistled back. "I shall, under one condition."

Ryon tensed. "Condition? What?"

"This is no ordinary wish. I need the queen to repeat after me—verbatim—if she wants to ensure our future." Orry tugged free from his arms and landed on the floor. She stalked forward on spindly legs. "Tell her."

He gulped. "Orry wants you to use her words exactly. It's the only way to bring Violet back."

Kayda tilted her head. "What words?"

"She wants to know what she has to say," he whistled.

"I warn you this will sound cryptic—but I promise you, it will work." Orry tilted her head to match the angle of Kayda's.

He rubbed his chin. "She says it will sound cryptic, but that it'll work."

Kayda's head swiveled toward Ryon. "These birds are your gods, aren't they?"

"Yes."

Kayda thrust out a hand. "Then I trust her. I'll say whatever she wants if it brings Violet back to us. Give me the feather."

Orry plucked a shining golden feather from her chest without waiting for Ryon to translate. Kayda's fingers closed around it.

Lark sniffled. "Sister, give me your other hand. I can draw blood without leaving a huge wound."

Kayda complied without a single shred of hesitation. "The words," she spat. "I'm ready."

Orry nodded curtly and sang, "Repeat after me..."

Thunderstruck

V iolet raced forward, the riders' alarm pealing through the air and pulling her toward the square like a mesmerizing lure.

Months that felt like years had passed since her life shattered. It took her days just to crawl out of bed. Weeks to work up the nerve to return to the square—to stand on the spot where Aylia's song was silenced.

She'd ignored her duty as a defender for all of it. Everyone had given her time, even Kai.

Especially Kai.

She'd never returned to his cabin. All these months later, she still couldn't stand the thought of it. No number of whispers in her ear that Kai needed her swayed her. He even refused to choose a new defender, risking his life every time he flew.

She hated it. But until today—until that alarm broke through the haze of her mourning—she couldn't make herself go through the motions of being a rider. Of being human...

That afternoon, the piercing cry blared through town, and something deep in her soul snapped back into place. Her feet began moving without her telling them to until she found herself standing in the square with her favorite bow in her hands.

Kai whipped around after securing Roc's saddle bags and jolted like he'd seen a ghost. He drew a deep breath, vaulted atop Roc's back, and thrust out a hand expectantly. "You're late."

Her chin quivered. "I know."

"You coming?" Kai's eyes softened. "If it's still too soon—"

She grabbed his hand. "Help me up, would you?"

Kai pulled her up and waited while she got settled. The other riders stared at them, whispering to each other, sending her nods and waves. She ignored them all and concentrated on strapping in. Slipping into the ropes felt like sliding on her favorite pair of boots—full of promise for the journey to come.

Adrenaline pumped through her veins as they lifted into the sky. It might be strange, but she'd missed this more than she cared to admit. The call to adventure. The promise of a fight.

Air whipped through her chest-length hair. Shrieks of monsters bled into the sky. Violet smiled. She'd mourned long enough. Now was the time for vengeance.

They emerged below a cluster of manticores. Vibrations pulsed over her skin as Roc released a hail of earth, scattering the beasts' venomous spines. Her arrows whizzed through the sky and fell the monsters one after another.

Before long, the battle took on the dreamy haze of a chore completed a hundred times. Her body moved by instinct, seeking the next target. Sinking the next arrow into flesh. Listening to the beast's dying screech.

It took the ominous rumble of thunder to break the spell.

"Flashes!" Kai kicked Roc's side until he banked sharply, turning away from the manticore they'd been chasing upward.

"Hey! We almost had it." Violet scowled as she watched the lone beast disappear into the cloud cover.

Kai's gaze went unfocused. "We chased that one too far."

She glanced around, noticing for the first time they'd been separated from the rest of the riders. If she squinted, she could make out their shapes in the air hovering near the distant village. Black clouds blanketed the sky in between, growing darker with every instant.

"We need to find somewhere to hunker down. Let the storm pass before we head back." Kai scanned below until his finger shot out, pointing to some mountainous terrain beneath them. "There. Roc says there are caves. We'll wait it out inside."

Her stomach churned. "Will we make it before the storm breaks?"

"We have to try."

Roc sped through the air, but it wasn't long before cold droplets pelted them. She shivered, holding on tightly as the storm broke, a raging tempest swirling wind and water in her eyes.

Lightning flashed, so close the hair on her arms stood on end.

Boom.

A massive blast of thunder rent the air immediately after.

Thankfully, Roc had little trouble navigating the storm, even when she was forced to close her eyes to a tiny slit. He wobbled slightly through the sky, making steady progress to their destination.

Then light blasted right on top of her. Pain exploded, searing through every cell of her body. Her mouth opened in a silent scream just before she collapsed.

Violet gasped, coming to with a jolt. Kai perched above her with his hands pressed firmly against her chest and his eyelids pinched closed. The ground beneath her vibrated. Outside, the storm raged, shooting flares of lightning so often she had no trouble piecing together that she was inside a cave, lying flat on the cold stone floor.

"W-what happened?" she croaked.

Kai gathered her in his arms and pulled her against his chest. "Thank the Maker! I thought I'd lost you." He settled her legs in his lap and rocked slightly, the motion so soothing she nearly shuttered her eyes.

It came back to her then. The battle. The race through the storm. The agonizing pain of being struck by lightning.

Plants crinkled against her chest as the hum in the ground cut off. Roc's sinuous head spun from the cave mouth. He examined her with one eye before turning back, watching the storm.

"You... healed me?" Even as the words slipped past her lips, she knew it was true. Not even an echo of pain remained in her limbs.

Kai cupped her face with one hand. "Of course I did. I couldn't lose you too." His body quaked, and she sensed from the warble in his voice it wasn't only from being soaked to the bone.

As she stared into his eyes, all the fears of the last few months came rushing back. "Let me go."

"No." His arm tightened around her back, not enough to crush her, just enough to let her know he was done listening. "I shouldn't have let you go to begin with." He pressed his forehead against hers.

She breathed him in, reveling in the strength of his embrace even though she ought to be pushing him back. "Please," she murmured weakly. "We shouldn't be doing this. We shouldn't be this... close."

Her trembling hands reached out, slipping around his neck and pulling him closer, belying her words. She couldn't help it. After months of self-isolation, Kai's touch was as mesmerizing as the alarm had been earlier.

"Why shouldn't we?" His eyes closed, his body relaxing into her arms.

He needed this too, didn't he? When was the last time he'd been hugged?

No. She couldn't forget what had kept her away. Her hands stilled, and she pulled back a fraction. "I don't want to lose *you*, that's why," she blurted, the words spilling out before she bit them back.

Kai's eyes popped open. "What? Why would you think that?" She lowered her head, her gaze downcast. Kai lifted her chin with a finger and forced her to meet his gaze. "Tell me."

"Everyone I've loved since I made that wish is dead. First Helka. Then Aylia." Tears pricked the corners of her eyes, and her voice thickened. "I-I'm scared," she admitted. "I haven't used my boon in months. Not since..." She choked down a steadying breath. "Not since the day she died. I heard it, Kai. I heard a death note in her song." She blinked back tears as her fingers closed in the wet fabric of his shirt.

"Death note?"

She nodded gravely. "I heard it before they both died. The same damn sound."

"Listen to mine." Kai loosened her hands and pulled them into his. "Right now."

"What?" She shook her head. "I can't."

"You can." His voice firmed.

She stared at him, swimming in the depths of his blue eyes. She couldn't do it... Didn't want to know if she was about to lose the one thread left in this awful world keeping her from unraveling.

"I'm right here." He gazed at her, expectant yet patient. Like he'd wait a thousand years. With his steady strength bolstering her, she finally gave in to the urge she'd been ignoring for months and called on her boon.

Kai's song wrapped around her. The percussion pulsed in perfect tune with her heartbeat. His melody sang, fluid yet frantic, and full of so much longing it made her soul ache. She drifted closer, and Kai's song responded, the tempo slowing until it became hypnotic.

"Do you hear it now?" he asked gruffly.

"No." She blinked, cutting off her boon. "But that doesn't mean I won't. I can't let it."

A tiny chuckle rumbled in his chest.

She scowled.

"Violet." He buried any trace of humor in his expression. "I've never been afraid of death. You can't be, living here, doing what we do. When my time comes, I'll accept it. But I can't accept living my life in misery or watching you be miserable. It ends today."

"But—"

"I'm not done." His warm palms closed on her cheeks. Her stomach fluttered, and her heart beat like mad. Kai stroked her neck with his fingers, his touch soothing and so unexpected it sent sparks racing through her flesh. "I'm sick of living half a life, hiding what I truly desire."

She closed her eyes as the truth hummed in her blood. That was exactly what she'd been doing for so long. Hiding her desires. Burying them so they didn't complicate her life. His confession brought them all screaming to the surface.

"When I thought I lost you to that strike, it felt like I was the one dying." Her eyes popped open as Kai's hand wrapped around the back of her neck. He met her gaze, staring at her with so much intensity she shivered. "Without you, I'm drowning. With you, it feels like I can fly."

Maybe it was wrong for her to accept the comfort he was offering her. To accept his love. But at that moment, her desire won.

She tipped her face up and sighed as their lips met.

Outside, the storm raged. In their cave, another tempest swirled, full of passion, whispered assurances, and so much pent-up longing it wasn't long before Roc took off, finding a new spot to ride out the lightning.

As the flares of light petered out, Violet curled against Kai's chest in the darkness.

"I want you back, Vi." Kai's voice thrummed with uncertainty, even after what they'd just shared. "We can find a new cabin, if that's what it takes."

She traced a hand lightly down his abs as a thousand conflicting thoughts bombarded her. Yeah, they'd lived together before. Still, agreeing right now felt like she'd be giving up on her life in Dracwood.

Should she say yes when she could be torn out of his life at any moment? Was Ryon still out there, trying to bring her back? Was she a fool to even consider it after so much time?

But how could she say no to Kai? He needed her—and it was past time she admitted she needed him too.

"What are you thinking over there?" Kai asked softly.

She shook her head. "Too much."

He threaded a hand through her hair. "I've got a cure for that." His hot breath trailed across her neck.

She giggled. "What happened to me being too scrawny to lie with?"

Laughter rumbled in his chest, and the vibration sent a shiver through her skin. "I never said that."

She gasped and shoved his shoulder. "Liar! You told me that the night you first suggested I move in with you and Helka."

"Huh." Kai lifted enough that she spotted his chagrined expression in the dimly lit cave. "I think I was in denial back then."

"Denial?" She shifted, propping her head up on her bent elbow.

He sank down on his back, lifting one hand to tangle in her hair. "I never told you what the oracle said to me, did I?"

Her stomach clenched. "No."

"When I went to see her, I was very young. But even then, I was settled. I'd met Helka, joined the riders, and found my calling. I don't know why I even asked her about my future when I had such a clear vision of what mine would look like."

Her pulse raced. The oracle had shared so much knowledge with her, but all of it derived from the past. This was the first she'd heard about her predicting the future. She trailed a soft touch across Kai's chest. "What did she say?"

"One of my ancestors was the oracle's bonded, long ago. During his life, he was cursed with a recurring dream—about me."

"That's incredible." Her pulse sped up. "What was it about?"

He grinned crookedly. "My love life, apparently. He dreamed about two women, one with dark hair. And one with hair so light it was almost white." He playfully tugged a lock of her silvery tresses.

"You're kidding."

"It's the truth."

She pursed her lips. "Of all the things he could dream about..."

Kai chuckled, but then his voice turned serious. "That's not quite everything."

"What else was there?"

"Well, for one, I laughed it off." He bit his lip. "No one has hair like yours in Lanwell."

"I can't imagine the oracle was too happy with that." Perhaps that was where his warning about being respectful had originated...

His eyes closed and his brow wrinkled, like he was trying hard to remember the exact words. "She was shocked that he'd dreamed about me at all. And for him to meet me so far in the future that he could share his vision was exceedingly rare. She told me it had to be important—but I'll admit, I left that day thinking the meeting had been a waste of time."

Her heart pounded. It was so bizarre... Oracles, dreams, prophecies, and riddles had all converged to bring her here. Why?

His eyes popped open. "Then, one day, there you were. Fighting against a horde of disanders with those pathetic little knives." He threaded their fingers together. "I was ... thunderstruck. I kept finding my gaze drawn to you. Probably looked like I was gawking at an illusion."

What did it all mean? She'd assumed breaking the ring was her calling and that she'd satisfied that when she came here. She'd kept busy, unearthing secrets that would be the key to defeating the evil back home. But what if there was more to it than that?

A niggling itch scratched at her as Kai continued reminiscing about the past. With his voice sliding around her, soothing though entirely unheard, she called on her boon again.

No. The death note thrummed in her ears. A tear slid down her cheek. Then another.

"Violet?" Kai cut off his rambling and cupped her cheek, brushing away her tears. "What's wrong?"

She forced a smile as she silenced his song. "Nothing. I just don't want this moment to end."

That was certainly true, but it wasn't the whole truth. She couldn't bear to tell him.

Kai was about to die... and it was all her fault.

The next morning, Kai pulled her into a hug after he finished strapping their bedrolls on Roc. He frowned as he released her. "You sure you're all right?"

"Yeah." She thumped into his chest and wrapped her arms around him tightly. She'd been too much of a coward to listen to his song again, but it hadn't stopped the death note from plaguing her dreams.

His hands slid down her arms soothingly. "Don't worry. We're close to home. We'll be back before you know it."

She sighed and tightened her arms as he pulled away. "Wait."

"What is it?"

She'd debated telling him. It had done no good with Helka. Maybe he'd be happier not knowing... Who wanted to know they were about to die?

She lifted her gaze to meet his. "Last night, I listened again." She blinked back tears. "And... I heard it, Kai. The death note."

Kai froze. She searched his face, desperate for some sign of his feelings. Finally, he blinked, and a lopsided grin crossed his face. "In that case..." His hand slid to her nape, and he lifted her to his lips, giving her a blistering kiss.

By the time he let her catch her breath, her tears fell in earnest. "No." She clutched him tighter and buried her face against his chest. "There must be something we can do..."

He brushed her hair off her forehead and kissed her softly. "Everyone has their time... If this is mine, then at least I went out on a high."

Her brows pulled down. "Kai, how can you—"

"Shh..." His gaze shot to Roc. Then he grabbed her hand and drew her further into the cave.

"What is it?" she hissed.

"Manticores. More than we can handle." He tugged her back as Roc attempted to cram himself into the cave opening. "With any luck, we can hide until they pass."

Violet nodded. Her heart thrashed in her chest. Was this it? The moment Kai was destined to die?

They huddled in the rear of the cave beside the small fire they'd let burn down to embers. A thin stream of smoke floated into the air, clogging the cave now that Roc had cut off the exit. Her nose twitched.

The not knowing drove her crazy as the moments slowly ticked past. She could use her boon. See if the note was still there. If it was louder or quieter—or if it had faded away into nothing.

Maybe she'd misheard last night. Maybe she'd been mistaken.

Fear held her back until another thought lodged in her mind and refused to disappear. What if Roc was in danger, too? What if *she* was? Didn't she owe it to them to use every advantage they had at their disposal?

As shrieks pierced the quiet in their cave, she called on her boon. She stared ahead, listening first to Roc's steadily thumping tune, as strong as ever. Try as she might, she couldn't hear a whisper of death among the percussion and bass.

Next, she turned inward, listening closely to the panicked cadence of her song. Her brow wrinkled. Nothing off there either.

She spun to Kai, breathing deeply as she opened her mind to his melody. It spooled around her, the tempo fast and frantic but just as lovely as ever.

The note—it was barely there. A tiny hum, fading fast.

Had she been wrong?

Relief rushed through her, and she sucked in a thready breath.

"Ah-choo!" She clamped her hands over her mouth, but it was too late. The death note exploded at the same moment Roc tensed, and the shrieks outside increased in volume and ferocity.

She cut off her boon, unable to stand the deafening clamor an instant longer. "Kai!" she hissed.

His eyes went unfocused, and his lips flattened into a thin line. He dug into his pocket. "I have a plan." He snagged her tunic and smashed his lips against hers. "Wait here."

Kai dug into the fire, wincing as he scooped up some embers.

"No!" Violet shook her head, scrambling to her feet as she spotted what he carried in his other hand. "Kai, don't!"

Her foot slipped in the ashes. Kai bolted forward as Roc shifted, giving him enough space to slip past the dragon to the cave's edge.

She arrived a heartbeat too late to snag his belt loop. Roc blocked her way, and no amount of scowling or pounding on his scales convinced him to move.

Light flashed. Beasts shrieked. And Roc finally moved, diving so swiftly she gasped.

"Kai!" she screamed, stopping at the edge of the cliff. Her eyes widened as she spotted him barreling down, straddling a manticore with charred wings. Another monster chased them, and a half-dozen bodies careened to the earth, their carcasses in various states of fiery decay.

Her training kicked in and she nocked an arrow. Then another. But after the third, they had fallen too far. Kai glanced up, and they locked eyes as a low cloud shrouded him, blocking her view. Roc followed a heartbeat later, swirling so much mist in his wake it obscured her view even further.

"No!" she shrieked.

She pulled at her hair and fell to her knees, smacking into the hard stone. The pain barely registered. It couldn't compare to the devastation searing her soul.

That didn't happen... She couldn't have just watched Kai...

Numbness settled in her limbs, and her chest caved. A keening wail spilled out of her lips.

She was so focused on the pain searing her heart that she didn't notice the predator sinking on her from above. The cave trembled beneath her.

Roc soared up, his majestic wings spread and a rain of rocks spewing from his mouth, knocking the manticore off course.

She blinked, forcing herself back into the moment. Her arrow flew, catching the monster in the side of its neck. With a gurgling cry, it fell, unable to stay airborne with its windpipe pierced and countless holes littering its leathery wings.

But the beast's death did nothing to calm the agony raging through her veins. Because Kai wasn't seated atop Roc.

He was gone.

Roc landed beside her and bent, his head spinning back to stare at her expectantly. She climbed on, praying against all hope that she'd find him.

Kai, where are you?

She spent the next few days searching high and low for any sign of Kai. A deep river sprawled below the cave they'd spent the night in. There was a chance he'd fallen in and drifted somewhere down the banks.

Roc had forced her to return to Lanwell when they didn't spot him by nightfall on the first day. By then, they weren't alone. Roc must have contacted one of the other dragons as soon as the manticores were spotted. Riders had arrived in force after he'd saved her in the cave.

Tora assured her they'd keep hunting for Kai—until they knew for sure it was too late. With Roc as his bonded, they'd know exactly when he died.

The fact that Roc still hadn't heard Kai in his mind meant he was out there somewhere, holding on to life. She wasn't sure how to feel about it. He was likely unconscious and on the brink of death. If he was in his right mind, he'd tell Roc where to find him. But as long as he didn't tell Roc he was gone for good, there was still a chance.

"Where is he?" she whispered into the breeze.

Hadn't she suffered enough? Would it be enough to spend these days searching, plagued with the knowledge that it was all her fault?

He didn't need to die, did he?

As Roc flew low, something unusual caught her eye. She kicked Roc's side, urging him to turn back.

They hovered over the top of a gorge, with a skinny land bridge connecting the two mountaintops overlooking it. A deep drop fell off, with a trickling river far below. Violet's pulse pounded as a flash of silver fluttered in the breeze below a lengthy crack in the rock.

She tapped Roc's neck. He turned, gazing back with one eye. She signaled frantically for him to land.

Roc thumped down on the widest spot available. Even so, he looked uncomfortable. The peak overlooking the gorge was cramped, but he squeezed in.

Heart thumping, Violet slid off, carefully keeping her balance. *Why did it have to be a bridge?* Her old fears came rushing back. It was a natural formation, not manmade, but it didn't stop her feet from shaking or her stomach from sinking at the thought of tumbling over the edge.

She almost whipped around and hopped back onto Roc's back. But the need to know drove her forward even while dread sought to paralyze her.

The wind whipped through the gorge as she shimmied on her hands and knees on the skinny overhang. She edged further out, clenching tightly to rocks just wide enough for her to crawl across.

Roc snorted, the noise managing to sound incredulous and concerned all at once. She ignored him, reaching out carefully.

"Got it!" she announced as the broken necklace touched her fingers. She tugged hard, dislodging it from the crack. "I thought this was lost for good..." Awestruck, she stared at the dingy, worn, yet miraculously intact feathers Ryon had lost so long ago.

This might be the answer to all her problems! She just had to think of the right wish.

What if she wished herself to Kai's exact location? But then how would Roc find her if she ended up somewhere dangerous, and she couldn't get Kai to wake...

She crawled back slowly, pondering the question as a gasp sounded from above.

Tora hovered on her black fire dragon, Legon, with a scowl on her face. "Flashes, Violet! Are you itching to be rescued too?" She crossed her arms and nodded to Roc. "He insisted we fly over and see what foolishness you'd gotten up to."

She stuffed the necklace into a pocket and carefully stood. "It's all right. I just thought I saw something. We'll get back to searching."

Tora's face fell. "Yeah... About that. I didn't mean to say anything with Kai missing, but when Roc said you were in danger, it just... slipped."

Violet cocked a brow. "Huh? You're not making any sense."

"I'm sorry, Vi. Roc is taking you back. He doesn't want you flying, under the circumstances."

She shook her head. "I really don't get what—" Her statement cut off as Legon sniffed loudly, his head aimed in her direction. "You're kidding..."

Tora shrugged. "He always knows... It's kind of his thing."

Violet scrambled back onto Roc's back. "It doesn't matter. I need to find Kai. I don't care what danger—"

"Kai doesn't want you out here either." Legon lowered enough to bring Tora to eye level, and when she met her gaze, Violet's hopes shattered. "I'm so sorry, Violet. It's too late."

Bent Rules

Ryon paced in the sitting room, his boots thumping dully against the new carpet. "I thought you said your words would work?" He sent an accusing glare to Orry.

Orry fluffed her wings, unperturbed. "They will. They likely already have. We just need to discover where she roosted."

He rubbed his temples. "Was it too hard to ask that she show up here instead of some random spot on our world?"

"We were already asking for much out of that wish. The rules will only bend so far."

Kayda cleared her throat. "What's all the whistling about?"

Mena tracked his movement across the floor, her head peeking through the open window. Kayda had insisted they move inside and grab a bite while they waited on word of Violet's return. She'd sent doves in all directions when it was clear Violet wouldn't pop up in front of them. But that was hours ago. They hadn't heard a peep yet.

Lark headed home for the night to nearby Greenvale, eager to spend time with her husband and son. Now they were left waiting for a sign while the sun slowly sank on the horizon.

Ryon dropped onto a fluffy couch. "I was just asking Orry why that wish couldn't direct Violet here." He sighed. "Guess she was asking it to do too much already."

"Do you have any idea what those words even meant?" Kayda smoothed a hand down her black gown.

A sinking feeling spread through his stomach. "Oh, I've asked. She just said, 'You'll see.'" He shrugged.

Honestly, Orry's cryptic nonsense grated on his nerves. It wasn't only that oddly worded wish, but half her answers lately hardly made a lick of sense. And from the labored way she hobbled around, he worried her time was shorter than he'd hoped.

Was Orry close to death? If that was the case, could they even trust her mind? They may have made a horrible mistake by using her wording...

Would Violet ever come home?

A knock on the door drew him from his morbid thoughts.

"Come in," Kayda called.

A teen wearing a tunic emblazoned with a dove holding a parchment in its beak rushed through the door. "Your Grace." He bowed deeply, then strode forward, offering Kayda a rolled parchment. "A dove arrived. The message was marked 'urgent.'"

Kayda waved Ryon forward. "Would you mind reading it?" She turned back to the boy. "See my steward on your way out. He'll have a tip for you."

The boy nodded gratefully, handed Ryon the parchment, and disappeared into the hall.

He unrolled the letter with shaking fingers. His gaze danced across the page, and he was too excited to read the overly verbose message verbatim. He summarized it instead, his voice rising in volume with every word. "It's from Magehaven. The willow in the village square cracked open today. There's someone inside..." He gasped.

Kayda stood abruptly. "Does it say who it is?"

"No. But they heard breathing coming from within. They sent a letter immediately, knowing you'd want to be informed." The parchment crinkled in his shaking hands. "It has to be her!"

"I think so too." She lifted her skirt and looped an arm against her waist. "Lead me outside. Mena will fly us there."

With a few short whistles, he filled Orry in. She flew out the open window and landed gracefully on Mena's back.

Then he took Kayda's arm, and together they scurried through the castle halls. A few silent guards looked on, but no one sought to stop them until they arrived on the grounds.

"Your Grace!" Guard Captain Gawain hurried over, his face flushed. "Looks like Mena is preparing to fly," he said sternly. "Please tell me you're not going on a pleasure cruise."

Kayda lifted a brow. "Oh, good. Gawain, would you mind giving me a hand up?"

"Where exactly are you going?" Gawain got into position despite his disapproving tone.

"We received word the willow in Magehaven cracked open." Kayda scrambled up, using Gawain's linked hands to boost her. "I'm taking Ryon to investigate."

"Investigating a tree... Your Grace?" Gawain's voice rose in pitch.

Ryon vaulted up behind her. "Violet might be inside." He stretched out his arms as he settled on Mena, and Orry hopped onto his lap, curling up for the flight.

Kayda added, "We're staying within the kingdom, Gawain. Nothing to worry about."

Mena began flapping her white leathery wings. The Guard Captain held his tongue, but judging by the deep crease in his brow, he wasn't pleased about their trip.

A swarm of conflicting emotions rocked him as they lifted off. Terror made his hands clammy and his breath come hard and fast. What if it *wasn't* her? Or worse, what if it was but she hadn't survived…

The absurdity of it all bubbled up in his chest. Why would Violet be sent back inside a *tree*, of all places?

But just as he worried he might pass out before they arrived, a wave of elation rose, calming his frantically fluttering heart. It *had* to be her. That meant he was about to see her again. He'd succeeded. Violet was home, and very soon, he would hold her in his arms again.

He spent the entire flight alternating between those extremes, barely noting their path over the forested countryside. When they arrived on the eastern coast of Dracwood, black dominated the sky, the moon a mere sliver dimly lighting their way.

His pulse sped as they flew low over Magehaven. Most of the homes in the picturesque seaside village sported the darkened windows of folk dead to the world. But one area was lit with dozens of blinking points of light. The willow stood in the center. Its vibrant green leaves shimmered slightly even when lit only by curious villagers holding lanterns and candles.

They descended beside the city square. The rhythmic scratch of wood being worked on carried on the breeze, blending in with the excited chatter of the townspeople who marveled over Mena.

Orry flew out of his arms with a parting whistle. "She's here, Ryon. I can feel it!"

Overcome with relief, Ryon hopped down as soon as Mena landed. Seeing a finely dressed man approaching, a blinding smile aimed at Kayda, he took off. She'd forgive him for not helping her down. He had to see Violet.

His boots slapped on the road, and his skin erupted with prickles. He raced through the crowd, elbowing past anyone in his way.

Men holding small saws and files crowded the tree. He charged straight toward them.

"Get back." One man turned with a frown. "We need room to work!"

"I'm here with the queen." Ryon raised his voice. "Move aside."

They parted hastily, and he bit back a gasp. The stories were true... Someone was inside. From afar, he could tell the unmoving form was human. The workers had whittled away enough of the bark to reveal a back and shoulders. The shapely curves looked feminine, though it was hard to say with so little of the person visible.

He marched closer, his eyes widening as he recognized the fabric sheathing the body. He'd only seen it's like in one place...

With shaking fingers, he pressed his hand flat against her back. Warmth bled into his palm—and he felt a reassuring twitch that let him know she was alive.

"It's her!" he shouted, likely loud enough to wake the whole village. At that moment, he couldn't care less. He approached a worker. "How long before you get her out of there?"

A man holding a crowbar replied, "Sooner if you get out of the way."

Ryon backed away. Kayda arrived at his elbow. "You can tell it's her? All Mena sees are her shoulders."

Relief pulsed through him so intensely it took him a moment to answer. "The clothing. It's the same fabric everyone wears in Lanwell. And Orry can sense her presence."

"Ah…" She patted his arm and smiled brightly. "Good." Then she cleared her throat and raised her voice. "Excellent work, all of you. Please remove her swiftly and safely. That's my niece inside."

Excited murmurs broke out, and the workers returned to their task with renewed vigor. Ryon waited impatiently while the men slowly chipped away at the bark, revealing Violet's hips. Then her arms. Once they'd widened the hole enough that the tops of her thighs were visible, he'd waited about as long as he could stand.

"Move aside." He strode forward and reached into the willow. His hands closed around Violet's hips, and he tugged.

A worker glanced back uneasily at Kayda. "Careful! She might still be stuck—"

Violet's body bent at the waist as he pulled her out. He grunted, struggling to free her from the awkward position. "A little help?"

Metal clanged on the ground as the closest man dropped his file and hurried to help tug her legs free. Another gripped her shoulders, easing her head out of the hole.

Ryon's heart raced when he got the first clear glimpse of her face peeking out of the hooded shirt sheathing her. "Violet," he whispered reverently.

It was her! She was back!

With the help of the men, he settled her softly on the ground. A gray-haired healer wearing sweeping brown robes rushed forward, shooing the workers away, but Ryon refused to move.

He couldn't tear his eyes off her lovely face. She still slept, oblivious to all the folk crowded around her.

Kayda kneeled beside them, her face pale. "Is she… all right?"

The healer's hands rested lightly on Violet's neck. He bent his ear by her face and pursed his lips. "She's alive." He lifted his head and scanned the rest of her body, frowning when his gaze caught on the lower half of her loose top.

The healer shuffled lower and swept his palms over Violet's abdomen. His eyebrows lifted, and a slow smile spread across his face. "They're both alive."

Ryon jolted, finally tearing his gaze off Violet's face. "What?"

"The babe just kicked me." The healer chuckled.

Kayda gasped. "Violet's *pregnant*?"

The words slammed into him like an avalanche.

He stared at the healer's hands on Violet's rounded belly. It was far larger than he remembered, like a woman midway through her pregnancy.

It shouldn't be possible. She'd been missing for days. There was no way. Unless his guess had been true. Time must truly move at different speeds...

Shock locked his limbs as he fought to reconcile the facts. They'd spent the night together before he'd left. If months had passed for Violet while days passed here... Joy bloomed in his soul so profoundly it brought tears to his eyes.

He returned his attention to her face with a smile. "A babe..." Violet was having his baby. His fingers slipped into her hood, and he leaned down, so full of joy he couldn't resist planting a kiss on her forehead.

But as his lips pressed against her skin, his stomach sank.

That wasn't right...

He pulled back her hood, revealing long strands of chest-length hair.

He forgot how to breathe... Pressure built, burning his lungs and making the edges of his vision blur.

They'd both been forced to shave their heads. There was no way her hair had grown that much in just a few months. It should be slightly longer than his, not this...

How long had Violet been there?

Who was the father of her child?

One thing was clear—it wasn't him.

Kayda's hand clamped on his shoulder, and Ryon inhaled deeply, though the action hardly brought him any relief. He felt numb... all over.

The healer spoke, his voice barely registering in his mind. "I don't recommend waking her forcibly." He nodded at the willow. "If she slept through that racket, she clearly needs the rest."

What happened to Violet on that world? He'd missed her so badly, but she'd led a whole life without him.

Would she even be happy they'd brought her back? Or would she wake up and rage, horrified they'd torn her away from her new life... and the man she loved?

"We should move her." Kayda pointed across the square. "There's an inn I've stayed at in the past that will suffice."

Ryon's legs quivered as he stood. Then he bent, scooped Violet into his arms, and headed to the inn, fighting the urge to weep.

What Else

When bright sunlight spilled into the open windows of her room, Violet stretched, reveling in the warmth. It must be one of the exceedingly rare moments the sun broke through the cloud cover—and she was missing it.

Her eyes popped open, and she gasped. She sat up in bed, blinking furiously.

This wasn't her room.

"*Hello, child.*" A musical voice rang through her mind.

Tears sprang to her eyes. "*Orry? I-I'm back?*" She'd forgotten how marvelous it felt to share her thoughts with her bondmate. How right. She slipped back into the habit easily, like picking up an instrument she'd mastered in her youth but hadn't touched since. A little shaky at first—but ripe with nostalgia and bursting with joy. "*Where are you? I'm not sure where I am...*"

She glanced around the wood-paneled inn bedroom, which didn't give her many clues. But when she lifted her nose, a pleasant tang of salt permeated the air. Seabirds cawed somewhere nearby.

"You're in Magehaven. As am I." Gold fluttered in the window, and she shifted in bed as Orry landed on the sill. *"I'm pleased you've returned at long last."*

"You can say that again." She rubbed her eyes, still a little muddle-headed. Then she wobbled in place like she'd awoken after sleeping off several strong drinks, though she could swear she hadn't touched a drop for ages.

She had a reason for that... but what was it?

The door swung open, and a man marched in, his gaze glued to the tray in his hands.

"Ryon? Blazes, it's good to see you!" Her heart expanded, and she smiled radiantly.

His gaze flew to hers. The tray wobbled. He rushed in, setting it on a table in the far corner of the room. Then he stayed there, hunched over the tray with his back facing her while the door swung under its own weight and slammed shut. "You're awake."

Her brow furrowed. That was all he had to say?

Orry spread her wings on the sill. *"You two have much to discuss. I'll take my leave. Call out if you need me."* With that, she lifted off, leaving Violet even more confused.

"I-I'm not sure what's going on..." She swallowed, her throat thick. "Did your head feel all scrambled when you came back, too?"

Water trickled into a mug. He finally turned, an unreadable expression painting his face. "It did. But I wasn't gone as long as you were." He slowly walked to the bed and stretched out the cup.

Her throat was beyond parched, but she ignored the drink. She threw her arms wide as she scooched out from under the blankets, intending to give him a hug.

"Oh!" A pang of discomfort shot up her side. Her hand landed on her belly, and her eyes widened.

"Hey, easy." The mug clattered on the bedside table.

She hardly noticed. The moment her palms landed on her stomach, a hundred thousand memories bombarded her. Years and years of memories.

Helka. Aylia... Kai.

She clamped a hand over her mouth, and nausea rose, nearly making her retch. Panic overwhelmed her next. If they'd used a feather for *her*... She spread her fingers over her stomach agitatedly, only relaxing when a strong kick pressed against her palm.

"Hey." Ryon kneeled in front of her, loosely holding her elbow. "You're all right. I'm right here."

Her gaze lifted from the floor and landed on Ryon. He looked so good. Exactly how she remembered, except for the simple brown traveler's attire. His hair barely reached his ears, just like it had the moment he'd left.

She reached out, unable to stop her fingers from sinking into his hair. Ryon flinched, but he let her trail her hand across his scalp. The short strands tickled her palm. "Have you kept up the habit of cutting it?" she asked hoarsely.

"No." Breath sawed out of his lungs as he released an enormous sigh. "You watched it get cut." He tugged on a strand of her long silvery hair. "How long ago was that for you, Violet?"

She met his eyes. "Almost ten years."

He rocked back on his heels. "Ten years?"

"Yes." She folded her hands in her lap, unable to meet his eyes. So much had happened in their time apart. He deserved to know the whole story. Yet, she just sat there, tongue tied.

How did you tell the man you'd promised you'd wait for that you lived and fought and *loved* for years, while only days passed for him?

Her head swam, and she shivered, wrapping her arms tightly around her middle.

Ryon retrieved the cup. The bed sank with his weight as he settled beside her. This time, she took it and drank deeply.

She stared down at the water in the half-empty mug. "I suppose we should fill each other in on what happened while we were apart."

Her pulse raced. Where to begin?

"I can go first. Sounds like you have a lot more to tell than I do."

Violet nodded gratefully. "All right."

He cleared his throat. "Your wish dropped me back where we left."

Her jaw fell. "Do you mean... the ring under the sea?"

"Yeah. I was exhausted. I barely managed to swim to the surface before I passed out. But before I did, I noticed the battle still happening. The sun was high overhead, at midday."

"You came back on the same day?"

"A few hours after we left. That was my first clue that something wasn't right..."

"What happened next?"

"A passing ship scooped me out of the sea. Luckily, it wasn't one of Jurdan's. They met up with Nox, and I woke long enough to tell them what we learned." He shook his head sadly. "While I was recuperating, they returned to Thalassia. And..."

She sensed from the weighted pause something was coming she wouldn't like. "Tell me."

He grabbed the cup, placed it on the bedside table, and enclosed both of her hands within his. "In order to free the Hilfolk, someone had to stay behind. There was no other way."

"Who?" She braced herself for horrible news. Nox and Mariun had been there... Kayda too. Was she about to learn she'd never see one of them again? "Who was it?"

"Your parents."

Her shoulders curled forward, and her chest caved. She'd almost forgotten. She'd spotted a glimpse of them before she'd swum for the ring. "Shadow?" Her voice escaped, merely a whisper.

"Nox saved him. And they saved hundreds of people before the city sank." He sighed. "By then, your mother was gravely wounded. Your father volunteered to stay behind."

"Blazes… I-I should've been here." Her chin wobbled. Devastation rose, searing her soul. She tugged her hands free and buried her face into her palms, weeping.

Was this part of her curse? More of those damned consequences coming back to bite her? When would it end?

Ryon's arms closed around her. "I'm sorry. I wish I'd been there too. Maybe if they'd waited until I'd recovered, it would've made a difference."

The tears fell faster then, in the face of his kindness. She didn't deserve it.

She pushed out of his arms, violently scrubbing her cheeks. "What else?"

He searched her face. "Losing your parents must be a lot. If you need a moment—"

"No. I want to hear it all."

She sat there numbly while Ryon recounted every detail. Waking on the island. Finding Orry and leaving to find Kayda. Convincing Kayda to make a wish using Orry's specific wording.

Violet cocked her head curiously. "Wait… what did she tell Kayda to say?"

Ryon furrowed his brow. "Something about bridges. I can't quite remember. Do you want me to ask her?"

She rubbed her neck and absentmindedly tugged on the necklace she'd worn every day for the last few months. Orry mentioned bridges once before... What did it mean?

Ryon squinted. Then he blanched. "I-is that what I think it is?"

"Hm?" She followed his line of sight and grinned halfheartedly. "Oh, yeah. I found it out in the wilds a few months ago." She tugged the necklace off and handed it to Ryon. "Here, I always intended to give it back."

He stared at the silver feathers in his hands. "I don't understand... If you found these months ago, why didn't you wish yourself back?"

She sighed. "I wanted to. Believe me, I can't tell you how many times I had to talk myself out of it."

"Why would you talk yourself out of it?" He stood, backing away. "Did you want to stay there, Violet?"

"No." She got up, standing in front of him while his shoulders trembled. "I wanted to come back... I always wanted to come back."

"Then why?" He shook the necklace at her. "You had the means in the palm of your hand."

Violet lowered her gaze and trailed her hands across her stomach. "The day I found the feathers, I learned I was pregnant. A wish on a silver feather changes one thing about yourself. Only, it wasn't just *me* any longer... I was afraid it wouldn't work for both of us." She smiled ruefully as another strong kick fluttered against her fingers. "I guess it would've, though. Just one more item to add to my long list of regrets."

Ryon stiffened. "I'm not so sure... I think that's why Orry made Kayda say all that stuff about bridges. She didn't wish you back." His gaze landed on her stomach. "She wished back the baby."

Violet sank back onto the bed as his words crashed over her.

Every day in Lanwell, she woke wondering why she was still there. Why had fate shown her those feathers at the exact moment she learned she couldn't use them? Why hadn't Ryon brought her back faster? Why keep her there so long she fell in love, and brought her and Kai together—just once—on the perfect day for her to conceive?

She stared down at her stomach in awe. Was it all for this child?

What does fate have in store for you, little one?

Shattered

"**W**here is he?"

"I told you already... Look for freshly dug earth in a clearing close to their cabin."

"Is he still alive?"

"We've been over this before. If he weren't, you wouldn't be speaking to me."

"I know... I'm just scared. Keep talking to me until I get there... please?"

Voices echoed in Nox's mind, but he couldn't talk back. He wasn't even sure he'd heard them truly. The wispy fragments floated away before he grasped them within the dreamlike trance he'd fallen under.

In the end, it was his most obscure boon that would save him—if anyone found him before his tiny supply of air finally ran out. Just before Jurdan buried him alive, he used the ability the bondmate who'd once betrayed him had gifted him—hibernation.

His heartbeat had slowed. His breathing had shallowed. And his mind drifted, falling into a state that was almost like a dream... but not quite the same.

Time passed glacially slow. The pain in his limbs radiated inward, pulsing and throbbing and making him yearn to move. But that was impossible now. If he did, he'd wake. If he woke, he'd breathe normally. And within the space of a few inhales, he'd suffocate.

He had no idea how long he'd lain there. Visions of Mariun plagued him incessantly.

One moment, he saw himself taking her home to his village in the Raimire jungle. She'd marveled at the teeming life. Blushed at the villagers' lack of attire. When he presented her with an orphaned jagoth kit he'd found, the vision faded, evaporating like smoke.

A horrible sight replaced it. Mariun tied up on a boat. Bloodred tears spilled down her cheeks. Thunder and lightning crackled in the sky before striking down and blasting her into smithereens. He screamed, and the image shattered like sea glass, only to be replaced with another.

On and on it went until he worried he'd finally gone mad. The ever-present fear overwhelmed him until he was presented with a vision more horrifying than all the rest.

His hands clenched around Mariun's delicate neck. They'd been there once before... but this time wasn't for show. Crazed rage burned through his limbs as he squeezed. She fell limp, her eyes open and staring blankly into his own.

No!

Nox jerked awake far too soon. Black dirt shrouded him. His lungs burned as he sucked in a deep breath. Likely his last...

"Please tell me you're out there," he asked weakly.

"No. You're supposed to be asleep. Go back to sleep!" Flint shouted.

Good advice. Nox looked inward. He fought to call on his boon like he had before. "*It's no use... I can't.*"

Gwen's voice shook. "*I'm out in the woods looking for you right now. Don't give up!*"

Nox closed his eyes. "*Funny. Thought I heard digging.*" His head grew heavy and his lungs ached, but even now, he still swore a rhythmic scratching echoed above his head. "*Must be my mistake.*"

If Gwen hadn't found him yet, then it was only wishful thinking. A massive storm had stopped her brothers from flying to his aid. Likely Jurdan's doing, to cover his trail as he stole Mariun away.

Her name gave him the strength to suck in another thready inhale. "*Tell her... I love her.*"

"*Nox, no.*" Gwen sounded panicked now. "*You'll tell her yourself. I'm almost there!*"

"*Hang on!*" Flint demanded.

But Nox couldn't reply. He was already slipping away.

A speck of dirt landed on his cheek. Then another. Then a whole pile of dirt crumbled above his head, caving in the tiny pocket of air he'd secured within his arms.

This was it... He was done for now.

He clamped his mouth closed, holding his breath for as long as he could. Yet he knew it was inevitable. His burning lungs screamed, demanding he breathe. Air or dirt—they didn't care which.

Then his body jerked. His wounds protested, sending so much agony flaring through his body the shock forced him to suck in a breath.

Cool, moist air filled his lungs.

Nox doubled over on the top of the dirt pile, breathing so fast and hectically dizziness washed over him. "*Gwen. You found me!*"

"*No, I didn't.*"

Nox rubbed the dirt off his face and rolled over. A pair of golden eyes stared back at him. "Shadow." He threw his arms around his brother's bondmate and wept.

"Shadow found me. I'm all right."

Even in death, his brother couldn't resist playing the hero. He had no doubt Conall had noticed when he went missing. That he compelled his bondmate to hunt him down. And he couldn't be happier to have his big brother looking out for him from beyond the grave.

"Thank you, Brother," he whispered to Shadow. "I owe you another one."

The sound of Gwen tromping through the forest echoed in the clearing, and Shadow tensed.

"It's all right. It's Gwen." He released Shadow and turned, wincing. *"I can hear you, Gwen. You must be close..."*

Shadow lifted his muzzle in the air and howled.

"Be right there." Gwen arrived swiftly, and she didn't bother to hold back her gasp when she spotted him. He must look a state, covered in dirt, dried blood, and bruises. *"What did they do to you, Nox?"*

"Not enough." He struggled to one knee. Agony in his limbs nearly made him weep again.

"Take it easy," Flint cautioned. *"You almost died."*

Gwen stopped beside him. With her to lean on, he hobbled up on his feet. *"They took her again. I have to save her."*

"You might want to reconsider that," Gwen said. *"At least, for now."*

"What? Why should I?"

"Well, for one, you look like you just crawled out of a grave..."

Nox lifted a brow. *"I'll heal."*

"But how fast?" Flint asked. *"Do you really think you should race to face Jurdan now? Be smart, Nox. Do you even know where they're going?"*

He shook his head. *"I'll start at Jolit Isle. Remember what that masked said?"*

"Sure. But what if you could get more clues?" Gwen curved her neck sideways, meeting his eyes with one of hers. *"When I dropped the big guy in Dracwood, we learned the spider is close to death. The diva thinks that if he could be healed, then the hold Jurdan has over him would be broken. Mena talked to me about it. They wanted to ask you to help by using my boon."*

Nox rubbed his temples. That was possible, judging by what had happened to him as a lad. But still... *"You want me to go back to Dracwood while Mariun is out there somewhere—with him."* He hissed out the last, unable to disguise the rancor in his tone.

"The key word is somewhere.*"* Flint sounded calmer than he had any right to be. *"Think about it. Jayan was Jurdan's second-in-command. If anyone was privy to his plans, wouldn't it be him?"*

"And that's not all..." Gwen's flanks trembled with excitement. *"Mena just told me some fantastic news. It's Violet. She's back! What if she learned something useful, too?"*

They made a good point. The bear admitted he was never trusted with important information... but that might not be the case for the spider.

And returning to Dracwood would allow him to heal. When he faced Jurdan again, he'd be armed with the knowledge of where to go, and maybe even a few tips on how to destroy him—for good this time. He'd make certain it was the last time they met.

He wouldn't take Mariun *ever* again.

Jurdan was a dead man... He just didn't know it yet.

Take It

Ryon's mind whirled as he sat beside Violet on the inn bed. As much thought as he'd given their future since she'd returned, he still couldn't wrap his head around what she'd gone through.

Ten years... How did she survive that long in a world overrun with monsters? What did she have to live through?

A part of him wanted to demand answers. To beg her to share every detail of her life while she'd been away.

But another urge rose above all the rest. He'd known he would make the offer as soon as the feathers had hit his hand. Because one thought kept reverberating through his mind, making nausea bite the back of his throat. *What if she didn't want to come back?*

His hand slowly stretched, and his fingers unclenched from the necklace. "Take it."

Her brow furrowed. "Huh?"

"I'll find out what Orry told Kayda. You can wish yourself back."

She stared at the dangling feathers but made no move to take them. "Why would I want to do that?"

His heart ached as he forced out the words. "If I'd known it'd been so long... I never wanted to destroy the life you'd made." Bitterness slammed into him hard, but he choked it down. "Take it so your child can be with their father."

Violet's eyes pooled with tears. "That's impossible." Her lip quivered. "Everyone I loved while I lived in Lanwell died because of me."

The depth of sorrow in her confession nearly tore him in two. But he couldn't swallow the surge of anger that rose with it. "There was more than one?"

How many men had she loved? He wanted to rage. To tear out of the room and find the first boat back to his island. Yet something held him back...

She blinked away her tears. "Yes... but not like you're thinking." She sighed. "First, I lost my best friend. Do you remember Helka?"

"Of course."

"She died in childbirth."

His heart twinged. It wasn't uncommon, but that didn't make it any less of a loss. "I'm sorry."

"Her daughter, Aylia, became very dear to me. I helped raise her. Watched her learn how to walk and talk. Nursed her when she was sick. She was a daughter to me in every way that matters."

Ryon's stomach churned. "What happened to her?"

Violet closed her eyes. "She was killed right in front of me. Snatched off the ground by a beast. I-I couldn't save her."

He dropped the necklace on the bed and took her hand.

Her eyes popped open, shadowed with pain and grief. "After Lia passed, I was a wreck. I could barely get out of bed. This little nagging voice kept telling me it was my fault. That the people around me were suffering as a consequence of my wish."

Ryon's stomach dropped to his feet. She'd used that wish to send *him* home.

He knew he should keep quiet. To let her tell her story in her own way. But he couldn't halt the question before it flew off his tongue. "What about the father? Did you love him too?"

Violet blew out a deep breath. "Yes."

He retracted his hand and jerked up, needing to move. His boots thumped on the floorboards as he paced the room while the world spun around him.

"I'm sorry. I know I said I'd wait."

"For years," he added blankly.

"I never stopped waiting for you. Loving you. Wishing you'd bring me back."

He halted in place and glared at her. "Are you sure? Because that looks like a lie from where I'm standing."

Violet shrank into herself, and he instantly regretted his words. Before he could snatch them back, she met his gaze and straightened her shoulders.

"I can apologize until my lips turn blue, but it won't change what happened. Living there, seeing how many people opened their hearts to more than one love... It made me want that too. And I guess after a while, I stopped trying so hard to ignore my feelings. But nothing happened until after Lia passed."

Ryon cradled his head in his hands and sank on the bed's edge.

Reaching for love in the wake of loss was certainly an understandable reaction. And deep down, he hated the thought of Violet spending all those nights alone. Lonely and loveless, dying to return home but stuck day after day with no answers. He wouldn't wish that on his worst enemy, much less the woman he loved.

Yet, he had so many questions. Did she love the child's father more than she loved him? When did their relationship start? How long did it last? But that wasn't what he asked.

"Was it Kai?" He knew the answer before she opened her lips. He'd sensed it all along.

"It was."

Ryon crossed the room to the window. He stared out, not seeing anything on the other side. His mind was too full of memories flashing in a loop.

The first day, when he'd seen Kai staring at Violet. Their heads bent closely as they joked during the test. Even that last day, when Kai arranged for them to spend their final night together...

Of course Kai fell in love with her. Violet was incredible. So caring that she'd become the surrogate mother of her dead friend's child. So purehearted that the girl's death had mired her in grief.

And Kai was there to comfort her—while he was long gone. Violet probably thought he was dead after ten years with no word.

He should've never left. He should've stayed with Violet until the end. They'd have found the silver feathers together and wished themselves back. And yeah... maybe Jurdan would still be in Thalassia terrorizing their world, but at least he'd have her. At least—

He shoved aside the resentful thoughts. Violet was right. They couldn't change the past. All that mattered was the future. He'd always assumed it would be *their* future... Now he wasn't so sure.

He spun around and met her eyes. "I love you, Violet. But it's only been days for me... Do you still feel anything for me after so long?"

"I do." She rose from the bed. "I never stopped."

His gaze fell to her belly, and his brow furrowed. "What about Kai? How did he...?" Curiosity burned within him, though he shouldn't care about the demise of the man who'd swooped in to take his place.

She froze, and the space between them felt more like an impassable gulf—not a few scant steps. "He died saving me." Her voice broke. "It took me a long time to get over that too. It helped that I could still talk to him, in a way."

"You could?"

She nodded. "He was dragon bonded, remember? With Roc and another rider there, we were able to talk. It wasn't the same, but it helped. He told me to move on. He didn't want me to stay shackled to Lanwell and the memory of everyone I'd lost there. After he said his piece... we said goodbye."

Kai could've clung to Violet, even in death. But he'd let her go. That was certainly admirable. And Kai had protected her when he couldn't, even when he'd paid the ultimate price. Deep down, he knew he should be grateful for that. But he couldn't stop a swell of fury from rising when he pictured Kai's face.

Violet swiped at her eyes. "I understand if you want nothing to do with me now. Even if we go our separate ways, you need to know that I still love you."

His hands trembled. He wanted to believe that more than any-thing...

Her voice rang out, thick with emotion but steady and strong. "All those years, I'll admit, I cursed your name a time or two. But even when I was miserable and heartbroken, I still thought about you. If you want to know everything that happened to me, I'll tell you. Every moment of every day."

He shook his head. "No." He didn't think he could bear it. At least not now. "Maybe one day."

She brightened slightly. "One day... So you want to see me again?"

Ryon's throat clogged. He stood there, wavering between two mo-mentous decisions.

Was what she'd done wrong? Or was falling in love and losing so much what she needed to suffer for her wish?

Did it really even matter when he loved her so much? Just yesterday, he couldn't stand the thought of not holding her in his arms again. If he closed his eyes, he could recall so vividly the bliss he'd experienced with her that last night in Lanwell. He could taste her lips on the night before they'd left Kings Keep, when he'd vowed to follow her anywhere. Those feelings didn't just disappear because she returned ten years older—and expecting.

Violet sighed wearily. "It's all right. I get it. It's too much to ask." She trudged back to the bed and sank down, her tone heavy with defeat. "I shouldn't have assumed the consequences would stop just because I'd made it back."

His soul shattered, splitting into a thousand jagged pieces. Was this the end?

A new future flashed in his mind's eye. He'd return to Avion alone. Spend the rest of his days in his childhood home, watching his mother putter around the kitchen styling hair. He'd visit his brother at the Aviary and listen to him sing.

It would be a good life—if Jurdan didn't show up someday to ruin it. But was it the life he wanted?

He pushed off the windowsill. Violet shifted, angling her body to hide her face behind the curtain of her hair as another future flashed in his mind.

They'd defeat Jurdan together. Then would come sleepless nights with a wailing infant. Soiled nappies to change by the dozen. And a babe staring at him every day, a living, breathing reminder of everything he'd lost by leaving without her.

His stomach tightened and his lungs constricted, making it hard to breathe. That future was coming—the evidence was right in front of his eyes. The only question was whether he'd be there... or just another consequence.

"No." The word exploded in the air, thick with finality as he finally worked up a response to her last declaration.

Violet's chest hitched and her shoulders drooped.

"Violet." He crossed the room slowly. "I won't be part of your suffering."

She lifted her tear-stained cheeks and gaped at him with disbelief. "Really?"

"If you never made that wish, then Jurdan would win. What happened after... I'm not thrilled I missed all those years of your life. And it might take me a while to wrap my head around... everything. But I'm glad you found someone who loved you when I couldn't."

"You are?" Sobs wracked Violet's chest again, but this time, her tentative smile made him certain they were happy tears.

Ryon sat beside her. "Yes. I love you, Violet." He placed his hand gently on her belly. "I'll love you both." He cradled her in his arms as she sobbed, and for the first time since he'd left her side, his life felt *right*. Violet was his one, and she was right back where she belonged.

Whatever It Takes

Nox clenched tightly to Gwen's thighs as they flew over the ocean with Crys and Ari flanking her sides. After Gwen's crazed flight to save him, he'd insisted she rest before flying back to Dracwood. It had given her brothers the time they'd needed to catch up.

Truthfully, each hour that passed had been torture. If not for his injuries—and the strong tea Balun had forced him to drink when he'd shuffled back into the village, bloodied and half-dead—he'd probably spent the entire night awake, wracked with fear and anxiety over Mariun's absence.

Luckily, the tea had helped him sleep soundly. The villagers had patched the worst of his wounds, and one of the Thalass refugees was kind enough to give him a fresh set of all-black clothes like so many of them favored. Now, he was halfway back to normal as he spotted the first sign of land on the horizon.

"*Mena says to land in the village square. They're waiting for us.*" Gwen flicked a glance over her shoulder as she swooped lower over the sun-drenched coastal village.

Nox's eyes widened when he spotted the enormous willow in the square. "*Wow. Guess they weren't kidding about where Violet ended up.*" A huge hole split the trunk in two, but the leaves shone as brightly as he remembered.

Gwen thumped down in the square. Nox hopped off and immediately headed for Crys. He'd strapped Shadow on Crys's back for the flight, knowing he wouldn't want to stay behind on the island when he could be with Violet.

Mena hustled over, rubbing flanks with Gwen and Ari. Crys's scales quivered, and he shifted slightly. Nox did his best to hurry so the impatient dragon could reunite with his siblings, eventually giving up his plan to untie the ropes, slicing through them instead.

Shadow bounded off Crys's back and shook out his fur. Then his muzzle lifted, and after a single sniff, he turned toward the dragons and froze.

Nox directed his gaze beyond Shadow's as a flicker of fabric flashed beside Mena. Then his heart stuttered as Violet jogged into the square, sheathed in a long, flowing white dress that made her unique violet eyes stand out like twin stars in the dark night.

"Squirt," he breathed, moving toward her.

But Violet only had eyes for another. She fell to her knees beside Shadow and buried her head in the wolf's fur, wrapping her arms tightly around his neck. "I'm sorry. I-I should've been here…"

The sound of her sobs broke his heart. "I was there with your parents at the end." Violet's gaze lifted to his as she blinked back her tears. "They told me to tell you they love you. And they're so damn proud of you."

Violet's chin quivered before she jerked her head aside, resting her cheek against Shadow's side.

Nox backed away, wishing he could say more. What was there to say? Her parents were gone. He knew nothing that would ease that ache... Violet needed the space to feel her grief. And as much as he might want her help to find Mariun and defeat Jurdan, the least he could give her was a few moments to truly live in her feelings.

Before she lifted her head, footsteps pounded the cobbles. Nox smiled at Kayda and nodded at Ryon as they arrived in the square.

Kayda didn't let him get away with such a lame greeting. She marched straight to his side and pulled him into a tight hug. "We'll find her, Brother. I promise."

Nox's chest tightened at the reminder. He could hardly go a few moments without thinking of her. He wasn't sure why when someone else brought up Mariun's absence, it made the ache more acute.

"I know we will." Nox pulled away with a smile, eyeing Kayda's simple green frock. She patted his cheek and returned the smile before her expression shifted.

"I understand Mena already told Gwen about our plan. But I must ask... are you willing to try healing Jayan?"

Nox drew in a deep breath. He'd waffled over his decision on the way over. Should he heal the man who had tried to kill his sister? A man who was complicit in so many of Jurdan's crimes—his second-in-command for two decades? He'd sat in that box by the Dark King's side and watched stoically while so many men and innocent animals died...

But then he remembered Mariun's story. How Jayan had stood up for her on the day she was forced to do the unthinkable. And he looked into Kayda's eyes and saw the affection she still reserved for her old friend. The man she'd sent on a mission, not knowing he'd be dumped into a world he didn't understand and courted by a madman.

"I'll do it."

Kayda's smile widened before dimming swiftly. "Are you sure? I know it's dangerous. Ryon said last time you passed out."

Violet finally lifted her face out of Shadow's fur. "I can help with that."

"Squirt." Nox lent out a hand, helping her to her feet.

Violet rose slowly, then thudded into his chest, wrapping her arms around him tightly. "Can you believe I even missed you calling me that, Uncle?"

Nox's smile faded as he noticed something strange. The flowing white dress had done a fair job of hiding it, but now that he held her, it was impossible to miss the extra weight around her middle. He pulled back, his brow furrowed. "Violet... are you—"

"Pregnant. Yes. And I have the child's father to thank for what I'm about to tell you."

Nox blinked repeatedly, and then his gaze flashed to Ryon. He stood behind Violet, his expression flat, but Nox thought he glimpsed suppressed emotion flash in his eyes.

Clearly there was more to this story than he could unpack right here and now...

He rubbed the back of his neck. "Sorry... I feel like I'm playing catch-up. Gwen told me you were back, but I didn't realize so much had changed."

Violet sighed. "You don't know the half of it. But it can wait. This is more important—if you want to heal Jayan without harming yourself."

Nox lifted a brow. "You know how to do that?"

She nodded. "Yes. It's all about choosing the right pieces of earth to draw on when healing. When you brought Mariun back, you grabbed the only thing you could find… and in a pinch, that will always work. But it will drain your strength at best, and at worst, it could kill you."

"How am I supposed to know which plants to choose?" He recalled a bit of the lore from the earth mages of old. But he'd never trained as a healer…

Kayda cut in. "Lark can help you. She's with Jayan now."

"All right. I think I can handle that." He turned to Gwen. "Guess we better prepare for another flight." With Jayan on the opposite coast of Dracwood, in Flamesmoat, it would be hours before they tried Violet's technique.

"No need to fly." Kayda grinned. "When we flew here for Violet, I gave orders to have Jayan transported to Magehaven. They arrived just before you did."

He wasn't surprised. Kayda had a knack for anticipating what needed to be done. Guess that came with the territory of being queen.

Nox clapped his hands together. "Well, no time like the present. Where is he?"

Kayda lifted two fingers to her lips and whistled sharply. Within moments, guards emerged from a nearby inn, carrying a stretcher between them. A woman wearing a dark-brown dress wrapped in a stained apron followed, a wan smile on her lips.

From the look Lark sent Violet, Nox gathered they'd already reunited. His guess was confirmed when she bypassed her completely and strode to him, pulling him into her arms. "Brother. I've missed you!"

Nox cringed internally, wondering what was on that soiled apron, but he didn't let it stop him from hugging Lark back. "I missed you too, Sister."

Lark pulled away, only to shove a handful of plants at his chest. "I'd love to chat, but I'm afraid there isn't much time. The crossing was hard on Jayan. If you're willing to save him, you need to do it now."

Nox's jaw clenched. "All right. Let's do this." He followed Lark across the square.

"Hey, Gwen. Can you help me out?"

She popped up from where she'd been rubbing flanks with her siblings. *"What do you need?"*

"I need you to summon so I can use your boon."

Flint's voice thrummed through his ears, thick with warning. *"Wait! That's not safe. Don't you remember what happened last time?"*

A phantom pain rattled his skull. *"I do... But Violet says she knows how to do it so I won't be harmed."*

Gwen tilted her head at Violet as she ambled across the square. *"She learned that while she was gone?"*

"Apparently." Nox's brows pinched as he got his first good look at Jayan. Lark wasn't kidding. If she hadn't told him he was still alive, he would've sworn he was staring at a corpse.

"Does that mean there were dragons on the other side of that ring?" Gwen shot another glance at Violet.

"Sounds like it. I'm sure she'll tell me all about it when we have the time." He placed the assorted plants on Jayan's chest.

Gwen replied, *"Right."* Then she opened her mouth, and the ground shook as a steady stream of pebbles spilled out of her mouth.

"Careful," Flint cautioned.

Nox closed his eyes and dug deep inside, reaching for the spot in his soul where his bond hummed with love. It was far easier this time now that he'd done it once before. The magic responded, the vibration increasing as it flowed up through his toes. And somewhere deep inside him it morphed, losing the shake and turning into pure heat that escaped as a pleasant warmth through the palms of his hands.

As quickly as the sensation washed over him, it subsided. Nox opened his eyes, half expecting dizziness to wash over him again and his head to slam into the ground. Gwen stopped summoning, and the square fell still.

Lark gasped. "It worked! Look. He's breathing normally already."

He glanced down, finally noticing the steady rise and fall of Jayan's chest. His skin, which only moments ago had been deathly pale and covered in sores, looked remarkably normal.

Backing away, he brushed the plant remnants off his skin. "If it's anything like last time, it'll take a while for him to wake."

Kayda lifted her chin. "Carry him inside, please."

The guardsmen obeyed, hefting the stretcher into the air.

"Should we head in as well?" Kayda asked. "We still have much to discuss."

They all agreed, and soon they'd piled inside a comfortable room that had clearly been decked out with all the best fabrics and tapestries Magehaven had to offer.

Kayda waved at the guardsmen. "Put him on the bed and leave us."

Nox settled on a finely upholstered couch next to Lark. Once they were alone, he turned to Violet, who'd taken a seat beside Ryon on a pair of wingback chairs.

"Vi, I'm dying to hear about everything that happened to you." That was the understatement of the century... "But first, I have to ask... Did you find out how to kill him?"

Violet settled a hand on her belly. "I think so."

"Don't keep us in suspense." Kayda sat on the edge of the bed next to Jayan.

"I met with an oracle while in Lanwell. She knew many things about the creatures we know as the Unseen. Most important is that they can't be destroyed while joined with a person."

Nox's stomach sank. That didn't sound promising...

Ryon leaned forward. "Joined? What does that mean?"

Kayda chimed in. "The Unseen wanted to join with Conall. When he finally agreed, that's when it revealed itself and tried to slither down his throat."

Violet continued. "In Lanwell, they called them murkborn. The dragons who'd built the rings found them during their travels from world to world. They were the reason they stopped using the rings. They didn't want to give the murkborn a chance to spread more."

"So those things came from another world?" Lark shivered.

Violet nodded. "They knew a few had sneaked through to other worlds, but they weren't sure where they'd ended up."

"It doesn't matter how they got here. We just need to figure out how to kill them." Nox's jaw clenched.

"I'm getting to that," Violet said. "The murkborn are a unique species that use blood magic to entrap followers. They can gift them powers, like healing and strength, but only in exchange for another creature's death."

Nox's gut clenched. "That's what happened with Chumy. And the crows Jurdan uses."

"Exactly." Violet swallowed. "But that isn't their true goal. What they always crave more than anything is finding the strongest, most powerful creature they can convince to join with them. Once they're paired with a host, both of them feed off each other and have extremely long lives. Even longer than dragons."

Lark blanched. "The Unseen told Conall he'd live forever..."

Violet's lip quivered, but she sucked in a big breath and barreled on. "That's why the murkborn always find a magical species that's vulnerable to... attach themselves to when they enter a new world. Then they siphon their power into the humans, trying to create someone powerful enough to become their next *vessel*."

Ryon's eyes widened. "That's what Jurdan did with the Hilfolk."

Kayda added, "And what the Unseen did to the dragon eggs he found in our land."

"Wait..." Nox's blood ran cold. "Is that why he won't let Mariun go? Is he planning to make her his next host?"

Violet's brow wrinkled. "Maybe. I'm more worried about what will happen now that Thalassia's been destroyed. Jurdan might track down another magical species now that he doesn't have the Hilfolk to drain."

Ryon's upper lip curled back. "He might go after the orecolns... Avion could be in danger!"

Nox's stomach sank. He couldn't handle the thought of those kind, peaceful people who'd helped them being harmed.

Who knew what Jurdan would do next? He might not even try for the orecolns. Maybe he'd go after the siltreak fish. Or some new species they'd never heard about on an island they'd never explored.

Violet pursed her lips. "I have a plan that might work. If we prove to Jurdan that the host he's in *isn't* the strongest, then we might be able to tempt him to switch."

Nox lifted a brow. "How do you expect us to do that?"

Violet speared him with a direct stare. "Not us... You. If this plan has any chance of succeeding, I'll need your help, Uncle Nox."

Nox's heart sped. But he was no stranger to putting his life in danger. "I'm in. If it helps us free Mariun from his clutches, I'll do whatever it takes."

She grinned. "Good. There's one more thing I learned that might help. But it means I need to get close to Jurdan so I can hear his heartsong."

Ryon cocked his head. "That might be a problem. We have no idea where to find him."

Rustling in the bed made everyone turn. Jayan's head lifted, and he stared across the room with a murderous look in his eyes.

Nox was about to jump to his feet and shove Kayda out of Jayan's way, when his deep voice reverberated through the room—hoarse and gruff but full of certainty.

"I can help with that." A sly smirk painted Jayan's lips. "I know exactly what Jurdan will do next."

Just Listen

Violet left Kayda's room and strolled into Magehaven square with a deep sigh while Shadow softly padded at her side. The dragons lounged beneath the willow, and the town lay still. They'd talked long into the night, going over every part of the plan in excruciating detail.

According to Jayan, Jurdan had been planning an attack on Dracwood for years. He used his crows to keep tabs on the country so he'd know when they'd be vulnerable to a strike. They figured with enough carefully placed "clues" dropped in places they knew Jurdan watched, they could trick him into striking at a time and place of their choosing. But instead of the easy assault he expected, they'd be there waiting in force.

Ryon had departed before her after volunteering to deliver a handful of Kayda's letters to the village courier. He'd sent her a weary smile as he'd left that set her mind at ease.

She was glad they'd come to an understanding. No, glad wasn't nearly strong enough. She'd been *euphoric*.

When he'd told her he loved her—that he would love them *both*—she almost passed out from relief. She'd hoped and prayed, but the understanding he'd shown was more than she'd expected.

That was Ryon. Wonderful... deep down to his bones.

Even if it took her another decade, she was determined to make it up to him. For every moment he'd spent sick with worry and racked with guilt, she'd give him a dozen moments full of happiness and devotion. She'd pull out her heart and show him every scrap of love she'd stuffed inside it over the years.

He deserved all that and more.

A curious sound drew her attention. Violet paused on her walk across the square from Kayda's inn to her own, turning her head toward the soft squeal.

It was coming from the willow.

She cinched the shawl Kayda had lent her tighter around her shoulders as she strode closer. "Hello?" The white dress swished around her legs louder than the noise, yet still it drew her in, playing on her curiosity until she couldn't stand hanging back. "Is someone there?"

"*It's just me, child.*" Orry's voice filled her mind, barely a whisper.

Violet's heart sank. "*Orry, what's wrong? Why do you sound so... weak?*"

Before she'd spotted her, she'd known what was coming. It still broke her heart to see her beautiful golden bondmate, sheltered inside the willow, her head hanging heavily as she roosted in the great crack spanning the trunk.

Orry had told her from the beginning her time was short. That every day she lived after bonding with Violet was an extra gift... one that none of the other Mother Oreas had been granted. Still, it didn't make the reality any less painful.

"My time is almost here, Violet. I'm sorry it had to be like this at the end."

"Shh." She curved the back of her hand across Orry's silky plumage. *"You have nothing to be sorry about."* Silent tears slipped down Violet's cheeks. She let them fall, making no move to wipe them away.

Though the action clearly pained her, Orry's head dipped shakily, and she plucked a feather off her chest. *"Here, take this. You'll know what to do with it."*

"I-I don't want to do this without you."

Orry's musical voice played in her ears. *"I'm afraid I won't be much help when you confront him. Not unless I pass before then. I doubt I'll have the strength to speak to you while I'm lingering between life and death."*

Violet's stomach wobbled. She'd be on her own... like all those years in Lanwell, and all the years before she'd met Orry. It shouldn't have felt like such an issue, and yet, it was a monumental loss all the same.

Sure, she'd had years to come up with her plan. She'd lain awake countless nights dreaming about exactly how it might play out. Thought about every possible scenario from every angle. That didn't mean she was ready. Look what happened the last time she called the shots. It had been her decision to wish Ryon back. That choice had brought so much pain into existence.

"Stop."

Violet flinched. *"What?"*

"I can practically hear your thoughts swirling from over here. Don't let them drown you."

She sniffed. *"How do you know I'll do the right thing? What if I make a mistake? If we don't stop Jurdan—"*

Another pitiful squeal echoed, reverberating in Orry's chest like a hound's toy. Shadow cocked his head, staring at her strangely with his golden eyes.

"*When it's time, you'll know, child. Fate chose this for you. Just listen.*"

Violet bit her lip. "*Do you want me to carry you inside?*"

"*No.*" Orry's black eyes lifted to the branches. "*I like it here. Such beauty. I'm glad... I got to see it.*"

She sensed Orry's strength fading. She didn't want to tax her. "*I'll leave you to rest, then.*"

"*Yes. Rest.*" Orry's eyes closed. "*Goodnight, Violet.*"

Violet clutched the feather against her chest and headed to her room, wondering if that would be the last time her bondmate closed her eyes...

Compelled

The next weeks passed in a frenzy for Ryon. He took to the challenge, first helping the villagers pack their homes to flee inland, then organizing the fighters who poured into the harbor.

Kayda had chosen the village as a staging ground for their offensive. As the days passed, boatloads of oddly dressed folk trickled in. Scantily clad Ramish set up tents in the fields beyond Magehaven's outskirts, while bearded Dolnmen in furs hunkered inside empty houses on the village's north side. They saved the south side for all the Dracians who arrived from the countryside. Everyone carried bows and staves, eager to help their queen protect the country from invaders.

The constant activity kept him from overthinking, yet fear was never far from his mind, lingering like a phantom just out of reach. He worried for his family. For the battle to come. And most of all, for Violet.

Things hadn't just magically become easy between them. But he wasn't afraid to put in the work to rebuild their relationship. And it appeared Violet felt the same. Every day she sought him out, no matter how busy they both were. They shared meals together. And they sat together beneath the willow, keeping Orry company as she clung to life with her final breaths.

He brushed a shimmering branch aside as he ducked beneath the tree that afternoon.

"You're late." Violet looked up from her spot on the grass, her legs curled beneath a simple blue dress. Shadow lounged beside her, his chin resting on his forelegs.

He grinned. "Got caught up hauling weapons off a boat from Joria. Why didn't you warn me those sandspears were so unwieldy?"

She tilted her head. "I wouldn't have thought a man with your strength would be such a whiner."

"Hey!" He approached a checkered picnic blanket decorated with a simple lunch of bread, cheese, and stew. "I'll have you know, all that strength didn't protect me from being poked with one of those curved blades—accidentally, of course."

She scanned him with her lips pursed. "I don't see any fresh wounds."

"And you won't. Just don't ask why I'm wincing while I sit." He sat gingerly on the blanket, his face an exaggerated grimace.

Violet burst into laughter. "You're ridiculous," she said finally, handing him a bowl. "Stop kidding around and eat."

A melodic trill filled the air, drawing his attention to the hole in the willow that Orry had seized for her own. "That sound... is a balm to my old... soul. Never stop making... each other laugh."

Violet asked, "What did she say?"

Ryon's heart twinged. Orry had lost the strength to speak to Violet mentally days ago. Each day, her breathing became more labored, and her words fewer. He'd never been more thankful for the first wish he'd made each time he shared another precious message with Violet.

"She said we should never stop making each other laugh." He met her gaze, knowing the statement would wash all the mirth from her expression as reality sank in.

Orry didn't have long to live—and there was nothing they could do. All the healing in the world couldn't stop dying of old age. Well, except for Jurdan's dark magic, but neither Orry nor Violet would ever consider that. Extending one's life at the sake of another's wasn't something any creature with a conscience would agree to.

Like he'd expected, Violet's chest caved. He wished he could take her pain away. Instead, he found himself blurting out a question he'd been holding back. He set down his half-empty bowl. "I've been meaning to ask... Are you sure about going to face Jurdan?"

She blinked. "Hm?"

He grabbed her hand, took a deep breath, and spoke from the heart. "It'll be dangerous. If anything happens to you, I don't think I could bear it..."

"I wish there was another way, but there isn't." Violet squeezed his fingers tightly. "I need to do this. To avenge my family." Her lip quivered, and she cradled her stomach with her free hand. "To make the future safe once and for all."

He could certainly understand her motivation. But it didn't make it any easier to know she'd be facing that villain without him.

"Ah, there you are." Willow branches fluttered as Nox shoved them aside. "I have news."

Violet perked up. "What is it?"

"A weather seer arrived this morning. She just informed Kayda that a massive storm is headed this way—and that it popped up out of nowhere."

Ryon hopped to his feet. "It's him."

Nox bent, his hand outstretched. Violet took it, slowly lifting off the blanket. "A seer? How many have arrived?"

"Three." Nox let go of her hand. "They're probably still sharing a meal with Kayda in her private dining room if you want to talk to them."

Violet flashed a half-smile at Ryon. "Do you mind? They may know"—a short, choppy breath spilled out of her lips as she corrected herself—"*have known* my mother."

He shook his head. "Go. I'll clean up." As Violet tore off toward the inn, Nox hung back, looking ill at ease. "You all right?"

Nox gritted his teeth. "I still can't believe I agreed to this." He lifted tortured eyes to meet Ryon's. "I should be the one saving her."

He clasped Nox's shoulder. "I won't let you down." Since Nox was needed for Violet's plan to succeed, he'd volunteered to take the lead freeing Mariun.

At first, he'd balked at the responsibility. After all, look what happened the last time he'd been put in charge of saving someone. But after reminding himself he *had* succeeded, and with some gentle cajoling from Violet, he'd manned up to the task. Nox hadn't been happy about it when they'd first laid out their plans—and clearly he still wasn't.

He squeezed Nox's shoulder tighter. "I mean it, Nox. She'll be back where she belongs after the day is through." He tugged the necklace Violet had returned to him out of his shirt. "And if we run into any trouble, here's our backup plan."

Nox's gaze caught on the silver feathers fluttering in the gentle breeze. "Keep her safe." Then he turned on his heel and stalked out of the square.

With a heavy heart, Ryon watched him go. *What if I fail again? What if I'm too late with Mariun like I was with Violet?*

No. He refused to let his fears weigh him down. He'd make sure Nox's days of worrying about the woman he loved were over. Hopefully after today, he'd be able to say the same for himself as well…

Ryon clenched tightly to Ari's back as they flew through a raging storm. Every flash in the sky made him flinch and pray to whatever gods were listening to see them safely through the tempest without being struck.

The storm had rolled in late that afternoon, hitting so hard branches splintered off nearly every tree in the village. Surf battered the beaches, kicking sand so far inland it coated the cobblestone roads. And lightning lit the horizon with near constant strikes, making the dark clouds flicker as if a thousand fires raged within the sky.

It had taken some convincing to get the dragons to attempt the short flight from Magehaven to the boat. Jayan had assured them one would be hidden inside the rolling waves and black clouds. By some twist of fate, they managed to arrive safely.

He slipped some smooth stones out of his pocket as they hovered above the deck. Though it was hard to see through the storm, he didn't miss the dozens of troops on board—or the arrows they sent sailing at them.

Ari wove through the air, deflecting the projectiles with blasts of ice. What few arrows made it past ricochetted harmlessly off his hard scales. The storm helped, sending many of the men's shots far off-kilter.

Ryon's heart slammed against his ribs. Those shots might be little trouble for a dragon, but it would only take one lucky strike to kill him or his friends.

Not if they picked them off first.

A rock flew off his fingers, making memories of flying atop Legon flash in his mind. In the short time he'd spent in Lanwell, he'd helped fell dozens of monsters while atop dragonback. And yet, it didn't stop his stomach from rolling when the first man slammed into the boards.

He couldn't linger over the guilt of killing a man. Not now.

He sent a stream of rocks down onto the ship. Beside him on Gwen, Violet's arrows twanged. Within moments, they'd cleared enough of the deck that they could land.

Nox kicked Gwen's side, urging her down beside a side rail. Ari landed beside her with a thump. Ryon slid off swiftly, then reached up, helping Shadow down.

Violet and Nox hustled over, and they huddled together behind the dragons' backs. Each of them were dressed in black and carried as many weapons as they could handle without sacrificing their agility. They'd come prepared for the worst, and it seemed they'd found it. Already, the dragons blasted ice and earth at dozens of masked who sought to attack them.

"Did you see anything?" Ryon shouted, needing to raise his voice over the smashing rocks and roaring storm.

"Mariun's up there." Nox's finger rose, pointing to the crow's nest.

Ryon gulped. What was she doing in there? And how was he supposed to get her?

Violet shouted, "He can't climb the mast. It'd be suicide."

She was right. From the sound of the magic the dragons kept blasting, the masked hadn't stopped coming. He'd never scramble up there without being picked off.

Nox fell silent for a moment. "Gwen will give you a lift."

They'd known the dragons couldn't stay for long. Those arrows might not be effective, but it wouldn't be long before the masked discovered something to wound the dragons. "What about you?" he shouted.

Nox pointed again, this time at a door close to their current position. "I saw Jurdan slip inside. We'll go after him." He clasped Violet's shoulder. "We run when the dragons take off."

"I'll help cover you." With a curt nod, Ryon turned toward Gwen. But he couldn't resist snagging Violet's hand. "Stay safe." He squeezed her fingers, then clambered atop Gwen.

Her massive green wings spread out as soon as he was seated. He ducked low, pressing himself tightly against her scales.

He counted silently in his head. *One, two, now!*

He popped up, flinging rocks left and right. Masked slammed into the deck, and even more ducked behind whatever cover they could find.

In the chaos, Nox, Violet, and Shadow raced for the door. Ryon's heart lifted. Nox snagged the handle and tore the door open, ushering the others inside. They were going to make it!

Out of the corner of his eye, he spotted an archer with his bow aimed straight at Nox's head. His bow arm was pulled back. No way he'd knock the shooter out before he—

Twang.

His hand shot out, flinging a rock instinctively. His breath caught in his throat as it sailed forward. His heart stuttered when the rock nicked the arrow end—just barely.

Nox cursed. The arrow that'd been meant for his head grazed his shoulder.

Ryon's shoulders sagged.

Slam. As the door closed, his heart pounded faster. Would their plan succeed? Or had he just sent the woman he loved to her doom?

Shaking his head, he shifted his gaze upward. He had a job to do.

Gwen climbed, flying higher than her brother. Soon it was high enough he spotted her, and Ryon's stomach dropped.

They'd tied Mariun to the crow's nest with her arms outstretched. What's worse, the storm appeared to be emanating *from her.* Blasts of light shot between her and the clouds, with no discernible pattern.

How was he supposed to get close enough to save her? The dragons were vulnerable to strikes. He couldn't hover above her and drop down...

He eyed the ropes attached to the rigging. "I have to jump," he muttered. He shifted his body, getting into position as Gwen slowly rose closer to the crow's nest.

Good thing he wasn't afraid of heights... Seemed Jurdan had done his research, setting Mariun in the one spot Nox would be scared to go.

But that monster didn't realize one thing. They were stronger together.

Ryon leaped, falling a fraction before he snagged a rope. His muscles screamed, but he held on as he dangled and swayed. Then he grabbed another rope, and his breathing evened.

This he could do. Hand over hand, he climbed, reaching the crow's nest swiftly.

His eyes widened as he drew close enough to see Mariun clearly. A torn black dress lashed against her skin in the blinding wind. Her body slumped, her face lined with exhaustion. If it weren't for the ropes tied to her wrists, she'd likely be unable to stand.

Yet, static poured off her, and the occasional strike flashed out the tips of her fingers, forcing him to close his eyes.

Was she controlling the storm? Why? And more importantly, how would he stop her?

He paused there, racking his brain until the answer came to him. At least, he hoped it was the answer. There was only one way to find out...

He climbed as close as he could to the crow's nest. With his heart in his throat, Ryon waited until just after a blast zapped from Mariun's fingers. Then he struck, tumbling into the nest and nicking Mariun's thigh with a small blade.

He ducked, covering his head and backing away as far as space allowed in the tiny nest. If his tactic failed—perhaps even if the effects took too long—then he needed to be ready for a strike.

After holding his breath for a few heartbeats, he chanced a glance at Mariun. Her slumped posture stiffened. The sky calmed, the lightning strikes fizzling out and the gray clouds lifting so quickly they were practically gone by the time he hopped to his feet.

He carefully sheathed the blade and pulled out a tiny vial filled with red liquid. Then he forced open Mariun's mouth, tipped her head back, and spilled the contents down her throat.

After grabbing a clean blade, he sliced through her bindings. "Easy," he told her. "Kayda said that stuff works swiftly. We don't want you falling."

Mariun's limbs gradually released from their locked state. "What was that?" She smacked her tongue against the roof of her mouth a few times while wincing.

"I used the same toxin on you that took down Jurdan." He shrugged. "That was the antidote."

She wobbled on her feet as he released the last rope.

"Why are you up here?" he asked.

Mariun gripped his shoulder. "Jurdan... I'm not sure how, but he *compelled* me to start that storm." Her eyes shone with tears. "I didn't want to. You have to believe me."

"I do." This was clearly another one of the fiend's powers. He'd sucked the magic out of Mariun like he had the Hilfolk. "It's all right. We'll fly to safety." He peered out of the crow's nest, looking for the dragons.

An arrow whizzed by his ear. "Guano!" He ducked, pulling Mariun down with him. "We're in trouble. Masked are climbing up here."

"We're not the only ones in trouble." Mariun's eyes widened, and she gripped his sleeve. "Where is Nox?"

"Below deck. He went after Jurdan with Violet."

Mariun groaned. "No!" She tore at her hair. "That's what Jurdan wants!"

His stomach dropped. "What?"

"Jurdan didn't only use me for the storm. He was planning an assault... and Nox was his target. You don't understand what he's done. What he *made* me do."

The muted sounds of violence carried on the breeze—coming from shore. Carefully, he peered over the nest's edge, and his heart shattered.

Dozens of the submersibles from Thalassia landed on the beach, and masked poured out. Their forces on land clashed with them in a bloody melee, painting the sand red.

What's worse, the dragons he'd been counting on to rescue them raced toward shore—and he had no way to call them back. He watched with dawning horror until another arrow sang in his ears, making him duck again.

"You powered those things?" he shouted.

"He made me!" She lifted a hand, and a pathetic shower of sparks buzzed faintly on her fingers. "Taking it without my consent drained me. I-I hardly have any magic left."

Ryon's heart raced. Their well-thought-out plan was playing right into Jurdan's hands! He needed to warn Violet, but how? He couldn't see any way to escape without a dozen arrows sinking into him like a pincushion.

As scrambling echoed below, his gut clenched. It wouldn't be long before the masked reached them.

How were they going to escape from this mess?

Too Easy

"*S*tay sharp." Flint's voice echoed in his ears. "*This feels too easy.*"

Nox bit back a groan. "*Tell that to my shoulder.*" They'd paused just inside the doorway long enough for Violet to wrap a makeshift bandage around his arm. He was lucky the hit had only been a graze. It still bled like crazy and stung more than he cared to admit.

"*A little pain ought to keep you on your toes.*" Amusement laced Flint's tone beneath his worry.

Violet paced ahead of him down a deserted corridor in the gigantic ship's interior section, following Shadow's lead. They'd brought the wolf, knowing his nose wouldn't lead them astray—and that Conall would want to be there with his bondmate when the evil plaguing their world was destroyed once and for all.

Suddenly, Gwen whooped with glee. "*He's done it! Ryon's freeing Mariun. The storm's stopping.*"

An immense weight lifted off Nox's shoulders. "Thank the Mother," he muttered under his breath.

Violet glanced back with a cocked brow.

"Ryon got her."

A grin flashed on her face before she turned back, all business. They both knew what was at stake. If their plan didn't work—

He buried the doubts before they fully formed. Their plan *would* work. It had to.

Shadow halted outside a doorway.

Violet bent, meeting the gray wolf's golden eyes. When Shadow bobbed his head, gaze glued to the door, she straightened and reached for the handle.

Nox's grip tightened on his short sword as she eased open the door. A vile feeling washed over him, even before a booming voice pierced his ears.

"Come in. I've been expecting you."

He glanced at Violet, making sure she was all right. A visible shudder worked its way through her body, but she stepped forward despite her obvious revulsion.

As soon as they passed the threshold, they spotted him. Jurdan stood in a crowded storeroom among boxes of all shapes and sizes tied down with rope. Nox's heart pounded as he pictured all the little nooks that might hide someone.

And yet... they were alone. Strangely, the entire length of corridor they'd traversed had been deserted as well.

Nox registered Shadow slinking out of sight in his peripheral vision. Violet froze, staring at Jurdan like she could see into his soul. She'd warned him that while she used her boon, it might look like she was in a trance. It would be up to him to buy her time.

He had to speak to the man who'd beaten him and buried him alive. Who'd stolen the woman he loved—twice.

Anger thrummed in his blood, and the claws emerged, digging into the hilt of his short sword. But he couldn't let the emotion rule him.

With a long stride, he drew closer, making Jurdan's gaze snap to his own.

"When I heard you'd survived, I almost couldn't believe it." Jurdan casually straightened his long purple robes, curiosity clear in his tone. "But look at you. Back again."

"What can I say? I'm full of surprises."

"*No!*" Gwen's voice rang in his head just when he needed to concentrate the most. "*They're attacking the shore!*"

He couldn't reply. Not when one wrong move might spell his doom. "Why don't you seem surprised to see me?"

Jurdan snickered. "Surely you'd come looking for your *love*... I hate to tell you, but she's bound to be a little sore with me after what I did."

Bile stung his throat. "What did you do?" If Mariun was hurt, he'd tear Jurdan limb from limb. Damn Violet's plan.

"Don't look so surprised." Jurdan paced closer, eyeing Nox closely with his black eyes. "If you hadn't sunk my ship, I wouldn't have been forced to use her power instead."

Nox's jaw clenched. "*Gwen, is Mariun alive?*"

"*Yes,*" she answered instantly. "*Ryon was just talking to her.*"

The knowledge slid over him like a soothing balm, tamping down his anger. She was alive. That was all that mattered. He had to keep a cool head.

His lip curled into a sneer. "She never wanted your power. She wants nothing to do with you." He remembered Violet's coaching. If this plan was going to work, he had to steer the conversation in the right direction. "You're not her father. You were never a true parent to her. Her *mother* is dead because of you."

Jurdan stiffened, and then his eyes narrowed. "Family..." He scoffed. "One day, you'll learn the hard way that no one can be trusted—just like I did."

Behind him, Violet's voice boomed, full of certainty. "Do it! Do it now!"

Nox backed away, using his boons to leap atop a crate. At the same moment, he slipped a feather out of his pocket.

Jurdan rolled his eyes, lazily tugging a string out of the top of his tunic. His stolen feather... "Two can play at that game. What are we wishing for?"

Nox's pulse pounded. He'd been worried the fiend had used it already. And even more worried that the feather Violet had given him wouldn't work. After all, Orry had told him he only got one. The very one Jurdan held in his grasp.

Except he recently discovered Orry had lied. It wasn't the feather that mattered. It was the wish. But if she'd let Nox wish Violet back when he'd asked, she wouldn't have been ready. Orry had lied because she'd known that Violet needed more time.

So when Nox slapped the golden feather in his hand to his injured shoulder, his flesh warmed to the touch. "I wish Jura knew everything written in the diary Violet found."

Hot, burning agony flashed through Nox's arm, radiating up his hand and through his veins to every place on his body. But soon after the sensation arrived, it vanished.

He blinked past the pain, turning his gaze to Jurdan.

Jurdan's hands tore at his scalp, his eyes flickering this way and that. "How?"

Nox jumped off the crate as Violet stepped forward. "I discovered your mother's journal in ruins on your homeworld." She stopped at Nox's side, compassion shining in her eyes. "She regretted not going through the ring with you. Can't you see? She *loved* you, Jura."

Jurdan shook his head. "No. Lies. It's all lies."

"It's the truth. You don't have to go on like this, Jura. You can still make her proud." Violet nudged Nox's shoulder.

His skin prickled. He didn't want to do this. If something went wrong...

No. It was the only way.

"Can't you see your chosen vessel is *weak*? Such a pity." Nox threw his short sword down, and it clattered off the wooden boards with an ominous *clack*.

Violet's voice rang out, full of empathy. "What I read in that diary broke my heart. Is your heart breaking too?"

Nox's tone was the complete opposite, thick with derision. "Have you tried leaving the ocean yet? Don't you know what happens to those who dream too often?" All magic had consequences. And the dream elixir came with one fatal flaw.

Violet said, "Jura, you don't need him. Don't you want to be free?"

"There's a reason the Winter Witch can't stray far from the coast. That body you're in is shackled to the sea too, isn't it?"

They circled Jurdan, playing both sides of him. The man—and the monster. One of them had to crack. Jurdan quivered where he stood, his eyes pinched closed.

Violet whispered, "She'd want you to be free, Jura. To be happy. It was her greatest wish."

"How can you stand being inside that weakling? Don't you want someone stronger?" His heart thudded madly as the next words slipped off his tongue. "Wouldn't you rather have me?"

Jurdan's head shot up, tormented black eyes landing on Nox. But when he spoke... his voice didn't come out of the man's throat. It echoed in Nox's mind, sinister and full of glee. "*You'll be my vessel?*"

Nox nodded, tongue-tied.

"*Say it!*" the voice hissed. "*Swear it!*"

With his pulse thudding in his ears, he blurted, "I swear I'll be your vessel."

As soon as the last word left his lips, Nox's limbs snapped into place. His entire body froze, and only a single part of his body moved. His mouth slowly opened so wide it made his jaw ache.

Across from him, Jurdan locked in the same position; mouth dropped, body fully immobile.

It was exactly what they'd hoped would happen. But Nox couldn't celebrate. Not while a voice echoed in his mind, the same horrid sound playing in his ears over and over.

That vile thing was *laughing*—glee pouring out so palpably Nox's skin crawled.

"You fool! I've wanted you all along. With your power, and a being who's truly worthy of your gifts, we can do anything. We'll rule them all!"

Nox stared with horror as an oily, snake-like creature slithered out of Jurdan's mouth. Its lithe body emerged, a black so dark it seemed to suck up all the light in the room like pebbles falling into an endless pit.

"Rot and decay. But you tried to kill me..." His gaze darted to Violet, desperate to warn her. But he couldn't speak. He couldn't even reach out to his bondmates. He had no way of telling them they'd made a terrible mistake.

"That was after you sneered at my gifts. After you stole what was mine. Don't you see... Now she'll be ours. *Forever."* The monster fully emerged from the man's mouth. As it slinked to the floor, Jura crumpled. He fell so wildly that he knocked Violet off her feet.

Then Nox was all alone, staring at the vile black serpent slinking across the floorboards. Even now, he promised him everything. What

Nox wouldn't give to live the rest of his life with Mariun, knowing she was safe and would stay by his side forever.

But at what cost? He'd have to allow that thing to use his body like a puppet. To hurt countless people and innocent animals in his quest for power.

Nothing was worth that price. Yet... with his limbs locked, he was powerless to stop him. All he could do was stare in horror as the ugly thing drew back, readying to climb up his body and slide down his throat.

A snarl rent the air. Shadow leaped out from behind a crate, snagging the murkborn in his jaw and biting down with a wet crunch. He shook his head, flinging the vile thing aside. Streaks of black blood littered the floorboards as the creature creeped off, hiding among the boxes.

Shadow coughed and rubbed his paws against his mouth.

This had happened before. Nox remembered his brother's tale of facing the Unseen. Conall had been freed from the stupor after Shadow attacked it. They'd been counting on it to happen again.

His stomach sank as his frozen limbs refused to move.

Had Shadow not injured this murkborn enough? Why was he still stuck, his mouth wide open and ready for the revolting creature's plans?

Jump

Frenzied thoughts stampeded through Ryon's mind. Though the storm had cleared, a dozen new problems cropped up in its place. One thing was clear. The dragons would be no help. Gwen and Ari were halfway back to the beach now. He had to find a solution on his own.

He scanned the ship, looking for anything that might help. There!

Turning to Mariun, he tightened his grip around his blade as Nox's lessons about sailing filled his mind. This ship was far larger than the one they'd sailed to find the dragon eggs, but hopefully the knowledge was still sound. "I need you to find them down below. Warn them. Tell them what you just told me."

Mariun's shoulders firmed at the same time her brows turned down. "But how?"

He grabbed a rope, slicing it free from the ones holding it in place. "Take this. Jump to the deck. It will slow your fall enough that you can land safely."

Her fingers trembled as she took it. "Are you sure?"

No. Not really.

"Yes," he shouted as the nest shook. No doubt from the weight of the archer currently climbing the rigging, ready to sink an arrow into their hearts. There was no time for second-guessing. He dug into his pocket, pulling out a handful of rocks. "On the count of three, jump. I'll cover you."

Mariun met his gaze, her gray eyes shining with determination.

"One. Two. Three!"

Holding tight to the rope, Mariun blindly leaped while he popped his head out of the nest, flinging rocks as fast as he'd ever thrown them.

The first he chucked at the fox-masked man climbing below them. The bastard held on, swinging wildly on the rigging. But he couldn't spare the time to land a killing blow. Not with Mariun dropping into a world of chaos. Yelps and thuds exploded everywhere as his hits connected.

That no one had been expecting a woman to come barreling out of the sky clearly helped. Half the men he felled just stood staring, making no attempt to attack either of them.

Mariun's boots slapped the deck, the rope slowing her decent enough that she landed easily. His pulse sped as she raced for the door below deck. He used the last of his rocks to pick off the few men he'd dropped who clambered back to their feet.

The door slammed.

She made it!

An arrow whizzing by his chin chased away the relief. He ducked, his heart racing.

He dug into his pocket, his stomach dropping when he found it empty. How would he pick off the fox when he climbed into the nest? He could fight him off, perhaps. Steal his bow if he was exceedingly lucky. If not...

The feathers! But what to wish for?

A thousand options flitted through his mind, each more outlandish than the last. He grabbed the necklace, slicing a feather off and nicking his palm.

Clattering echoed just beneath him. He was out of time.

Was this fate lashing out? Heaping one more horrible consequence on Violet's shoulders? He never should've come here…

Guano! If only the dragons hadn't left, he wouldn't be in this mess. They could just fly away.

Flying. That was the answer!

A black-gloved hand clamped on the edge of the nest. He had to move—fast.

He drew a deep breath, snagged a rope, and leaped out of the nest.

His foot connected with the fox's head, sending a shock wave up his leg. He kicked off the poor man's mask, desperate to gain more distance. The rope swung him outward as he simultaneously slapped the feather against his skin and let go.

He careened through the sky, yelling, "I wish I could fly!"

Time seemed to slow as he waited for the flash of warmth that signaled a wish taking hold. Only the sensation never came.

His gaze darted wildly as he plummeted from so far up. Terror took hold. Especially when he spotted a flash of silver fluttering above.

He'd dropped it! Somewhere during his hectic leap, he'd lost the damn feather!

He scrambled for another, desperately digging into his shirt. Yet even as he reached for it, he knew it was too late. His body was rushing to greet the sea far too swiftly. His limbs flailed in a poor position for a dive.

This was it. He'd hit the water hard and snap his neck.

Violet... I'm sorry. His eyes pinched closed as the dark waves filled his vision. Regret slammed into him so hard it nearly overpowered the pain that smacked into him as he landed. "Oof."

That wasn't water... His eyes popped open as he grabbed on for dear life. Rough white scales met his fingers, and it took every iota of his strength to keep from sliding off.

A hand gripped his sleeve, dragging him upward.

"Kayda!" he grunted, scrambling into a seated position behind the queen, who perched on Mena's back, wearing form-fitting silver armor with her long red hair flowing behind her. His gaze immediately fell to the boat. Masked perched at the deck rails, aiming bows at the shore. More arrows whizzed in the air, yet Mena did a fair job dodging them.

His brow furrowed. Why weren't the masked headed below deck, eager to help their leader? Whatever the answer, he was glad for it. Violet needed all the help she could get.

But now that the storm had cleared, the archers were a danger to the fighters on shore. They had to do some—

Fire blasted from Mena's mouth, and he tore his gaze away as screams erupted and sizzling flesh invaded his senses.

So that was why Kayda had come... It was pure fate that she'd caught him—and he couldn't be happier for it, despite the carnage he'd just witnessed. Dozens of burning masked plunged into the sea, dousing the flames searing their flesh. Others ran wildly, tossing water on the fires racing across the deck.

A pang of distress struck him. "Violet's still in there! If the fire spreads—"

Kayda barked, "It won't." Mena turned, headed back to shore. It seemed their plan had been to wreak havoc rather than destroy—and it'd certainly worked.

He held on as Mena flew to shore. Jurdan's boat was perched in the harbor, close enough to the fighting that a few hard strokes of the giant dragon's wings brought them abreast of the fighting.

They flew low over the melee. Grunts of pain and clashing steel competed with the roar of the surf for dominance. He watched a ring of Sul warriors slashing out at masked with their pole knives, landing so many strikes his black clothes were in tatters. A bearded Dolnman fought another, his battle axe shearing through the masked's abdomen like it was parchment.

And yet, neither masked collapsed from the deathly wounds. His eyes widened with dawning horror as the masked shoved the Doln-man's axe away and snatched a low-flying crow out of the air. The snap of bone echoed in his ears as the masked's flesh reformed before his eyes.

The blood magic. He shivered. This was Jurdan's doing. How long would they last against a foe so *unnatural*?

Mena slammed into the ground behind a low barrier they'd erected in the sand. Ryon slid off, trying to come to terms with the madness.

Kayda clamped his shoulder as her boots hit the sand beside him. "You did well. They'll come through. Have faith and"—she raised her voice to a shout—"hold the line!"

Whoops filled the air, momentarily overpowering the grunts and screams.

"What do you need me to do?" he asked.

The queen nodded to Gwen. "Stick with her. Aim for the temples."

His stomach roiled. That was right. Only a killing blow would drop Jurdan's men. At least with Gwen, he'd never run out of ammo.

As he jogged across the sand, a thread of unease tugged at his heart, demanding he turn back. He listened, whipping around as a shark-masked man leaped over the barrier, bow drawn, an arrow aimed straight at Kayda. She had her back turned, her head bent beside Mena's. Neither of them saw the danger creeping up on the queen.

Guano! Killing the queen would ruin morale. It might enrage Mena—causing her to light up friend and foe alike in her grief. Worst of all, it would *destroy* Violet.

He thrust out a hand and took a running step as the arrow whizzed through the sky. Even with his strength, he couldn't jump hard enough to make it back in time.

"No!" a familiar voice shouted. A dark-skinned man leaped into the arrow's path—Jayan.

Thunk.

The arrow sank into Jayan's chest, and he collapsed into the sand, rolling into a ball. Kayda spun, her eyes bulging as Mena's gaze landed on his blood-soaked tunic. "Jayan!" She sank into the sand beside him.

Fighters on the other side of the barrier descended on the shark, burying him in a cascade of steel.

How many more of their friends would fall? Ryon glanced at the boat in the harbor while fire smoldered inside his chest. *Please be all right in there... We need you.*

Play

V iolet struggled to sit. She shoved purple robes off her arms and untangled her legs from the man who had tripped her.

"Sorry," a dazed voice muttered. It was Jurdan's voice—the same timbre and tone—yet the cadence of the word differed completely. And what's more, that horrid crawling itch she always felt in the Supreme's presence was entirely absent.

It worked! Their plan to separate the man and the monster had actually worked!

"Jura?" she asked softly.

Dark-brown eyes glanced at her. Then those lips that so often sported a sneer trembled as he stared at his hands. "You don't know how long I've dreamed about this... being *me* again. Thank you for giving me another chance."

She'd sensed it as she'd listened. While Nox goaded him—them—she'd concentrated hard on their song. She'd heard it when Nox said, *Mother.* In that instant, Jurdan's heartsong split, becoming two distinct melodies, one filled with so much longing she nearly wept. That was when she knew it would work. That the man within still cared for something more than he cared for dominance.

Bang!

The door flying open broke her train of thought. Mariun rushed in. "Nox!" She went to him, her eyes widening and steps slowing as she drew closer. "What's wrong with him?"

Violet blinked as she took in her uncle's locked position. "It's not supposed to happen like this..." Getting to her knees, she shuffled to Shadow's side as she spotted him coughing.

"You!" Mariun's voice dropped so low it vibrated through the air like she'd kicked a drum. "You did this!" She stalked across the room to Jura, drew back her fist, and clocked him hard in the nose.

"No!" Violet dropped her waterskin on the floor, the liquid spilling everywhere. "He's not Jurdan!"

Mariun froze, her fist pulled back for another strike. "What?"

Behind her, Shadow lapped up the spilled water. Violet rushed back. "We released him from the murkborn."

"No!" Mariun jerked back, hurrying to Nox. "That's what he wants. It's what he's wanted all along."

Violet's head spun. She felt like the ball in a child's game, bouncing from one place to the next.

Jura cradled his bloody nose. "She's right. In the end, he didn't want me. Danger was baiting you by taking her. He wants Nox. Wants to *be* him."

Horror flooded her, turning her blood to ice. "Blazes!"

Mariun stood in front of Nox, her gaze flitting around like she expected a monster to pop out of the shadows at any instant. "We can't trust him. Don't believe a word he says!"

Violet turned back to Shadow and kneeled at his side. "Are you all right?" At Shadow's nod, she patted his head. "Find it." Shadow sniffed and zeroed in on the black sludge tracks tracing the floorboards.

Jura timidly said, "You can trust me. I see now how wrong I was."

"How can you say that after what you did?" Mariun's voice wavered, thick with anguish. "Never. I'll never forgive you."

"Here." Jura reached into his tunic and plucked out the golden feather Violet had embroidered with her own hands. He dragged the string off his neck. "We can use this to kill him, can't we?"

Mariun glanced from the feather to Nox and back again. "Give it to me. I'll do it. I'll wish him dead."

Violet gasped. "No. You can't..."

Her chin quivered, but Mariun's eyes were full of resolve. "I have to. I'm the only one with a wish left." She thrust her hand out to Jura, but her gaze stayed locked with Violet's. "I've suffered enough, haven't I?"

She shook her head. "For life and death? No, you haven't. None of us have." She didn't even need to listen to Mariun's song to know it. Life and death were not meant to be tampered with... even with bloodfeathers. The consequences were always dire.

Jura held the glimmering feather at eye level. The tiny picture of Flint flashed, making Violet glance at Nox.

He'd not moved. Not spoken a whisper. But she sensed the emotion pouring out of him as if he were screaming and stamping his feet.

"You can't, Mariun." She nodded to her uncle. "It would destroy him."

Mariun spun to face Nox, twin tear tracks spilling down her cheeks. "I'm sorry." She pressed a swift kiss to his bottom lip. "I can't let you die for me—or worse. You've sacrificed enough."

Violet's heart gave a pathetic thump, then clenched into a tight fist. She couldn't let Mariun do this... could she?

Mariun's voice hardened. "I swore I'd see that vile creature destroyed, even if it was the last thing I did." She turned back to Jura, thrusting out a hand. "I meant it."

Jura stared at the feather, seeming mesmerized. "You're wrong about one thing."

"What's that?" Mariun hissed.

Jura met her eyes. "You're not the only one with a wish left."

Mariun lunged for him. They collided in a mad tumble, rolling and smashing into crates. A flash of gold flew into the air.

Violet snagged the feather and cleared her throat. "Stop!"

They both froze, clothes askew and eyes wide.

"Give it to me!" Mariun demanded.

"Let me make amends," Jura said.

Mariun scoffed. "You can't trust him!"

Shadow barked, drawing their attention to the far wall. He nosed at a hole likely leading to a rat's nest.

"It's in the walls." Shivers chased down Violet's spine. Would they ever find the murkborn Jura had named Danger? Was it hiding nearby, waiting for the perfect moment to strike? Or would it abandon Nox and seek a new vessel for its twisted plans?

Mariun opened and closed her fingers. "Please, Violet. I need to end this."

"Don't make her do it. I'll kill Danger. I swear it." Jura's voice rang with eagerness... but could she trust him?

"Wait!" With a deep breath, she called on her boon. She stared at both of them, frowning.

Nothing. She heard nothing beneath the clamor of a single note. The death note reverberated so piercingly it overwhelmed everything else. Whoever made that wish wouldn't survive. She'd known it before. Having the confirmation only made the decision harder.

How could she choose if she was drowned out by death?

Orry's advice from so long ago returned to her. She'd said, 'Once you've mastered your boon, you'll be able to hear the song in your own heart.'

Violet closed her eyes and looked within. She dug deep down to the quiet center of her soul and conjured every instrument she could imagine within the black nothing behind her eyes. *Play*, she instructed, listening with her heart.

Softly the music rose, starting quiet as a whisper. It built in layers, each note ringing out until a grand symphony coalesced. And within the breathtaking beauty of everything that she'd witnessed and all the knowledge she'd scraped and scarified to find—the answer emerged.

Her eyes snapped open. She stalked forward, pulling a dagger from her belt and thrusting the feather at Jura.

Mariun shook her head. "No! He'll—"

Dust rained from the ceiling. It was the only warning before the wood panel gave way right above Nox's head. The single panel set off a chain reaction, knocking several pieces around it. Something black and awful fell with the wood. The bile rising in her throat confirmed what it was, even as Nox slammed into the floor, hidden under the fallen ceiling—with the monster.

"No!" Mariun shrieked, leaping to her feet. But she'd never tear the debris off Nox in time.

It didn't matter. Not so long as her song was right.

She stared at Jura as he snatched the feather and blade. He slashed the back of his fist and smacked the golden feather onto his skin. Then he bent his head, his mouth moving, the soft-spoken words lost within the clatter of scratching wood.

Mariun tore at the wreckage, making little headway. "Help!"

Violet couldn't pry her gaze off Jura. What did he say? He could've wished for anything.

"Help me!"

Mariun's plea finally unfroze her. Violet grabbed one half of the beam Mariun was struggling with. With a grunt, they shoved it aside, revealing Nox laid out on the floor, a writhing mass of black sitting just beside his open mouth. The creature shrieked, a bloodcurdling sound that she was sure would live on in her worst nightmares.

Mariun kicked the disgusting thing aside and gathered Nox's head in her lap. "Wake up! Please."

Violet's pulse thundered as she hovered atop them. Nox lay motionless, his mouth still gaping unnaturally wide. The moment the murkborn finally fell still, her uncle's jaw snapped closed and his limbs unlocked.

"Rot and decay." He groaned, fighting to sit up. Mariun burst into tears.

Violet's heart warmed, but she left the pair, not wanting to intrude on their privacy. She turned to Jura, and a heavy weight settled on her shoulders.

She sank beside him. "Are you...?"

He coughed weakly. "Dying?" Blinking, he shifted his gaze away from the pitiful lump of goo shrinking on the wooden floor. "I think so."

Violet shuddered. The murkborn's corpse reminded her of a worm caught in the bright morning sun. *Good riddance.*

She glanced back at Jura. A wave of empathy crashed over her hard and fast. She'd told the others about his mother's journal, but none of them had read it like she had. It painted the picture of a young man bullied and forced to scavenge to survive. When he'd been gifted a rare power—the same power Mariun shared—it had corrupted him.

She'd always wondered if his mother's journal could be trusted. Was Jura just a misguided youth, drunk on power and courted by a monster? Or was she clouded by maternal love and seeing what she wished her child had been, while ignoring the facts?

Now, as she stared into the dark eyes she'd once feared, it was like looking at an entirely new person. The journal wasn't wrong... but it seemed they'd never learn how different the two beings were.

"I'm sorry," she whispered, taking his hand. If any small piece of Jurdan still remained, her skin would be crawling. But all she felt as she cradled his clammy palm was sadness.

"Don't be." He gazed once more at Mariun. "I—"

His words cut off, replaced with a coughing fit that ended with him hacking a gout of blood.

"Jura." Violet squeezed his hand. "Your mother would be proud. She'd be proud that you set things right." As his fingers slipped out of hers, their slack weight falling against his motionless chest, she prayed he'd heard her. That those last words gave him a modicum of peace.

Shadow sidled up beside her, nudging her gently with his head. Violet met the wolf's kindly golden eyes and sent him a wobbly smile. "Let's get out of here."

Still the Same

Ryon's shoulders sagged. A carpet of black feathers and downed men littered the beach, snagging in the surf and tangling with seaweed washing ashore.

He could still scarcely believe it. One moment they'd been fighting, and the next, the men who'd just been practically impossible to kill crumpled like marionettes cut from their strings. The crows followed, plummeting from the sky lifelessly. Even when he knew that it would likely happen when Jurdan was destroyed, witnessing it still made him gasp and rub his eyes.

Now, they were left with the aftermath. Dozens of wounded men and women moaned, surrounded by healers. Lark flitted among them, bending close to any she deemed to need the rest, while the people around her covered their ears.

Yet, there were a few who'd never rise again, no matter how many healers attended them. Jayan was among them, his wound so severe there was nothing to be done. Ryon wandered to the spot where Kayda sat with her old friend as he drew his last labored breaths.

"Don't go." Kayda scrubbed her cheeks with the back of her fist. "I only just got you back." She patted the sand until she located his hand. Then she picked it up, pressing his palm against her cheek.

Jayan gazed at his queen with bottomless devotion shining in his gaze. Kayda would never see—Mena had flown out to the boat to collect survivors—but Ryon couldn't miss the love pouring out of the man. Love that seemed far greater than the usual affection of a warrior for his regent.

"I-I'll see you again, P-princess. I know I-I w-will." Jayan took one last shuddering breath and fell still, his sightless eyes still locked on Kayda's face.

Ryon slowly approached, bending down to tug Jayan's eyelids closed. "I'm sorry."

"He proved who he truly was in the end." Kayda's spine stiffened, and she gently placed Jayan's hand on his chest. "A good man through and through."

"He was." He breathed out a deep sigh. Violet would be glad to learn her initial judgment about the spider back on Avion proved true. Once she returned...

His gaze shifted to the horizon. The evening sky blanketed the sea, awash with oranges and pinks. Just no dragons—yet.

They knew the plan had succeeded. It was clear the moment their enemies fell. But anything could've happened on that boat. He wouldn't rest easy until he knew she was safe.

What was taking them so long?

"They'll be all right." Kayda rose, brushing sand off her armor. "Mena can hear them coming. There's a hole in the hull. Sounds like it's taking them a while to climb out."

Anxiety pinged within his chest. "Are they sinking?"

Kayda's brows pinched together. Then she shook her head. "No. The vessel is sound. Just some damage to the inner deck."

Were they hurt when the outer deck caved in, or while climbing out? He should've insisted Mena take him back. He should be there, not waiting on the beach.

"They're out." Kayda's face lit with an enormous smile.

"All of them?"

She nodded. "All of them."

He exhaled, and it was like all the worries he'd grasped so tightly escaped with that single breath. It was over. Finally, truly over.

Though he wished it hadn't required so much death and sacrifice, it had all been worth it in the end. Now they could exist without the threat of annihilation hanging over their heads. They could go back to living a normal life. He couldn't ask for a better gift than that.

As the dragons lifted into the sky, he said a silent prayer to the gods of his youth. In truth, the holy birds he'd grown up worshipping weren't all that divine. He could see that now, after all his travels. But they'd still set him on the path that led him here. They'd led him to his one. He'd never stop being grateful for that.

Sand kicked up, whirling against his legs with each great beat of the dragon's wings. He raced forward, scarcely able to wait until their claws settled on the ground.

"Ryon?" Violet's head bobbed on her shoulders as she attempted to see past Mena's flapping wings.

"I'm here!" He wove around leathery scales, desperate to reach her.

Violet spotted him, and her face lit up, relief shining so strongly in her eyes it was practically blinding. He reached up at the same moment she slid down. Then she was in his arms, hugging him so fiercely he knew she'd been as worried for him as he'd been about her.

"Tell me we don't have to be apart again," she muttered against his chest.

"Never." The single word slipped past his lips and wrapped around his heart like the truest of promises.

When she lifted the loveliest eyes to meet his, he cupped her face and stared down at her. Since she'd returned, they'd taken things slowly. In many ways, it felt like getting to know her all over again. Yet their time together taught him one valuable fact; the years she'd lived without him, the life she'd carved out for herself as a castaway, didn't change a thing.

She was still the same woman who'd brave uncharted waters to save someone she loved. And he was still the same man, willing to follow the woman he treasured anywhere, no matter what life threw at them.

Violet's courage and kindness were boundless. He was lucky to have her in his life, and he needed her to know it. "I love you, Violet of Greenvale." He didn't wait for her to say it back. Her answer stared up at him, shining in her expressive eyes. Instead, he pressed a kiss to her lips.

A tiny gasp hit his skin. Then her arms snaked around his neck, pulling him closer. When they broke apart, the satisfied smile she flashed made him weak in the knees.

She glanced at the sky and sighed softly.

"What is it?"

She grinned. "Just remembering the last time we kissed while the sun set." She cocked her head. "If someone told you back then that the next time it happened, we'd be surrounded by a ruined army, would you have believed them?"

He twisted his lips. "I don't know about that. I can tell you the next time it'll happen, though."

She lifted a brow. "Did I miss you wishing to glimpse into the future?"

He shook his head. "No. I'm just planning on making this a daily ritual." He dipped his head, stopping with their lips almost touching. "What do you think?"

"I think that may be the best plan I've ever heard." Their lips met again, and for that single moment under the sunset, all was right with the world.

Home

H and in hand with Ryon, Violet strolled past the battlefield and into the town square. The willow stood waiting, a silent witness to the battle that just ended.

"Orry?" Her brow furrowed as she ducked beneath the fluttering branches. Then her breath spilled out in a gasp. "Where is she?"

Ryon froze beside her, both of them staring at the willow's trunk. "Are you seeing what I'm seeing?" he asked, mouth agape.

She nodded, swallowing hard. The tree trunk—which only hours ago bore a massive hole—was completely solid. It was as if she'd never been plucked out of a hollow in the bark. And like a magical bird had never roosted within it.

"Don't fret, child. I'll be with you... always."

Violet clasped a hand over her mouth as her bondmate's voice filled her head. She knew what it meant, but she couldn't stop herself from asking, *"Does this mean you're... you're..."*

"Dead?" Musical laughter tinkled through her ears. *"I'm afraid so."*

She glanced back at the tree. *"And the willow?"*

"My final resting place. A fitting spot, don't you think?"

A lone tear slid down her cheek. *"I do."* Frankly, she could think of nothing more perfect. The shining willow held special meaning for her people. It marked the spot where the last battle ended—and all the mages of old banded together for a greater purpose. Where they chose healing over more violence.

Now, the beautiful tree held even more meaning for her. It wasn't only the place where she'd been returned, welcomed back by her family and friends. That tree was the lone spot of comfort during one of her dearest friends' last days, cocooning Orry within its magical embrace.

Her hand dropped to her swollen belly. She suspected the willow had done far more than that, if the words of the seer she'd met before the battle could be trusted. She'd find out soon enough...

Ryon cleared his throat. "Is Orry gone?"

Violet nodded as conflicting emotions swarmed her. "But she's returned to my thoughts."

"That's good, at least." He wrapped an arm around her shoulders, pulling her into his warm embrace.

"Yeah. Yeah, it is." She sighed.

"Violet?" Orry asked.

"Hm?"

"There's one more thing I need you to do."

Violet closed her eyes, willing the weariness in her muscles to subside. *"What?"*

When Orry answered, her voice was wistful. *"You must return to the Aviary."*

"Funny, I was already planning to."

Melodic chuckles filled her ears, making her smile. *"Good... I'm pleased we're of the same mind."*

Ryon stared at her, the corner of his mouth lifting when he spotted her grin. "Everything all right?"

"Yes. Do you think the dragons will agree to one last trip across the sea?"

He brushed a strand of silvery-white hair behind her ear. "I dunno. Shall we go find out?"

"*We're back,*" she announced softly.

"*Good. You know what must be done.*"

The dragons touched down in the massive field ringing the Aviary. Ryon helped her slide off Ari's back, her boots crunching softly in the grassy meadow. Then he turned to untie Shadow.

More footsteps thumped behind her. "I can't believe I let you talk me into this, Squirt." Nox shook his head. "I should be home by now, relaxing in my own bed."

She flashed a crooked smile at her uncle. "Then you'd miss all the fun."

"Think if we stick around long enough, they'll throw us another feast?" Mariun tugged her skirt around her ankles before she slipped her arm through Nox's elbow. They'd all donned skirts before leaving, not wanting to offend the brothers' sensibilities.

Ryon chuckled. "I don't doubt it." He leaned in with a stage whisper. "My people are always looking for an excuse to celebrate."

A door in the brothers' squat rectory swung open. Violet's smile widened when she recognized the man who came out to greet them.

It was impossible not to, when he shared the same features as the man she loved.

Rovan hurried across the field, smiling warmly, until he spotted his twin. "Ryon? I almost didn't recognize you..." His gaze caught on his brother's head. "You haven't seen Ma yet, have you?" From the way he narrowed his eyes, Violet gathered Vera might riot when she saw Ryon's dark locks shorn.

"Not yet." Ryon ignored the typical Avion greeting and pulled his brother into a tight hug. "Violet needed to come here first. Orry's orders."

Rovan nodded sagely. "Ah." He thrust out an arm toward the Aviary. "Mother Orea has been expecting you."

Violet's eyes widened. "She has?"

"Yes." Rovan marched toward the Aviary, and they followed. "She was adamant that you be allowed to do whatever you deem necessary." He spun back, eyeing the dragons curiously. "All of you."

Nox scratched his head. "I'm glad someone seems to know what's going on here."

Violet chuckled. "Guess that's my cue to explain, huh?" She'd put off telling them in her eagerness to get everyone there without complaint. But there was no reason to hold back. Especially not when she needed their help.

"Let's hear it." Nox grinned, watching her expectantly.

"When I was in Lanwell, I learned a lot about the rings connecting our worlds. On each world that they traveled to, the dragons built four."

Ryon froze. "Four?"

"Yes. The people in Lanwell destroyed all of their rings when they realized how evil the creatures were they'd unleashed into them. Now that we've rid our land of the last murkborn, I think we should do the same."

Mariun drew a deep breath through her nose. "That seems wise. But how are we supposed to find them?"

Violet tilted her head. "The oracle explained how they chose the spots to place the rings. Each location was always selected to represent a place on that world where one of the elements was most powerful."

"So the ring you two went through was likely the water ring." Nox rubbed his chin.

"And it's pretty clear the first ring was in Dracwood. The underground lava that heats all the hot springs on Dracwood's eastern coast would be the perfect location for the fire ring. Luckily, judging by my father's tales, that one's already been destroyed." Violet paused, her gaze lingering on the circular structure ahead. "What better spot for the earth ring than atop a mountain?"

Ryon gaped at the Aviary. "You don't mean... But the Aviary looks nothing like the ring in the sea."

She shrugged. "The oracle said they could be any size." The crumbling exterior appeared to be far older than the surrounding buildings. And the gray rock was nothing like the red-orange mountain stones. "When I heard that, I just knew." She walked the final steps to the colossal structure and placed a hand on the side. "This is it. The Aviary is the earth ring."

As she touched the mysterious building, a sense of rightness washed over her. When she'd first come here, she'd wondered why her eyes were so drawn to the Aviary. Why that sense of wonder she'd experienced standing in its presence never abated. There had to be a reason... This was it.

Rovan stopped beside her. "What are you planning?" His voice wavered, and she wondered if she told him she intended to tear it down, if he'd put up a fight. No matter that the new Mother Orea instructed the brothers to allow her free rein.

Luckily, she didn't need to test the limits of his devotion.

"Don't worry. The structure won't be destroyed. The oracle told me how to break the magic safely. But we have to close the path." She turned to Nox. "Can you ask the dragons to summon? I need them to open the ring like they did before."

"Think I can handle that." Nox fell silent and crossed the field to where his bondmate and her siblings lounged in the grass.

Ryon stiffened. "Wait... Isn't that dangerous? What if you get sucked in like last time?"

With a soft smile, she stretched out a hand. "I won't. This time, I'll have an anchor."

His calloused fingers slipped into hers. "Together?"

Warmth seeped through her chest. She tore her gaze away and told Rovan, "You might want to warn the orecolns to make themselves scarce. Unless they're eager to travel to another world..."

"Good idea." He hurried into the Aviary. Within moments, whistling interrupted the delightful chorus of birdsong emanating from the structure. Then, birds burst forth, elegant silver bodies flying out of the many holes in the pockmarked building.

Soon they'd all landed in the meadow, their beady black eyes trained on Violet. Rovan emerged, his long robes fluttering in the wind with a beautiful golden bird perched in his arms.

A pang of regret jabbed her chest. "*The new Mother Orea looks so much like you.*"

Why didn't they have more time?

"*Ah... but she will never be me. Today, you grant her a glorious gift. She'll never again venture beyond those walls. Not like I have. Like I'll continue to, through you.*" Orry's words made the regret subside into a dull ache.

Rovan stopped beside Ryon. "Ready."

Violet lifted a brow at Nox. "Are the dragons agreed?"

"They are." His lips thinned. "Just... see that you don't get pulled into that thing, will you? I've had about all the rescues I can stand."

She chuckled, squeezing Ryon's hand tighter. "Don't worry. We'll be careful."

The dragons circled the building. In unison, they flew up, hovering where a roof would've been on a normal building. Then their jaws snapped open, and they summoned, sinking their magic right through the middle of the Aviary.

The meadow came alive with opposing sensations. The ground rumbled beneath her feet, moisture and static filled the air, and a chill spread across the back of her neck. She shivered, waiting until the swirling magic coalesced, just like it had that day while the waters parted.

Unlike the Aviary, this ring lay on its side, with the round opening facing the sky. Yet with the holes littering the sides, it was simple enough to watch the magic spin. Once the whirling slowed and finally stretched taut like a multicolored skin, she stepped closer.

Ryon walked with her, his grip on her hand tightening. She knew what he must be thinking. The same thoughts whipped through her endlessly.

Where does this lead? If something goes wrong, will I ever find my way back home?

Ryon squeezed her fingers. "Whatever happens, I'm with you. Now and forever."

She met his gaze, reassured by his unwavering faith. Then she stretched her hand out, pressing it firmly against the rough stone.

This time, it required far less energy to conjure the magic lying dormant in her blood. Magic she'd been so certain she'd lost long ago after she'd used it to fulfill her destiny. But when she reached for it, calling forth the light, it came readily, blasting through her flesh and pouring out of her hand.

Excruciating pain seared her body, there and gone in the space of a heartbeat.

Blazes... She wobbled, so full of relief that the awful experience was over that she almost collapsed.

At that moment, the vortex dragged her forward. Her breath caught. Not again... It was pulling her in!

"Oof!" She slammed into Ryon's chest. He backed away, hauling them both to safety.

She watched, fascinated, as the light invaded the magic, forcing the vortex to shrink. Then she blinked, and it was gone. The air stilled as everyone, human, dragon, and orecoln alike, held a shared breath.

"*Thank you, child.*" Orry's grateful voice triggered her exhale.

Ryon cupped her cheek. "You all right?"

She nodded. "Yeah."

"Don't get me wrong. I'm glad that's over." Ryon raked a hand over the scruff on his head. "But I don't understand how you did it... I thought you said your magic was all used up after you broke the last ring."

"It was."

Mariun rubbed her brow. "Then how did you do that?"

"The willow." Violet sighed. "I think somehow it gave me more. When I woke after I returned, I felt different. I couldn't put my finger on why until I met with a seer before the battle. She told me my aura was purple again, when it should've just been red."

Her hand slipped to her belly as she recalled what else the seer had spotted. But that revelation could wait.

Nox frowned. "Fair enough. By my count, that makes three rings down. What about the last one?"

"The air ring." She smiled at the dragons. "Can you ask them to keep an eye out for it? I hear they liked to build those in the sky."

He fell silent, then met her gaze. "They're on it. Guess it'll turn up eventually." Nox tilted his head. "What about you two? Got anywhere else you need to be?"

She shook her head. "Not really. But I was thinking…"

Ryon chuckled. "Why am I worried I won't like the sound of this?"

"I thought you'd follow me anywhere?" She patted his chest and smirked. "I've been thinking someone ought to finish filling in that map my aunt and uncle started. You up for another adventure?"

They still had months before the baby arrived. It might be their last chance before a whole new adventure in parenthood found them.

Ryon grinned crookedly. "Sounds like fun. When do we leave?"

Orry interrupted. "*You haven't left yet, have you?*"

"*No.*" Violet sent Ryon an apologetic glance and held up a hand. "*Why?*"

"*There's something for you in the Aviary. Head inside and pull back the center stone on the altar.*"

Adrenaline pumped through her veins. "I need to go in. Orry left me something."

"Let's see what it is." Ryon and the others followed her inside.

She shuddered as the bare walls greeted them. If she thought it was eerie before, with countless beady eyes staring down at her, it was worse with the building empty. Still, she followed Orry's instructions, ignoring the loud clatter of their boots in the echoey chamber.

Her fingers quivered as she spotted the center stone on the wide gray stone altar. Intricate drawings of birds decorated nearly the entire surface, but that stone was completely smooth.

It slid out easily, leaving a dark hole behind. She reached inside, implicitly trusting Orry not to lead her to danger. Her fingers encountered something small and square. She tugged, dislodging a wooden box.

"What's inside?" Nox asked, his voice thick with awe.

Heart pounding, she lifted the lid and gasped. Dozens—maybe even hundreds—of bloodfeathers were crammed within the small space. Most shone brightly silver in the light spilling through the Aviary's open roof. Yet she spotted a few gold feathers mixed in.

"*This is for me?*" Violet asked, unable to hide the shock in her tone.

"*A gift for the one. Use them yourself. Share them with the worthy. Pass them down to your heirs. The choice is yours.*"

With tears shining in her eyes, she snapped the lid closed. "*Thank you.*"

They walked out, and Ryon made arrangements with Rovan for them to stay the night. She stopped outside, clutching the box to her chest while her mind spun. Then Shadow ambled over, nudging her hand with his head.

She smiled at the wolf, almost feeling like her parents were right there beside her. "You were right..." she whispered.

It seemed like so long ago that they'd sat her down in the kitchen and told her she was destined to save the world. Back then, she'd been so excited. She never suspected the adventure she craved would tear her away from her world and make her wish more than anything that she could just come home.

Then somewhere along the way, she'd realized a greater truth. Home wasn't just a place. It lived within the hearts of the people she loved. With her family and friends by her side, no matter how far she ventured, she'd always be home.

Ryon stretched out a hand. "Ready?"

She grinned. "Definitely."

Light in the Dark

G wen touched down on the shore of his homeland, scattering tiny stones in her wake. Nox breathed deep, soaking up the fragrant perfume of flowers and fruit the ocean breeze did little to hide.

"Where are we?" Mariun asked as he helped her down.

"Stoneshore. My family lives just over that hill." He pointed at the steep rock wall topped with thick jungle hiding the village from view. "Come on. I can't wait for you to meet them."

Mariun tentatively took his hand, allowing him to lead her up the stone stairs cut into the hillside. "Are you sure they'll like me?"

"Positive." He squeezed her fingers, wishing he could wrap an arm around her shoulder but unable to on the steep stair. "They're gonna love you."

A chorus of giggles greeted them as they ascended onto a jungle path. Children wearing sheer green clothes hovered nearby, their little faces lighting up when they recognized him.

"Nox! You're back!" a little girl sporting pigtails declared.

The boy beside her gaped down at the beach, his big brown eyes wide. "Is that a *dragon*?"

"Who's your friend?" another girl chirped.

Nox chuckled, waving back to the beach. "That's Gwen." He finally managed to wrap an arm around Mariun's shoulders. "And this is Mariun."

The girl's pigtails bobbed as she performed a cool once-over. "You're so pretty," she gushed, leaning in. "Can I braid your hair?"

Mariun flashed a wobbly smile, her hands tangling in the windswept length of her black hair. "Um... Thank—"

Another boy jumped in, not giving her time to finish. "Where did you come from? Can you tell us about it? Is it Slinas?"

The first boy punched him in the shoulder. "She ain't from Slinas." He scanned Mariun's clothes. "They don't wear dresses like that in Slinas."

Nox wove through the crowd, dragging Mariun forward. "Hold the inquisition, would ya? We'll all meet round the fire for story time—after we've settled in."

"They seem nice." Mariun waved at the children, a tiny smile on her lips and a deep blush on her fair cheeks as she scanned their see-through clothes quickly before averting her eyes.

"They are. I think you'll like it here."

Her awed gaze flitted all over as they hiked through the jungle. She giggled at the orange tree monkeys chittering in the canopy, her eyes widening with delight at every new bird and flower they passed. But the closer they drew to the village, the more her shoulders tensed.

"What's wrong?" He bent to study her expression. "You don't need to worry. My family is your family now. I promise they'll love you, just like those kids did."

She twisted her fingers in her dress. "I'm sorry. I don't mean to be ungrateful... I'm just not used to this. I lived my whole life in fear. Now I get to have a normal life. A family. It's all I've ever wanted." She smiled at him, tears in her eyes. "I just can't help worrying it's too perfect to belong to me."

Nox pulled her close. "Hey, trust me, it's not. The jungle isn't some perfect paradise. There are dangers here, too."

"Really?"

"Don't worry, though. You've got a jungle expert here to protect you."

She shoved his shoulder. "And he's so humble, too."

A low chuckle rumbled his chest. "See? Not perfect at all." Nox tilted his head, sensing there was something else weighing on her. He grabbed her hand, squeezing it lightly until she lifted her gaze to his.

"My power is gone." She lowered her gaze to the road. "Jurdan stole it in the end. If it was meant to come back, wouldn't it have by now?"

He'd worried when all the masked fell that Mariun would, too. She'd been connected to him in a way—like the masked. They could only guess that since she'd never agreed to it—since he'd *stolen* her power—that she'd been free from the slaughter. Perhaps that was why he was always so adamant that those under his power agree to his *gifts*.

He tipped up her chin. "Isn't that what you wanted? To be normal? To have a regular, boring life?"

She rolled her eyes. "I never said *boring*."

He cocked a brow.

She sighed. "You wield so much power with your boons. And now you're dragon bonded, too. And I'm just... me."

Nox's heart clenched. He wasn't surprised her insecurities were cropping up. After all, it must be hard to feel confident when the people meant to love her gave her up, letting a monster raise her.

He cupped her cheek. "I love *you*, Mariun, not your power."

She blinked, those big doe eyes searing his soul the same way they had the first moment he'd spotted her while locked in a dank prison cell. "I love you too, Nox."

He leaned his forehead against hers, releasing an enormous sigh. "Good. Because I have lots of plans, and they all revolve around you."

"They do?"

He nodded. "Yep. Gwen and I already discussed it. After we spend a little time with my folks, we're taking you to see the world. I'll show you all the places and creatures you missed while you were locked away beneath the sea."

Her face brightened. "Really? I'd love that."

He grinned, entwining their fingers. "I was hoping you'd say so." He tugged her into motion, and they leisurely strolled hand in hand toward his parents' hut.

He'd always thought he'd been cheated out of the chance to be a true hero. When the opportunity arose to dig deeper into the mysterious evil plaguing their world, he'd jumped in with both feet.

Who knew it would take him traveling halfway around the world to discover what he was really missing? And that the greatest evil the world had ever known would still bring him something to be thankful for? Defeating Jurdan showed him that even the darkest of places might still hide a kernel of light.

Mariun was his light. His love for her lit the black spaces in his soul and made him into the hero he'd always longed to be. And he couldn't be more thankful for that.

Epilogue

Princess Dayna flicked her red hair over her shoulder as Ari landed outside the quaint Dracwood village of Greenvale. She slid down, blinking quickly as the bouncy curls sprang right back into her eyes.

Everyone always told her she was the spitting image of her late grandmother. When she stared at the grandest portrait in the Royal Corridor of Kings Keep, and the freckle-faced Queen Kayda stared back, she could certainly see the resemblance, though she'd inherited her Doln grandfather's blue eyes.

Sometimes she wished she'd not received so many of her predecessor's qualities. Like now, when her unruly hair refused to cooperate. But there were a few perks too...

"You sure he's here? This place looks deserted." Her bondmate settled in the overgrown grazing field, his twitching scales betraying his impatience.

"Uncle Bowen was never a great fit for running the farm." She frowned, lifting the blue skirt of her simple day dress so it wouldn't

pick up grass stains. "*I wonder if those farmhands Mother hired aren't working out?*"

Her great-uncle was one of her oddest relations. Most of the family steered clear, dubbing him the unofficial black sheep, but she'd always enjoyed his fantastical stories. If only he would stop insisting they were all true—to anyone who would listen.

More than half a century had passed since the last great war. When it ended, Bowen hadn't even been born yet, and most of the old-timers from that generation had long since passed. The people living in their kingdom had gone a long time since witnessing the magnificent feats of magic told in those old stories.

She knew better than to think them all myths. Especially after she discovered in her late teens that she'd inherited another power from Queen Kayda. The bonding ability that skipped her mother hadn't skipped her.

She'd been bonded to Ari for years now. But with the kingdom in peace, she hadn't needed to call on him very often. Except for the occasional joyride. A smile spread across her lips. Now if she could only find her favorite passenger...

"Uncle Bowen?" she called out, ducking around the barn doors swinging in the breeze. "You busy?"

Metal and wood clattered loudly within. A wild mop of salt-and-pepper hair popped into view, among a sea of strange bits and bobs. Bowen was always crafting something—odd inventions that rarely worked, and served as a source of embarrassment for the rest of the family more often than not.

"That you, Dayna?" He waved a tool reminiscent of a back scratcher, the clawed metal foot attached to a pole so long it had to be unwieldy.

"Yep." She bounced on her feet with a grin. "Thought you might need a break."

He shook his head, the wrinkles in his lined forehead deepening as his brown eyes narrowed. "I'm far too busy, I'm afraid."

"Sure I can't pull your leg?" She cleared her throat, then hit him with the rest, her tone a playful singsong. "I brought Ari..."

Bowen wiggled his brows. "Did you now?" He set down the odd tool with a clatter. "I suppose I could spare a few moments if we're flying."

Her grin spread until it was blinding. "I knew you couldn't resist."

"You know me too well." He followed her out of the barn, brushing the sawdust off his worn overalls. He kneeled beside Ari, folding his hands into a makeshift step. "Up you go."

Soon they'd both clambered atop Ari's back, and he lifted into the sky. Dayna's pulse pounded, the exhilaration of flight seeping into her skin and filling her heart with delight.

"Have I ever told you the tale of my warrior mother, Violet, and her grand adventure slaughtering monsters on a world beyond our own?" Bowen asked, slipping into the easy cadence of a born storyteller.

"Many times. But I don't mind listening to it again." She smiled as her great-uncle spun the epic tale full of lost love, horrid beasts, death, and disaster.

"*What's he blabbering on about this time?*" Ari asked.

She bit back a giggle. "*You know Uncle Bowen. He's always got a story.*"

"*It's the manticores again, isn't it?*" Ari snorted, the exhale loud enough she caught it even with the wind whipping past her and Bowen chattering in her ear.

"*I don't mind,*" she replied. "*His stories are... fun.*" No one really believed him. Her parents warned her not to trust his tales as gospel. But sometimes she wondered...

"And that's why Ma always said I was special," Bowen explained as he wrapped up. She'd listened to this story at least a dozen times. Now was the moment where he'd proudly wax poetic about all the creations he was working on. How he was determined to make the world a better place. It was his *destiny.*

She peeked over her shoulder when the rest never came. Instead of grinning widely, puffed up with imagined self-importance, Bowen's chest caved.

"Special..." He sighed. "I'm beginning to think Ma was full of shit."

"Blazes, Uncle! Watch your language."

He grimaced, chagrined. "Sorry, dear."

"*Hey. Do you see that up ahead?*"

She jerked her attention forward. "*What is—Oh! I do! Is that a circle made of clouds? How curious...*" The shape hovered in the air, a massive ring of dark clouds that crackled with static in an otherwise clear sky.

Ari halted in place, hovering in the air. "*I-I found it!*" His gleeful voice rang in her ears.

Bowen squinted at the structure. "We going through there?" He pointed at the center. "Looks like fair weather ahead."

"*I finally found it! I have to go back. Find the others.*"

"*Wait!*" Her gaze snagged on the ring. Something about Bowen's suggestion struck a chord within her. An undeniable urge to fly through filled her. "*Shouldn't we see what's on the other side? We owe it to everyone to fully investigate, don't we?*"

Ari hovered in place for another moment before he slowly creeped forward. *"You're right. It can't hurt. No way that ring will open without all of us here, anyway."*

Dayna smiled. She'd make Ari explain that cryptic statement in a moment. Adventure was calling.

"Let's fly."

Craving more adventures in the world of Dracwood? The Palisade Trilogy follows Conall, Kayda, and Lark as they grapple with dangerous magic, venture across a landscape teeming with mythical creatures, and face terrifying betrayals while fighting to reunite and save their world. Read the full trilogy, starting with Shadows That Bind Us, out now.

Thank you so much for reading Bloodfeather Symphony! As an indie author, reviews are everything. If you enjoyed this book, please take a moment to leave a rating or share your honest thoughts in a review. I am grateful for all feedback from my readers.

Also by

Binge the complete Palisade Trilogy now. An epic fantasy adventure, full of unique magic, animal companions, dragons, betrayal, and a quest to save the world.
Shadows That Bind Us — Palisade Trilogy 1
Muses That Align Us — Palisade Trilogy 2
Lines That Drew Us — Palisade Trilogy 3

Sign up for my newsletter for a free standalone prequel novella that tells the story of how the Palisade was built centuries ago.
You'll find the link on my website amberlwerner.com

Standalone Short Story

Somewhere In Between

The Blood Song Trilogy

The Odyssey Ring – A Blood Song Trilogy Prequel

Bloodfeather Lullaby — Blood Song Trilogy 1

Bloodfeather Heartsong — Blood Song Trilogy 2

Bloodfeather Symphony — Blood Song Trilogy 3

About the author

Amber L. Werner loves to write about magic, monsters and mythical creatures. She lives in Norristown, PA with her husband and two children. Read more of her work in the Blood Song Trilogy, and The Palisade Trilogy, her complete debut series.

Follow her Facebook page Amber L. Werner
Or Instagram amberlwerner

Sign up for her newsletter and receive a free novella.
Find it here amberlwerner.com

www.ingramcontent.com/pod-product-compliance
Lightning Source LLC
Chambersburg PA
CBHW061333310726
48974CB00001B/21